THE LIBRARIAN'S SECRET SCANDAL

BY
JENNIFER MOREY

AND

DR COLTON'S HIGH-STAKES FIANCÉE

BY
CINDY DEES

MILLS & BOON

Dear Reader,

It was a true privilege to work with so many talented and friendly authors on THE COLTONS OF MONTANA. This was my first continuity. Not only was it fun, it was also a challenge. The corroborative effort was rewarding and showed me a new side to writing. I love to be pushed like that. Growth is an essential ingredient for me as a writer, because I am a firm believer that you should never stop learning and trying new things.

The Librarian's Secret Scandal is special to me because it involves a wounded heroine who refuses to crumble. Bad things happen to us and still we have to move forward. Sometimes that isn't easy. It's hard to stay afloat on a raft of positive energy when that energy seems to have all but dried up. It takes strength to throw that negativity overboard and adjust your course, set your sights on happier times and never let the bad ones drag you under. Sure, there may be some rough spots along the way, but you'll arrive at the end of your trip stronger than ever.

Lily Masterson faces adversity and never gives up. What a worthy addition to THE COLTONS OF MONTANA. I hope you'll feel the same.

Jennie

THE LIBRARIAN'S SECRET SCANDAL

BY
JENNIFER MOREY

To my homey. There is no other hero for me. Patience and Keyren
for inviting me to participate in this romping continuity. Susan, for her
never-ending brainstorming energy. My twin sister, Jackie, and the
rest of my family for all their support. And as always, Mom,
who got me going down this path.

First published in Great Britain 2011
Harlequin Mills & Boon Limited,
Eton House, 18-24 Paradise Road, Richmond, Surrey TW9 1SR

© Harlequin Books S.A. 2010

With special thanks to Jennifer Morey for her contribution to *The Coltons of
Montana*.

ISBN: 978 0 263 88514 9

46-0311

Harlequin Mills & Boon policy is to use papers that are natural, renewable
and recyclable products and made from wood grown in sustainable forests.
The logging and manufacturing processes conform to the legal environmental
regulations of the country of origin.

Printed and bound in Spain
by Litografia Rosés S.A., Barcelona

Chapter 1

The smell of stale air and cleaning chemicals lingered as Lily Masterson left Montana State Prison. Sunlight made her blink a few times, bringing her out of a fog of hugely unsettling emotions. She couldn't even begin to categorize them. Her nerves were a jumbled tangle of friction. Her stomach still churned. Her heart still beat heavily. A sob lodged in her throat. She hated that.

"Maybe you should wait a few minutes before you drive back to Honey Creek," the victims' officer said.

Lily didn't know what a typical prison worker was supposed to look like, but this one resembled more of a schoolmarm with her short, curly brown hair, round glasses and short, plump frame. The woman had met her at the prison entrance when she'd first arrived and stayed close through the parole hearing.

"I'm fine." It was a lie, but all she wanted was to get away from this place.

"Are you sure? Most victims don't come to these hearings alone. We usually meet them somewhere in town and drive them here."

Well, Lily wasn't like most people, then. She refused to succumb to that kind of weakness. It made her helpless, and she wasn't.

"Yes, I'm sure. Thanks for asking."

The truth was she'd barely made it through the hearing. While one part of her struggled with the reminder of the trauma she'd suffered, the other was mad as hell. She'd thought she was over this by now. Facing Brandon Gates shouldn't have been as hard as it had been. That's the part that made her mad. Why was she crumbling after she'd worked so hard to be strong? She'd gone through extensive therapy and aggressive self-defense classes. She'd picked herself up and started a new life and damn it, no one was going to take that away from her. Not again.

But being that close to Brandon Gates for the first time in fifteen years had thrown her. Crushed her. Talking about how he'd violated her and its devastating effect on her while he stared across the room like a dead deer was even worse. He hadn't looked at her, but his demeanor, his presence, still bothered her.

The victims' officer kept pace beside her. Lily thought she'd walk her to the exit and then let her be on her way, but apparently the woman was going to escort her all the way to her truck. Lily didn't want that. She'd talked to the woman before the hearing and they'd had a nice conversation, but it was time to leave.

"I can make it from here," she told the woman with a forced smile.

"Sometimes seeing them after so long is more disturbing than you think, and that's okay. It's perfectly natural to feel that way."

Lily was sure the officer had seen a lot of women break down after testifying at their rapist's parole hearing, but she didn't want to be one of them. "I'm fine, thanks."

Lily walked with the officer a few more steps and then stopped. The officer stopped, too, and seemed to understand Lily's growing impatience.

She handed her a business card. "All right, but if you need to talk to anyone, just give me a call. I can help you find someone good."

Lily took the card even though she had no intention of using this. She'd already gone through therapy. She refused to depend on that again. She'd moved on. This was just a minor setback. Chances were he wouldn't be released anyway. What board would do that after hearing her testimony?

"You'll be notified of the board's decision in about a week. Maybe less."

Lily nodded with another forced smile and started walking again. "You take care now," the woman called after her.

Lily kept walking, glancing back once to make sure she was finally rid of the woman. Seeing the officer heading back toward the prison settled her nerves a notch.

Reaching her Dodge Ram pickup truck, she kicked the front tire on her way to the driver's door to vent some of her frustration. It wasn't supposed to be like this. She was supposed to go to the parole hearing and hold her head high, show that dirty rat how strong she was. Climbing into the truck, she sat there for a minute, unable to shake her tension. She couldn't let her daughter see her like this. Not on top of all the talk flying around Honey Creek. She'd expected some talk around town, but she hadn't expected it to be as bad as it was. That was *two* things she'd underestimated.

Starting the engine, she wiped an escaped tear and backed out of the parking space. She drove toward the end of the row a little faster than she should have. Okay, a lot faster. She couldn't wait to get away, to put the prison behind her and out of sight. The residual image of Brandon's face lurked in her mind, the way he stayed focused on the parole board and ignored her. Would it have been better if he had acknowledged her?

Her stomach churned with nausea. Maybe once she returned to Honey Creek she'd recover.

A black SUV crossed in front of her. She didn't see it coming and didn't have time to avoid a collision. She slammed on her brakes, but her truck hit the SUV broadside. Her airbag exploded and her mind blanked for a second.

When she could think again, she saw that she'd sent the SUV head-on into a light pole. Its front end was crushed. So was the passenger side. Her truck didn't appear to have sustained much damage and the engine was still running. Her heart hammered and the shock of the wreck intensified the tremble in her limbs.

A man stepped out of the driver's side of the SUV. He was tall and muscular but lean. Lily opened her truck door and hopped out, steadying her wobbly legs as she approached the man.

"I am so sorry. Are you all right?" she said.

Rubbing the back of his neck, he stopped when she did, his eyes full of annoyance.

When he didn't answer, she asked, "D-do you want me to…call for help?" She'd left her cell phone in the truck. She started to turn.

"No. Don't do that. I'm okay."

She faced him again. He'd lowered his hand and now his gaze took her in, a slow and observant once-over.

She stiffened a little. At least he wasn't as annoyed anymore. "Your neck…"

"It'll be sore for a few days but I'm all right."

After studying her face a bit longer, he glanced back at

his SUV and then walked to the front. There, he stood and surveyed the damage.

Lily was mortified. She wanted to crawl out of her skin and escape until this was over.

"I have insurance," she said quickly.

He looked at her.

"I—I was...I guess I was...a little distracted," she stammered.

"Places like this have that effect," he said.

Was he kidding? She didn't know what to say.

"It's probably going to be totaled," he said.

Great. She couldn't remember what her deductable was. A thousand probably. And her rates would go up after this, too.

"That's all right." As if.

"I liked my SUV," he said.

She hadn't thought of it like that. "I'm sorry." Could she disappear now?

The victims' officer came running toward them. She must have barely made it into the building when she'd noticed the crash.

Here we go, Lily thought. Lord, she wanted to go home.

"Oh, my God...are you two okay?" The officer stopped, breathing rapidly from exertion.

"Yes, we're fine," Lily said. "Neither one of us is hurt, but I'll call the police for an accident report and we'll be on our way." She tapped the toe of her shoe on the pavement and looked toward the road leading to the checkpoint.

The officer followed her look and then her gaze passed over the wreckage of the man's truck. "One of you isn't going anywhere without help. You'll need a tow."

"We probably need an accident report," Lily repeated, knowing she sounded harried. "You know...for insurance. So as soon as we call...." She could drive home.

"We don't need to call anyone to come out here," the man said.

She stopped tapping her foot. "Really?"

"No one was hurt, and this is a private parking lot. All we need to do is stop by the sheriff's office and fill out a form for insurance."

"Oh. Okay. Good." Then all they needed was a tow truck. How long would that take?

His eyes grew more curious and then he really looked at her. It made her nervous. As if she wasn't nervous enough.

"Maybe I should get someone to drive you home," the officer said to her. "You look a little shaken."

"No. I can drive."

"You were just in an accident."

This lady was really starting to irritate her. Did she hound all the victims who came here? Lily didn't respond, just looked toward the road again. Oh, to be on it, driving away from here, on her way home.

"Wait a minute," the man said, which brought her head back around. "You look familiar."

How could he possibly know her?

"Where are you from?" he asked.

She didn't want to tell him.

"Wes Colton." He stuck out his hand. "Honey Creek County sheriff."

Momentarily stunned, she numbly took his hand. Colton. He was a Colton?

"You're from Honey Creek?" she asked, her astonishment coming out in her tone.

He smiled. "Yeah. You're Lily Masterson, right? You took over for Mary Walsh at the library."

"That's me," Lily said, cringing inside. The resident bad girl. There was only one reason he recognized her. All the gossip. Honey Creek was rampant with it these days.

"You know each other?" the officer cut in.

"No," Lily all but snapped.

"Not really," Wes answered conversationally. "We both live in Honey Creek. It's not far from here."

"I know where that town is." The officer smiled. "Quite a coincidence, wouldn't you say?"

Quite.

He nodded toward the prison. "Might be a bad sign that we're both here."

Lily was getting good at forcing humor. She laughed.

Great. Would he guess why she was here? If the victims' officer didn't give her away.…

She glanced at the woman. Her eyes had widened but she remained quiet.

"What brings you here?" she asked Wes.

"I came here to see my brother."

Of course. She remembered. Damien Colton was in prison for murder, except the man he had supposedly murdered had recently turned up—dead again. Damien was Wes Colton's brother. Talk about his impending release was all over town. Lily looked more closely at him. He was handsome and young. She thought she remembered someone saying he was thirty-three, which was too young for her forty years.

"What about you?" he asked, and she wished she would have kept her mouth shut.

"Oh.…" How was she going to answer that? No one from Honey Creek knew what had happened to her. "I was just… visiting a friend."

The officer angled her head a little, a silent question in her eyes.

Lily ignored her, but she couldn't ignore Wes. The amusement that had pulled a smile from his mouth faded.

Surely he'd heard all the rumors. Some weren't rumors, either. Before she'd left Honey Creek, she'd done anything and everything to spite her holier-than-thou parents. That was so long ago, though, and so much had changed since then. She'd changed. Why was it so hard for everyone to see that?

"What kind of trouble did your friend get into to land himself here?" he asked.

She thought fast. "Robbery."

The officer's eyebrows lifted.

"Must be someone close to you if you're willing to visit him here."

"He's just a…a…friend."

The officer's eyebrows lowered and her eyes turned sympathetic. She knew why Lily was lying.

Lily met her gaze and hoped she read the message not to say anything. When the officer remained a silent observer, she didn't know if that was worse. Pity was for the vulnerable.

"You've been away from Honey Creek for a while," Wes said, appearing oblivious to the exchange. "What brought you back?"

Another subject she didn't particularly want to discuss. But he wasn't pressing on her reason for being here so she wouldn't complain. "My dad. His health isn't so great right now. Stage two stomach cancer. He's gone through the surgery, but he's still in treatment and we don't know how things will progress from here. I came back to help him. Without Mom around it's hard for him to care for himself."

He nodded and his blue eyes showed his admiration. They also showed self-assurance and intelligence that went along with his honorable reputation. She checked his left hand. No ring.

"That's very kind of you to do that," the officer said, sounding out of place in the conversation. Was that because she'd noticed Lily looking at Wes?

Checking for a ring. Oh, lord….

He had really nice hands. She'd heard he was a nice man, too. And a sheriff….

Something about that appealed to her.

She stopped herself short. Why was she thinking like this? She hadn't been back in Honey Creek long, and was too caught up in the gossip going around about her to pay much attention to potential love interests. She didn't want to get involved with anyone. So why had those thoughts even crossed her mind? Was she interested in Wes? He was attractive, but…

Lily tipped her head back and looked up at the big, blue sky. "At least the weather is nice."

Wes looked up with her, but not for very long. He was studying her again.

"Sure is," the officer said, drawing out the word *sure* suggestively.

And Lily snapped her head down to see the officer smiling.

The officer turned to Wes. "So, you're a sheriff?"

"Yes. Honey Creek County."

"Oh, well," the officer beamed, "Lily's in good hands then."

Wes chuckled.

Lily loved the sound. "Should we call for a tow now?"

"Of course," the officer cooed. "And then maybe you could let Sheriff Colton drive you back home in your truck, Lily," the officer suggested, doing a bad job of pretending to be nonchalant. "He'll be needing a rental car anyway." Her smile was more genuine now, but held a tinge of slyness. Maybe she understood why Lily had lied and only wanted to make sure she made it home all right.

Not.

The officer had noticed their exchange and was now match-making. Was she like this with all the victims?

"Sure." Anything to be gone from here as soon as humanly

possible. She looked at Wes. "I can drive you back to Honey Creek."

He dipped his head. "I'd appreciate that."

After the tow truck had left with Wes's SUV and the prison worker had gone back into the building, Wes got into Lily's pickup. As she started the engine, he covertly looked at her. She had thick, long black hair and a pair of amazing blue eyes. Her breasts were just the right size and shape in the short-sleeved collared cotton shirt she wore, and she looked nice in the knee-length jean skirt.

She started driving. He hadn't argued over who should drive. He thought he should, but he also had the impression she needed the control…or the sense of it. He faced forward. The truck was quiet and she stayed focused on the road.

It was strange thinking of her as the wild and uninhibited woman she'd been before she left town. She seemed like such a lady now. Professional. Friendly, if a little nervous. He wasn't sure if it was the accident or the real reason she'd come to the prison. He knew she hadn't been telling him the truth when she said she'd come to see someone. She got a scared look when she'd told him. And the way she'd said *just a friend* signaled a lie. *Just a friend,* yeah, right. Whoever she'd come to see, he wasn't her friend. Besides, that whole exchange with the prison officer had been weird.

He'd gotten good at recognizing when someone wasn't on the up-and-up. Too many times he'd trusted his first impressions only to learn it was all a facade, especially with women.

Now he was more than a little curious about what had brought Lily to the prison. He'd make a call in the morning. He knew people at the prison.

"Have you always lived in Honey Creek?" Lily asked.

Good. She felt like talking. "No, I moved away after high

school and joined the navy." He didn't want to get into his SEAL training. It had been a youthful impulse, but as soon as he'd grown up enough he'd realized the daredevil employment wasn't really all that impressive. It didn't pay well, either. Neither did being a sheriff in a little town like Honey Creek, but he liked the sense of community and being close to his family—however dramatic they could be at times.

"How did you go from the service to law enforcement?" she asked.

"After I was with the navy, I went through training and worked as a peace officer for a while. Worked my way up the ranks and then ran for sheriff here."

"You've been back some time then?"

"A few years."

She nodded conversationally.

He was glad she didn't ask more about his background with the navy. "You have a daughter, don't you?" he asked just in case, redirecting the topic.

The smile that formed on her profile was warm and lovely. The sight revved his interest. When he'd first seen her get out of her truck, he'd almost forgotten all about the wreck. She was tall, which he liked since he was six-two, and slender and she had smooth skin.

"Yes," she answered. "May. She's fourteen going on thirty. Or so she thinks."

Wes smiled in return. "Sounds normal. I put my parents through hell at that age, too."

"She's adorable until she opens her mouth. And boys don't have those hormones affecting their emotions."

He chuckled. "It's different, but I think the torment is the same."

Now she chuckled. He liked the sound. It was soft and genuine.

"How long has it been since you left Honey Creek?" he asked.

"Fifteen years."

That sparked his interest. "You were around when Mark Walsh was supposedly murdered."

"Yes. I remember that."

Some of the gossips said she'd slept with him, too. He saw her lips tighten and she adjusted her grip on the steering wheel, almost as if she were preparing herself for questions; or maybe she wondered if he thought what most others thought and didn't like it.

"When was the last time you saw him?" he asked, watching her.

She gave him a warning glance. "Are you wondering if I knew where he went instead of dying like everybody thought?"

"I'll try anything if I think it might help me find his killer."

"The last time I saw him was at the post office with his wife, about a month before he died…or everyone thought he did."

"He never contacted you after that?"

"No." Her voice sounded sharper. She knew why he'd asked that question. The rumors. Could she blame him? He had no way of knowing unless he asked.

Before he could explain that, she added in the same sharp tone, "And just for the record, I didn't sleep with him."

He almost smiled at her defensiveness. He'd bet his badge that she was telling the truth. When some people lied, their defensiveness gave them away. But Lily's was driven more by vulnerability. He wondered if she knew that about herself… that she protected her vulnerability with defensiveness.

The way his interest kept intensifying the longer he spent with her made him check himself. He believed her about

Walsh, but how much of the other rumors were true? There were a lot. He didn't want to involve himself with a Jezebel. But if the talk was exaggerated...

"Is it true you danced naked in front of the market on your twenty-fifth birthday?" he asked, making sure he sounded teasing.

She gave him two quick looks as she drove, without smiling. "Trying to find out if all the gossip is true?"

"What if I was?" He was serious now, because he really wanted her to tell him.

"I'd want to know why."

"I think you know the answer to that." He looked at her suggestively. He wasn't asking in the capacity of sheriff.

She concentrated on driving. He waited for her to reply, but she didn't. Maybe she didn't like it that he'd asked. Maybe she wondered if he was like many others in Honey Creek, buying all the talk. He never took rumors to heart, but right now he wanted the truth.

"Aren't you going to answer my question?"

"Yes."

"Yes, you danced naked in front of the market?"

"And I went sailing for two weeks with a man I met in Vegas. Two of his friends went with us. I jumped from airplanes. I went on a safari in Africa and survived a hurricane in Barbados. I raced dirt bikes. I got in fights with other women. I even tried mud-wrestling." She stopped talking and he found himself absorbing everything she said. She'd left a couple of things out. "Oh, and I drank a lot of whiskey, smoked pot and broke up a couple of marriages."

Wes knew that one of the women whose husband she'd taken was still angry and not at all happy she was back in town. "The quilting group had a lot of fun with the sailing thing," he said. And the rumors were X-rated.

Lily rolled her eyes. "I heard about that group."

"Quilting's just their excuse."

He liked how that made her smile. But she didn't say any more.

"Not going to comment on the sailing thing, huh?"

"What do you want me to say? It's all true. Is that what you want to know? Is that why you're asking me all these questions? Yes, I went sailing with three men."

He stared at her. The rumors hadn't been kind. She'd gone sailing with three men and had sex with all of them. More than once.

She looked over at him, her expression matter-of-fact. She wasn't denying anything, nor did she appear ashamed. But he was pretty sure that was a cover-up. She wasn't proud of her early adulthood.

"How did the quilting group find out about that?" he asked.

"I was friends with your sister Maisie back then." She sent him a challenging look.

His older sister could get a little overbearing sometimes. "She does love a good tabloid tale."

"She tried to turn me into one."

"Sorry, but she didn't have to try very hard."

"I've changed since then," she said, sobering.

"I'm starting to see that," he said, making sure she saw he meant it.

Soft satisfaction made her eyes glow warmly and she resumed her concentration on driving.

"Why did you do it?" he asked.

"What? Behave that way?"

"Yes." He didn't want to hear any more about her sailing trip.

"You didn't grow up in my household."

Her father was a minister and her mother didn't work. "Too strict?"

"Strict. Judgmental. Relentless. Yeah. Nothing I did was good enough. So I thought it'd be neat if I showed them what bad really was."

He heard the regret in the form of sarcasm in her tone. "You wish you hadn't done the things you've done?"

"Not everything. The safari was a great experience. So was rock-climbing and jumping from planes and even sailing, except for the company I had."

Her hands adjusted on the wheel again, and now she seemed to be getting upset. He didn't want to upset her, especially since he was enjoying this, and her. He didn't question her further.

Looking ahead, he noticed they were almost at the outskirts of town.

"Will you just drop me off at the sheriff's office? I have a Jeep I use for work there. I can drive that until I take care of my SUV."

"Sure." A few minutes later, she pulled to a stop in front of his small office, a redbrick building with white trim and a sign that said Honey Creek County Sheriff.

"It'll be interesting explaining this to my deputies," he said, more to keep her from leaving before he could ask her out on a date.

"If any rumors start that I had a tryst in Deer Lodge, I'll know where it started." She smiled, but he could tell she didn't want that to happen.

"No deputy of mine would do that, and I certainly wouldn't. I'll just stick with the truth…I met this beautiful woman at Montana State Prison…."

She started laughing. Once again, the sound reached into him, this time strumming a stronger infatuation.

"Yeah, that would stir up a few questions." She grew somber as she said it.

"Nobody needs to know we met there. I'll just tell them you totaled my SUV."

He loved the flirtatious glint in her eyes. "And you can tell them I wrecked you for any other woman."

"You might have."

Her eyes blinked in response, an indication of the flurry of thoughts, and, he hoped, some warming emotions his reply had set off.

"Do you have any plans Friday night?" he asked.

Her smile came and went on her face, as if the idea first tantalized her and then made her shy away. "You're asking me out on a date?"

"Is that so hard to believe?"

"No…well, yes…I mean, you're the sheriff."

"Amazing, isn't it? Me, sheriff of Honey Creek County."

"I don't mean that. It's just…you're… And I'm…"

"I'm a man and you're a woman. Are you trying to tell me you're…" He lifted his eyebrows and let his expression finish his meaning, even though he was teasing.

"No!"

"Then go out with me. Dinner. Friday night. I'll pick you up or we can meet somewhere. Whatever you're most comfortable with."

She stared at him. And then turned and looked through the windshield.

"Come on. It'll be fun. I can already tell," he coaxed.

"I don't know…"

"I promise I'll behave."

Finally she looked at him.

"Friday night. Seven o'clock," he said.

Again, she seemed to waver between accepting and not. "I don't think now is a good time. With all the talk around town…"

"All the more reason to go out with me. It's like you said, I'm the sheriff. It'll be good for people to see you with me."

"Or bad for you to be seen with me," she countered.

"I don't care what people say. It's the truth that matters."

Her eyes grew soft with warming affection. Just what he wanted to see. He grinned. But she was going to turn him down. He could tell.

"Think about it," he said.

She smiled a little and nodded. "I will."

"Think hard." He smiled.

She laughed, as soft as the look in her eyes. Damn, he liked her.

He opened the truck door and stepped out, turning to face her. "At least I know where to find you." The library.

"Don't you dare." But her lovely smile proved she was kidding.

"See you soon, Lily Masterson."

The last thing he heard before closing the door was another warm laugh. Feeling good, he headed for the office with a little extra verve in his step.

When he reached the door, he looked back. She hadn't pulled into the street yet. She was still watching him with a soft smile. And that told him all he needed to know.

Chapter 2

"One of the boys at school asked me if I was as good as my mother."

Damn. Would it ever stop?

Lily looked across the truck at her fourteen-year-old daughter. Her blue eyes and black hair mirrored her own. May was only five-four for now, but she'd probably grow another four inches to match her height, too.

"What did you do?"

"Nothing. I walked away."

"Good girl. What comes out of people's mouths isn't important unless it's true." Realizing that's what Wes had told her, she shook off thoughts of him. "It's your actions that mean more. You show them who you are. You don't crumble."

"You're always saying that," May retorted.

"Arguing and getting into fights isn't the way to handle this."

"But it's true, what they're saying about you."

"Some of it used to be true. It isn't anymore. They'll see that eventually, as long as we don't let them beat us down."

"I don't know why you wanted to come back to this stupid town. It sucks here."

"Watch your mouth."

"Everyone thinks you're a slut."

"Well, I'm not. And I told you to watch your mouth."

"They call me a slut, too."

Lily gave up. "You aren't a slut."

"I don't have any friends because of you!"

That broke her heart in two. "You have Peri." She was a cute little redhead that May said was an outcast like her.

"Peri is a dolt."

Pulling to a stop in front of the school, Lily watched May's face go grim with dread.

"Hold your head high and do well in your classes. You'll meet some friends who won't judge you the way the others do." When May didn't move to get out of the truck, Lily said, "Go on. You're better than this, May."

May turned her head and looked at her. "I don't like it here."

"We aren't moving. We just got here."

With a heavy sigh, May opened the door and hopped out.

"I love you," Lily said.

May looked at her and didn't say anything before slamming the truck door. Lily watched her until she disappeared inside the school building, and then drove away.

That was the hardest part about all the talk in town. She hated what it was doing to May. But they'd get through it. The talk wouldn't go on forever.

She headed for Main Street. Bonnie Gene Kelley had called this morning and Lily had agreed to meet her. Parking, she got out and started walking down the street. Bonnie Gene had an uncanny ability to pry out whatever was bugging her. It had been a week since the hearing and still Lily was having trouble dealing with seeing Brandon in person.

Walking down Main Street, Lily was vaguely aware of people turning their heads to look at her. She passed the Corner Bar and jaywalked across the street toward the West Ridge Hotel. Next door was the Honey-B Café, where she'd agreed to meet Bonnie Gene. For once they weren't meeting at Kelley's Cookhouse, the restaurant Bonnie Gene and her husband ran.

Bonnie Gene was one of two people in town Lily trusted enough to call friends. She had stuck by her through everything over all these years, starting out as more of a mother figure, but as Lily grew older, their friendship had grown. She was the only person who knew about Brandon.

Lily wasn't sure if that was a good thing. As soon as Bonnie Gene discovered she'd testified at Brandon's hearing, she'd picked up on how badly it was affecting her. And Bonnie Gene didn't take no for an answer once she made her mind up about something. So, whether Lily liked it or not, which this morning she didn't, she had to meet her friend for breakfast before heading to the library for work.

The thought of eating breakfast soured her stomach. She'd just die if the parole board decided to release Brandon after the agony of her testimony. He hadn't done a very convincing job pleading his case. As far as she was concerned, he'd been cold and deliberate, stating that he'd received treatment while incarcerated and he was reformed and ready for society. He'd even had a plan. Move back to his hometown in North Carolina and work for his dad's remodeling company.

Ready for society. More like ready to hunt down more women in society. He'd just come out of a fifteen-year drought.

Surely he was eager to assuage his evil cravings. She hoped the parole board hadn't been fooled.

Pushing open the door to the café, Lily looked around for Bonnie Gene and spotted her at a table, waving a hand, her dark brown hair brushing her shoulders. For a sixty-four-year-old, she still looked good. Lily went toward her, dreading having to talk about Brandon. She sat across the table, seeing Bonnie Gene's light brown eyes soften with sympathy. Sometimes sympathy was worse than anything else. She wished people would just treat her like a normal woman.

"I'm all right," she almost snapped.

"Don't get all defensive with me," Bonnie Gene said. "I know what this is doing to you."

Lily felt her shoulders sag and she leaned back in the chair. A waitress stopped by the table.

"Nothing for me," Lily said.

"Two Western skillets," Bonnie Gene told the waitress. "And some good strong coffee."

"I'm not hungry." Especially for Honey-B's ham-and-cheese-laden Western skillet.

"You have to eat." Then to the waitress, "Two skillets."

The waitress glanced once at Lily, then scribbled the order and left. Lily wondered if that look was because of the rumors rather than Bonnie Gene's bulldozing.

"You've been doing so well up until now," Bonnie Gene said.

"I'm fine."

"There you go again, all defensive. It's okay to be upset about this, you know. Anybody would be."

"I'm over it."

"You're strong and you've done well with your life. You never let it get you down, but seeing him in person like that…"

She'd overcome the trauma of her rape, but now it felt as if she were going through it all over again. Reliving it.

"What was it like seeing him again?"

Lily angled her head with a do-you-have-to-ask look. Bonnie Gene was trying to get her to talk.

"I mean, how was he toward you?"

"Actually, he never looked at me. If I didn't know better, I'd say he seemed uncomfortable that I was there."

"Really?"

She nodded.

"What if he was?"

"He was acting." For the sake of the board.

"I've heard some criminals get that way at their parole hearings."

"That's a crock." She'd never believe Brandon was miraculously cured. Anyone who could do what he'd done to her and have no remorse couldn't possibly be normal, even after spending so long in prison. Especially after that.

Bonnie Gene looked at her for a while. She didn't have to say anything. She was still worried about Lily. "When do you find out what the parole board decides?"

"Any day now."

"No wonder you're such a mess. Not knowing must be killing you."

It was, but she'd get through it. She would.

"You sure you're going to be all right?"

"Yes." She wouldn't have it any other way. "Promise."

Bonnie Gene smiled. "You might have been a wild child before you left this place, but you were always strong. Not too many women could recover to the extent you have."

"Oh, I don't know about that. Survival is a pretty good motivator." It had been for her.

The waitress reappeared with coffee and another long look at Lily. Lily ignored her until she left, lifting the cup and taking a tentative sip. It went down all right. That was a good sign.

"Somebody told Maisie Colton that you dropped Wes off at the county sheriff's building last week."

Lily looked at Bonnie Gene. Great. Just what she needed.

"She asked him why," Bonnie Gene said.

Remembering what he'd said, she wondered if he'd stayed true to his word. She hadn't seen him around town since that day, despite all his charm in asking her out. But maybe he wasn't on a timetable. He was a man, after all. And it had only been a week.

"What did he say?" she asked.

"That you ran into him outside of town."

She couldn't help smiling. That wasn't exactly a lie. Montana State Prison *was* outside of town.

"That's what I thought," Bonnie Gene said, and Lily knew her smile had given her away. "Spill it, girlfriend."

"There's nothing to spill. I wasn't paying attention and I ran into him and wrecked his SUV so I drove him to work."

Her friend's mouth dropped open. "What? You got in a wreck? What happened?"

"I wasn't going fast, only about twenty miles an hour." Which was pretty fast in a parking lot.

"What happened?" Bonnie Gene repeated.

Lily didn't want to tell her too much. What if it got around town?

"Come on. It's me." Bonnie Gene pointed at herself and looked injured. "You ran into our hunky sheriff and you didn't even tell me."

"It was no big deal."

"Did he ask you out?"

"Bonnie Gene…"

"Oh, this is getting good. Where were you when you ran into him?"

Lily cocked her head, not wanting to talk about this. She'd much rather lie and get on with her day. But it was so hard lying to Bonnie Gene, her one true friend through everything.

The waitress returned with their food and left.

"Where?" Bonnie Gene demanded, scooping up a forkfull of eggs.

"Outside of town." She pushed her eggs around on the plate.

"Wes just said that to protect you." Lily watched Bonnie Gene's eyes and knew she was starting to figure things out.

"When did you run into him?" she asked.

"A few days ago."

"What day?" Bonnie ate more eggs, chewing and looking at her expectantly.

Darn it! "A week ago." She hesitated. "Today."

Bonnie Gene swallowed as her puzzle came together. "A week ago today? Was it the day of the parole hearing? Come to think of it, I haven't seen Wes driving his SUV since…."

"Oh, all right. It was the parking lot of the prison, okay? He doesn't know why I was there, though, so don't be spreading any rumors. I don't want anyone to know."

She set her fork down. "Honey, have I ever failed you yet?"

Lily relaxed. "No. I'm sorry."

"You're just a little rattled right now. I understand."

Before Lily could respond, a woman appeared next to their table. Her pear-shaped body was stuffed into peach-colored stretch pants and a dark purple T-shirt that clung to rolls of fat. Shoulder-length red hair framed angry pale green eyes adorned by too much makeup.

"You have a lot of nerve," she said to Lily.

Lily tried to place the woman but didn't recognize her. She looked at Bonnie Gene, who shrugged her shoulders.

"I shouldn't be surprised you don't remember me," the woman said.

Oh, no. Another piece of her past was about to rear its ugly head.

"Karen. Andy Hathaway is my husband?" The woman said it like a question.

Then memory came rushing back. A brief affair packed with lots of naked writhing at a downtown hotel. Andy Hathaway had been hung like a Hoover hose.

And, my oh, my, was she uncomfortable now. "Karen, I…" What could she possibly say? Sorry for humping your husband? But it was so long ago….

"Save it. You think anybody is glad to see you back? I don't know why you bothered."

"It's been a long time," she said, knowing it was feeble.

Sure enough, that only managed to anger Karen more. "It would be better if you left town. I never wanted to have to lay eyes on you again after what you did."

"I can understand how you feel, but—"

Karen leaned over and pointed her finger in front of Lily's face. "You don't know the first thing about how I feel."

Lily moved her head back as Karen jabbed her finger too close.

"You didn't give a rat's ass how I felt back then and you don't give a rat's ass now. I want you gone from here."

Lily wanted to tell her she was being ridiculous after so much time had passed.

"Lily's not the same as she was before she left," Bonnie Gene said.

"You stay out of this. It's none of your business."

"Karen…I don't know how to say this but…I'm sorry. I really am."

Karen's mouth tightened until her lips turned white. She picked up a glass of water from the table and tossed it toward Lily's head. Water splashed and ran down her hair and face. She wiped her eyes and looked up at Karen.

"I want you gone, you hear me?" Karen hissed, and then turned her back and marched out of the restaurant.

Still numb, Lily noticed the entire café had gone silent and everyone was staring at her.

"Does she really think she can make you leave town?" Bonnie Gene asked. "Seeing you must have really riled her."

Dabbing her face with a napkin, Lily didn't know what to say to that. She felt bad and yet…there wasn't a thing she could do. People started whispering around them.

"You ready to go?" Bonnie Gene asked.

"Yeah. Now would be good."

Bonnie Gene put down enough cash to cover their check and stood. Taking the napkin with her, Lily followed her outside, wiping the front of her shirt.

"Good thing it's just water," Bonnie Gene said.

"Yeah, it could have been a gun."

She exchanged a look with Bonnie Gene.

Lily pushed the library door open and dug in her purse for her ringing cell phone. The strap slipped down her arm, causing her to adjust her hands like a juggler. She found the phone.

"Lily Masterson?" a woman queried.

"Yes." She slung her purse strap back over her shoulder. It slipped back down to her elbow, nearly yanking the phone away from her ear.

Some days nothing ever went right.

"This is Karla Harrison from Montana State Prison?" the caller said, her inflection rising at the end.

The mention of the prison stopped Lily's breath and a tiny shock wave made her stomach turn and her heart jump into faster beats. She stopped walking.

"Yes?" She remembered the woman. The victims' officer who'd walked her to the parking lot.

"Is now a good time to talk?" Karla asked in an overly gentle tone, as if she had to walk on eggshells in order to talk to a poor, helplessly traumatized woman.

Lily hated being treated like that. She started walking again.

"Of course." This *was* turning out to be a real crapper of a day. She kicked her office door open. It bounced against the stopper and swung back toward her, tapping her arm and knocking her purse off her shoulder again.

"The parole board has reached a decision in Brandon Gates's hearing."

Now consumed with apprehension, Lily walked to her desk and sat down, letting her purse slip to the floor beside her chair. "Yes?"

"I'm sorry to have to tell you this, but they've decided to release him. You'll be getting a letter in the mail."

"You're *releasing* him?" How could they?

"It was the board's decision."

Apprehension morphed into outrage. "What did they base it on?" Prison overpopulation?

"He went through treatment while he was incarcerated and according to the board, has a valid plan for reentering society."

"Plan?" she all but shouted. *Valid plan?* It was maddening. "What plan? A rapist tells you he's moving to North Carolina and that's enough for you to set him free?"

"The board is very careful when they make decisions like this, Lily. Please try and understand that. They wouldn't have released him if they didn't think he'd do his best to stay rehabilitated."

"I don't believe for one minute that he's *rehabilitated*." A hundred images assailed her, all of them from the endless hours she'd spent in that cabin. Tears burned her eyes.

"I'm sorry, Ms. Masterson. I know this is hard for you. If you'd like I can give you the name of a good counselor near your home town."

"I don't need a *counselor*," Lily snapped. "Stop talking to me like that."

"I'm sorry, Ms. Masterson, I—"

"When?" Lily swallowed the lump of hurt in her throat.

"Excuse me?"

"When will he be released?"

"Next week. Friday. It's all in the letter."

Lily never hung up on anyone, but today she did. She ended the call and held the phone in her palm, staring down at it, shaking, lost in a maelstrom of old pain and a deep sense of injustice.

She wiped a tear that had slipped from her eye.

There was no punishment that would change what she'd endured, both during her assault and after. The month that followed it had been the worst, with no one to turn to and nowhere to go that felt like home. No wonder she'd tried to obliterate the experience with a one-night stand. It wouldn't have been her first.

Having sex with a stranger had been a mistake, an attempt to somehow minimize what had happened to her. Instead, that last wild night—like so many she'd had before her rape—had done the opposite. It had made her feel dirty and cheap and had thrown her into a severe state of depression.

Hearing a sound, she looked up to see Emily, her assistant, standing in the doorway. She blinked her eyes clear.

"You okay?" her assistant asked with a worried frown.

"Yes. Fine." Lily held up the phone. "Just a personal call."

Emily didn't look convinced. "We got a couple of boxes of books from a donor yesterday."

"Good. Let's get going on sorting them." She could use the distraction right now. Putting her phone down, she stood and moved around the desk.

Brandon Gates was going to be released. It didn't seem real. It was so unfair.

"They're all romance novels. I don't think we have enough room for all of them."

Lily forced a smile. "We won't keep them all. Just the ones in good condition." She passed Emily and headed out into the main library.

Karla's news hung inside her like low, dreary fog. It was what she'd been dreading since the hearing. Her worst fear had come true. Would he really go to North Carolina? Or would he risk going back to prison to come and find her? That would be very stupid, unless he thought he could get away with it. Lily had to smother a shiver with the thought of him finding her. And she hated that, her reaction, what he was still capable of doing to her.

Did he know she'd lived in Honey Creek back then? She'd never told him that night, but maybe he found out later. Did he know she'd moved back?

"Are you sure you're all right?" Emily asked.

Lily had forgotten her assistant had followed her. "Yeah." She bent to pick up a few books from the first box and turned to place them on a table in alphabetical order by author name.

"Who were you just talking to?"

She sent a look over at Emily, letting her know she was prying too much.

"Sorry," Emily said.

The sound of someone behind them made Lily turn. So did Emily.

Wes Colton stood on the other side of the boxes, holding a book in his hand. The sight of him stole her breath and shards of excitement chased her bleakness away.

"Looks like you got some new inventory." His voice was masculine and as appealing as she remembered. Maybe more so.

What was he doing here? Her insurance company was handling the transaction with his SUV. Of course, he had another reason, but she wasn't sure she was ready to face that.

"Wes." She hoped she didn't sound as schoolgirlish as she thought.

Emily glanced from her back to Wes.

He held up the book, the picture of a bare-chested man looking down at the soulful face of a brunette. "Interesting cover art."

Lily snatched the book from his hand and dropped it back into the box he'd taken it from. "It's popular fiction."

He didn't say anything, just grinned his amusement and something else. Was he flirting with her?

"Uh…I'll go help at the checkout counter," Emily said, smiling secretively as she wandered off.

Uncomfortable with the way Emily left them alone and the realization that she'd picked up on Wes's flirting, too, Lily had to force herself to look at him.

"How are you?" she asked.

"Good. You?" Was he nervous, too, or was this small talk a way for him to get a conversation going?

"Good," she played along.

He smiled wider. "I came by to see you."

His announcement dispelled the awkwardness. Gladness expanded and bloomed in her chest.

"I bought a new vehicle in Bozeman yesterday," he added.

"Oh, that's good. I hope you like it as much as your last SUV."

"More so. Cost me a little more than I expected, but it's worth it." His gaze floated over her face. "It's good to see you again."

Another charge of excitement tickled her. She smiled and saw how he noticed. "It's good to see you, too."

Losing herself as she met his smiling eyes, feeling his attraction match her own, it took her a moment to realize how they were behaving. She glanced around. Emily was busy with someone at the checkout counter. There was no one standing near them. No one had noticed them ogling each other.

Reality came down a little harder. Did she really want to encourage Wes? Aside from the folly of him getting involved with what everyone considered the town floozy, she would be no good for any man right now.

The news of her rapist's release had robbed her of her strength. She was vulnerable again. The same struggle she'd overcome so many years ago was returning. Would she be able to go home and not feel as though she had to lock every door and window and double-check them periodically? She hated that kind of weakness, the power Brandon Gates still had over her. Would she ever be free of that part of her life? It was disheartening.

No. She refused to succumb to irrational fears. He was moving back to North Carolina. That was far away from here, and he'd be foolish to try and make contact with her again. He had to know she'd expose him if he did.

"Don't worry, our secret is still safe," Wes said.

He'd given her a brief distraction from her troubles, but they weren't going to magically go away. "You shouldn't have come here."

"Would you rather we go back to the prison?"

He was trying be funny, but he had no way of knowing how upsetting the reference was for her. She looked down at the floor.

Wes was quiet for a few beats. "So…how do you like the library?"

Back to safe topics. He had a way of easing her into those and keeping her enchanted.

She glanced around at the dark wood shelves and Emily helping someone else now at the checkout counter. Something about this place made her feel good. It soothed her. Maybe it was her love of books. They'd installed new computers a few months ago. Some of the floor had been carpeted and some refinished with new hardwood. New lighting had been installed, too. It was cozy. Fresh. Clean and bright. "I like it." She looked back at him. "I like the work, too."

"How long have you been doing this line of work? I never got a chance to ask you that when you drove me to my office."

"I went to college after I left Honey Creek. It's been about ten years now." He was doing a good job of taking her mind off that phone call, drawing her out of darkness and into the light of his purpose in coming to see her. The Sheriff of Honey Creek County was interested in her.

"It suits you."

Did it? She took in his chest in his sheriff uniform, his height, and even though he was flirting, he had a commanding presence.

"Being sheriff suits you." She couldn't believe she'd said it. "I mean—"

"I know what you mean," he cut her off. "And I like that."

Oh, boy…

"Why did you leave the navy?" she asked, more to divert the conversation.

"I wanted to come home."

"You planned on running for sheriff?"

"Not at first."

"What did you do in the navy, anyway?" How had he gone from that to law enforcement?

He hesitated and the glint of infatuation left his eyes. She wondered if this was a sore subject.

"I joined the SEALs."

Her brow rose. She couldn't help it. "Wow. You passed that training?"

Was he studying her? He seemed as though he was suspicious of her. Did he wonder why she'd asked? Why did it matter?

"I worked with a team for a while," he finally answered, "but I didn't like the travel."

"And the danger?" Did he like that?

"That didn't bother me so much. I was careful."

Careful? "You sound so confident."

"You have to be."

"Is being sheriff of this little town enough of a stimulus for you?"

"I was young when I joined the SEALs. I don't need adrenaline rushes to stay interested anymore. So, yes, I like what I do now. And there's a lot to be said about dodging fewer bullets."

"You've dodged bullets in Honey Creek?"

"In a manner of speaking."

And he'd dodged them as a SEAL. "Didn't you like being a SEAL?" He was sure acting strange about it.

"I liked it. I just wanted to come home," he answered curtly.

She decided not to question him further on that. He obviously didn't want to talk about it.

"When is your brother going to be released?" she asked instead.

A woman looked at them as she passed. Lily wondered if she'd heard what she'd asked.

Wes didn't appear to notice, in fact, his tension eased. "I should have the court order in the next week or two."

"That's great."

She could only imagine what it would be like to watch your brother spend so much time in prison for something he didn't do. There would have to be some kind of effect on Damien. It had to have changed him somehow. Hardened him. Would he be dangerous?

She didn't want to find out. Instead of continuing to question Wes, she steered clear of the more detailed questions she was dying to ask.

"You must have been pretty young when he was convicted."

"Eighteen."

"Is that why you joined the SEALs?" Did he want to learn how to fight? To kill? Had he planned to go after whoever was responsible for wrongly convicting his brother?

He took a moment to answer and she inwardly kicked herself for asking. She hadn't meant to bring that up again.

"It might have had something to do with it. I never stopped believing Damien was innocent. I didn't know what to do. Maybe I joined the SEALs because it gave me a sense of control, whereas with Damien's situation, I've never had control."

"Even though you wanted it."

"Yes."

"I think everyone does the things they do in life for a reason, whether they know it or not."

"You became a librarian for a particular reason?"

"I love to read."

"Is that the only reason?"

She had to stop herself from fidgeting. She'd admitted to no one what had led her down this path. "It's what pointed me in that direction."

"When did you start reading a lot?"

"It wasn't until later, after…after I left." Now she was getting really uncomfortable.

"It was probably a good thing you did leave."

She just looked at him. If only he knew.

"I mean so you could find something to do with your life."

Did he mean other than being a wild woman?

"Without the pressure of…" He seemed at a loss for words.

"I should really get back to work."

He looked at her a moment. "Scared you away again, huh?"

"No, it's not that." What a lie that was. Brandon's release was hurtling her back in time. How could she have a normal relationship with any man if every reminder made her feel vulnerable?

"Then have dinner with me. Tonight. What time do you get off?"

"Oh…that's sweet, but…it's just not a good time."

"You're shooting me down again." He said it playfully.

"I'm afraid so." She couldn't help laughing. "Besides, did you know I'm forty?"

"Wow, your life is over."

She shook her head. "You're only thirty-three."

"Word gets around. You're old enough to be my sister."

"Stop that." But she laughed.

He grinned and she got the distinct impression that he

wasn't about to give up on her. There was something appealing about that. There was something appealing about a man who wasn't afraid of rejection. It showed boundless ambition and self-confidence. A humble ego.

There was a time in her life when she would have jumped headfirst into a relationship with a younger man, but things had changed.

He backed away. "I'll be back."

"People are going to talk," she said.

Emily had finished with the person at the counter and now watched them.

"Let them." He backed up some more.

She wasn't so sure, but his teasing was infectious. "Easy for you to say."

He took another step back. "It'll give them something else to talk about besides you."

"Oh, yeah? How do you figure that?"

"I just got a bug in me to start reading more."

Meaning he'd be stopping by the library more often. Her first reaction was to tell him no, but the delight he'd made her feel stopped her. She didn't try to sway him.

Wes left the library wondering if he'd misread the back-and-forth emotions from Lily. Sometimes she flirted with him and at other moments she withdrew. Was it their age difference? He wasn't that much younger than her. And she had good skin. Hell, he'd probably look older than her when he was forty.

He'd been trying to contact the victims' officer ever since the morning after Lily had plowed into his truck. She'd seemed to know Lily so he'd called a friend he'd made over the years Damien had been incarcerated and asked for her contact information. The minute he learned she was a victims' officer, he'd gotten more interested in finding out the real reason Lily had gone to the prison. But the officer had gone on a weeklong vacation the day after Lily had wrecked his SUV. He'd planned to wait to go to the library until after he spoke with her, but the truth was, he couldn't stay away any longer. What if Lily started thinking he wasn't interested?

He just hoped she wasn't messed up with an inmate at Montana State Prison. She said she'd changed but…

It'd been a week. He'd call the victims' officer again.

He drove to the west side of town and pulled to a stop in front of the Honey Creek County Sheriff's office. Getting out, he walked into the building, passing the front counter and heading to his office directly behind that, and sat behind his desk. He leaned back and let himself stare at nothing for a while, thinking about Lily. Maybe he should start to worry about how much he was beginning to like her.

The legal pad on his desk caught his eye. It was full of scribbled notes about Mark Walsh's murder case. He'd jotted them down earlier. Some were centered around the money-laundering angle the FBI was investigating, others were on the note found on the body of the man who murdered Jake Pierson's partner. Jake was the first FBI agent assigned to the money-laundering investigation and Jim Willis had been his partner. Since this whole thing started, Wes had gotten to know both of them. Jim had been a good friend to both him and Jake. He shouldn't have died like that, shot by a hit man who was after Jake for information the investigation had uncovered.

The note found on Jake's partner's body hadn't been signed, but it was on a special kind of stationary that had bothered Wes ever since he'd seen it. The stationary was expensive. Not just anyone would use it. He'd been all over town tracking down possible sources. One lead had taken him to the Colton ranch, where he'd found some in his dad's office. Was that significant? Probably not. The stationary could have been ordered from an office-supply catalog. Anyone could have ordered some. It would be tough narrowing down a suspect that way. And of course, there were no prints on the paper other than those belonging to the hit man.

A knock on the open door brought his head up. Deputy Ryan King stood there. He was a six-foot lean-framed man with fine, light brown hair whose light green eyes kept the women coming around, but he never strayed from his wife.

"Come in," Wes said.

Ryan closed the door and moved closer to Wes's desk. "Sorry to bother you, Sheriff. I'm not one to give gossip much thought, but my wife told me something I thought you'd want to hear."

Leaning back in his chair, Wes waited.

"She goes to that quilting group that meets in town. You know the one?"

"Yes. What about it?"

"Well, Terri said there was talk about you and that Masterson woman spending time together. Someone saw her drop you off here at the office and said you looked like you were getting along really well."

How long before it got around he'd just left the library? Wes chuckled. Didn't those women have anything better to do than talk about people?

"Some people take offense to you getting messed up with someone like her," Ryan said. "You're the law in this town. If people don't respect you...."

"It's been fifteen years since Lily left this town."

"That doesn't matter. It's your integrity in question."

"She isn't the same person. She's grown-up now. People will see that after a while."

"But if you continue to see her..."

Now he was beginning to get annoyed. "It's just talk."

"People are wondering where you were with her, where you could have met her."

"It doesn't matter how or where I met her." He looked pointedly up at his deputy. "I could have met her anywhere in town before that."

"I'm sorry, I know it's none of my business. It's just...your reputation."

"I'll worry about my own reputation, but thanks for letting me know."

"Come time for reelection..."

Wes looked up from the pile of papers on his desk and lifted his brow.

Ryan frowned, but relented.

When his deputy had left, Wes couldn't focus on the mound of work he had to do. Maybe he should pay more attention to what the town was saying. What if something got around that would hurt Lily? What harm would it be to use Ryan as a way of monitoring the gossip? He didn't care what was being said, but Lily did. And that was reason enough for him.

He picked up his phone and dialed Ryan's extension.

Chapter 3

"You've got one of the best pair of blue eyes I've ever seen." Levi Garrison came into step beside her. "Has anyone ever told you that?"

May Masterson rolled those blue eyes that were so like her mother's and didn't slow down on her way to her next class. Levi easily kept up with her. He was tall and had a long stride.

"I'm serious. I meant to tell you that the other day."

"When you were making fun of my mother?" Jerk.

"Yeah, well, about that…"

"Say anything smart and I'll knock your front teeth out," she said without looking at him. He was one of the most popular boys in eleventh grade. He was a football player and active on committees. He was smart, too, but not as smart as her. May knew her GPA was higher than this yokel's.

"I've been meaning to apologize for that. You took it all wrong anyway."

"How else am I supposed to take it when someone asks me if I'm as good as my mother?"

"That wasn't me. I didn't say that."

"No, you said I was prettier."

"You are."

She sent him a glare.

"You took it wrong. I wasn't after you that way."

"You said I had a nicer tail."

"I was just havin' fun. Who cares if your mom was easy when she was in high school? That was a long time ago."

May stopped and curled her hand into a fist. She raised it and brought it back for good momentum.

Levi caught it as she began to swing. Her fist fit into his hand.

His green eyes flared with something hot. "I'm sorry, okay? I didn't mean to make you mad."

"What do you care?"

He made the mistake of letting his gaze fall to her chest before meeting her eyes again.

She pushed him with her free hand. "Leave me alone, you jerk!"

"Hey." He let go of her fist. "I'm trying to be friends here."

"I don't want any friends." Not here anyway. She missed her friends in Sacramento. No one called her a slut there.

She pivoted and marched down the hall again, dodging other students, bumping someone's shoulder. A girl narrowed her eyes at her as they passed each other. May flipped her off.

Levi took hold of her wrist and pulled her to the side of the hall, twirling her smoothly. Her back came against a locker, but not hard at all. Levi was agile in the way he handled her. She didn't want to like that about him.

He put his hand on the locker above and beside her head and leaned closer. "I said I was sorry."

Her breath got stuck in her throat.

He leaned back and offered his hand. She looked down at it and back up at his cute face.

"What do you want?"

"Your friendship."

"That sounds like a line." Except he seemed sincere. Wouldn't it be great if one of the most popular boys in school liked her? "What do you really want?"

"To take you out. But that can wait. I'll settle for being friends for now."

"And once we're friends? Then what? You try to get into my panties?"

"No. I'm not after you like that, I told you."

"I don't believe you." But she wanted to.

"Just start by taking my hand. If all you can offer is hello in the halls, that's fine by me."

She eyed his hand again. What harm would it be to accept his apology? She could be reasonable. It felt good to have someone on her side for a change.

But what if he wasn't? What if he was just playing her? What if this was some kind of joke?

"Come on. I won't do anything drastic. I promise."

Deciding to give him a chance, she gave him her hand. He grinned as he shook her hand.

"You're gonna be late to class," he said, still smiling as he strolled down the emptying hall.

She watched until he disappeared into a classroom and then started to turn to head for hers.

"What do you think you're doing?"

May stopped and saw Sherilynn McTeague and one of her friends standing nearby. Sherilynn had long, blond hair and light brown eyes. She was a pretty girl in a prissy sort of way, and, like Levi, one of the most popular kids in school. But not so bright academically.

She was also Levi's girlfriend.

"Last I checked this was a public school," May said. She wasn't afraid of this prom queen.

"You stay away from Levi."

"Yeah," chimed in her friend, a slightly chunky, short-haired girl with big cheeks. "Go find your own boyfriend."

"Levi isn't my boyfriend. We were just talking. Not that it's any of your business." May turned to walk to her classroom.

"Careful how you talk to me, ho," Sherilynn called to her back.

Anger fired up in May like wind over a brush fire. *Ho?* Slowly, she pivoted, tensing as she moved closer to the two.

"If you're looking to get laid, do it with somebody else," the girl continued. "There are plenty of other boys who'd love to oblige you."

"Yeah," her chubby friend said. "Like mother like daughter. Isn't that what they say about people like you?"

Stopping, May's temper flared hotter. She was sick of *holding her head high* and not reacting to these unwarranted barbs like her mom always told her to do. She'd hold her head high all right. *After* she kicked both of these girly-girls' behinds.

Fisting her hand, she slugged the chubby girl right on the mouth. The girl's head jerked to the side and she stumbled backward, nearly losing her balance. See if she talked nasty ever again.

Sherilynn shoved May against one shoulder. May had to take a step back, but now she turned her attention to this girl. She swung her fist again, catching the side of her head. Then she hit lower, aiming for the soft part of her stomach. Sherilynn grunted and pulled May's hair. May yelled and slapped her hard across her cheek. Sherilynn stumbled and bumped into the chubby girl, tripping over her feet and falling. May stepped over her, meaning to straddle her and keep hitting, but the chubby girl pulled her by the arm. May yanked free and backhanded the girl on her nose. The girl retreated with a screech and held her bleeding nose.

Sherilynn was starting to sit up and climb to her feet. May lifted her foot and planted it against her chest, shoving her back to the floor. Then she straddled her and started slugging. See if she smiled pretty for any guy for a while....

The chubby girl pulled her off just as May spotted a teacher charging toward them.

"All right, in the principal's office. Now!" the teacher yelled. "All three of you!"

Sherilynn got to her feet, holding her side with one hand and her face with the other. "She started it!"

"Yeah, she hit me first," the chubby girl said.

"Is that true?" the teacher asked.

"Yeah. They were calling me names! I'm not a whore!"

"You're just like your slutty mother," Sherilynn said.

May lunged for her again.

The teacher stepped in her way, though, so all May could do was glare at the girl around her shoulder. "Wait 'til after school. I'll finish you off."

"May Masterson." The teacher grabbed both her shoulders. "You will stop this right now!"

"Make *them* stop. I didn't do anything wrong."

"Fighting isn't the answer."

"Her mom fought all the time," the chubby girl said snidely.

"How would you know, you weren't here," May retorted.

"No, but my mom was. She told me everything."

"My mom isn't like that anymore. You need to mind your own damn business."

"May, you don't swear in this school."

She zeroed in on the teacher's gaze. "Tell them to back off then."

"Why don't you tell the principal to do that." Moving one of her hands to May's elbow, she held tight and walked her down the hall, saying over her shoulder, "You girls are coming, too. Follow me."

Three days after seeing Lily, Wes walked into the West End Café in Deer Lodge, Montana. He'd searched for Karla Harrison, the victims' officer who'd come out of the prison after Lily had wrecked his SUV and had finally gotten hold of her. Once he told her who he was, she'd agreed to meet him here. She remembered him, but more importantly, she remembered Lily. He could tell she genuinely cared about her and was sure that was the only reason she was meeting him.

A few other tables were filled and talking joined the sound of dishes clanking and workers busy in the kitchen. The wood tables and chairs were scratched with age and the blue linoleum floor needed updating, and he was sure some women liked the lacy white valances above the front windows but he thought they could go with the floor.

The entry door opened and Karla walked into the small café. When he'd called her he'd asked if she'd meet him here rather than the prison. He didn't want anyone to know what he was doing, least of all Lily.

When she saw him, recognition showed on her face and she headed for his table.

"Sheriff Colton?" she asked.

He stood and took her hand in a shake. "Thanks for meeting me."

She sat down. "I have to admit, you have me curious. You didn't really say why you wanted to talk about Lily."

He sat across from her. "She's grown important to me since the accident."

Karla smiled softly. "I could tell there was something going on there." Then she sobered. "She seemed like such a strong woman when I first met her. I thought she'd do all right going to that parole hearing all by herself, but I could tell it was hard on her afterward."

There it was, the missing piece. "What parole hearing?"

"Oh…I thought you knew." Her expression turned worried. The waitress came and he ordered coffee. So did Karla, but in an absentminded way.

"Lily told me she went to the prison to see a friend," he reminded her when the waitress left.

"Oh," Karla hedged. "Yes, I remember."

"I could tell that wasn't the truth."

"I see." She poured sugar into her coffee and stirred. "I thought she'd have told you by now."

"She hasn't. I think it's too difficult for her. I was hoping you could tell me the real reason she was there."

Stopping her spoon, Karla stared at him, her hesitance etched over her expression. "I'm not sure how much I should tell you. What if she doesn't want me to?"

"Like I said, she's grown important to me. I want to help if I can."

Slowly Karla's expression smoothed. "That's very kind of you, Sheriff."

"If you aren't comfortable talking to me, you can give me the name of the inmate case manager."

He watched her process that. He was a sheriff. He had his ways of finding out what he needed with or without her help. Now that he knew Lily had gone to a parole hearing, and what day, he wouldn't have much trouble tracking down the case manager.

"No, no need for that. Lily's one of those special victims to me. A real fighter when all's said and done. I care about what happens to her, and I would love to know that she's happy. You want to know why she was there that day? She testified at Brandon Gates's parole hearing. She was the only victim who had the nerve to come forward out of all those women who testified at his trial."

Wes didn't like where this was heading. *Out of all those women...*

"Who is Brandon Gates? What was he in for?" he asked, fearing he already knew.

"Sexual assault."

"He raped her?" He supposed he shouldn't be surprised, as wary as Lily was around him, and as reluctant as she was to go out with him. Being with men had to be hard for her. Trusting them even harder.

Karla nodded. "It's so sad working with some of those women. And then the ones who seem so strong come along, like Lily, and you think they'll be all right, but…"

"When did that happen?" His mind raced to catch up. She'd left the area so long ago.

"Fifteen years ago, I think."

He could only stare at Karla. No wonder Lily had run into him with her truck. It must have killed her going to that hearing and having to face the man who'd hurt her so seriously so long ago. Surely she hadn't seen him since the trial. It must have brought it all back.

I was just visiting a friend, she'd said. That meant she didn't want anyone to know why she'd gone to the prison. It also meant she was ashamed of it. Why?

May was fourteen. He inwardly cursed. What she must have gone through if a rapist had fathered her child…

"You care about her."

His focus returned to Karla, but he decided not to answer her. "Was he released?"

Her eyes grew sad. "Yes."

It explained so much. "Where is he now?"

"He has family in North Carolina. One of the guards told me he was going to live there and stay with his brother. Apparently, his father has a remodeling company."

He nodded. Good. He was far away from here.

The waitress came to refill the coffee and he sipped.

"What happened?" It was a question he didn't want to ask, but had to. He needed to know. If he wanted to see Lily, he had to know what he was dealing with. She might be the first genuine woman he'd met in a long time. What kind of cruel irony would it be to discover she couldn't get past her tragic experience?

"She was out drinking with a friend one night. The friend went home with someone, a man. Brandon Gates abducted Lily in the parking lot and drove her to a remote cabin, and…"

He was glad she didn't elaborate. "How did she get away?"

"Late that night, she got free of the rope he used to tie her and left him sleeping. She hiked ten miles down the mountain to a main road and got help."

It took real grit to do something like that. Hike in the dark after being raped. Survival instinct had to have taken over, but not many women would be able to do something like that. She must have had experience in the back country before. Probably followed a stream or found her direction with the moon or stars. Given all the stories he'd heard about her adventurous escapades, he wasn't the least surprised.

Maybe he did have a shot with her after all. She was certainly brave enough.

"You'd be good for her."

Wes emerged from thought to look at Karla. He appreciated

her concern for Lily and her devotion to her job, but this was getting too personal.

"You being sheriff and all," Karla went on. "She'd feel safe with a man like you."

As corny as that sounded, he had to agree.

Lily walked into the main office of the high school and went to the counter where a woman waited.

"Are you May's mother?"

"Yes." She couldn't believe this. She was so angry she could spit.

"Right this way."

Lily followed the woman down a short hall just past the counter and entered the principal's office. The short-haired blonde woman in her fifties behind the desk looked up at her with obvious disdain. May sat in a chair in front of the desk. She looked sullen, causing Lily to check her anger.

The principal didn't smile. "Have a seat."

Lily sat in the chair next to May.

"They started it," May said right off the bat.

Lily pointed at her. "You be quiet." Then to the principal, "What happened?"

"Your daughter got into a fight with two other girls over a boy."

"That isn't true!"

Lily snapped a look at her daughter. May saw it and pursed her lips before looking away.

"They argued. May hit a girl named Brit Andrews first and they started to fight. Sherilynn McTeague tried to stop her but May hit her, too. Broke Brit's nose. Her mother is contemplating pressing charges."

"They called me a ho," May cut in.

Lily sent her daughter a warning look before turning back to the principal. "Is that true? Did they call her names?"

"They claim they didn't."

"That is a stinking lie!" May shouted.

"May?"

May sulked, her mouth downturned and her gaze dropping to the principal's desk.

Lily turned back to the principal. "So you've questioned the other girls?" It was all she could do not to get in the woman's face. But she didn't want to exacerbate May's situation and start another round of gossip about how her daughter was following her mother's footsteps.

"Yes."

"And what disciplinary action have you taken with them?"

"She let them go," May snarled, eyes on fire again.

"I suspended them," the principal corrected, eyeing May with impatience.

"As if that's going to stop them," May sneered.

Lily ignored her daughter's outbursts. At least the other girls were being reprimanded. But May had thrown the first punch. What kind of punishment did the principal have in mind and how much of it would be influenced by Lily's reputation?

She looked down at her daughter. "How many times have I told you not to get violent?"

"What am I supposed to do? Let them call me names and taunt me? No! I'm not going to anymore." She'd leaned over the arm of her chair, putting her face defiantly closer to Lily's.

Lily saw May's passion and decided to table the argument for now. She didn't really blame May for being upset, but she had to learn to do things the right way.

She turned to the principal. "I'm really sorry about this. I'll discipline her myself."

"I'm considering expulsion."

Lily lowered her head, feeling rage and disappointment. She wanted to tear into this biased woman for not understanding what prompted May to fight back. And she wished May would have shown more decorum. The worst part was that Lily could relate to her daughter's predicament. The familiarity stung. She'd been in this type of situation so many times. She'd deserved her punishments, and May was in danger of following the same path.

She slid her gaze to her daughter, who met it with another flash of defiance, but that quickly turned to contrition, as if she'd seen how this was affecting her mother.

Lily looked at the principal. "I'm asking you to give us one more chance. Just one. I'll work with May. She's having a hard time adjusting, that's all. This won't happen again."

"It will if they keep getting in my face about the way you were when you lived here before!" May retorted. "They think I'm the same way. I'm sick of taking it."

"We've talked about this."

"They're mean to me!"

Lily turned back to the principal. "Please."

The woman met her eyes for a while and Lily could see her seriously considering what to do. Here the woman was, staring the town Jezebel in the face, thinking she was raising another one, and thinking she should come down hard enough so that it made a solid enough impression on May that she wouldn't do this again.

"May is nothing like I was when I went to school here, and after," Lily said. "She knows better. She'll come around. Please give us another chance. All I'm asking for is one. If she does it again, I'll expel her myself."

The principal's eyes blinked but Lily saw how they softened. She waited.

"All right," she finally said. "One more chance. I gave the other girls a week of suspension. May will have the same."

Lily sighed and sank back against her chair.

"That is so unfair," May said.

"You can go now," the principal said.

May stood up with all the attitude of a slighted teenager and marched out the door ahead of Lily.

Lily followed more slowly, reaching her truck after May, who now stood at the passenger door with her arms folded, glaring at her mother. Lily felt worry slither through her.

Oh, God. What would she do if her daughter rebelled to the extent she had? She'd been so careful to raise her with an open mind, not the way her parents had raised her. Had she miscalculated somehow?

She climbed into the truck and waited before starting the engine.

"You don't get it."

Lily took in her daughter's fiery blue eyes. She had to get through to her somehow. "May, do you realize you're acting exactly the way the other kids expect you to?"

That only seemed to inflame her further. "What did you do when you went to school? When everyone called you names, what did you do?"

"I fought and got suspended. More than once."

"See?"

"See what? The answer to this isn't fighting. It didn't do me any good getting into fights and it didn't stop the talk. If anything, it made it worse."

"I'm not going to end up like you, but I can't let those girls walk all over me, either. They won't stop unless I make them."

"May…"

"You want me to be a wimp."

"No, I don't. I want you to be mature. You can't *make* anyone think the way you want them to. They'll form their own opinions no matter how many times you punch them in the nose."

"See? You don't get it."

Lily sighed, struggling to come up with something to say that would reach her.

"I'm not going to sleep around and go wild like everybody says you did," May said.

"No, but you're going to slug your way through high school and end up with a bad reputation anyway."

"I already have a bad reputation. Just being your daughter does that."

Lily had to catch her breath. That hurt so much. She'd worried coming back here would stir up talk, but she'd hoped it would fade as soon as they saw her working at the library and not going out to the bars and out with lots of men or on wild adventure trips.

She started the engine and began driving.

"I'm sorry."

Surprise made her glance at May, who met her brief look with the apology still in her eyes. It touched Lily. Maybe there was hope after all.

"I know you aren't like that anymore."

"Promise me you won't get into any more fights. If for nothing else, at least to prevent an expulsion."

May turned her face toward the window as Lily drove toward home.

"May?"

She looked at her but didn't say anything.

"I won't tolerate your being expelled from school. Do you understand that?"

"Yes."

"Then no more fights."

"Okay."

"Okay" wasn't a promise, but that was all she'd get for now. Lily knew her daughter. She just hoped May would have the good sense to listen to her.

Chapter 4

Wes left his office after talking on the phone with the new FBI agent assigned to their money-laundering investigation. The agent worked remotely and had an informant somewhere in town. Wes had tried to get him to say who that was, but he'd made a song and dance about needing to protect his informant. Wes was the sheriff. Did the agent really think he'd jeopardize the investigation? The agent was keeping the informant secret for a reason. Safety was one thing, but there was more to it than that. The agent wanted an ace in the hole, which meant the identity of the informant would come as a surprise to everyone. Maybe that person was someone prominent in town, someone everyone knew. Someone who could do a lot of damage or cause a scandal. And in Honey Creek, that meant it could be just about anyone.

What Wes wouldn't give to have Jake Pierson back on the case. But Jake had his own issues to deal with, the best one being his wife, Mary. Mary was one of Mark Walsh's daughters and had a vested interest in finding her father's killer. Mary and Jake had fallen in love when he was working the investigation, which ran into a few problems when Walsh was murdered.

Walsh was supposed to contact Jake with information about a potential money-laundering operation at Walsh Enterprises, but someone had gotten to him first. Jake had tapped into computers at the company, but nothing conclusive had turned up. Who was behind it? Now that Walsh was dead for good this time, they might never know. Jake had gotten close, but his and Mary's probing had led to his partner's death. And losing Jake's partner was a hard blow to everyone close to the investigation.

Wes climbed into his Jeep and started driving. All he needed was a break, just one big break. Some clue that would tell him who was behind Walsh's murder. He had a hunch that the murders of Jake's partner and Mark Walsh were connected to something big enough to make Mark disappear. Maybe it was the money-laundering operation. He was hoping the new agent and his informant would be able to shed some light on that. And soon.

But Wes's call to the new agent had produced nothing new on the money-laundering operation. He was tired of all the dead ends he'd encountered since finding out Mark Walsh had been murdered—for real this time.

His cell phone rang.

He put the BlackBerry to his ear. "Wes."

"Sheriff," one of his deputies said. "We got a call from Jolene Walsh this morning. She wants to meet you."

"Did she say why?"

"No. She insists on meeting with you personally. Only you."

Jolene had been among those he'd considered potential suspects, but there was nothing concrete to connect her to

Mark's murder. She'd been married to Walsh before he'd vanished fifteen years ago, and he hadn't been a model husband.

"Tell her to meet me at the office in two hours."

"She asked me to tell you to come to her house as soon as possible. Like now."

"She just wants me to drop everything and come to talk to her? Did she say why?"

"Only that it had something to do with Mark Walsh, and she's afraid to come to you because she doesn't want Mark's killer to get suspicious of her."

That made him take his foot off the gas pedal. "Did she say anything else?"

"No."

"All right. I'm on my way."

He turned onto a side street off Main and turned around. As he came to the stop sign at Main, he saw Lily enter the Honey-B Café. He checked the clock on his stereo. A little past noon. Impulse took over. It had been days since he'd seen her.

What harm would it be to make Jolene wait about an hour?

He parked on the street and walked toward the café.

Opening the restaurant's door, Wes searched inside for Lily. She was at the checkout counter and the cashier was handing her some change.

"It'll be just a few minutes," the cashier said.

"Why don't you make that two?" Wes asked, stopping the cashier midturn.

"Afternoon, Sheriff. What kind of dressing would you like with your salmon salad?"

Anything other than a salad would have worked. He looked at Lily, whose blue eyes blinked up at him. He turned back to the cashier. "Make that a Philly with cheese."

The cashier grinned. "You want that to go, too?"

He looked back at Lily, who still seemed surprised to see him...or was she happy to see him and trying to cover it up?

"Why don't you stay and join me?" he asked.

Her eyebrows lifted. "Uh...I—I was going to take it back to the library."

"I'm sure the library will be fine without you for an hour. Come on. There's a table over by the window."

She looked there.

He turned to the cashier. "Will you have our lunch brought to us over there?"

The cashier sent Lily a disapproving glance before turning back to Wes with a stiff smile. "Of course." No doubt she was miffed that the sheriff of Honey Creek County was cavorting with the likes of Lily Masterson.

Wes wondered if his lunch with Lily would make it around to the quilting group. He stepped aside and held his arm out, indicating her to precede him, hoping she would. She hesitated, but—much to his satisfaction—walked toward the table.

Sitting across from her, he watched how she quietly analyzed him.

"You don't give up easily, do you?" she asked.

"Not when it matters."

That won him a soft smile. "Don't you have work to do?"

"Yeah, but it's lunchtime. A sheriff's got to eat just like everybody else."

"So you just happened to decide to come here for lunch?"

He liked the flirty light in her eyes. "Are you wondering if I followed you?"

She fiddled with the cardboard menu display in the middle of the table. "Did you?"

He chuckled. "No. I was driving out of town after a call from my deputy, and I turned around to head the other way when I saw you."

Setting aside the cardboard display, she said, "So you did have work to do."

"It can wait."

A waitress came with glasses of water, eyeing the two of them.

"Where were you going?" Lily asked him after she left.

"Just following up on a possible lead."

"About Mark Walsh?"

He never discussed his investigations with anyone not directly involved. While he didn't want to make her wary by being too secretive, Lily didn't need to know any details.

"Possibly," he said.

"Can't talk about it, huh?"

"Not yet."

She sat back and observed him, no longer fiddling. He didn't try to hide the smoldering effect the sweetness of her attention had on him, especially when she relaxed like she did now. He sat back like her and treated her to the same appreciation.

"You're beautiful like that, you know." He couldn't help telling her.

She smiled. "Like what?"

"When you let your guard down."

"My guard is down?"

"You know it is."

Her eyes lowered, a hint of coyness, and then lifted to meet his again. "I think it's sweet that you came in here in the middle of a busy workday."

"And yet, you won't go out with me."

A breath of a laugh escaped her, soft and brief. "If you keep this up, you just might get your way."

That appealed to him immensely. He wanted to ask her if she liked being chased, but thought better of it. No, she would not like being chased. That wasn't what this was all about. She needed time. And she needed him to take things slow.

"Thanks for letting me know," he said.

He watched her study him and felt her curiosity build, as if his patient pursuit of her was beginning to open a closed door. He liked that. He liked that a lot. Once she opened herself to him completely, he'd be one happy man. Winning her trust would be one of the most gratifying things he'd ever achieved. Only with Lily, he couldn't really call it an achievement. *Gift* was a better word. Her gift to him. He wanted that so much, for her to want to give him that.

"Have you ever been married?" she finally asked.

And the question jarred him. He hadn't expected her to ask him that yet. Was she ready for this? The dating questions.

He was making progress. "No."

"Why not?"

"I haven't found the right woman yet." Maybe he was picky. Maybe he just worked too much. But one thing was for sure. He wanted to get it right the first time.

"How many relationships have you been in?"

"I don't know."

"You don't?"

He hadn't thought about it. "What do you mean 'relation-ships?'" He could understand her need to interview him, and he wanted to do well.

"Anything that went beyond a few dates."

"I've had a lot of those. Most lasted three months."

"You've never had a longer relationship?"

"Yes, I have. I was with a woman for four years in my early

twenties, and then I was with another woman for two years. That ended a little over a year ago."

Leaning forward again, she fiddled with the salt and pepper containers, uncomfortable again. He didn't like that.

"Are you afraid of commitment?" she asked.

"Only when I think I'm in danger of committing to the wrong woman."

"And who would that be?"

Was she worried he might consider her one of the wrong ones? If not now, then down the road? No one knew for sure what would happen as a relationship grew. "I think you know when you know."

"But what are you looking for? What was it about those other women that didn't work for you?"

"My first relationship ended because we were just too young to know what we wanted. The other…" He wished he hadn't brought this one up. It wasn't something she wanted to hear, he was sure.

"What?"

"It just didn't work out."

"Why not?" She smiled as his hesitation went on for too long. "Were you too different?"

"No. We got along. At first anyway."

"Then what was it?"

He picked up his water and sipped, taking in her playful expression.

"Sex?" she asked.

Now he wanted to squirm in his seat. When was the last time a woman made him feel like that? When was the last time anyone had made him feel like this? Cornered. Uncomfortable. Second-guessing himself. Maybe it was her history. He didn't want to offend her.

"It must have been sex."

He put his water down. "Do we have to talk about this?"

She laughed and he imagined part of the old Lily was resurfacing. That was encouraging. He didn't want her to be uneasy with sex because of her experience, so the fact that she could talk this way was a positive sign. But he wanted to be careful.

"It must have been good because you stayed for two years."

"It was good until it stopped," he confessed.

"Stopped, as in…you went days without it? Weeks?"

"Days I could handle. It was months."

"That is a long time. But you stayed."

"For a while."

She contemplated him as if she were studying a diagram in a page from a textbook. "How important is sex to you?"

The waitress appeared next to their table again, her eyes shifting back and forth between them again. She put their food down. "Can I get you two anything else?"

"No thanks," Lily said.

Wes shook his head.

When the waitress left, Lily looked expectantly at him.

So, he wasn't going to get out of answering her question. He kept his voice down. "As important as it is to anyone. She lost interest and I wasn't connecting with her anymore. It doesn't take a genius to figure that out. She just didn't have the courage to be the one to do something about it."

Lily nodded her understanding. "Sex is overrated."

Fighting the instinct to talk about her past, he chose his words carefully. "Not if you're with the right person."

Her gaze met his and darted somewhere across the café.

"I take it you haven't found that yet," he said. He didn't think he was pushing boundaries since she'd been the one to broach this personal, intimate topic. Besides, a little pushing just might be what she needed.

"I've never been married if that's what you're asking."

"Afraid of commitment?" He softened that with a grin. Let her know he was teasing.

She smiled back. "No."

"How many relationships have you had since you left Honey Creek?"

"Not very many. Three short-term ones and a few dates. I have May…"

He knew better than to press her about never being married by forty. He already knew why anyway. "Why didn't they work out?"

"The guys ended up leaving."

Because of sex? She'd already hinted she hadn't had great sex. Anybody who said things like "sex is overrated" couldn't have experienced it the way they should.

She began to seem uncomfortable so he didn't say anything about that. He was curious about one thing, though.

"What about before you left Honey Creek?"

"What about it?"

There was that sassy defense mechanism that always surfaced when she faced down her past and all the rumors.

"I don't mean to pry—" even though she had with him "—but you seem so different now. I can't help wondering…" He let the rest hang. She knew darn well what he was asking.

"What?" she challenged him. "You want to know if I had good sex? Well, all right. I'll tell you. Yes, I had fantastic sex. I loved it back then. Couldn't get enough of it. Satisfied?"

Was she telling the truth? "I'm sorry." And he was. "I didn't mean to upset you."

"You didn't." Her tone dripped with derision.

He just lifted his brow, the only sign he'd give that he knew she was upset.

She turned away. "I'm not that girl anymore."

"I know. You're someone much more mature and interesting."

When she faced him again, he saw that she'd mellowed some.

"And I'd be lucky to be the one to make you love it again."

"I don't want to love it like that again."

"It would have more meaning now." Because it would just be with one man instead of several. But he knew better than to voice that fact.

Her defensiveness slipped away with the return of her flirtation. "You seem awfully sure about that."

"Like I said, I'd be lucky."

She contemplated him, as though wondering if he'd say that if he knew what he was up against. Maybe she also wondered if it was even possible to enjoy sex again. He'd give it his best. He dreamed of the things they'd do together.

But first things first. He hadn't even convinced her to have dinner with him yet.

The warm humming sensation that hadn't abated since leaving Wes at the café energized Lily's stride as she entered the library. She supposed that conversation was her fault since she'd been the one to bring up sex. But she'd genuinely wanted to know about him. The way a man answered questions like that said a lot about his character. Wes had passed that test… except for the part about not getting enough of it. Could she even keep up with him? His drive might be different than hers.

Why was she thinking like this?

She passed the checkout counter and went into her office, going to the window.

I take it you haven't found that yet.

She'd known he wasn't asking about her marital history when he'd said that. What if he was right?

The idea of having a normal sex life scared her. But talking to Wes made her wish for it.

"You're settling in just fine, it would appear."

Lily turned and saw Mary Walsh standing there, red hair and pretty amber eyes shining.

"The library looks great," Mary said.

"Everything's running smoothly. No problems with personnel, either."

"Yeah. You have some good ones here."

Lily knew Mary hadn't stopped by to check in on her for this reason, but she played along. "How's Jake's new security business going?"

"Started out slow, but things are beginning to pick up. Damien's release has helped."

Lily smiled at the sarcasm she heard in her friend's tone. But at the same time it reminded her that Brandon was going to be released soon.

"Maybe I should give him a call," she said absently.

"Are you afraid of Damien, too?"

"No." Too late she realized her blunder. "It's just…with all the talk…"

"Yeah. That's why I wanted to stop by. You holding up all right?"

"Yes. A little gossip never hurt anyone." Well, not physically anyway.

"A little gossip, huh? Is it true you've been seeing Wes? I never make a habit of trusting what this town goes ape over."

"I wouldn't say I'm *seeing* him."

"Do you want to?"

"I'm not sure. He's seven years younger than me." And she was dealing with so much right now.

"He's not that much younger. Jake is six years older than me."

Call her old-fashioned, but it was different when the man was older. "I can handle a couple of years of difference, but seven…it seems like a lot."

"Wes is a nice man. He isn't after a twentysomething hottie. He and Jake got to be pretty good friends. I think you two would make a great couple."

"Thanks for the vote of confidence. You're probably the only one in town who thinks that." She laughed to cover the hurt that reality caused.

"No, I'm not. Bonnie Gene thinks so, too."

"Okay, so there's two of you."

Mary laughed this time. "That'll pass. You know how this town can be."

Boy, did she ever.

Emily appeared in the doorway, holding a vase of red roses. "This just came for you."

"Wow," Mary cooed.

"Delivery guy just left." Emily smiled a huge smile.

Lily was stunned. Had Wes done this? Already? He must have called right after he'd left the café. Unless he'd called before he'd gone into the café? That made more sense.

"Wow is right." She took the flowers by the vase.

She turned and placed the vase on the desk in front of her chair and sat down. There was a card. She slipped it free of its plastic holder and opened it up.

Roses are red and so are you.

Lily reread the card. What did it mean? It wasn't signed. If Wes sent these, he had a weird sense of humor.

What if it wasn't Wes?

"Lily? Are you all right?"

She looked at Mary. Who would send red roses other than Wes? Was this a practical joke? Roses cost a lot of money. Who would spend that much on a practical joke?

Maybe it wasn't a joke.

A chill accompanied the realization, running down the skin on her arms and sprouting goose bumps on her thighs.

Mary walked to the roses. "Who sent you those?" She read the card and turned to Lily.

Lily shrugged. "Someone who doesn't like me."

"You should call Wes."

She didn't want to do that. "It's probably just someone in town messing with me." Someone who didn't want her here? That was three-quarters of town. It would be next to impossible to figure out who sent them.

"It's not funny, Lily."

"I'm not laughing."

"Call Wes."

"I'll think about it." If she called him, it might give him the wrong message. She didn't want to encourage him by leading him to think she was using the flowers to get closer to him... appeal to his protective nature.

Mary angled her head in silent admonishment.

"It's a harmless prank."

"What if it isn't?"

Brandon wasn't due to be released yet so it couldn't have been him. He'd be the only one she'd be afraid of.

"No point in worrying unless there's really something to worry about." It wasn't as if someone had tried to kill her, like what happened to Mary and Jake.

Mary considered her a while. "Be careful, all right?"

"I will."

"I came by to see if you and Wes would like to double for dinner sometime. But first I had to make sure you were really seeing him."

"Oh. I… Wes and I aren't really dating."

"It doesn't have to be this week. Just let me know when you're ready."

She sounded so sure the date would happen.

Mary smiled. "I'd better get going."

Lily said goodbye and after Mary had left, sat behind her desk, staring at the roses.

Since there was only one florist in town, she might be able to find out who sent them. She picked up the phone and called.

"Daisys," Daisy Ray answered.

"Hi, Daisy, it's Lily from over at the library."

There was a slight hesitation. "Oh…hi, Lily. Do you like your flowers?"

Daisy sounded nervous. "They're beautiful. Except the card wasn't signed. How am I going to thank the person who got them for me?"

"Well, now, I—I don't know. You have a secret admirer it would seem." Daisy's tentative laugh spoke volumes.

"Who bought them for me?"

"I don't know who it was. They paid cash."

"You don't know who it was?"

"It was a young boy. Maybe fifteen or so. I don't know his name."

Was she telling the truth? Lily wasn't sure how much more she should press the woman. She seemed uncomfortable. Why? Did she think Lily was at it again? Back to her old ways? Carousing around town, hitting on men? And now they were sending her flowers?

Except that isn't what this was about. Lily was beginning to think this wasn't an innocent delivery. *Roses are red and so are you?* That could be construed in any number of ways. Red could be a symbol of beauty or passion, or one of death.

Lily shook that last thought off. Someone was just trying to scare her and she wasn't going to let them. The flowers were beautiful. She'd put them on her desk and forget the rest.

Wes stepped to the door of Jolene's farmhouse and rang the bell. Seconds later, the door opened.

"I've been waiting for you," she said.

"Sorry. I had a lunch meeting I couldn't miss." She didn't have to know it was with Lily. He was sure everyone would find out before the end of the day anyway.

"Come in."

He passed her in the entry and then followed her to the kitchen, where a cassette player lay. That was interesting. A cassette player in this day and age.

"I found it this morning," Jolene said.

And he had to assume she meant a tape. He leaned over and pressed the rewind button, but the cassette had already been rewound. He pressed Play.

"I was cleaning out the attic and found this in a box of old hats and gloves and scarves. Mark must have put it in there before he disappeared."

Wes looked at her. And she had just stumbled across it?

She was wringing her hands in front of her as she stared at the cassette player. Why was she so nervous?

"Hi, Mark," a feminine voice said from the player. It was grainy and a little muffled.

"Hi, Tina. Come on in," Mark Walsh answered.

"He had the cassette in a case and wrapped in a box," Jolene explained. "Probably why it's preserved so well."

"When did he record it?" Wes asked, hoping to trick her in case she knew more than she was telling, like maybe she knew about the tape and the reason Walsh had made a recording.

She shrugged. "Had to be sometime before he disappeared. That hat box has been in storage for years."

"You said it was important," Tina said.

Who was Tina?

"Sit down."

Muffled shuffling sounds garbled the recorder. Mark must have placed it close to wherever they sat. The voices were a little clearer now, too.

"I got to thinking about what you told me," Mark said.

"It has to be over, Mark. You're married."

"It's not about that. I want to help you, Tina."

"Help me?"

Wes just bet there was something he wanted in return, too. That was how Mark Walsh operated. He might have been murdered, but *nice* was not a trait he'd been known for.

More shuffling noises garbled the recording.

Tina inhaled sharply. "What is this?"

"It's a passport."

"A driver's license, too?"

"Yes. And anything else you need to get a fresh start. You no longer have to be Tina Mueller."

There was a long silence.

"What are you talking about?"

Good question. Wes couldn't wait to hear the answer to that one.

"There's something I want from you. You don't have to agree, but if you don't, you have to leave your new identity here and leave town."

"What identity? I don't need a new identity."

"Oh, yes, I think you do, Tina Mueller."

"Why do you keep saying my full name?"

"I know all about your past, my love. You know the one I'm talking about?"

Another long silence ensued. "Bastard."

Mark chuckled. "I bought you a house, too."

"You're crazy."

"And you'll let me in whenever I come over."

"What for? To be your mistress? Go to hell!" More shuffling suggested Tina had gotten to her feet.

Mark must have stopped her.

"You'll do everything I tell you. No one knows you in Honey Creek. You can make a nice life for yourself there."

"But only if I spread my legs whenever you show up and God only knows what else? No thank you."

"I discovered one of my wife's diamonds is missing."

Tina's hesitation spoke volumes. "So? Buy her another one."

"I know you took it."

"No, I didn't. I was only at your house that one time."

"Yes. And I saw you take the ring. You thought I was sleeping, but I wasn't."

Tina didn't say anything.

"What would the police say if they knew?" Mark asked.

"You don't understand. I had a good reason for taking that ring. I chose you because you have a lot of money. You wouldn't miss a ring your wife never wears. It wasn't even her wedding ring."

"How do you know she never wears it?"

"She has a hundred other ones."

"You stole from me."

"Please, Mark. I didn't do anything wrong back then, but the police won't believe that. If you really want to help me, you won't tell anyone I took that ring. It will give me the break I've been looking for."

"Is that all you wanted from me? Money?"

"I needed the ring."

"And you slept with me to get it."

"Don't take it personally. Someone like you doesn't care about a little old ring."

"That little ring is worth over a million dollars."

Again, Tina remained silent.

"Have you sold it yet?"

After another hesitation, she said, "Yes."

"Take my offer, Tina. It's the only one you'll get."

Tina sighed. Long seconds passed. "How do I know I can trust you?"

"Do what I ask and this stays our secret. Cross me, and the deal is off. It's simple."

She didn't say anything and Wes could imagine the thoughts that had gone through her head.

"You can make a good life for yourself," Mark told her again. "What I ask of you won't be too much of an imposition. You'll be free of your past and you can do whatever you want with the money from the ring. I won't stand in your way unless you refuse me. It's a generous offer. One both of us will benefit from."

Him more than her. He was essentially lining her up to be one of his minions. Sex probably would have nothing to do with it, despite what Tina thought.

"All right, what, exactly, do you have in mind?"

The recording ended.

Wes ejected the tape and turned to Jolene. "Mind if I take this?"

She shook her head. Her arms were folded and she looked small and vulnerable. What was she afraid of? Or was hearing the tape between her ex-husband and one of his lovers disturbing to her? He wondered if she was telling him the truth about how she had found the tape. What if she'd known about it all along and kept it secret?

Why would she do that?

The tape was irrefutable evidence that her husband had had a lover. Was that enough to give her motive to kill if Mark had contacted her recently? Or had he contacted the lover and given that woman the motive? If Jolene was aware of the reunion, she also knew it could shift the blame off her.

She could have done this fifteen years ago, too, so Wes was inclined to believe she'd only recently found the tape. And the lover had ample motive to kill Mark if he'd contacted her from his not-so-dead grave. He doubted she'd been the cause of Mark's disappearance, but his reappearance might have threatened her enough that she would do something drastic about it. After living for so long free of his ultimatums, his return would be a bitter pill to swallow. Especially if she had made a nice life for herself as Mark had given the opportunity to do with his offer.

"I don't know anyone named Tina," Jolene said.

"Mark helped her change her identity." He'd get all he could on Tina Mueller, hoping something would turn up to lead him to her.

"I searched his financial records for the house he talked about, but didn't find anything."

"I'll see what I can find."

"I almost feel sorry for her."

Wes thought she seemed sincere. "Why?"

"She was so close to pulling it off."

"Pulling what off?"

"When she met him she must have known he had money and decided to use him. For once he was the one being used. It must have really gotten under his skin, knowing that a woman used sex to get into his house and steal something valuable. I have to hand it to her."

"You're happy she stole your ring?"

"I don't care about the ring. He deserved a taste of his own deceitfulness."

He nodded. "Do you think he deserved to die for it?"

"No, of course not. That's not what I'm saying."

There was nothing more he wanted to ask her right now. "I'll let you now what turns up." He headed for the door.

"Wes?"

He stopped with his hand on the doorknob.

"I didn't kill him."

Right now he had nothing to prove otherwise, but he wasn't going to tell her that. Until he knew for certain who the murderer was, he wasn't going to eliminate anyone as a potential suspect.

Chapter 5

Lily glanced over at her dad. She bet she could count on one hand how many times Seamus Masterson had spoken to her since her return—the words *yes* and *no* excluded. Everybody called him Shay for short. Sometimes she felt like calling him that instead of Dad. She had called him Shay as a teenager and it had annoyed him.

He'd aged a lot since her mom had died. He didn't even look like the same man. Where once he'd been tall and big-framed, now he was still tall, but wiry and frail. As a child she'd been intimidated by him. Maybe that was why she'd rebelled to such an extreme. It had certainly played a role. His lack of acceptance of her had been the catalyst; that and her mother's prim way of allowing him to destroy her self-esteem. Or at least trying to.

Shay sat on the couch holding a newspaper, his thick glasses magnifying his blue eyes. He didn't acknowledge her when she sat in the chair next to the couch. Not even when she said

"Good morning." She might as well not be in the room. It was Saturday and she had the day off. She was hoping to spend an hour or two of family time with him. Break a little of that ten-foot block of ice separating them.

She looked around the room. It was cozy for such a staunch man. Bookshelves spanned the entire north wall behind her, and antique furniture over a red mosaic-patterned rug faced a wood-burning fireplace. Windows filled most of the east wall and reached the vaulted ceiling. A French door next to the bookshelves led to a wooden balcony. There was a den in this house with a television and stereo, but her dad liked to spend his time in here reading. Maybe that was his way of escaping his lonely existence. He might have seemed like a cold-hearted bastard growing up, but he'd loved her mother to the core of the earth.

Lily turned to look at him again. He still had his face in the newspaper.

May would be down any minute. They'd talked about going out for lunch and then shopping in Bozeman. The getaway would be good for both of them. It would get Lily's mind off Brandon's release, which would have happened yesterday, and May's off her troubles at school.

The sound of May's feet thudding on the stairs to the walkout basement preceded her voice. "Mom? Can I get a pair of hiking boots today?"

It irritated her that now her dad put the newspaper on his lap and looked up at May with a smile.

"Sure." She needed a pair of hiking boots anyway.

"Hi, Grandpa," May said.

"Mornin', pumpkin."

"I'm too old to be a pumpkin." But May laughed anyway.

"You're my pumpkin."

"Are you coming with us today?"

Her dad's smile faded and he glanced at Lily. It was brief. "You girls go on your shopping spree. I'll be here when you get home."

"You always stay home." May pouted.

"You get to be my age you'll understand."

"May's right, Dad. You do always stay home. Maybe it would do you some good to get out every once in a while."

Cold eyes found hers. "I'm happy right here."

"You could spend more time with May."

"I'll spend time with her tonight." His voice was starting to rise.

Lily decided not to push the subject in front of May. She'd been careful not to put too much emphasis on the conflict between her and Shay; May didn't need to be involved in all that. Lily wanted her daughter to have a good relationship with her grandfather. And the way Shay was responding to her was a good sign.

She stood. "You ready?" she said to her daughter.

"I'm hungry."

"Didn't you eat breakfast?"

"I had cereal."

And it had already worn off. The metabolism of a fourteen-year-old was something to marvel at. "We'll stop somewhere for an early lunch." It was already eleven anyway.

Lily grabbed her purse and keys and led her daughter to her truck.

"How come Grandpa never talks to you?" May asked when they were on their way.

Lily never knew how to answer these questions. The last time May had asked why she'd never met her grandfather before now, Lily had said she hadn't been close to him as a child. The next question had been, "What about my grandmother?"

She'd gotten past that one by telling May her grandmother had died.

"I suppose he doesn't know what to say."

"Why not? He talks to me."

"I told you, we weren't close when I was growing up."

May was silent for a few minutes. "Is it because of the way you were?"

Lily parked in front of Kelley's Cookhouse and turned the truck engine off. She looked over at her daughter. Maybe it was time to tell her all of it.

"My dad was very strict when I was growing up."

"Like you?"

Lily grunted a laugh. "No. Worse. He and your grandmother were religious but they were also…" *Narrow-minded and stiff* didn't seem like the right way to say this. "They wanted things to go their way or no way. If I didn't play by their script, I heard about it. Sometimes I was punished."

"They beat you?"

"No." Not physically. "When you're a parent you have to teach your children, not dictate to them."

"Grandpa did that?"

"He's changed, May. He's learned and grown over the years. If I'd known that sooner, I would have brought you back before now."

"What about Grandma? What was she like?"

A pang of sadness built in Lily's chest. She wished she could have had a better relationship with her mother. "She loved your grandpa. She did what he wanted."

"She treated you the same?"

"She didn't have to. She let him have control."

Lily watched her daughter think about that. "I would never do that."

May couldn't have paid her a higher compliment. "Then I did something right with you, honey." She smiled her love.

Her daughter smiled back. "Do you think Grandpa will change his mind about you?"

"I don't know. He never accepted me for who I was. I don't know if he'll ever get past that."

"What did he want from you?"

"I wish I knew. Good grades didn't matter. He didn't agree with my interests or opinions. They were different from his, you see."

"I'm glad you didn't let him control you, Mom."

God, she loved her daughter. "I didn't let him control me, but I made a mistake in the way I rebelled against him. That's why I got so mad when you ended up in the principal's office for fighting."

May rolled her eyes, but it was without annoyance. "Are we going to eat or what?" She swung open the truck door.

Lily laughed and got out with her. That's when she saw Maisie Colton walking down the street toward them. She was still beautiful at forty. Tall and slender with long, brown hair, she moved like a movie star. No one would ever guess she had a crazy streak by looking at her.

"Lily Masterson? Is that you?"

Maisie knew damn well it was. Lily stopped in front of the entrance to Kelley's Cookhouse, her daughter beside her.

"Hello, Maisie."

Maisie turned to May. "And who is this?"

"My daughter, May." Nothing like stating the obvious.

"Hello, May." Then to Lily, "I didn't know you had a daughter."

Lily smiled because that wasn't true. Maisie knew well and good she had a daughter. She probably also knew her age and speculated, just like many others, that May was one of Mark Walsh's children, scattered in a wide radius from Honey Creek County.

Maisie ignored her silent look and turned to May. "She's

so adorable. And she looks so much like you." Then to Lily, "How old is she?"

"I'm fourteen," May said.

Maisie's eyes told Lily all she needed to know. With all the theatrics of a movie star, her eyebrow lifted as she looked at May and then her condescension slid to Lily. She thought Mark Walsh was Lily's father.

Lily didn't even try to correct her.

"You left town in such a hurry, I never had a chance to say goodbye," Maisie said, and Lily sensed May looking up at her.

"I had an opportunity to attend Drexel University in Sacramento," Lily said. The opportunity had come much later—after she'd been in Sacramento for a while. But Maisie didn't need to know that.

That seemed to give Maisie pause. Honey Creek's bad girl had cleaned up her act enough to go to college.

"And now you're a librarian." She said the word *librarian* as if it were beneath her standards.

"She's *head* librarian," May cut in, all sass and attitude. It was so sweet to be defended by her daughter.

"Yes, so I've heard," Maisie said, scrutinizing Lily. "I also heard you and Wes are getting to be quite the item."

She'd known this would come sooner or later, the not-so-subtle queries that would feed the constantly churning gossip mill. "Really? I haven't heard that."

"How did you meet him?"

"I ran into him outside town." Lily couldn't stop her smile. If it hadn't been for her purpose for being at the prison, this would be funny.

"Wes told me you got into an accident with him, but he wouldn't elaborate."

"I wasn't paying attention."

"It's so peculiar…you two are being so secretive. Why? Where did the accident happen?"

"It's none of your business," May sneered.

"May," Lily admonished, even though she inwardly cheered. Ahhh, the candor of adolescence.

May looked up at her with all the fiery spirit of a hormonal teenager. "Tell her to back off, Mom."

"Don't be silly," Maisie said. "I was only trying to make conversation. You should try it sometime."

May squinted her eyes, making it abundantly clear that she didn't buy it, nor did she like Maisie.

Maisie grunted haughtily before turning back to Lily. "Wes must have been on his way back from the prison to see Damien when you met him. He rarely leaves town for any other reason. I still get so upset about that. Damien and all. But isn't it just wonderful that he'll be released?"

"Yes. Wes is happy about that, too." She could have bitten her tongue for letting that slip.

"You must be getting close to him."

Lily didn't respond.

"Who'd have thought…you and Wes."

Taking May's hand, Lily squeezed, a silent message to stay quiet.

"Mom?"

"We'd better get going," Lily said to Maisie. "We have plans after lunch. Good seeing you again, Maisie." It was a total lie, but she refused to let anyone take her down.

"You, too, Lily."

"Stop letting these old hags drag you through the mud!" May hissed as they headed for the door of Kelley's Cookhouse.

"Maisie is my age, May."

"Maisie who? Who is she?"

"Maisie Colton."

May's mouth dropped open and she gaped at her. "She's related to the sheriff?"

"She's his sister."

"Oh, my God. You should tell him to get lost. Is he like her?"

"No, May, Wes is a very nice man." With no agenda to slander her. At least, not so far.

Wes sat behind his desk reading a background file on Tina Mueller. Born and raised in Atlanta, Georgia, she was the only child of a plumber and a waitress. She hadn't graduated from high school and Wes couldn't find anything else on her after that. She had a couple of juvenile offenses that suggested her upbringing hadn't been stable.

His desk phone rang.

"Sheriff Colton."

"Sheriff, this is Nina Barker from Fulton County Juvenile Court in Atlanta. You called a couple of days ago?"

"Yes. Thank you for calling me back."

"I found the file you were looking for, but there's a note with a contact and a request to route all inquiries to a detective Grant Isaac." The woman gave a number to him. "This note is pretty old, though. He might not even be around anymore."

"I'll try to get a hold of him. Thanks."

He disconnected the call and entered the new number. His gut told him this was going to lead to something. After two rings, someone answered.

"Detective Isaac."

Luck was going his way today. "Sheriff Wes Colton from Honey Creek County in Montana."

"Afternoon, Sheriff. You're a long way from Atlanta. What can I do for you?"

"I got your name from Nina Barker over at juvenile court. I'm conducting a background check on someone you were investigating more than fifteen years ago. Do you have a few minutes to talk?"

"Who is it you're investigating?"

"Tina Mueller."

The detective's hesitation said he might be recovering from an unexpected surprise. "Tina Mueller, huh? That case has been cold for so long I thought it'd never see the light of day again. How do you know her?"

Wes explained about the Walsh murder and the tape Jolene had given him.

"And you think the Mueller woman may have killed him?"

"That's what I'm trying to find out."

"Do you know if she's still in Honey Creek?"

"No, not yet."

"Do you know what name she's using now?" the detective asked.

"No. Detective, why did you say her case was cold? Which juvenile offense is still open?" As far as he could tell both counts were closed. She'd done all that had been required of her.

"I wasn't investigating her juvenile cases. She was eighteen when her stepfather was murdered."

Wes nearly choked on his own saliva. "Murdered?"

"Yep. Ed Mueller was the stepfather's name. He was stabbed fourteen times while the mother was out with her weekly cards group."

Wes's mind filled with too many unanswered questions. He didn't know which one to ask first.

"You must not have received a full report," the detective said.

"I guess not. You think she did it?" And did he know why? But he'd save that for later.

"It hasn't gone to court yet, but a couple of years ago we

did some advanced DNA testing on some preserved evidence. Should prove her guilt if we ever get a chance to test for a match."

Wes started writing notes. "What was the mother's name?"

"Janet Mueller. There was a long history of abuse in the family. There are hospital reports on both the mother and the daughter. One day Tina must have had enough and waited until her mother left to use a butcher knife to stab her stepfather while he slept on the couch. He drank a lot so he must have passed out first."

"What kind of evidence do you have?"

"Prints on the knife that turned up in a Dumpster not far from their house. Blood. He must have gone a few rounds with her before he was killed. His knuckles were bloody and it wasn't his. I doubt she could have overpowered him if he fought her before she stabbed him, so my guess is she waited until after he passed out."

"So when she found out you recovered the murder weapon, she panicked and ran," Wes said.

"Yep. On one hand, I can hardly blame her. On the other, she should have gone to the police. Done things the right way."

Wes had to agree. "Where's the mother now?"

"Still living in Atlanta last time I checked."

"Do you know if she's been in touch with her daughter?"

"I doubt it. When I questioned her, she was more upset about her husband's death than the well-being of Tina."

"What about now? When's the last time you spoke with her?"

"Oh. It's been, what...something like five years now."

"You have a phone number?"

The detective gave it to him and he jotted it down with the rest of his notes.

"Will you let me know if you find her?" the detective asked.

"Yes, I will."

"Thanks for calling, Sheriff."

Wes hung up and sat back in his chair. When his mind settled, he looked up and saw his deputy standing in the doorway.

"I knocked," Ryan said.

"Come in."

"Sorry to bother you, but I think you'll want to hear what I have to say."

More gossip. What now? "All right."

Ryan didn't sit down. He stood just inside Wes's office. "My wife met up with her friends from that quilting group again last night. One of the women there said she talked to Maisie, who I guess ran into Lily on Saturday."

Wes put his elbow on the arm of his chair and rested his chin between his thumb and index finger, trying not to get annoyed. Why wouldn't those women leave Lily alone? And Maisie. Why did she have to go and stir up trouble all the time?

"She said Lily got in a wreck with you the same day you went on one of your visits to Montana State Prison."

Wes dropped his hand and straightened in his seat. Damn Maisie. He'd have to be careful what he told her from now on.

"They're hyping up the connection to the prison," Ryan continued. "One of the ladies went so far as to say you probably met Lily there. It's causing quite a commotion."

What did they think? That he broke Lily out of jail? This was getting ridiculous.

But what would it do to Lily if word got out that she'd gone to her rapist's parole hearing? So far it didn't seem that anyone knew she'd actually gone there, but how long before that changed? This kind of talk might not be good for her. As long as no one talked, it would be hard to prove Lily had been at the prison, much less that she'd gone to a parole hearing. But he'd warn Lily anyway.

"That's the same day you met Lily, right?" Ryan asked.

"Yes."

"Did you meet her at the prison?"

Wes stood up. "Thanks for telling me." He wasn't going to give away any more than he needed to.

"Sure thing." Ryan looked disappointed.

Moving around his desk, Wes stopped before Ryan. "I need you to check on something for me."

"Okay," Ryan said. "What is it?"

"See if you can get the names of every woman who moved to Honey Creek in 1995."

"Any particular type of woman you're looking for?"

"Not sure. Get me every name and I'll go from there."

"Will do."

Wes headed for the door.

"Where you going?" Ryan asked.

He paused and looked back. "The library." He grinned over his shoulder. He was going to stop by and see Lily today anyway. Ryan had just given him an excuse.

Ryan shook his head and didn't return Wes's grin.

Outside the building, Wes climbed into his SUV. He drove the short distance to the library and parked in front. Inside the building, he looked around for Lily, but didn't see her. Was she even working today?

Her assistant sat behind the main counter and saw him approach.

"Is Lily here?" he asked.

"Yes. She's in her office."

He looked where the girl had glanced and thanked her before heading for the hallway.

"I should probably tell her you're here," the assistant called after him.

He ignored her. In the open doorway of Lily's office, he stopped. She looked up, dark hair thick and silky around her face, blue eyes growing big when she caught sight of him. She got more beautiful to him every time he saw her.

"Wes?"

"Hello, Lily." He noticed a bouquet of roses on her desk.

"What brings you here?" she asked, that soft smile of hers emerging. She stood and came around her desk to stand closer to him.

"I was in the neighborhood."

That made her laugh a little. "Sure you were."

He grinned. "Would you like to go for some coffee?"

"I can't. I don't have time today."

"That's what you always say." It wasn't, but he wondered if she was avoiding him.

"No, really, today I'm pretty busy."

"Then you'd go otherwise?"

Her head angled and her eyes sparkled coyly. She didn't answer. He bet he could have talked her into going with him if she wasn't so busy. That pleased him.

Looking pointedly at the bouquet of roses, he returned his gaze to her and struggled with an attack of jealousy.

"It seems I have an admirer," she said.

She went to the flowers and pulled the card from a plastic holder, handing it to him.

He took it and read the cryptic line, looking at her when he finished. "Who sent you this?"

"It wasn't signed and the florist didn't know who'd bought them."

He didn't like it that someone had shown such animosity toward her. It had to have been someone in town; Brandon Gates wasn't released from prison yet.

"Mind if I keep this?" he asked Lily.

"No."

He tucked it into his shirt pocket.

"What would you have done if the roses were from a male admirer?" she asked.

He heard her teasing tone. Wasn't she worried about who sent her the flowers?

"I'd have bought you lilies."

And he was rewarded with a warm, flirtatious smile. He'd definitely have to get her some lilies.

"I heard you ran into Maisie Saturday," he said.

That cooled her mood a bit. "Yes. I know she's your sister, but…"

"No need to apologize. I'm a little annoyed with her right now myself." Or maybe he was being overly protective of Lily.

"Why's that?"

"She knew I went to the prison the day I met you, and now she's got the town wondering if that's where our accident occurred."

She met his gaze and a silent question floated between them. He wasn't going to say that he already knew the real reason she'd gone to the prison that day. She wasn't ready for that. But he could see how the prospect of the entire town knowing bothered her.

Wandering to the window behind her desk, she looked through it and didn't say anything.

He waited a few beats, but when she didn't move, he went to stand behind her. She looked up and over her shoulder at him when he touched her arm.

"If I could stop the gossip, I would," he said, and he meant it.

When she turned to face him, he saw how his declaration

had eased some of her tension. Moving closer, she touched his face with her hand. "I believe you."

His cell phone rang.

Really bad timing.

"Colton."

"Sheriff."

It was Ryan.

"The court order came through."

Excitement and satisfaction coursed through him. Damien was coming home.

Chapter 6

On her first day back after suspension, May saw Levi leave school ahead of her and tried to ignore her disappointment. Had he even noticed she was back? He probably already forgot about her. Why did she even care about a jock like him anyway? She didn't want him to like her, did she? He wouldn't. He wouldn't want to risk his reputation. Hanging out with her might ruin any chance he had of becoming class president.

She left the building and stepped out into a clear afternoon.

"You doing anything today?"

Peri Carter jogged to catch up to her and then walked beside her. Peri had been hanging around her more and more lately. She wasn't very popular in school, either. Everybody teased her about her curly red hair. It was really thick. And really red. Her eyelashes were red, too, and her pale green eyes were almost creepy. But she was smart and nice and didn't talk about May's mother.

Her dad was a doctor in Bozeman. Gynecologist. The boys liked to give her a hard time over that one. It was so stupid. Boys were stupid.

"Going home," May said, looking around for Levi again.

"You want to take our bikes and get ice cream?"

May spotted him leaning against a tree, looking right at her. Her heart jumped and she lost a little breath. He was so cute.

Why was he over there? Was he waiting for her? She tried to stop her excitement.

"Maybe. Let me go home and ask my mom," she hedged. What she really wanted to do was be with Levi.

"You rode your bike to school today, right?"

"Yeah, but I have to ask her." Why was she doing this? What if Levi wasn't waiting for her?

"Don't you have a cell phone?"

"I forgot it today." She had, so it wasn't a lie.

"Okay. Well, call me when you get home."

May smiled. "Okay."

Peri jogged toward a waiting line of buses and May stopped walking and looked over at Levi.

He pushed off the tree and started toward her. Her heart hammered faster in her chest. He was coming over to her. *Her!*

Wearing a white T-shirt and holey jeans, he made her want to drool. Then she realized what she was doing. She'd be dumb to trust him. What if this was some kind of joke? What if he and Sherilynn were having a good laugh over the way he was starting to make her think he liked her?

"Hey, May."

She loved his voice. "Hey."

"You going home?"

"Yeah."

"I'll walk with you."

"I rode my bike."

"Then I'll push it for you."

To heck with it. She'd see what he was all about and then worry about the rest later.

"Okay."

She walked beside him to the bike racks and found hers. He pulled it free after she unlocked the chain, and they headed down the street.

"I heard about what Sherilynn and her friend did," he said.

"Oh, that. It was nothing." Yeah, right.

"I'm sorry about that. For some reason she thinks we're still going out."

"You aren't?"

"No. I broke up with her a couple of weeks ago."

"Oh." She tried to sound like it was no big deal.

"Has she bugged you since then?"

"Nope. And she better not."

"She thinks she's tough but she's not. I'll say something to her so she doesn't do it again."

"Thanks."

A boy rode past them and looked back, staring. Levi walking her home would be all over school tomorrow. She held back a big smile.

"You want to catch a movie sometime?"

Was he asking her out on a date? What would her mom say? Would she let her? Then another thought deflated her excitement.

Was he just trying to get into her pants?

"Only if you want," he said.

"I'll ask my mom."

He stopped and she realized they were in front of her house. Her mom was still at work.

"I'll see you at school tomorrow," he said.

"Okay." She smiled and took the bike from him when he leaned it toward her. "Thanks for walking me home."

"I'll walk you home tomorrow, too." He grinned and she loved it.

"Okay."

Lily was bone-tired after closing the library. Early-September evenings in Honey Creek cooled with the approach of winter and tonight was no exception. She walked to her truck. A Ford Expedition parked across the street made her stop. She squinted her eyes to see better. She couldn't tell what color it was, but there was a man sitting in the driver's seat. It had to be Wes.

She crossed the street, feeling little sparks of excitement igniting the closer she got. Now she could see his new SUV was dark gray with shiny chrome trim. He rolled his window down and she leaned her forearm on the frame.

"Are you stalking me?" she teased.

He grinned. "Just making sure you're all right."

"A likely excuse." But she knew he hadn't liked the note that came with the roses.

"I also wanted to see if you were hungry."

"Oh...."

"Have you eaten dinner?"

She was a terrible liar so she stuck with the truth. "No. I was going to stop at the market on the way home. May and my dad will already have eaten." And her dad, she was sure, hadn't gone out of his way to save any for her.

"We could go over to Kelley's Cookhouse."

Where everyone would see them together? "I was just there with May over the weekend."

"How about McCormick's, then?"

McCormick's was a small pub on the other end of town. It attracted some regular drinkers and served typical pub fare.

They'd be safe from the quilters there. Besides that, the entire town was abuzz over Damien's homecoming. The focus wasn't on her anymore, or at least not for a while.

"All right." Why not? It was just dinner. She wasn't going to go home with him, as she might have done all those years ago.

"Climb in. I'll drive you back here when we're finished."

She opened the door and got in. The Expedition had that new-car smell and Wes reached for the radio to turn down the music. Country.

"Why don't you wear a cowboy hat?" she asked.

"Just because I listen to country music doesn't mean I have to wear a hat."

"A Montana sheriff should wear a cowboy hat." Plus he'd look good in one.

"I was never comfortable wearing them. I don't like anything on my head. Gets in the way and makes me sweat. Besides, I'd look a little funny driving an SUV in a cowboy hat."

She laughed. "Fair enough." She didn't think it would matter what he drove, though.

It never took long to get where you were going in this town. Wes parked his SUV and she got out before he reached the passenger side, leaving her purse and taking her sweatshirt.

He opened the pub door for her. It was dim inside the long and narrow bar and a football game played on two TVs above shelves of booze. Bar stools lined one side of the establishment and small, tall tables lined the other. Four men sat at the bar and a couple and two men sat at two of the tables. She didn't recognize anyone. Before she'd left Honey Creek, she'd done most of her carousing in Bozeman.

McCormick's wasn't the kind of place that had a hostess, so Wes led her to a corner booth in the back. It was the only booth and the biggest table in the place. Some turned to look at them as they passed, but no one showed any further interest than that. For the first time since returning to Honey Creek she felt normal in public.

The bartender came to get their order. She ordered a burger and Wes ordered the same.

"Has anything else happened since you received those roses?" Wes asked.

"No." Hopefully whoever sent them had had their fun and was finished now. But she knew that wasn't why Wes was asking. He didn't think she'd confide in him at this stage of their relationship.

"Getting protective of me now?" She kept her tone light, but really she was touched that he cared so much.

"Part of my job." He grinned.

She was glad he recognized her teasing. That made it easier on her to explore him a little deeper.

"Doesn't that make this too personal for a sheriff—involving yourself with your girlfriend?"

The residual traces of his grin renewed and twinkling humor reached his eyes. "You said it. Just remember that."

This wasn't how she wanted it to go. She hadn't meant to say that. She fumbled for a response, damage control.

He chuckled. "Freudian slips don't have to count for now."

He was so good at that, easing her mind. "How is it possible that you've escaped marriage for so long?" The question came to her mind as naturally as she voiced it. "You'd think a woman would have come along and snatched you up by now."

"Are you volunteering?"

The bartender came with waters. The interruption was perfect. She used it as an out not to respond.

But when the bartender left, he said, "Just for that I'm going to spend more time at the library."

She laughed softly and was surprised that the idea didn't bother her.

Their burgers arrived and they ate in silence for a while.

"When is Damien going to be home?" she asked.

"Tomorrow. I'm going to pick him up."

"I'd say I'm relieved everyone's talking about him now, but I know it can't be easy for him. Or you for that matter." In one respect she could see why some in the town were leery about his return. Innocent or not, he'd spent fifteen years in prison. That had to harden a man.

"I never care what people say. I only care what the truth is."

He'd said as much before, and that probably helped to make him a good sheriff. "How will Damien feel about it?"

"He already knows what he's coming home to. He'll be fine. He just needs some time to adjust, just like everyone else who has a negative opinion about his incarceration."

"Fifteen years is a long time."

"He'll have his moments. But Damien is a strong man, and not everyone is against him." His expression grew more somber. "What worries me is his anger. I don't blame him for wanting justice, but I don't want him doing anything stupid."

Like resorting to violence to avenge himself? Lily knew what it was like to want that.

"Are you going to let him help you with the investigation?"

"I'm sure nothing will stop him from his own inquiries. I'll keep him updated on my progress, though. Hopefully that will be enough."

She didn't know what to say to that. She didn't know enough about the case to judge. Or about Damien for that matter.

She could tell the talk about his brother upset him. Maybe

he felt guilty for not being able to prove his innocence. Maybe he was worried about how Damien would handle his anger and bitterness. It wasn't a good situation, but she remembered the Coltons as bold and ambitious. Some of them carried that boldness a little too far, but none of them were the backing-down type.

Wes was no different, except he had a softer side, one she noticed more and more. He caught her looking at him and she wanted to turn away from that direct gaze. No shyness there. His interest was clear and building, if the heat that came into his eyes was any clue.

The way that made her feel was almost foreign. She'd forgotten what it was like to have a man look at her like that, and to enjoy it. Had she felt this way at all since the rape? Had a man ever stirred such a warm glow before? No. Even before that, she couldn't recall a time she'd felt a response this intense to someone.

The bill arrived and she let herself absorb the sight of Wes while he was distracted. But when he finished, he met her look and the heat renewed. Averting her head, she walked ahead of him to the door. Outside, his hand took hold of hers, and she let it. All the way to his SUV, he held her hand. That was it. At the side of his SUV, he held the passenger door open for her and didn't try anything as she climbed in.

He was taking it slow, being a perfect gentleman. Or was *cautious* a better word? More likely he was afraid she'd shoot him down again. Or was that what she wanted to believe? Because right now she didn't feel like telling him not to call. And that was a new one for her.

She held back a smile as he got behind the wheel and drove toward the library. All the way there she felt his presence beside her. Energy hummed. Sexual energy. It had been so long since she'd felt this way—without the usual stiffening. Relationships hadn't been easy on her after her rape. She'd had to work at them. This felt different. Easy. Natural. Should she be worried? Even their age difference didn't matter as much anymore.

Wes pulled to a stop beside her truck and she froze as she looked out the window. Someone had used spray paint to write all over her truck.

Whore covered the driver's and rear passenger doors. It was written on the hood, too. On her pretty truck.

Tears sprang to her eyes. She heard her own hitched breath.

Wes swore from the other side of the SUV. "Stay in here."

She struggled to hold back her crying, but it was too much. Why wouldn't everyone leave her alone? She was so tired of being labeled. Jezebel. Rape victim. Outcast.

Watching Wes walk around the truck, scanning the parking lot as he did, Lily wiped her cheeks. He came full circle and pulled out his phone, dialing a number then lifting the phone to his ear.

He opened the passenger door and looked at her with concern in his eyes. Concern and anger. He put his hand on her knee, a comforting gesture. She listened to him ask his deputy to come gather evidence. When he finished with that call, he made another one to arrange for a tow.

How sweet. He wasn't going to let her drive the truck any-where, sparing her any embarrassment.

When he hung up, he put his phone away and placed his hand on the headrest behind her head. He was so close.

"I'll find whoever did this," he said.

A swell of affection rose up in her. Odd how his nearness didn't make her feel suffocated. That was usually how she felt when she was with a new man. It was a struggle to overcome anxiety over his intentions. But not with Wes.

He lifted his hand from her knee and touched her cheek.

Just when she thought he'd kiss her, headlights shone on them. Wes's deputy had arrived.

Wes moved back and waited until the deputy emerged from his car, then he walked toward him. They spoke a moment, the deputy nodding every once in a while, and then Wes returned to his SUV, going around to the driver's side.

"Ryan will take care of it. I'll drive you home."

She avoided looking at her truck as Wes started driving.

"Do you need a ride tomorrow?"

She hadn't thought about it yet. "I'll get a rental." She could walk to the car-rental company.

"You can drive my Jeep. I'll bring it by in the morning."

"Really?" He was going out of his way for her. After a brief hesitation, she decided to go along with it. "Are you going to use that as an excuse to see me?"

He kept his profile to her. "Yes." But he was grinning as he turned the SUV off Main and headed east out of town. She didn't question how he knew where she lived. Her father had lived in the same house for years.

A few minutes later he pulled to a stop in front of the house. All the windows were dark. She hadn't called May to tell her she was going to be late.

She got out of the SUV and turned in the open door to say goodbye to Wes, but he was already shutting the driver's door.

Her heart leaped into a faster rhythm. He was going to walk her to the door?

The idea was both tantalizing and frightening. It also felt a little juvenile. Had a boy ever walked her to the front door before? She couldn't recall a time when that had happened. Men had walked her to her door, but that was only when she was going to let them in. No way was she going to let Wes in, and that was what made this night so different from others in her past.

She heard him walking behind her on the sidewalk that led to the front step and porch. He took her hand when she reached the door. She faced him, as nervous as a teenager on a first date.

"I had a nice time at dinner," he said.

"So did I." And it was true. She'd enjoyed every second with him up until she saw her truck. And even that hadn't been as bad as it would have been without him.

Letting her hand go, he slid his arm around her waist and pulled her closer. His movement was nonthreatening. Slow. Gentle.

He kissed her, a soft touch that was far from invasive. And it was over as soon as it began. The sweetness of it made her fall for him even harder.

"Good night," he said.

"Mmm," she could only utter. She put her fingers on her lips as he walked to his SUV. She turned before he reached it and opened the front door. The entire exchange was clichéd, it had been so simple.

Man and woman go out on a date. Man walks woman to front door. Man kisses woman and says good-night. She wondered if that's why it worked for her. It was undemanding. Easy. There that word was again, popping into her head. Wes was easy to be with. Easy on her eyes. Easy to talk to. Easy to feel good with.

Floating into the house on those thoughts, Lily closed the door and turned. Her father was standing in the entry between the living room and the kitchen. She saw his silhouette in the dim light of the interior.

"You're home late," he said.

"I went out for dinner after work." She didn't want to talk about the truck.

"Who with?"

Did he care? "Wes Colton."

"Wes Colton." It sounded like a sneer.

She didn't respond, just put her purse down and slipped out of her shoes.

"You're shooting kind of high, aren't you?"

She straightened. "Excuse me?"

"Going after the sheriff. Don't you think that's awfully bold?"

He thought it was bold of her to want to be with a sheriff. She shoved her hurt feelings aside. "I'm not going after him. He drove me home, that's all."

"I saw you kiss him."

"He kissed me."

"You didn't seem to mind."

"Dad, it's been a lot of years since I left here."

"You haven't changed."

If he couldn't see how wrong he was by now, she wasn't going to bother arguing. She started to head toward the stairs.

"Is he the only one you're chasing around town?"

Stopping at the top of the stairs, she turned. "I'm not chasing anyone."

"Don't be breaking up any more marriages. I don't need that kind of embarrassment at my age."

"I know, Dad. It has always been about you." Talk about never changing….

"You watch your mouth in my house."

Lily sighed. What was he going to do? Kick her out? He needed her and he knew it. He had no one else, even though he wished he did.

"Why didn't you drive yourself home?" her dad asked.

"My truck…broke down. I had to have it towed."

"And you went to the sheriff for help? Or maybe you planned it that way. Maybe there's nothing wrong with your truck."

"Wes was in the parking lot when I left work."

Her dad grunted.

Lily faced him fully and folded her arms. "Why do you hate me so much?"

He didn't answer, but his smirk eased a bit.

"I think you've hated me since the day I was born."

"That isn't true."

Nothing would convince her of that. Not with the way he talked to her just now. But he had his mind made up. He had his version of her all lined out in his mind, with no second chance in sight.

"I'm sorry you don't believe me," she said, dropping her arms and turning to go to bed.

"Give me a reason to, Lily."

That stopped her. She looked back at him. "What do you think I'm doing?" He was a big reason why she'd come back to Honey Creek. She wanted his love as much as she wanted the demons of her past to stay in the past.

She watched her question register on his face. He knew what she meant. And yet, he didn't acknowledge her.

Leaving him standing there, she tried not to let the crushing heartbreak of their damaged relationship ruin the enchantment of her evening with Wes. But her father thought she was shooting too high. What if he was right?

Chapter 7

In the early afternoon of the next day, Wes waited in front of the prison for his brother to emerge. Damien was five minutes late. Getting out of the SUV, Wes walked around to the other side of the vehicle, stopping when he spotted Damien exit the prison. His longish dark brown hair was on the messy side, giving him a hard look even from this distance. He wore the jeans and black T-shirt Wes had delivered for him. Damien smiled as he approached. It was a rare sight.

Wes put an arm around his brother for a brief hug. "I've waited a long time for this day."

Hard eyes that weren't softened by his smile met Wes's. "Thanks for never giving up on me."

The words were spoken devoid of emotion, as if prison life had drained Damien Colton. He wasn't a weak man, but he had a thirst to find Mark Walsh's real killer, to find justice and even retribution. How different would that effort be after enduring so much? How differently would Damien handle it now versus the pre-imprisoned Damien? More than once he'd expressed his disappointment in his family for not doing more, their dad in particular. Darius hadn't gone out of his way much to help Damien. Maybe he felt he couldn't. Maybe he doubted his son's innocence. But Wes had never doubted Damien. Neither had Damien's twin brother, Duke.

"You get anything more about why Walsh was going to meet that agent?" Damien asked when they were on their way.

"No." The reply landed like a dry thud inside the SUV.

Damien glanced over at him and Wes felt his cynicism. "You have nothing to go on?"

"Jolene gave me a tape Walsh recorded shortly before he died. One of his lovers stole some jewelry from his wife and he caught her. She admitted to it in the recording."

"And Jolene waits fifteen years to hand it over?"

"She says she only recently found it among stored items in her attic."

"Do you believe her?"

"I think she's afraid of becoming a suspect in the murder. A blackmailed lover has plenty of motive. Turning over the tape shifts the suspicion to the lover."

"He blackmailed her?"

"He never said on the tape, but my guess is he recorded her admitting to the robbery for insurance. Maybe to make sure she did what he wanted. You know, use her in some way with his business dealings, on a personal level. Something like that."

"Who's the lover?"

"Her name is Tina Mueller, but she changed her identity after she met Walsh. At least I think she did. The tape suggests Walsh offered to help her and she agreed. I won't know until I have something solid, though."

"Can I hear the tape?"

"Sure. As long as you keep it to yourself."

"I want Walsh's murderer just as much as you do."

More so. For Damien, it was very personal. It was still personal for Wes, but he also had a job to do.

He went on to tell Damien about his talk with the Atlanta detective, particularly about the murder Tina had allegedly committed there.

"How do you think she ties into Walsh's murder?"

"I don't know if she does. But think about it. Tina's stepfather abused her. If she killed him she did it to get away from him. If Walsh came back to Honey Creek after fifteen years being gone and she had been successful in starting a new life, she wouldn't be happy to see him. What if he contacted her? Suddenly her new lifestyle is threatened."

Damien nodded. "Yeah, she may have murdered him now, but we still don't know who let me take the fall fifteen years ago."

Hearing the anger in Damien's tone, Wes stayed silent.

"If he wasn't murdered back then, why didn't the evidence show something?" Damien asked, frustration coming out in his tone. "You'd think something would have come up to cast doubt during my trial. But it didn't."

"There was nothing fair about your trial."

"You can say that again. Somebody set me up."

"And we're going to find out who."

Wes wouldn't stop until he had all the answers. With the new FBI agent's help, he'd get to the bottom of it. This time they had Walsh's body—his real body, not a heaping pile of circumstantial evidence. Something was bound to break.

Wes drove into town.

"Mind if we stop at the Corner Bar?" Damien asked.

Wes glanced over at his brother. He was going to start drinking now?

Damien sent him an *oh-please* look. "I just want to taste a beer again. You'd want to celebrate a little, too, after spending the prime of your life behind bars."

Unable to argue that, Wes parked down the street from the bar.

As they walked down the sidewalk, cars passed by and there were a few people out and about. Some looked more than once when they saw who was with Wes. He noticed how Damien didn't miss it, either, and couldn't tell how it affected him.

His release had caused quite a stir in town. Wes couldn't imagine Damien would be happy with the less-than-thrilled reception he was about to receive.

One of Mark Walsh's sons, Peter Walsh, and the CFO who had taken over for Mark at Walsh Enterprises, Craig Warner, exited Kelley's Cookhouse just then. It was lunchtime.

Sure enough, Peter's face showed his displeasure at seeing two Coltons walking by, one of them none other than Damien, the man originally accused of killing his father.

"Afternoon," Wes said.

"Sheriff," Craig answered with a curious glance at Damien. Peter didn't say anything. Maybe after a while he'd come around. Things might be awkward at first, but Wes hoped everyone would see that Damien was a good man. The same applied to Lily.

Lily.

Just the thought of her made him want to be with her. If he didn't think he'd scare her away, he'd see her every day.

A couple came out of the hardware store and stopped short when they saw Damien.

Damien met their stares and glanced at Wes. "I can see some things never change."

The town was still a gossip mill. "Yeah."

They entered the Corner Bar and heads turned. Two patrons sat at the bar. All of the other tables were empty.

Tall and tattooed, Jake Huffman paused in the act of filling a glass with ice and nodded his welcome from behind the dark, polished-wood bar.

Wes followed Damien on a worn wooden floor through the dimly lit bar, past booths and tables. Damien chose a table and sat. Wes sat across from him just as Jake approached.

"What can I get you?" He didn't seem affected one way or the other by Damien's presence.

That seemed to ease Damien's tension from seeing Craig and Peter. He ordered a dark microbrew.

The bartender looked at Wes. "Water for me."

"Comin' right up." Jake left the table's side.

Wes leaned back in his chair. "What are you going to do now that you're out?"

"I don't know. Work at the ranch for a while. Eat a lot of different food. Sleep in my own room."

Wes chuckled. "Sounds like a good start.

The bartender dropped off the beer and water.

Damien lifted the mug and sipped. "Mmm," he murmured, then set the glass down on the table and looked across at Wes. "Simple pleasures are sure going to feel great for a while."

Wes smiled. More power to him. He hoped he went all out and enjoyed his freedom. But that made another thought come to mind. "Have you heard from Lucy Walsh since her father was murdered for real?"

"Nope."

"I wonder how she feels about that now."

"Really, all I want to do is live my life again. If the Walshes can't let go of the past, there's nothing I can do to change that."

Wes couldn't tell if his brother was hiding some buried emotion where Lucy was concerned. He'd been angered and hurt by her quick and easy belief in his guilt. Their breakup hadn't been clean. Now that she was proven wrong, what would she feel when she reflected on the past and the love they'd shared?

"That, and I want to find Walsh's real killer." His eyes grew driven and resolved. "I want that more than anything."

"Who can blame you?" He wanted that, too.

"I'm not leaving town until I can put that to bed."

Wes grew more alert. "You're planning to leave?"

"I was thinking about it. As soon as this is over, I'm not sure I ever want to see this place again. Or the people. Especially if they hold a crime I never committed over my head."

"It might just be the fact that you were in prison so long. Something like that changes a man."

"How? By turning an innocent man into a murderer?" he scoffed. "They just need something to talk about."

True, but once Damien adjusted he might not want to leave, especially since his family was here.

"Duke's looking forward to seeing you. He would have come with me but something came up at the ranch and Dad kept him."

"I'll see him when we get there. I talked to him before you came to get me. He told me about Dad." Damien shook his head. "Sometimes I just want to hit that man."

And Wes had to agree.

Lily stood from her desk at nine and started toward the door. What a long day. It was time to close the library.

Something crashed behind her. Glass shattered. With a strangled yell, she turned and saw a flaming ball hit her desk and roll onto the floor in front of her feet. She'd been sitting at the desk just seconds before that. She might have been hit in the head.

Running out into the library, she found a fire extinguisher and ran back to her office. Flames swirled over the surface of her desk, burning the papers she'd studied only moments before. More flames burned the carpet where the ball of fire had come to rest. Smoke began to fill the office. She sprayed the fire extinguisher just as the fire alarm went off and the overhead sprinkler shot on.

The fire was extinguished.

Lily heard her own breathing along with the sprinklers and felt her pulse ricocheting against her ribs and throat.

She went to the broken window and peered outside. She didn't expect to see anyone, but she did. A shadow standing behind the library. Pushing up the window, she coughed and waved the smoky air as it floated past her and out the window.

The shadow moved, taking the shape of a person running down the alley.

Lily ran from her office, jumping over the charred floor. She raced down the hall and burst through the back door. Sprinting down an alley, she skidded to a halt where it ended at a side street.

A car engine fired up. She ran toward it, trying to see the license plate. It was dark so she couldn't see much of anything. The car pulled away from the curb and sped away. It looked like a midsize car, a Buick or a Toyota. It was a dark color, too. Black or blue or green, maybe. She couldn't tell.

She stopped running, breathing hard from exertion.

The sound of sirens made her turn and head back to the library. Reaching the back door, she went inside the smoky-smelling library and made her way to the front. By the time she got there, a fire truck had arrived. Outside, she approached the first fireman she saw.

"We got a call from someone who said they saw smoke," the fireman said.

"Someone threw something flammable through the window of my office," she told him.

"Is anyone else inside?"

She shook her head. "I was just about to lock up and go home."

Another siren sounded and Lily watched Wes's SUV come to a stop behind the fire truck, parking at an angle in his haste, a thin bar of lights flashing along the top of the windshield.

"You wait here while we check inside," the fireman said.

She absently nodded and the fireman left to do his job, though he and his team would find no fire to battle. They'd ensure the building was safe and be gone before too long.

As Wes neared, she saw the worry etching his expression.

"What happened?" he demanded.

She repeated what she'd just told the fireman and he cursed.

"I ran after the person, but it was too dark to tell who it was."

"You what?"

She ignored his temper, knowing it stemmed from concern. "I couldn't see the license plate, either. And I couldn't tell what kind of car it was, only that it was midsize and dark-colored."

"You went after the person who tried to burn the library down with you in it?"

"I…" He didn't like it that she had taken it upon herself to chase her arsonist.

"You could have been hurt. Or worse."

"Someone clearly doesn't want me here. I wanted to find out who that is." She wondered if Karen Hathaway had been the one to send her flowers, but hadn't given the thought much credence since she wasn't the only one who wanted her out of Honey Creek. The same thought had crossed her mind when her truck had been vandalized.

"Oh, my God," she murmured. If Karen would go to those lengths…

"What's the matter?" Wes asked.

"I think I know who's behind all this. The flowers. The vandalism. And now this."

"Who?"

"Karen Hathaway. She…" Lily stopped short as the fireman she'd spoken with moments before reappeared. She didn't want this getting around town.

"All's clear," the fireman said. "But you're going to need some repairs."

She already knew that. The other firemen were getting back on the truck. This one said his farewells and joined them.

Lily watched them drive away.

"I want you to come with me to my house and stay there for a while," Wes said.

She turned to look at him. The idea shocked her as much as she was sure it would stir the talk around town. "What?"

"You heard me." He was adamant.

"No. No way. I can't do that."

"You'll be safe there."

"Wes…"

He stepped closer to her. "This is getting serious, Lily. The flowers were an innocent enough prank. Writing on your truck was bad, but nobody tried to hurt you. This is different."

"Wes…I…I have May, and…my dad."

"We'll pick them up. I'll wait while you all pack. Anything else you need you can get tomorrow."

She was stunned into silence. "My dad will never agree to this."

"Then I'll make arrangements for someone to take care of him."

Apart from her. As unpleasant as he'd been to live with so far, she wasn't ready to give up trying to close their rift. Someday she hoped he'd be able to see her for the person she'd become, not the one who'd left Honey Creek with a bad reputation. And he was beginning to show an interest in May. She'd noticed it the day she and May had gone shopping. Before they left, he'd been a real grandfather for a few moments. That was so important to her.

She didn't have to live with Wes long. This wouldn't last forever. So maybe it wouldn't hurt to stay with him a while. The security did appeal to her. She had to think of May, after all. It wasn't only about herself. If anything happened to her daughter she'd just die.

"Let me talk to your dad," Wes said.

She focused back on him. He'd do that for her?

"Come on," he said, and started toward the library.

Lily followed him inside. She hadn't exactly told him she'd go with him, but that didn't seem to matter. He'd made up his mind and she was following him. After he helped her close up, he led her to his SUV. He was sure taking charge. Normally, this commandeering attitude would turn her away, but coming from Wes, it felt good. Like a safe place to land.

"What were you going to tell me about Karen Hathaway?" Wes asked when they were on the way to her house.

"I saw her at the Honey-B when I met Bonnie Gene there. She came over to our table. She wasn't happy to see me."

"Why not?"

"She's married to one of the men I…had…relations with before leaving town."

"What did she say to you?"

She was glad he didn't judge her for having an affair with a married man. "Basically she told me she wanted me to leave town and threw water in my face."

He looked over at her. "She threatened you?"

"In a way, yes."

He shot her an admonishing look. "Why didn't you tell me this sooner?"

"I didn't think much of it."

"Didn't you?" He sounded incredulous. "You should have told me about that when you received the flowers."

"I—"

"How long after you saw her was it that you got the flowers?"

"I don't know. A couple of days maybe."

Wes sighed hard.

"Sorry." Maybe she should have told him. "I didn't think there was anything you could do. I didn't think there was anything anyone could do."

"I'll talk to her in the morning."

There he went again, taking charge. It was such a new experience for her. Usually she was the one in control, calling all the shots. Until now she hadn't liked to feel out of control. But for some strange reason it was different with Wes. She was afraid to think too far into the future.

Wes reached over and put his hand on her knee. She looked at him, surprised by the softening change in him.

"Don't worry. I'll take care of it," he said.

And a warm rush of something too close to love consumed her.

After thirty minutes of talking to her dad, Wes finally got him to agree to come stay over at his house—at least for one night. All the way there Shay had complained, but she'd seen the way he'd looked at her when Wes told him about the fire. He hadn't flinched when he heard about the flowers and the vandalism, but someone trying to burn the library with her in it had gotten his attention.

She followed her dad and May into Wes's house. It was a sizable white-pine-log home. The entry opened into a huge room with a rock fireplace that rose to the exposed purlin log roof. Pine steps on three sides lowered to a dark brown–carpeted seating area with sofas patterned in a rich-looking brown and deep blue fish design. A moose head hung on the rock above the fireplace. Past the living area was a dining table and chairs backed by floor-to-ceiling windows. The kitchen was open to the dining area. Stairs to the left of the entry led to an upper level, and next to those more led to a basement.

"Wow," May exclaimed. "You're loaded."

Lily elbowed her daughter, who grinned up at her and giggled.

"Shay, you'll probably be more comfortable in the bedroom down here." Wes didn't seem affected by May's comment. He pointed to their right, where an open door revealed a bedroom. "It has its own bathroom."

"It'll be nice not to navigate any stairs," Shay said.

"There are two bedrooms upstairs and one down in the basement." Wes looked from Lily to May.

"I want down," May said, which left Lily in the room too close to Wes.

She looked at him and then at her dad. Wes didn't seem to think anything of it, but her dad sort of scowled and, with a grumble, went to his main-level bedroom with his carry-on-size bag.

May headed for the stairs leading down beside the main entrance.

"There are two rooms off the rec area. One's an office. The bathroom's in between."

"Okay," May yelled as she skipped down the stairs.

Now it was just her and Wes. Lily rubbed the back of her neck.

Wes bent to lift her luggage. "Come on. I'll show you your room. It has its own bathroom, too."

Good. She could use a shower before bed. Her hair smelled like smoke.

Upstairs, from the loft, a log banister permitted a view of the lower level. Two doors led off the landing. Wes pushed open the far door and she entered before him. It didn't feel right with him in here, not in a bedroom. He put her luggage down and went back toward the door. The sudden flash of anxiety that had begun to build faded and was gone before he turned.

"Good night," he said, and her heart melted all over itself.

He was being so careful with her. As soon as the thought came she wondered why. Why was he being so careful with her?

Was it because he knew she wasn't comfortable with their age difference? Or had he picked up on something, something in the way she behaved? She had turned him down a few times. Maybe he wondered why, since she also liked him a lot. He probably saw that, too.

"Good night."

He closed the door.

Alone now, she turned in a circle. The room was neutrally decorated in tans and white, complementing the log furniture and knotty-pine armoire and dresser. There was a flat-screen TV and a computer, too.

Taking the smaller of two bags from the bed, she went to the bathroom just past the dresser and desk. After showering and slipping into her cotton, knee-length black nightie, she crawled into bed, so tired she fell asleep almost immediately.

He entered the dark room. She smelled him. He was tall and big and through the shadows she could see his head was hairy and he had fangs. Like a wolverine. He reached for her, his talonlike fingers clawing the air in front of her. She ran from the room, down a maze of hallways that stretched farther and farther. She felt lost and trapped. She heard him running behind her. Felt him, too. His evil presence.

Then he appeared in front of her. His face leered, light-colored eyes glowing. She dug her feet into the carpeted floor, but couldn't stop moving toward him. Closer and closer. Her hands came against him. Closer and closer, until his body was pressed hard against hers.

She screamed and writhed to get away, but she couldn't. She didn't know why. He wasn't holding her.

Finally, she was running outside. The dirt path illuminated by moonlight ended when she ran out of the trees. Now she ran through tall grass that hindered her escape. A cliff appeared on her left. The roar of rushing water frightened her. The water was dark. The river was wide and deep.

Rock broke away from the cliff where she ran. She slipped.

She was falling through the air. Fear tasted tinny in her mouth. She couldn't stop the fall.

She was falling. Falling. Closer to the churning water that rushed toward a raging waterfall. She didn't want to hit the water. It was dark, deep water. And if she fell over the waterfall…

She came awake with a grunt. Her stomach still plunged from the residual effects of the dream. Her heart hammered. She swallowed between gulping breaths.

No way was she getting back to sleep anytime soon.

Flinging the covers back, she dug out her robe from her suitcase and shrugged into it. Maybe some milk would help.

The floors on the upper level and stairs were carpeted, but downstairs the hard wood was cold on her feet. A light was on in the kitchen. Wes sat at the table.

She stopped short when he looked up from the papers he had strewn before him, pen in hand over a legal pad.

"Did I wake you?" he asked.

He wasn't wearing a shirt. She stared at him, unable to

form a response. The edge of the table concealed some of her view, but she could see he at least wore black fleece pants.

Shaking herself out of her trance, a little confused by the strength of his effect on her, she moved toward the kitchen. "No." In the kitchen she stopped again. "I couldn't sleep and thought I'd try to rummage up some milk."

He stood up from the table, putting the pen down, and walked past her to open an upper cabinet for a glass. He got a carton of milk out of the refrigerator and poured her some.

Lily rubbed her forehead, feeling a headache building. The dream still had her out of sorts. It made her think of Brandon. He was a free man, living life the way he pleased despite the harm he'd caused to others. It wasn't fair. She clutched the robe closed where it lay open below her throat.

"You okay?"

She looked up to see Wes holding the glass of milk for her. "Yes." She took the milk. "Thanks." Sipping, she kept her gaze low, struggling to push bad thoughts from her mind.

"Why don't we go sit where it's warm?" He gestured toward the living room.

She looked over to the sitting area and only then noticed the gas fireplace was running, the sound of a fan blowing warmth into the room subtle and soothing. It was too appealing to resist. Plus, what else would she do other than lie awake in bed?

She sat on a big chair nearest the fireplace, holding her glass. The fire held her gaze.

The dream still had her in that in-between state, still unable to separate it from the here and now. Dreams like that always reminded her of that night.

Drinking at a Bozeman bar. Meeting Brandon. He was another conquest. He was someone interesting enough to pursue. It hadn't taken much back then. As long as the man wasn't timid and seemed to be halfway ambitious both physically and professionally, she was interested. And an opportunity to go on a new adventure was always irresistible to her. Brandon had said he liked to hunt in Argentina. She'd never been to Argentina.

She'd left with him and he'd knocked her unconscious when they'd reached his car. No one had seen him do that and no one had any reason to be suspicious.

She'd woken to the beginning of a nightmare.

"You sure you're okay?"

Snapped out of her downturning thoughts, she looked over at Wes, who'd taken a seat on the sofa that faced the fireplace.

"I couldn't sleep."

"Why not?"

"I had a bad dream."

She watched him contemplate her response. "Not surprising after what happened."

At first she thought he was talking about the rape. Then she realized he meant the fire.

She looked away. She'd much rather have nightmares based on that. But this nightmare had been based on something real. Waking in that cabin, bound, cold. Frightened, not knowing where she was. And then Brandon had come into the room. He'd smiled when he saw that she was awake. And that's when the horror had begun.

Lily shut her eyes and fought the demons in her mind. She was so tired of fighting them. Again. She'd been doing so well until the parole hearing. It was so disheartening.

"It wasn't the fire," she said, weary. She didn't understand why she felt a need to reach out to someone. To Wes. She'd never felt that way before. She'd never trusted anyone enough to reveal such a dark secret about herself.

"What was it?" he asked.

She didn't look at him. "I didn't go to the prison to visit a friend." Did she really want to tell him this? *Yes,* her heart cried. She did. She needed to. She needed to get rid of it somehow. She turned her head to look at him. "I went there to testify at Brandon Gates's parole hearing. He raped me fifteen years ago."

Wes's expression didn't flinch. "I'm sorry, Lily."

"It's the reason I left Honey Creek. I couldn't face anyone after that, not when I was so…not when my reputation was so…" She couldn't finish.

"It's okay. I understand." He moved over on the couch. "Come over here and sit by me."

Both a command and an offer of support, she found she couldn't resist. She put her glass on the coffee table and stood and moved to the couch, sitting next to him. He put his arm behind her on the back of the couch. She scooted closer and let her head rest between his chest and biceps.

"I met him at a bar and when I left he knocked me out and drove me to a cabin near Trout Creek. I escaped just before dawn."

Wes reached over with his free hand and slipped it between her clenched ones on her lap. She let him, feeling him first give her hand a small squeeze before simply holding her.

"There were several other women who came forward after his arrest. He got the maximum sentence and wasn't eligible for parole until now. The parole board granted his release. The victims' officer told me he went back home to North Carolina. He's a free man."

"I'm so sorry, Lily. You shouldn't have had to go through any of that."

"It changed me," she went on. "Something like that would change anyone." Strange, how it felt good to tell someone about it. Even Bonnie Gene didn't know the details. "I came back to Honey Creek for about a month, but I couldn't stand how I was treated. The same as before, but I wasn't like that anymore. So I packed my things and drove to Bozeman. Got a part-time job and stayed until the trial was over. After that, I moved to Sacramento."

She looked up at Wes and saw unspoken questions in his eyes. He moved his hand from the back of the couch to her shoulder. She knew what he was wondering.

"I was desperate to feel normal again. I was too ashamed to tell anyone. It was bad enough having to talk about it in court. I needed some kind of relief. I thought if I went back to the way I was before I was raped that I could put it behind me and go on as if it never happened. So one night I went to a bar. It was scary at first. That's how I'd met Brandon. But facing my fears would help me heal, right?

"I made a mistake thinking I could do that by picking up a guy and sleeping with him. It backfired on me. The intimacy. I wasn't ready. It only intensified my trauma. The guy was nice, but he didn't have much going for himself. He didn't have a job. He drank too much. By the time I found out I was pregnant, he'd moved. I sent him a letter telling him about the baby, but he never responded or tried to contact me."

She stared at the fire again, sighing as contentment washed over her. It felt so good to rid herself of the burden.

"What was Gates like during the hearing?" Wes asked.

"Docile. Nothing like he was fifteen years ago. Could have been an act."

"Some sex offenders are nervous about facing their victims during their parole hearings, especially the ones who've changed. They want to get out of prison and live normal lives."

"I'd rather he stayed in prison."

"I agree, but it doesn't always work out the way you want. You have to move on."

"I never questioned I would. I did move on. And I'll do it again now that he's free."

"You've done well for yourself. And for May. It'll only be a matter of time before everyone else in town sees that."

She tilted her head up and smiled. "Thank you."

"For what?"

"For listening. For being here. Now. Tonight."

Leaning toward her, he put his fingers against her jaw and urged her to move her head closer to his. She let herself get lost in the warm desire of his amazing blue eyes. He lowered his head, bringing his mouth oh so close to hers. Hot, sweet anticipation tickled her senses. She closed her eyes to it, and felt his lips touch hers. He kissed her softly. His breath came faster and she became aware of her own breaths. She parted her lips, tentatively, uncertain but curious. He pressed firmer.

She spread her hand on his bare chest, feeling the hard muscle beneath. Need mounted to a feverish pitch and she sought more of him. She opened her mouth more and heard him suck in a breath of air before he slid his tongue into her mouth. He toyed with her, pulling a gruff sound from her. She wanted him.

Wanted him.

Enough to get naked with him.

Have sex with him.

This kind of urge hadn't overcome her since her younger days. And that thought snapped her back to full awareness.

Breaking away from the kiss, she stared up at him, as breathless as he was.

"Sorry," he murmured.

"Wes." She wasn't ready for this.

He slid his arm from behind her and stood. "Sorry."

"No…it's okay." She stood, too.

"I'm going to get back to work," he said, stepping back.

"Yeah. I think I'll go back to bed." As if she'd ever get to sleep now.

"Okay. See you in the morning."

"Okay."

As she headed for the stairs, she couldn't remember ever feeling this disconcerted with a man.

Or this desired by one.

Chapter 8

Karen Hathaway opened the front door of a baby-blue-and-white modular home in dire need of repair. She was in dire need of repair, too. She wore faded jeans that were too tight and a bright pink T-shirt that molded to her body and exposed her stomach, which hung over the rhinestone belt at her waist.

"Mrs. Hathaway?" he said.

"Yes?"

"I'm Sheriff Colton. Mind if I ask you a few questions?"

"About what?" She blew a bubble with her chewing gum, smacking the glob back into her mouth when it popped.

He cleared his throat. "You ran into Lily Masterson at the Honey-B, isn't that right?"

"I heard about you two. Is she trying to get you to come after me now?"

"Did you confront her?"

"Yes, and I threw a glass of water in her face. Did she tell you that, too?"

"I need to talk to you about some things that have happened since then. Is now a good time?"

Her eyes became slits between bags of excess skin that trembled as she chewed her gum. "What things?"

He removed his notebook from one of his pockets along with a pen. "Your husband had an affair with Lily in the past, is that right?"

"You know it is. Everybody in town knows it."

"And are you still angry about that?"

"I wasn't until I saw her in town. I don't want her here, prancing around and tempting my husband."

Her husband had looked a lot better back then than he did now. Lily wouldn't have been with him otherwise. She was an attractive woman. "Then you have good reason not to want her in town."

"You bet I do."

"Did you send her roses with a note?"

"No. Why would I do that? Send her flowers." She scoffed. "I wouldn't send her flowers."

"Her truck was also vandalized. Someone painted the word *whore* on it several times."

Wes saw in Karen what he would call smug irritation. No awkwardness or anxiety that would give away her guilt. "Are you accusing me of doing that, too?"

"I'm asking you *if* you did."

"No."

"Are you aware that the library was set on fire last night?"

"It was?"

Did he imagine how hopeful she sounded? Before coming here he'd done a background on her and discovered she'd had a juvenile record in Bozeman along with a robbery charge that had been dismissed in court. He waited for her to answer his question.

"No, I didn't know anything about that." She paused. "Is she okay?"

"Yes. The fire was put out before it did much damage, and Lily wasn't hurt."

Her expression drooped almost imperceptibly.

Wes remained focused on his purpose. "Where were you between eight and ten last night?"

"Here." Her smugness had returned.

"Alone?"

"No, I was with my husband."

"Is he here now?"

"No. He left a half hour ago."

"Is he at work?"

"He has the day off. Said he was going fishing." She didn't appear to care one way or the other.

"Thank you, Mrs. Hathaway. That's all I need for now." He put away his pad and pen.

She looked stunned by his abrupt dismissal.

"Good day." He nodded once and left the house.

Andy Hathaway was a middle-school janitor who spent his time off at the Corner Bar. Just past ten in the morning, Wes took his chance that he'd find Andy there now, not fishing.

Parking in the only space left in front, Wes glanced around at the quiet street and entered the bar. There were three men at the bar, one of them Andy.

"Sheriff," the bartender, Jake, greeted.

Wes said hello and stopped beside Andy. "Andy, will you join me at a table?"

Andy looked up, his reddened eyes startled. "What for?"

"I'd like to ask you a few questions."

The other two men at the bar looked from Wes to Andy. The bartender slowly wiped the bar surface.

"About what?"

"Come on over and I'll explain." Wes walked to a table a good distance from the bar and sat.

All four of the other men stared at him. Andy slid his drink from the bar, picking it up and carrying it with him. Dark liquid spilled as he set the glass down on the table and pulled a chair out.

"I ain't done nothin' wrong." He drained the drink and banged the glass down.

That's what everyone was saying to him. Wes kept his frustration to himself. "Mind if I ask where you were last night?"

"Why you want to know?"

"Just answer the question."

"Am I in some sort of trouble?"

Was he expecting to be? "No. I just need you to answer a few questions."

"Maybe I should get me a lawyer first."

"Do you need a lawyer?"

Andy fell silent. Then he turned his head over his shoulder. "Can I get another?" he called toward the bar.

Wes kept his expression neutral as he waited for Andy to decide what to do. The bartender delivered another drink and Andy drank half of it.

"I was home last night," Andy said.

"Where was your wife?"

"She was home, too."

"All night?"

He smirked. "Yeah. Where else would she go?"

Wes wasn't impressed with their relationship so far. "What did you do? Anything?"

"No. Watched a game on TV and went to bed."

Wes looked down at the drink on the table and then back up at Andy. "Were you drinking?"

Andy's smirk grew more sardonic. "Why you want to know that?"

"Were you?"

"Yeah. I have a few every night after work. Helps me unwind."

Wes wondered what it did in the morning. "Did you fall asleep early?"

"I was tired after working. Yeah. I fell asleep while my wife watched TV. She was next to me."

"When you fell asleep," Wes finished.

"Yeah. What about it?"

Wes wanted to ask if his manhood was threatened. "Someone tried to burn the library down with Lily Masterson in it last night."

"Yeah? What's that got to do with me?"

"Your wife threatened Lily three nights ago. Did you know that?"

"No." Andy swore. "Serves that Masterson woman right, though. Worst mistake I ever made was sleepin' with that whore. Been payin' for it ever since."

Wes took a moment to jot down some notes. Had Andy felt strong enough about that to write it all over Lily's truck?

"So, you support your wife's threat?"

"She hadn't done it, I might've." Andy took a swig of his drink. "Shouldn't have come back here, all the trouble she left behind. Damn near ruined my marriage."

Wes looked down at the near-empty drink and back up at Andy's pasty face and wondered what Karen loved about him. And what he loved about her. It amazed him to see people let their lives dwindle to empty shells without doing anything to make them better. Nothing improved without effort. And strength. It didn't appear Karen and Andy were capable of either. They settled for what they had and beat each other up for it.

"Thank you, Andy. You've been a big help." Wes stood.

"You gonna arrest my wife?" he asked.

"Not yet."

"Way I see it, Lily got what she deserved. Karen didn't hurt her. Lily should listen to her and leave town. Nobody wants her here anyway."

Without acknowledging Andy, Wes turned and left the bar.

Driving down Main Street, he saw a familiar truck in front of the sheriff's office. Damien was there. He was driving his old pickup.

Wes parked and walked into the building.

"Damien's here," Deputy King said, standing behind the counter. He looked and sounded annoyed. "He went into your office."

"I know." Wes saw Ryan approach, veering around a desk to intercept him.

"I got what you asked for," he said.

Wes took the piece of paper Ryan handed him. It was a printout of a spreadsheet with a list of names. He stopped walking to read. Each row listed a woman's name and the columns were filled with personal information. The year she had moved to Honey Creek. Her age. Her marital status. The year she'd married—if she'd married. Her address and phone number. Her profession.

There were five women.

He looked up at Ryan. "Good job."

Ryan smiled. "Damien asked me a lot of questions. I didn't tell him anything."

Meaning he hadn't told anyone about the list. Wes nodded and folded the paper, tucking it into his back pocket. "Okay."

He went to his office. Damien was sitting behind his

desk, his fingers typing away on the keyboard in front of the computer.

He looked up when Wes entered. "About time you got here." He stood and came around the desk to stand before Wes.

"Find anything good on my computer?" He was a little irritated that his brother had taken the liberty.

Damien chuckled. "Relax. I was just checking out places to live outside Honey Creek."

"You're serious about moving?"

"Very."

"How're you doing otherwise?" He didn't want to talk about Damien leaving. After so many years without him around, he preferred to have him near.

"Good. My house feels like a mansion and my refrigerator is my own private delicatessen. I have a little of everything. Mexican, Italian, American. Lots of chips and dips. Every kind of cheese you can imagine. Cookies. Brownies. Ice cream. Soda, juice, iced tea, chocolate milk. I didn't realize how much I missed variety in my food."

"Don't get fat," Wes teased.

And Damien chuckled again. "I drank beer with Duke, too. I tried a new pilsner. Sure is good to hang out with him again."

He seemed happy, and that made Wes feel good. "You come by just to tell me what you're eating and drinking?"

"No, I came by to see if you learned any more about that woman. Tina Mueller."

"Not yet. I have some people I'm going to talk to, but nothing definitive yet."

"Who're you going to talk to?"

Wes angled his head. He didn't want to get Damien into a froth unless there was something to froth over. He'd check these women out and see if any of them were worth investigating further. "Just some women who might turn out to be Tina."

"I want to help."

"Let me handle this part of it. If I find out if we have something solid to go on, I'll let you know."

"Why not tell me now what you've got?"

"I don't want to scare Tina away before I've had a chance to talk to her."

"I wouldn't do anything rash. I'd ask her questions, just like you. Or I'd just go with you. I want to be involved."

"Let me do my job, Damien. Have a little faith in me, would you?"

Damien stared at him a while and Wes could read his thoughts. There'd been times when he'd had very little faith in any of his family.

"I can't sit back and do nothing," Damien said.

Wes didn't respond. He wished he hadn't said anything about Tina Mueller. But this was Damien. He deserved to know what was going on every step of the way. However, it was too soon. Wes didn't know enough.

"Damn it, Wes."

"Put yourself in my shoes for just two seconds. What would you do?"

He watched Damien think about that. And finally he relented. His eyes grew less perturbed. "Yeah. I can understand where you're coming from, little brother. And I'd probably do the same thing, especially if I didn't know much. You're the sheriff, not me. Just promise me you'll tell me when you know something."

"I'll keep you updated. I promise."

Damien nodded and turned to leave.

"And, Damien," Wes said, catching his attention. "Tina might not have killed Mark Walsh." He had to prove that first.

Damien took a moment to digest that before he said, "Don't worry…I'll be keeping my eyes and ears open for other possibilities."

"That's the best thing you can do to help right now."

"Call me when you've talked to them." With that, Damien left the office.

Moving behind his desk, Wes pulled out the folded piece of paper and sat. He flattened the page.

Margaret Jefferies. Forty-eight. Married twenty years. Housewife. That meant she'd moved here with her husband. Three kids. One in college. Unlikely that she was Walsh's lover. The oldest child would have been about five when they moved here. Walsh hadn't provided a new identity for an entire family. Only Tina.

Audrey Damascus. Forty-five. Married ten years. Veterinary assistant. She'd have been thirty at the time of Walsh's recording. Two kids, seven and nine. She was a possibility.

Eileen Curtis. Thirty-eight. Divorced. Married seven years. Real estate agent. No kids. She was a possibility, too.

Betsy Grant. Eighty-five years old! Widowed. Retired, obviously. Wes knew her, too. Definitely not possible. Mark Walsh would not have had an affair with a seventy-year-old woman.

Amy Fordham. Forty-one. Divorced. Waitress. Married five years. One child, a ten-year-old. Another possibility. He had three women to question.

Wes would begin with the veterinary assistant. Her job required no formal training and there'd be no background check required. She could easily slip into her new life without anyone knowing.

He leaned back against his chair. He couldn't call any of the three women a suspect, but it was a good start. Hopefully, Tina hadn't left town.

Checking the time, he put the paper into a folder and filed it in his drawer. He was supposed to stop by Maisie's tonight. He'd much rather be with Lily. That kiss hadn't left his mind all day. But she hadn't wanted to go with him to Maisie's. He'd have to be content with the memory.

A Linkin Park song blared from a ton of tiny speakers spread out from an entertainment center. It was new and the sound was awesome. May was going to ask her mom why they didn't keep up with the times. She smiled up at Levi as he led her from the throng of dancing teenagers. Even the unwelcoming faces she passed didn't bother her. Some took notice of who she was with. That rocked.

Levi found a space against the wall. She stood beside him.

"I'll go get us a beer," he said.

She'd never had a beer before. Her mom didn't drink and had always told her not to.

Alone by the wall, May watched a group of kids dance. Some sat on a couch. Most moved around and talked and laughed while they drank beer.

Then she caught sight of Sherilynn. She stood beside two other girls, arms folded, face all pissy.

May stared back at her. She wasn't afraid. They weren't at school this time. There'd be no meeting with the principal.

As if reading her expression, Sherilynn turned away, saying something to one of the girls.

Levi returned, handing May a cup of keg beer. She took a sip. It was bitter, but had a flavor that wasn't unappealing.

"Do you like it?" Levi asked.

May nodded. "It's all right." She wasn't sure she'd try it again, though. Levi smiled. One of his friends interrupted the moment by stopping in front of them.

"Hey, Gavin," Levi said.

"You and Sherilynn break up?" Gavin asked, eyeing May.

"Yeah."

Gavin eyed May again.

"This is May," Levi said.

"I know. Hey, May."

May ignored him, not sure if he was another enemy or not. He still eyed her funny, checking her out, but not in a good way. He didn't like her. She could tell. Jerk. He didn't even know her.

"I heard your mom and the sheriff were gettin' it on."

May rolled her eyes. "What do you know?"

"Gavin," Levi said in a warning tone.

"My mom said Lily got in a wreck with him after one of his trips to Montana State Prison."

"Get lost," May sneered.

"Was your mom at the prison, too?"

May fumed inside. She was so sick of everybody saying bad things about her mom.

"Was she visiting somebody? A guy?" Gavin laughed. "Maybe that's why she never got hitched. She's been pining over a dude in jail." He laughed again.

"You're an asshole," Levi said, which May appreciated but it wasn't enough.

"My mom testified at a hearing there," May informed him.

She felt Levi's quick glance and saw Gavin's surprise with the lift of his brow.

"Why did she testify?" Levi asked. "What hearing?"

Because he was the one who asked, she looked up at him and contemplated telling him. Maybe knowing would change the way everybody thought of her mom. She wanted that more than anything.

"My mom was raped before I was born." She turned what she hoped was a haughty look at Gavin. "That's why she left Honey Creek. After we came back, she had to testify at her rapist's parole hearing to try to keep him from being released. She met Wes right after that, when she was leaving the parking lot."

"Whoa," Gavin exclaimed.

Levi stared at her, stunned. "That's awful, May."

"Is that who your dad is?" Gavin asked.

And May felt her face start to heat. "No," she snapped. "It happened way before I was born."

"Yeah, right. That's what your mom probably told you. Guess what comes around what goes around," Gavin said, laughing, yet again.

May couldn't stand it anymore. She slapped him. His head jerked to the side a little but his smile went away.

"Asshole," she said, tossing her hair over her shoulder as she marched toward the door. Outside, she would have kept walking toward home, sure that Levi would side with his stupid friend.

But he didn't. She heard him jog up beside her.

"I'm sorry, May. Gavin's a friend but he isn't one of my best ones."

Over and over again Levi was proving to be someone unlike many at school. "Now it's going to be all over school that my mom was raped and she had it coming."

"I don't know about that. I think it'll make most people change their minds about her. See that she's changed. It's terrible what happened to her. I'm sorry, May. I really am."

May stopped and faced him. She moved closer, putting her hand on his chest. "You're a nice person, Levi."

He stepped closer, too, and now their bodies touched. Excitement and apprehension fired through her. She'd never been kissed by a boy before.

He leaned down. "I like you, May." And he kissed her. He

touched her mouth with his. It felt soft and warm and made her tingle all over.

She stared up at him when he lifted his head.

"Get in. I'll drive you home."

She caught her breath and got in his car. Still feeling that kiss, engulfed with the memory, she turned to look out the window.

A shadow caught her eye. Someone was standing in the trees in front of the house. She couldn't tell who it was. Sherilynn, probably. That stupid girl kept hovering whenever she was with Levi. Fine. Let her. May wasn't going to let her beat her down. Nobody would. She wouldn't let them.

Lily looked out the front window again. Still no lights. May had told her she was going to Peri's house and would be home by nine, but she'd called there and Peri's mother said Peri was home alone. May wasn't there.

Lily was worried sick. It was after ten.

Wes was up at his sister's house. He'd invited her, but she'd declined. The last thing she needed was to spend an evening with Maisie Colton. And she was still so out of sorts after last night.

Confiding in Wes that way, and then that kiss. She could have gone to bed with him. After she had gone to bed alone, she'd wished she had slept with him. It was long past time for her to reclaim her sexuality. She hadn't had good sex in so long, but she felt as though she could have it with Wes.

Trusting him was hard for her, though. Trust was hard for her with any man. But never had she come closer to trusting one than she was with Wes. It both frightened and excited her. What if it didn't work out with him? What if he discovered he needed someone younger, or someone with less drama to carry around?

What if it *did* work out?

That's the part that tickled her insides and made her breathless.

Car lights appeared on the dirt drive that led to Wes's log home.

Lily waited. She kept the light off in the front entry.

The car stopped and a boy got out. He opened the passenger door and May emerged from the car. The boy held her hand as they walked toward the door. There, Lily had a close-up view of them.

The boy put his hands on May's waist. May put hers on his shoulders, and slid them around his neck as the boy leaned in for a kiss.

Lily wasn't sure what to think of her fourteen-year-old daughter kissing a boy. What should she do? The boy didn't look much older than her. Maybe fifteen or sixteen. But he was old enough to get her daughter pregnant.

The kiss lasted a minute or two and then the boy said good night.

He stepped back and watched May open the front door.

Lily stayed out of sight until the door closed. May's dreamy smile vanished when she saw her.

"Mom."

"Where were you?" Lily demanded. She was mad as hell.

"At Peri's. I told you."

"You were not at Peri's. You lied to me."

"I was, too."

Lily walked to stand right in front of her daughter. "I called there."

May's mouth closed and she said nothing. What could she say? She was caught.

"I knew you wouldn't let me go out with Levi."

"Levi? Is he your boyfriend?"

She put her hands on her hips. "Mom—"

"Is he?"

Her hands dropped to her sides again. "Yes. A-at least…I think so."

"How long have you been seeing him?"

"Not long. A couple of weeks."

"Have you had sex with him?"

May's face colored. "No! Mom…!"

Good. What a relief. Lily could see her daughter was telling the truth. Thank God.

"Are you going to?"

"No! I like him, that's all."

"If you end up liking him long enough and want to have sex with him, you tell me first. I don't want you getting pregnant."

"Mom, stop it." May marched past her.

Lily stopped her at the top of the stairs, taking her by the arm. "You haven't told me where you were." She smelled the air close to May. "Have you been drinking?" Lily was appalled.

"No! What's the matter with you?"

"You smell like beer."

"I do not."

"How much did you drink tonight?" Lily demanded.

May rolled her eyes. "I just had a couple of sips of beer. It was no big deal."

"No big deal?" Lily's head spun. "First you get into a fight, now you're going to parties and drinking beer. What's next, May?"

"I'm not doing anything wrong."

"Oh, really? That's what you think?" Lily pointed her finger in front of May's face, still holding her arm. "You're fourteen years old. You lied about where you were going and you *drank alcohol*."

May let out a grunted breath.

"You're grounded."

"Mom!"

"You're grounded and you will not see that boy until I say you can. Do you hear me?"

"Mom, don't."

"No friends. No calls. You come home after school and that's it."

Just then Wes walked in the door. Lily let go of May's arm and turned. Seeing him was like a breath of fresh air, though he stole hers. May disappeared down the stairs, her angry steps loud, Lily was sure, on purpose.

"Everything all right?" Wes asked.

"Just having a teenager moment." Disconcerted by how good it was to see him, she headed for the kitchen. "You're home late." She inwardly cringed because she thought she sounded like a wife.

"Had something come up. I got a call to leave during dinner with Maisie. That didn't go over well. She accused me of using it as an excuse to go home to you."

"Did you get a chance to eat?"

"Not much."

"I'll make you something." Hearing him behind her, she poured herself a glass of milk and turned with the carton. "Want some?"

"No thanks. I'll just make myself a sandwich."

"I'll make it for you." She told herself it wasn't because she felt like his woman. She was only grateful for his hospitality.

"Thanks." A long sigh came from him as he sat at the kitchen table.

Taking out everything she needed to make him one of her favorite club sandwiches, Lily went to work. "What happened tonight?"

"Got a call from a woman who said her husband was drunk and she was worried what he'd do. By the time I got there, he had already left. I caught up to him after he left the Corner Bar. Had to arrest him on DUI charges."

"I'm sure his wife was delighted."

"She decided to let him stay the night in jail."

"Can't say I blame her."

Finished making the sandwich, she brought it over to the table and sat next to him. She wouldn't be able to sleep right away anyway. It wasn't because she'd missed him tonight and was happy to see him. It wasn't.

The warmth in his eyes made her smile.

He lifted the sandwich and took a bite. "Mmm." He chewed. "You make great sandwiches."

"You sure you don't want anything to drink?"

"Actually, a beer would be good."

But when she started to get up, he put his hand on hers. "I'll get it. You wait here."

She felt inexplicably warm and tingly while he got a beer and returned. And she couldn't stop smiling.

He grinned. "I'm glad to see you, too."

Fighting a girlish blush, Lily looked down.

When Wes's hand slid over hers again, she looked up.

"And I could do this every day," he said.

Every day. Lily felt herself fall into what she was afraid to call love.

Chapter 9

After three days living with May's attitude over being grounded, Lily was ready for a break. She entered Kelley's Cookhouse, leaving the cool chill of late September behind. Bonnie Gene was at the restaurant with her husband so Lily asked if she could spare a few minutes. Wes had called and said he was working late, and her dad had agreed to keep an eye on May.

She didn't know how she felt about the way things were progressing with Wes. She wasn't even sure she wanted anything to progress, not in the direction of love. When he'd called, it had warmed her with affection. How sweet of him to think of her. But then she'd realized him thinking of her that way had too much of a domesticated feel. She was—in effect—living with him. He'd called to tell her he'd be home late from work. He didn't have to do that.

Not only that, her dad had begun responding to questions she asked him. He always shut her out when she tried to have a conversation with him, but things were improving. Was it because of Wes? Did he see how well he treated her? Did that make a difference? If she gave in to fantasy, she'd dream of staying with Wes the rest of her life, caring for her dad and raising May. It felt right. And then it didn't. Most of the time it felt as if she were risking too much. If she allowed something to develop between them, how long before he started wanting someone younger? Would she find herself in her sixties facing life as a single woman again? She didn't want that.

No one had threatened her after the fire, and she was beginning to wonder if it was time to go home.

She entered Kelley's. People turned to look at her. She recognized a few of them. Mary and Jake Pierson were there, having dinner with Lucy Walsh. Mary saw her and something in the way she looked at her piqued Lily.

She went to the table, feeling other glances on the way. Something weird was going on. What didn't she know that they did?

Mary stood from the table. "Lily, I didn't know. I'm so sorry." She hugged her. Lily felt every muscle in her body stiffen.

Mary leaned back. "Are you doing all right?"

"Yes. How are you?" She wanted to deflect whatever had Mary concerned, having a bad feeling about it.

"I'm fine. Jake is keeping me out of trouble." She looked back at him and winked.

"That's good. No one's tried to come after you again?" Lily asked.

"No. What a relief that is." She met Lily's eyes. "Look, if you ever need to talk…"

Lily didn't like her leading inflection. "Thanks," she said abruptly. "I'm meeting Bonnie Gene today. Have you seen her?"

"No, I haven't."

"She's over there, talking to some customers." Jake pointed.

Lily saw her the same time Bonnie Gene turned and saw her. Bonnie Gene smiled and waved and then said something to the seated couple she'd been talking to. Stepping away, she indicated a booth nearby.

Lily looked at Lucy and Jake, and ended with Mary. "I'll catch up to you later."

Mary nodded, sympathy still in her eyes.

Oh, God. Lily couldn't breathe. What had happened? What rumor was passing around town now?

She saw Bonnie Gene and felt relief spare her. Her friend was like a beacon. A safe place to get away.

But as she slid onto the booth seat, she saw the same look in Bonnie Gene's eyes.

"What?" Lily asked.

"Oh, Lily. Everybody knows."

"Knows what?" But she didn't have to be told. Tears of humiliation burned her eyes.

"Gavin MacGregor told his mother. It spread from there."

"Who is Gavin MacGregor?"

"He's a junior at Honey Creek High. Levi Garrison is one of his friends. Levi and May were at the same party last weekend. Apparently they talked to Gavin."

May had talked. May told someone about what had happened to her? Her own daughter? Surely it hadn't been on purpose.

"They know you were raped. Some are saying May is your rapist's daughter. Oh, Lily, I'm so sorry. I know how upset this is going to make you."

Lily could only stare down at her hand on the table.

"I've told everyone I know that May's father isn't who they think it is."

Which was only going to make things worse. As soon as the details emerged—and they would—they'd know it hadn't been that long after her rape that she'd slept with May's father.

Lily looked around. Almost every eye in the place was trained on her. Some looked away when she caught them, others didn't. Some turned to talk with their tablemates.

A tremble began in her limbs. She wiped a traitorous tear from her cheek.

"Lily?"

She wanted to get up and walk out of here, but that would mean parading in front of everyone. She felt like a rape victim again. Helpless. What was she going to do?

She didn't know. She only knew she was lost and afraid. The front door opened and Wes walked in. Her heart overflowed with need. She needed him so much right now and he was here.

He searched the restaurant until he found her. His face was set and grim.

He knew. She needed him. He'd known, and he'd come for her.

Another tear rolled from her eye and more followed. There was no stopping them now.

Wes strode toward her, all purpose and brawn heading her way. It was the most beautiful sight in the world to her.

"Oh, my…look at him," Bonnie Gene said.

Lily's emotions overwhelmed her. He was going to rescue her. That's what it felt like. Unless she was wrong and he had another reason to be here. But she doubted that, especially when he reached the table and extended his hand.

"Come with me," he said.

She wiped her cheek again and gave him her hand.

"Bonnie Gene," he said.

"Wes. Your timing couldn't be better."

"I tried to catch you before you got here," he said to Lily.

She let him put his arm around her and escort her toward the door. He must have called home again, after learning what was going around town, and worried she was in the middle of spectator hell. She was. The restaurant was quiet as they passed, all the way to the exit.

Maybe moving here had been a mistake after all.

Wes opened the door for her and she got into his SUV. He shut the door and moved to the other side. When he sat behind the wheel, he looked over at her. After a minute, he started driving. But just outside of town he pulled off the road onto a side street and parked along the side of the dirt road.

She looked over at him, wondering why he'd stopped.

His face was intent as he hesitated. "I'm sorry this is happening, Lily, But I have to ask. Why, after fifteen years, do you still need to keep a secret?"

Bowing her head, she stared at her clasped hands in her lap. "You know why."

"It wasn't your fault."

"Yes, it was. I picked him up at a bar. I did that all the time."

"You were young."

"I should have known better. Things weren't great at home, but taking personal risks wasn't the way to fight back." She lifted her head and turned toward him. "I hurt myself more than I hurt my parents. That's what I was trying to do. Hurt them. And look what it got me."

"You have to stop blaming yourself, Lily."

"I'm over it. I am. It's just…with Brandon's release and all…it set me back, that's all."

"Yes, it set you back, but there's more to it than that. You've kept this buried too long."

"You think I shouldn't mind if the whole town is talking about me…about *that?*"

"No. I don't think anyone would like that. I think you should stop blaming yourself."

She did blame herself. She'd never thought of it that way, but now she realized she did. Sleeping around the way she had, it was hard not to hold herself accountable. But she hadn't set out to get raped. No woman deserved that, no matter how debauched her lifestyle.

Yet again, Wes had done something incredibly sweet. He cared about her. He'd rescued her. He was still rescuing her. Helping her heal. Never before had she trusted a man this much.

Removing her seat belt, she leaned over the console. His face was close to hers now.

"Don't stop holding your head high," he said.

She slid her hand along the side of his face and ran her fingers into his rich, brown hair. He didn't make a move, which only sweetened the moment more.

She pressed her lips to his. He let her have control. He responded to her kiss, but didn't push further. She parted her lips and pressed harder.

He answered her.

Soon his arms were around her and she was arching toward him. It felt so good. And safe. He was the first man in fifteen years who made her feel that way.

She broke away to unbutton his shirt. When she slid her hands over his chest and pushed the material off his shoulders, he put his hands over hers.

"Lily."

She looked up into his impassioned eyes. "I want this."

"Not here."

Yes, here. It was a rush to feel like her old self again, only this time she was in control. This time she wasn't doing anything to rebel against her parents. This was real. It meant something.

Climbing into the backseat, she sat and patted the space beside her. Wes had twisted to watch her, and now he hesitated.

His hesitation only made her want him more.

"Come here."

"Lily…"

"Please."

At last he climbed into the back, his big body not fitting between the seats as well as hers had. He sat beside her. She crawled onto him, straddling his thighs.

He put his hands on her hips.

She kissed him.

"I don't have anything," he said.

"Diseases? Good," she teased, kissing him some more.

"That's not what I meant."

She laughed because she already knew that, pushing his shirt down his arms. "It's okay." He shrugged out of his shirt, still looking uncertain. Pulling her long-sleeved white T-shirt over her head, she dropped it on the seat beside her, loving how his gaze fell.

When his eyes lifted, she unbuttoned his jeans. He didn't look so uncertain anymore.

Climbing off him, she took off her jeans and removed her underwear. The sound of his breathing was an aphrodisiac. On her knees, she waited for him to get naked. When he left his jeans and boxers on the floor, she climbed back onto his lap, positioning herself on the length of his erection, but nothing more. She needed a little more time.

Kissing him, her pulse grew heavier as his hands roamed. She tipped her head back when he put his mouth on her breasts. His hands kneaded her butt, moving her against him. The slow and steady grind against his hardness heated her. She moved with him. He groaned and found her mouth, kissing her deep.

She continued to move with his coaxing. Urgency made her ache unbearably for him.

Now she was ready.

Raising up on her knees, she reached down and put him where he needed to be, and then let her weight slowly draw him inside. He fitted her perfectly and let her keep the pace.

But she was clumsy in her movements, as if it were her first time. In a sense, it was. She'd started her life over after her ordeal. The sex partners she'd had since then had been all wrong. Stiff and unpleasant. This was the opposite. Right. Warm. Exquisitely pleasurable.

Wes held her hips and began to thrust his own upward. She put her hand on the roof to keep her head from hitting it. Tingles of ecstasy sailed through her. An orgasm grew, rapid and out of control. She shouted when it burst over her. Wes rammed his erection into her until a sound from deep in his throat told her he'd reached the same peak.

Sagging against him, she laid her head on his shoulder and basked in the wonder while her pulse slowed and her breathing came back to normal.

It had been beyond her hope ever to feel like this again. But somehow Wes had overcome that obstacle. How frightening to realize the significance. How frightening to realize the significance of him. Wes. Could he really be hers?

A long-buried part of her cried, *yes.*

Lily didn't come down from Wes's room until late the next morning. He'd already left for work. She'd barely awakened when he'd leaned over the bed and kissed her. But now the memory of that and of what had transpired after they'd come home last night had her floating inside.

Seeing her dad and May at the kitchen table, she was a

little embarrassed. If either one of them had gone upstairs, they'd know where she'd slept.

Her dad and May stopped talking when she neared.

"Don't you have to work today?" her dad asked.

He was actually talking to her? "I have the day off." Thank goodness. She couldn't have woken up early after last night. She turned to May, "Why aren't you in school?"

"I told her she could take the day," her dad said.

"What gives you the right to do that?" Lily snapped.

"I wanted to talk to you," May said.

Lily went into the kitchen and poured herself a glass of iced tea from a pitcher that Wes kept in his refrigerator. She was still upset with May and hadn't decided how to deal with it.

"Keeping things bottled up is never a good thing," her dad said. "Neither is moping in your room all day."

She turned and looked from May's somber face to her father's. May must have told him everything. "I wasn't going to stay in there all day."

"You should have told us what happened back then."

"You and Mom? What would you have done?"

"Helped you. Something."

"Really?" She couldn't subdue her animosity. "I doubt you'd have done anything but blame me." Her parents had never really been there for her. She'd never felt as if she could turn to them. And while she'd moved here to mend that relationship, the reminder that the whole town was gossiping about her rape put her in a foul mood.

Her dad looked annoyed. "You made it hard for us, Lily, with all your gallivanting. But we wanted the best for you."

"You wanted me to be someone I wasn't."

"That isn't true. We wanted you to succeed."

"Nothing I could have done would have made you think I succeeded."

Her dad sighed. "Well, that part about you hasn't changed. You're still as hardheaded now as you were then."

There it was, his disapproval. She'd known it would come up sooner or later.

"My mom isn't hardheaded," May put in.

But Shay ignored her. "If you'd done something to make us proud, we would have been," her dad said.

"Like what?"

"Get good grades. Go to college."

"I did get good grades." She'd had a B average but that hadn't been good enough.

"You had no aspirations other than going to parties and being with boys."

It would have been different if her parents had loved her for who she was. But she didn't comment on that. Instead, she sipped her tea.

"I hate to say it, Lily, but it's no wonder you were raped." Her hand trembled and she almost dropped the glass.

"What I can't figure is how you could have gone out and done it again right after that."

Meaning how she'd gotten pregnant with May.

"I don't regret that."

"No, you have May, but...hell, Lily, have you no respect for yourself?"

"Stop it!" May yelled and then she pointed at Shay much the same as Lily did when she was mad. "You leave her alone."

Shay pushed back his chair and stood. "There's no talking to you, Lily, you never listen." With that he left the room and then the house, the front door shutting with a thud.

Lily turned toward her daughter.

"Mom, I didn't mean to start anything."

The look of heartfelt appeal on her daughter's face seared her. "I know you didn't."

"It's just that that boy kept saying bad things about you and I couldn't stand it anymore."

So she'd thought she'd defended her mother telling that boy about her mother's tragedy would make him stop thinking of her negatively.

"And your reaction backfired. When are you going to learn to stop lashing out in a difficult confrontation?"

"I'm not like you, Mom. I'm not going to sit back and let anyone slander me. Or you."

"And now everyone will look at me like I'm weak and vulnerable. I didn't want that."

"I know." She still looked pleading. "I'm sorry."

Lily moved closer and hugged her daughter. "You don't have to be sorry. I know you didn't mean any harm. I love you. The talk will pass."

The sooner the better.

Sitting in his SUV, Wes tried to concentrate on the entrance to the veterinary clinic where Audrey Damascus worked. He wanted to catch her when she left. But he kept sinking into heated memories of Lily. He couldn't stop his brain from going there. Checking his watch, he figured he had a few minutes, so he finally gave up and leaned his head back against the seat and shut his eyes.

The last thing he'd expected was that Lily would want to have sex in the back of his SUV. It resembled the old Lily, and yet it didn't. Some of her adventurous spirit had returned, but rather than a reckless impulse, growing trust in their relationship had compelled her. Wes had felt it with her, and it had drawn him closer than ever. After connecting with her like that, he was worried about what it would do to him if she ever turned away from him.

And then they'd gone home and she'd slept with him. At around three he'd awakened to find her watching him, and this time he'd taken control. She hadn't been afraid and that had arrowed straight through him. Making love with her was intense that time. He couldn't wait to do it again.

Wes opened his eyes and watched the clinic. He wished he could leave right now.

Just then, Audrey Damascus emerged. It was five-fifteen. Good. The sooner he got this over with the sooner he could go home to Lily.

He got out of his SUV and approached her as she reached her car, a dented and fading Honda Civic. He had known from her driver's license that she was a little on the heavy side, but he would never have guessed she was this overweight. If she'd been involved with Mark Walsh, she must have been a lot thinner. Or maybe Mark had secretly liked heavier women.

She stopped at her driver's door and saw him.

"Audrey Damascus?"

She eyed him in surprise.

"I'm Sheriff Colton." He showed her his identification.

She glanced down and then looked up at his face. "I know who you are."

He took out his notepad and pen. "I need to ask you a few questions. Do you mind?"

"What about?" She appeared genuinely perplexed.

"Did you know Mark Walsh?" he asked.

Her brow creased above her nose. "The guy that was murdered?"

"Yes."

"I know *of* him. It's a small town. Are you asking me if I knew him personally?"

"Yes."

A breath of a grunt accompanied the wonder in her eyes. "No, I didn't. Why are you asking me that?"

"You moved to Honey Creek in 1995, isn't that right?"

"Yes. How did you know that? Why are you checking up on me like this?"

Her voice didn't sound like that from the recording, but the tape was old. "Why did you move here?"

She hesitated as she searched his eyes for answers he could only guess were swimming in her head. "My husband has family here. We were just dating back then, but I moved here with him."

That would be easy enough to check. "What was your maiden name?"

"Murdock."

He jotted that down.

"Look, Sheriff, I've done nothing wrong, especially where Mark Walsh is concerned. I didn't even know him."

"You never met him? Not even once?"

"No."

"Do you know anyone by the name of Tina Mueller?" He watched her face for telltale signs.

She shook her head. "Never heard of her. You gonna tell me what this is all about?"

This was a waste of time. Wes knew it right then. Her bewilderment was too real to miss. She didn't know anything and she'd never been involved with Mark Walsh.

He closed the notebook. "Thanks for your cooperation."

"Wait a minute. What made you ask me about Mark Walsh?" Audrey asked as he walked toward his SUV.

He turned. "Sorry to have bothered you."

She put her hand on her hip and looked frustrated that he refused to tell her anything. It was better that way. He faced forward again and made it to his SUV. He didn't want to alert Tina Mueller that he was on to her. Hopefully he'd find her before word got around that he was asking about her.

Next on his list was Eileen Curtis and then Amy Fordham. He drove the short distance to Curtis Real Estate Agency, but didn't get out right away. It was almost six now. If he got home too late, maybe he'd wake Lily up. He wondered if she knew he wanted her to sleep in his bed from now on. If she didn't, he'd have to make sure she did. Like, now.

He pulled his phone from his pocket and called her. She answered on the second ring.

"Hi," he said when she answered.

"Wes?"

"How are you?"

"I'm fine. Just leaving work. How are you?"

"I had to hear your voice."

"Oh." She sounded tentative, as if this transition in their relationship was too new for her. "It's good to hear your voice, too."

He wanted her to mean that. But he wasn't sure if she did. Maybe she needed time to get used to this. He was okay with that. He was a patient man. "This is turning into a long day. I have to talk to some people and then I have to finish up at the office. I'll be a little late getting home. I wanted to let you know."

"All right. I'll wait up for you."

His heart soared. "That would be great." She might be a little skittish right now, but she was still attracted to him.

He could hear her breathing. They didn't say anything, but he could feel the energy between them.

"I'll see you when you get home then," she said, her voice sultry now.

"I can't wait."

"Me neither."

He was the luckiest man alive. "Bye."

"Bye," she whispered, and he could picture her smiling.

He disconnected. That was more like it. Looking toward the old house that was now a business, he steered his focus back on work.

He got out of his SUV. Eileen had done well for herself over the years. She lived in a refurbished old house in town and her real estate business had grown to service other towns in the county. He had seen Eileen around Honey Creek, but he'd never had a chance to talk to her and get to know her. She had a reputation of being friendly to everyone, Colton or Walsh, it didn't matter. Once, a long time ago, a rumor had traveled around that his dad had had an affair with her, but that turned out to be false. His mom had had a hard time with that, but things had mellowed after it was discovered Eileen had gone to Vegas the weekend they were purported to be together. Ryan had filled him in on that, compliments of his gossipy wife.

Wes stepped to the door of Eileen's real estate agency and opened it, a good sign she was still here. The living room was a seating area with a desk on one side. This room opened to what once had been the kitchen but now was a conference room. Two other doors were open, one off the conference room, the other off the living room. Through that door he heard the sound of someone tapping on a keyboard.

The tapping stopped when he shut the front door.

Eileen Curtis appeared a few seconds later. Her short hair was dyed blond, a little on the harsh side. She had green eyes. Dressed in expensive-looking brown slacks and a cream-colored turtleneck with a brown scarf around her neck, her trim body showed her healthy lifestyle.

"Good afternoon, Ms. Curtis."

"Sheriff?" she queried. "Don't tell me you're looking for a new house. I can't imagine there's a better place for you to live than your ranch."

He smiled. "I'm not here to find a new place."

"What a relief." She smiled back, straight white teeth another clue to her healthy and successful lifestyle. Her image lived up to her reputation in town.

"I need to ask you a few questions."

"Wow. Should I be flattered?"

"It's about Mark Walsh."

Her smile faded. "Oh, that. I heard he showed up dead again. I'm so sorry. Your brother…"

"Thanks. We're all really happy he's free."

"That must be so hard for him. After all these years…"

"Yes."

She swung her arm toward the conference table. "Would you like to sit down? Can I get you some water or anything?"

She wasn't flustered at all. Wes went to the table. "I don't need anything to drink, but thanks."

He sat and so did she, across from him.

"You have me at a loss," she said. "What do you think I know about Mark Walsh?"

"Did you know him?"

"Me?" She breathed a laugh. "No. It's a little hard to get to know a dead man, isn't it?"

Wes smiled at her attempted humor. "You moved here the year he was supposedly killed the first time, didn't you?"

"Was that when it was?" She lifted her head and looked upward as though searching her memory. "Yes, I think it was the same year."

"And you never met him?"

"No. What makes you think I might have?"

"I'm not sure. That's why I'm asking."

"Are you asking every woman who moved here the same year he was killed?" she asked.

"Something like that."

She considered him a moment. "I heard he had a lot of lovers. Are you questioning all the women who might have gotten involved with him?"

Why had she brought that up? She'd denied knowing or ever meeting Walsh so asking her wouldn't do him any good. If she had been involved with Walsh, and she was Tina Mueller, she'd deny it.

"Where are you from originally?" he asked instead.

She eyed him curiously before answering. "I was born in Austin, Texas. I lived there until I came here."

"What made you choose Montana?"

"I wanted to stay west, but I didn't want the heat."

"And Honey Creek?"

"Why Honey Creek?" She looked upward again. "I moved to Bozeman originally, but after checking the area out, I fell in love with this town. It gets a little trying knowing everyone who lives here and them knowing everything about you, but I love the small-town feel, and when no one is taking jabs at others, it's a supportive community."

So she didn't like her privacy invaded? "What about your family?"

"I was an only child and both my parents are dead now."

"I'm sorry."

Her soft smile said she appreciated his condolence.

"You're divorced, is that right?"

"Yes."

"Is Curtis your married name?" He knew this, but asked anyway.

"No, I kept my name when we married."

Wes nodded. "Where's he now? Your ex-husband."

"He moved to Billings."

Wes jotted that down on his notepad along with his name, which Ryan had already given him.

"Do you mind my asking what all this has to do with Mark Walsh's murder?"

"Maybe nothing. I'm just trying to gather all the information I can," he said, standing. "I think that's all I need. Thank you for your cooperation."

"Anytime, Sheriff." She stood with him and smiled.

He nodded his farewell, wondering if she was another dead end. She didn't seem to have anything to hide, but then, some liars were better than others.

Wes sat at a table in Amy Fordham's section. The hostess hadn't seemed too pleased with his request. The tables were filling up, but he wasn't going to take long. It was already after eight and he was anxious to get home to Lily.

He missed her and it hadn't even been twenty-four hours since he'd last seen her. And she had baggage he was afraid she wouldn't be able to drop. For once he found a woman he thought would fit in his life, and she had a traumatic past and issues with their age difference. He'd never had to go after a woman this hard before, but he swore he'd do it with Lily. Because one thing he was sure of…he wanted many repeats of last night.

He hoped she felt the same.

The waitress approached his table.

"Hi, I'm Amy. Can I get you something to drink to start out?"

Her voice was a little gravelly from smoking and she seemed a little rough around the edges.

"Actually, I won't be long." He showed her his badge. "Sheriff Colton. Will you have a seat for a minute?"

She glanced around at the other tables.

"This won't take long," he said, and pushed out the chair next to him.

She looked at him. "Did something happen?"

Her curly hair was clipped back and her skin had a slight sheen to it from sweating, but she was an attractive woman, in good shape and looking young for her age and smoking habit. He could imagine Walsh going for a woman like her. Big breasts and all.

"You've heard about Mark Walsh's murder?"

Her confused nod answered him.

"Please, sit down. I need to ask you a few questions."

"I didn't have anything to do with Walsh's murder."

"Where are you from?"

"Why are you asking me that? Am I a suspect or something?"

He smiled as kindly as he could. "No. Not at all. I'm just trying to piece some things together."

"And you think I can piece them together for you?" Her eyes grew dubious. "You must not have much to go on."

"Sit down, Amy." This time there was no invitation in his tone.

She sat, eyes a little more apprehensive now.

"Where are you from?" he asked.

"Bozeman."

"What brought you to Honey Creek?"

"My mom lived here. I came here after my first divorce."

He asked what her ex-husbands name was and she told him.

"What is your maiden name?"

"Why do you need to know that?" She looked from his notepad where he was busy writing to his face.

"Was it Fordham?" he asked.

"No, that was my second husband's name. We had a child together."

"What was your maiden name?"

"Smith."

Was she lying? Amy Smith? Well, he hadn't expected anyone to tell him her maiden name was Mueller.

"How long have you been divorced from your second husband?"

"Seven years."

"Is he from here?"

"He was. He moved away after our divorce."

"Where did he go?"

"Why would I care? He cheated on me. He probably moved to his lover's hometown in Boise."

He was careful not to feed on her emotions. "Did you know Mark Walsh?"

"I heard his name around town. I never met him, though."

"Why did you and your first husband divorce?" He was fishing for a connection to Walsh. If she had an affair…

"We were too young when we met. We grew apart."

"Did you have an affair with anyone?"

She laughed cynically. "You mean with Walsh? No. Guys like that don't turn me on. I like them younger than me—not the other way around. My boyfriend is three years younger than me."

He studied her for a moment. There really wasn't anything else to ask at this point. He had enough to go on for now. He could corroborate her answers with her ex-husband's, and maybe one of them would reveal something.

He stood from the table. "Thank you. That's all for now."

Her eyes followed his movements. "Why do you think I knew Walsh?"

"You've lived here long enough to have met him," he said, knowing it was noncommittal and vague. He nodded a farewell. "Thanks again." And with that, he left.

Maybe something would turn up on her, maybe something wouldn't. Eileen had been willing to cooperate, maybe too willing, and Amy had been apprehensive and had the hardened persona to go with a Tina Mueller past. Eileen was much more refined and a lot more successful. Not the makeup of a woman capable of killing a man. Or men, if she had, in fact, killed her stepfather and then Walsh.

He didn't want to think about all that anymore tonight.

All he wanted was to go home to Lily. Unfortunately, he still had things to wrap up at the office. With any luck, he'd get home by ten or a little after. Lily said she'd wait up for him. He hoped it wasn't too late when he got home.

Chapter 10

Lily took the rolling cooler from the passenger seat of the Jeep and pulled it toward the sheriff's office. Her heart beat in tune with her nerves. Maybe this impulse was too much too soon. It was his phone call. It was so sweet. She hadn't been able to get him out of her mind ever since. So she'd packed dinner for two and driven to his office where he'd said he had to finish up. She wasn't even sure he'd be here yet, but she wanted to surprise him.

Inside, the office was quiet. Tugging the cooler along, she moved around the front counter and headed for the only office with a light on.

At the entry, she stopped. Wes stood behind his desk, stuffing a folder into a narrow, soft leather briefcase. The sight of him stole over her, like an electric current of love.

He looked up and grinned. "I was just thinking about you."

The warm gush that greeting gave her nearly made her face heat up.

He glanced down and saw the cooler. "I was about to leave and come home."

Should she have waited for him? "Have you already eaten?" As busy as he was, she didn't think he had.

Moving around the desk, he shook his head. "No. I haven't had time."

God, he was sexy. She wheeled the cooler into the office, stopping in front of him.

His eyes took in her face. "There's a table in the conference room." His voice was all gravelly and made her tingle.

"Here's fine." She knelt to unzip the front compartment of the cooler. Inside, she took out a blanket and spread it on the floor, glad to have something to keep her busy.

"That's handy." He knelt down beside her and then sat, leaning against the office wall. "Guess there are some parts of the old Lily that haven't changed."

She looked over at him and was relieved to see he was teasing.

"Your adventurous part," he added. "That's all I meant."

Smiling, she unzipped the top compartment of the cooler and took out the bagged sandwiches and a container of crab salad. Next came a bag of chips.

"In case you can't tell, I don't cook much," she said.

"Looks like we'll be spending most of our money at the deli counter then."

"I can cook some things. Boiled eggs. Hamburgers. Hot dogs."

When she'd finished arranging everything, she leaned against the wall beside him. Handing him a roast beef sandwich on a paper plate, she dished him up some crab salad. Next, she took care of her own plate.

After they'd eaten for a few minutes, she asked, "Don't you get tired of working so much?"

"It isn't always like this. There's just a lot going on right now."

Meaning Mark Walsh's murder. The fire in the library…

"I feel like I'm partially to blame for that."

"Not to blame. I want you safe. It's my job."

"I feel safe with you." She smiled and loved how he noticed.

"Good. That's quite a compliment."

"Why do you say that?"

"A woman with your history? It can't be easy." He bit into his sandwich.

He meant the rape. "No, but I don't want to be treated like I'm helpless, either."

Looking at his face while he chewed and swallowed, he said, "I can tell that about you. And it's commendable."

"There are some who wouldn't agree." She took another bite of her own sandwich.

"Like who?"

She waited until after she swallowed her bite. "Like the victims' officer at the parole hearing. She was awful."

"She meant well. She cares about you."

Lily thought that was an odd thing to say. "How do you know that?"

"She told me." He put his sandwich down, abandoning another bite.

Lily froze. "What did you say?"

Slowly, he met her eyes.

A chill of foreboding chased her euphoria away. "When did you talk to her?"

He hesitated. "After I met you."

"After?" She put her sandwich down on her plate.

"Lily, don't be upset. I knew you were lying about why you were at the prison and I just wanted to know why."

"So you…you…you went behind my back? You…you checked up on me?" Without telling her? Why had he kept it from her? That stung. Disenchantment swirled inside her. And here she'd been beginning to think he had real potential.

She removed her plate from her lap and put it on the blanket, no longer hungry.

"I wanted to know why you were at the prison."

"That was none of your business."

"I made it my business. I've been interested in you since the first day I met you."

"So you wanted to…what…make sure I wasn't involved with a criminal?"

He didn't answer. "Lily, please. It was a harmless inquiry."

Harmless? Her rape was an intensely personal matter. "What did she tell you?"

"That you testified at Brandon Gates's parole hearing." He paused. "And why."

Lily's now bloodless face felt cold. "You knew. All this time, you knew."

"I…"

She felt betrayed. "Why didn't you tell me?"

"I wanted you to be ready to tell me on your own."

"And I did." She remembered how much it had meant to her, to unburden herself, to trust him enough to do so. And the whole time, he'd already known. She felt humiliated. She'd bared her soul to him and he'd already known. A lump of hurt gathered in her throat.

"How could you?" Absurdly, she felt like crying. She didn't want to be a baby about it.

He put his plate down next to hers and propped his weight

on one hand as he leaned toward her. "Lily, I was only being respectful. I knew how hard it was for you to confront it."

His face was too close to hers. "I've confronted it."

"No, you haven't. You can't stand it that the town knows. You can't stand it that anyone knows. Including me."

"It's *personal*."

"You aren't over it yet."

"Yes, I am. I went through years of therapy. I'm *fine*."

Wes studied her face. "Usually when a woman says *fine* like that it means the opposite."

She was starting to get really mad.

He held up his hand. "All I'm saying is you tell yourself you're fine when you aren't."

"That's because his *release* bothers me, and why shouldn't it? It would bother anybody. But I'm over being raped. I'm past that. He doesn't hold that over me anymore."

"Then why do you have to keep it a secret?"

That stopped her. He already knew why. It was her Jezebel past. She understood his point even though she didn't want to. He was right.

"It isn't your fault," he said in a deep, gentle voice that strummed her feelings for him.

But he'd betrayed her. "Why did you let me go on when I told you about it? Why didn't you stop me? Why didn't you tell me you already knew?"

"Lily…" He ran his fingers through his wonderful hair and sighed. "I'm sorry. I wanted you to tell me when you were ready."

He'd already told her that. "I trusted you."

"You still can. Nothing's changed."

"Talk about keeping secrets. How many others are you keeping from me?" She sprang to her feet and looked down at him, deep hurt engulfing her.

Wes stood, too.

She turned and would have left the office had he not taken hold of her arm just above the elbow and stopped her.

"Please. Let's not end the day like this," he said.

"I'm going back to your house to pack and get May and my dad."

"Lily…" But he released her arm.

"I'm going home, Wes." She turned again and once again tried to make it to the door, not caring that she left the cooler behind.

Wes took hold of her arm again, a little firmer this time, pulling her around to face him.

"I can't let you do that," he said.

Tugging her arm free, she stepped back and sent him what she hoped was a mean look. "What are you going to do? Force me to stay with you?"

"I don't want you alone right now."

"I have my dad and May."

"Two people who depend on *you,* not the other way around."

So many things were bouncing around in her head she couldn't keep up. How he'd pursued her. How careful he'd been with her. Because he'd known. And he hadn't told her.

He hadn't forgotten her past, either, the one that painted her reputation red. It's the reason he'd felt compelled to seek out the victims' officer. Instead of asking her, he'd gone behind her back. Because he didn't trust what she'd tell him.

"I know what you're thinking," he said. "I never questioned your integrity. That's not why I went to the victims' officer."

"No?" Her eyes began to sting with moisture.

His grew imploring. "Okay, maybe that was part of it. But you lied, Lily. I didn't think you'd tell me the truth if I asked you."

He was right, she probably wouldn't have. The realization

of that only upset her more. Maybe she wasn't over what happened to her. If she was, she wouldn't care so much that her secret had gotten out.

Fifteen years.

After all this time, she still wasn't over it. She'd done a great job of convincing herself that she was, but the truth wasn't going to change—no matter how much she wanted it to, no matter how much she tried to be strong. Her efforts were merely a smoke screen.

Wes moved closer, and in her distraction, she didn't think to escape him as he slipped his arms around her and pulled her close. "You're not the same woman you were when you left this town."

A tear slipped down her cheek. "That's not what you thought when you checked up on me behind my back."

He held her face between his hands, using his thumbs to wipe her tears—silent, unwanted tears.

"No. I knew you had changed. I knew that the day I met you, after I started talking to you."

She shook her head within the embrace of his hands. He couldn't have. He would have questioned her personally. Instead, he hadn't trusted her, Honey Creek's wayward wild child.

"We met at a prison, Lily." He sounded pleading. "I had to be sure."

She refused to let him break her resolve. His actions told her more than his words ever could.

"Then you should have told me after you were sure," she said quietly.

Pain and regret shadowed his eyes. This time when she slipped free of his arms he didn't stop her as she turned and headed for the door. But he followed her all the way to the Jeep.

When she opened the driver's door, he moved to stand

beside her. "Wait for me at home. At least do that much. I'm right behind you."

She didn't agree, nor did she disagree. She didn't know what she'd do. If she went back home, he'd no doubt have constant surveillance on her. Maybe he himself would provide the service. Continuing to stay with him would be hard, though. Knowing how he'd betrayed her trust, something that was already so fragile.

"Don't stop anywhere on the way home and keep your doors locked," he said. "After I pack up our things, I'll meet you there."

She looked straight ahead through the windshield.

"Lily?"

He wouldn't move unless she assured him. Finally she looked at him. She didn't want to assure him and she didn't want the sight of him to melt her.

"If I have to come after you, I will," he said.

And she knew he meant it. "It's just a little vandalism. No one is out to hurt me."

"I'd be inclined to believe that if the acts stopped with your truck. But someone tried to set the library on fire with you in it. That's a lot more serious."

Yes, it was serious, but she wasn't fooled. He was concerned out of more than his responsibility as sheriff. He had feelings for her. And that churned up conflict in her.

"Wait for me," he said again.

She met his eyes and didn't answer. It would be hard to pack her things and drag her daughter and her dad back to their house at this hour.

It wasn't until he shut her door that she realized the way he'd spoken. *Home. Our things.*

She looked at him through the driver's window. He stood with his arms at his sides, his face an expression of hard determination. She was the center of all that emotion.

Love and hurt waged a battle in her chest. More tears filled her eyes. She wiped them when they slipped free and put the Jeep into gear.

After throwing all the picnic paraphernalia back into the cooler, mentally kicking himself the entire time, Wes drove home faster than an off-duty sheriff should and finally pulled his SUV to a stop in front of his house. Leaving the cooler in the garage, he went inside.

It was surprisingly quiet. The Jeep was still in the driveway so he knew Lily hadn't left yet. He went upstairs to his room, hoping beyond hope that she'd had a change of heart and was there waiting for him. She wasn't. He went to her room door, wanting to knock.

"She's in there."

He turned to see May standing there.

"She was crying when she came home. She didn't see me."

Wes sighed hard and heavy and rubbed his tired eyes with his fingers.

"What happened?" she asked.

He lowered his hand. "Nothing. I just made a mistake, that's all."

The girl didn't look placated. Wes wondered if she was worried about Lily or something else.

"How much longer you grounded for?" he asked.

"Another week." She rubbed the toes of her right foot over the carpet, fidgety.

He looked from there to her face. Slowly May looked up at him. "Is she upset because…because of what everyone is…"

Dawning came over him. "It isn't your fault the rumors started in town, May."

Just as he'd thought, that was the crux of the girl's troubles. Her face sagged and her lower lip quivered.

"It was bound to get out sooner or later," he added.

"Yeah, but if I'd have kept my trap shut at that party…"

"You mean the party you should have never gone to?"

Her face reddened, probably more because he was a figure of authority rather than embarrassment over being caught at a party.

"I'm sure you didn't mean to hurt your mom."

"No."

"She's already over it." That wasn't true, but May didn't need to be bothered with that.

"Is she still mad at me?" May asked.

"She isn't mad at you for that. She's mad at you for lying and going out without telling her." And until he found whoever started that fire in the library, he wanted to make sure she didn't do it again.

"You still seeing that boy?" Lily had told him all about it.

"I see him at school."

"Are you going to go out with him again?"

She rubbed her toes over the carpet again, as though drawing an invisible line there. "I don't know."

"What will you do if he asks you to another party?"

"Tell my mom."

Good girl. "What will you do if she says no?"

She grunted and angled her head with growing annoyance. "It's stupid for her not to let me go out like all the other kids."

"It's not stupid. People haven't accepted her coming back here yet. She's concerned for your safety."

"Levi wouldn't let anything happen to me."

"What will you do if your mom says you can't go out with him?" he asked again.

She grunted cynically. "I won't go."

"Good, because if you don't listen to your mom, it'll be me coming to get you."

With that, May pivoted and started for the stairs.

"May?"

She stopped at the top of the stairs.

"I mean it."

The annoyance trying to make its way onto her face eased and she conceded with a nod before going downstairs.

Wes hoped to hell she'd do as her mom asked from now on. Otherwise, he was going to have his hands full.

Late the next day, Wes took the background checks on Amy Fordham and Eileen Curtis from Ryan and went into his office to start reading. He'd asked for a detailed search. Copies of everything. Birth certificates, Social Security numbers, marriage certificates. All of it. And it didn't take long to discover Eileen had some serious discrepancies in her past.

Eileen Curtis had grown up in a mountain town in southern California and had married in her early twenties. Wes found the marriage certificate which confirmed her married name— Williams. He looked through the file for a divorce decree and found none. Nowhere in the file could he find any indication that Eileen had divorced and taken back her maiden name.

If Eileen was really Tina, she was about the right age. Whoever had devised the ghost identity had known what they were doing except for the issue with Eileen's maiden name. Had Mark Walsh been that man or had he solicited the help of someone else? Wes would bet the latter.

He checked the file on Amy Fordham and confirmed what he thought he'd find; everything was in order. She'd had a rough go of things so far in her life, but she was an honest citizen with no criminal record.

It took him an hour to study the documents. When he'd

absorbed all he could, he dropped his pen down onto the stack and leaned back for a stretch. It was hard concentrating when his mind kept drifting to Lily.

He hoped he hadn't blown it with her. This morning he'd called home to make sure she hadn't packed and fled. When he discovered she hadn't, an overwhelming urge to see her hadn't left him alone. After he'd ordered her a dozen lilies delivered to the library, he'd had to force himself to stay focused on work. But now he was finished and all he wanted to do was see her. He also wanted to know if the note he'd sent along with the flowers had made any impact.

He checked the time on his computer. Five-forty. Her dad had said she was working until six tonight.

Grabbing his keys, he left.

When he entered the library ten minutes later, he searched for her. She wasn't in her office and he didn't see Emily. In fact, the library was nearly empty tonight.

He found her in the nonfiction section with a rolling cart of books she was putting back on shelves. She saw him as she turned to lift another one, going still, her eyes widening.

"Lily." He went to stand closer to her, the cart between them.

"What are you doing here?" she asked, resuming her task.

"I was going to see if you wanted to go get a bite to eat."

"Dad and May are cooking tonight."

Stiffness radiated from her. She was turning her back on him, but it took some effort. He almost smiled at that. Maybe the flowers had done some good.

"I'm sure they'll manage without us," he said.

She slid her eyes his way for a glance.

"Let's go out for dinner."

She put another book onto the shelf. "By the way, thanks for the flowers."

Okay, so she wasn't ready to agree to dinner. But she hadn't shot him down yet. "Don't mention it."

"I appreciate you apologizing, too." She rolled the cart farther down the aisle, seeming indifferent, or pretending to.

He followed, leaning a shoulder against the shelving, watching her beautiful profile. "Does that mean you won't move out?"

She looked at him. "I haven't moved in."

Not yet. Not technically. But now wasn't the time to tell her that's what he wanted. She'd only shoot him down, the way she was so good at doing.

"I would never do anything to intentionally hurt you. You know that, don't you?" he said.

After sliding a book onto the shelf, she bent her head.

"I didn't mean to hurt you, Lily."

"Well, you did."

"I'm sorry. I meant what I said on the card." He'd written that he'd done what he thought was right, what he thought she needed, but he was wrong and he was sorry. Would she please forgive him?

Her hands hadn't moved off the shelf after putting the book there. Slowly her head lifted and she met his eyes.

Touching her face with his hand, he caressed her soft skin with his thumb. "Please. Give me another chance."

Her eyes closed for a long blink. Then she opened them. "You're such a man."

"Thanks," he teased, but he knew what she really meant. Men could sure be stupid sometimes. When it came to women, sometimes they just didn't get it.

His cell phone started ringing. Bad timing. He didn't want to answer, but when he saw it was Ryan, he knew he had to.

"Sheriff."

It was Ryan and he could tell something was wrong. "Yeah. What have you got?"

"Just got a call from Kelley's Cookhouse. Damien's causing trouble with Amy Fordham."

"What kind of trouble?"

"Apparently he got in her face about a woman named Tina Mueller. Her boyfriend is with her and it doesn't look good."

"I'm on my way." He disconnected and looked at Lily. "Will you come with me?"

Her brow lifted. "To break up a fight?"

"No, I'll break up the fight. You wait for me and then we'll have dinner."

"There?"

She needed to face the world someday. The more time he spent with her the more it convinced him that's what would cure her once and for all of her past. She'd taught May to hold her head high, but she wasn't following her own advice. Avoiding places where the gossipmongers frequented was a sure sign of that.

"It's as good a place as any," he said.

She searched his face. "In case you haven't noticed, I'm working."

"It's six."

A tiny smile inched up on her face. "Let me guess—my dad told you that's when I got off."

He grinned. "He did."

"I wonder whose side he's on."

"Mine for sure."

She laughed softly. "Then how can I resist? When the men gang up on the women…"

"The women gang up on the men. Come on, let's get going before Damien tears the place down."

Leaving the cart, she walked toward the front. Emily was behind the counter.

"Call if you have any trouble closing," Lily said as she passed.

Wes followed her to his SUV. His heart burgeoned with gratification at her easy agreement in going along with him. He was making headway with her.

Getting there ahead of her to open the passenger door, he let her in first and went to the other side. Then he drove fast to Kelley's.

After parking in front of the restaurant, he got out and headed for the door, Lily right behind him.

Kelley's sounded more like a bar when they entered. People were shouting and talking loud and fast. Wes spotted Damien in a brawl with someone. Amy Fordham stood nearby, tears streaking her cheeks. Another Colton brother, Finn, was there, too, trying to talk to Damien. The two must have come here together while Finn was in town for a visit. An E.R. doctor in Bozeman, Finn was too brainy and congenial to do anything as Neanderthal as getting involved in a physical fight. He dressed impeccably and spoke well. His thick, light brown hair was a mess on top of his head, but he still managed to look groomed.

"Wait here," Wes said to Lily.

Watching the scene unfolding before her, she nodded.

Nudging people aside to get through the throng, Wes reached Damien and pulled him off a man.

"You're as crazy as your sister!" the man yelled at Damien, blood smearing on one side of his mouth.

Damien tried to yank free of Wes's grip, but Wes held firm. "What happened here?"

"Nothing. I heard her tell her boyfriend that you questioned her about Mark Walsh. All I wanted to do was ask her some questions."

"I don't know anything about Mark Walsh!" Amy yelled, and the man he'd fought with moved toward her, taking her into his arms. She cried against his chest while the man glared at Damien.

"What the hell, Damien?" Wes demanded, letting go of his arm.

"I didn't come here to fight. I asked Amy if I could talk to her and her boyfriend got between us. He said I couldn't talk to her, and I asked her if that's how she felt. Before she could answer for herself, her boyfriend shoved me and told me I should go back to prison. I shoved him back and he punched me."

"So you hit him back."

"Yes. He hit me because he knew who I was, not because of what I said to Amy."

Wes let that slide. "I already cleared Amy, Damien."

"Yeah, well, you didn't tell me."

"I was going to. You didn't give me a chance."

Damien looked over at Amy, who eyed him warily, a look that was becoming common whenever he appeared in public. The town didn't know what to think of him, and when he cornered people like this it didn't help. No doubt Amy would say he'd harassed her, the ex-convict who was supposed to be innocent now.

"It didn't get ugly until her boyfriend interfered," Finn pointed out.

"He got in her face!" the boyfriend snapped. "Amy told me all about him after you interrogated her."

Wes held up his hand, not liking the man's temper. The boy was new in town and obviously hadn't taken any time to question the gossip. Then he looked at Damien.

"That's true," Damien said. "Nothing would have happened if he hadn't lost his cool."

Wes looked over at the boyfriend. "That's bull crap," the man snapped.

"I was sitting at the table right next to them," said an older man, standing just behind Amy and her boyfriend. He pointed at Damien. "That man walked over to her and told her who he was and then asked her if she minded if he asked her a couple of questions. Her boyfriend got up and told him to get lost."

The boyfriend glared at the older man. Amy's sniffles began to ease.

Damien turned to Wes. "I just wanted to know what was going on."

Why hadn't he waited to talk to him? Did he doubt his abilities as sheriff? "You could have waited and asked me."

Damien's face eased into resignation.

Wes turned to Amy and her boyfriend. "I'm sorry about all of this. You can go now."

Amy looked indignantly from him to Damien, and then her boyfriend led her to their table, where they gathered their things and headed for the door.

Wes faced the crowd. "That's it, folks. Time to break it up." The people who'd gathered dispersed. Wes spotted Donald Kelley returning to his position behind the bar.

"Everyone's going to love that *he's as crazy as his sister* part," Finn said, earning a warning look from Damien.

Wes faced Damien. "I'll call you tomorrow. Good to see you, Finn."

Finn angled his head in acknowledgment, ever the gentleman, but clearly amused by the evening's happenings.

Wes turned and headed toward Lily. She smiled softly as he approached and the sight of it melted him all the way to his core.

He located the hostess. "Could you get us a booth?"

The slim blond woman nodded hesitantly. "Right this way."

At a booth, Lily slid onto the seat and he sat beside her. Damien appeared across from them, making room for Finn. Wes sent him a questioning look.

"You still have some explaining to do," Damien said. "And I don't want to wait until tomorrow."

"Mind if we join you?" Finn asked with a touch of sarcasm. He looked at Lily.

"I don't mind," she said, looking up at Wes.

Wes checked on Donald Kelley standing behind the bar, who nodded his consent. Apparently, the fight hadn't gotten too violent, or Donald would have wanted Damien to leave.

"Lily—Damien and Finn. Damien and Finn—Lily," Wes introduced them.

"Good to meet you, Lily. I've heard a lot about you," Finn said.

Wes inwardly grimaced at the innuendo.

Lily looked warily from him to Damien, who slouched against the seat, lazy and content. If Finn's comment bothered her, she did a grand job of hiding it. Instead of responding, though, she removed her silverware from the rolled napkin.

Damien eyed her before looking at Wes. "You never mentioned you had a girlfriend."

"It never came up."

Wes checked around the restaurant. Some people still glanced their way and talked, but others had resumed their evening. At least Damien hadn't busted anything.

"What do you do, Lily?" Finn asked.

"She took over for Mary Walsh over at the library," Wes answered for her.

"Lily Masterson. Yeah, now I remember you," Damien said.

Lily fingered her fork and lowered her gaze.

"Don't worry, I know what it's like to have the whole town talking about you."

"You have such a way with words, Damien," Finn said.

And Damien scowled at him. "And you don't?"

Finn looked perplexed.

A waitress arrived at their table, looking at Damien as she handed each of them a menu and put down four glasses of water.

Damien caught it and turned his scowl on her.

"I hope she doesn't spit in our food," Finn said.

He ignored his brother and turned to Wes. "Why don't you think Amy is the one who killed Walsh?"

"Her background checks out. There are no suspicious gaps and her maiden name checks out." He contemplated how to say what was next. "But Eileen Curtis's background gave me some different results."

"Eileen?"

"The real estate agent?" Finn asked, straightening in his seat. "Are you sure?"

Wes agreed Eileen was the most unlikely suspect. Her reputation was pure and everyone liked and respected her. She also fit the bill for someone motivated to ghost her identity. If she was, in truth, Tina Mueller, she had a criminal record from her youth that she wanted to escape. She wanted to assume another person's identity and live a normal life. But if she'd recently killed Mark Walsh, she hadn't deviated from her criminal ways and that made her dangerous.

"No, I'm not sure. Not yet." He looked pointedly at Damien. "I'm going to question Eileen again. Once I've done that, I'll call you."

"Thank you." Damien turned away and went a little still.

Wes followed that gaze and saw Lucy Walsh enter with three other people.

"Perfect," Damien muttered.

Lucy smiled as she talked to the man beside her. He was tall and lean with medium brown hair, and was dressed in jeans like her. Craig Warner and Jolene Walsh followed behind them. They were seated across the restaurant, but in plain view. Lucy happened to look their way and her smile drained when she saw Damien.

"I thought you didn't care about her anymore," Finn commented.

"I don't." But he sounded contemptuous.

The waitress returned to their table. "You folks ready to order?"

They did, with Damien still watching Lucy.

Lily turned to Wes, a question in her eyes. He wondered the same. How did Damien really feel about Lucy? He put his hand over hers and gave it a gentle squeeze, wishing they were alone and he could just stare at her.

Finn looked from their hands to Lily and then Wes. Wes ignored him and turned his attention to the table that had Damien so riveted.

Lucy leaned close to the man beside her. Steve Brown. Wes was pretty sure that was his name. Craig caught Wes's gaze and gave him a nod of acknowledgment. Wes tipped his water glass before taking a sip.

Steve said something to Lucy, caressing the top of her hand on the table and taking her hand in his.

Jolene's turn came. She noticed that everyone else at her table was looking somewhere so she did, too. And then her mouth opened and her eyes grew rounder. She seemed scared out of her skin. Wes didn't like the way the Walsh family had shunned the Coltons after Mark Walsh's debauched murder trial, but he also understood its source, and he knew with time that would all pass. Damien was innocent. They had all thought Damien killed Mark, but now things were different. Jolene had helped Wes by turning over the tape, and though he was inclined to believe she'd done it to protect herself, she'd also done the right thing.

A few minutes later he noticed Lucy say something to Steve, who glanced toward Damien and then said something in return. What had them so skittish? Or was it something else? Maybe Lucy didn't know how to handle Damien's return now that she knew he was innocent.

"Is he worried you're going to take her away from him?" Finn asked.

"I wouldn't take her back if she was the last woman in Montana."

"I wonder what she thinks of you now?"

"She probably feels bad for thinking you killed her father," Lily said.

Damien glanced over at Lucy, catching her staring at him. "She's probably afraid of me. She was so quick to accept the verdict, and she knew I was angry, and now, all these years later, come to find out she was wrong. Everyone was wrong."

Their food arrived and Wes dug in. Beside him, Lily did the same.

"What if Lucy does feel bad?" Finn asked. "Maybe she wants to talk to you, but doesn't know how to approach you?"

Damien turned his irritation on his brother. "That would be her problem. I forgave her a long time ago. And I've moved on."

"Yeah, it sounds that way to me," Finn quipped.

Wes knew that Damien felt betrayed by the town in which everyone had so easily believed his guilt, and Lucy's betrayal had been perhaps the hardest for him to take. Seeing her for the first time in fifteen years had to be a blow, whether he was over her or not. It had to dredge up old emotions and memories he likely didn't want cluttering his head.

No wonder he was irritated. Wes would be irritated, too.

"You both were so young back then," Lily said. "People

change over fifteen years. And no one can call you a guilty man anymore."

"Maybe she's afraid you'll ruin her newfound happiness," Finn said. "She might think you still have feelings for her. Or maybe she still has some for you."

"I don't think so. If she cared at all for me back then, she would have believed me."

Finn shrugged, chewing and swallowing before he spoke. "Well, all I'm saying is seeing you might bring a lot of memories back."

"I was in prison for fifteen years, Finn. I know that's easy for you to forget, but it isn't for me."

"I wasn't implying—"

"She's probably afraid I'll break into her house and strangle her," Damien said without waiting for Finn to finish, popping a French fry into his mouth.

That's how he thought the whole town perceived him, Wes thought. He couldn't stand that people couldn't accept his innocence. He was especially angry with their dad, who had barely done anything to help him. It was as if Darius had agreed with the jury like everyone else.

Darius Colton was a powerful man who liked to have his way and to have everyone in the family obey him. Some would call him selfish. Egotistical, even. But Darius Colton was also smart and relentlessly driven. Maybe success had made him callous. Wes didn't know. He was their father, that's all, whether or not any of them liked it. He had his redeeming qualities, but mostly he was just plain hard to please. Damien going to prison had only exacerbated that quality.

Lily leaned toward him and her scent reached him. Instantly, his attention floated to much more pleasant ground.

"For once the talk won't be about me," she said.

Meeting her eyes as she smiled at him, he thought he could look at her for hours and not get tired of the sight. She returned to her salad, almost finished with her meal, like him. The anticipation of going home with her permeated his senses. God, he loved her.

And it hit him.

He *was* in love with her. How did he feel about that? His mind reeled. Should he be more careful? What if she couldn't overcome her skeletons enough to accept him? To open her heart fully to him? What a cruel twist of fate that would be. For the first time ever, he'd found a woman he truly felt could go the distance and she might not feel the same.

But he wasn't going to give up. She was coming around. Her forgiveness over his going to the victims' officer proved it. She had feelings for him, she just hadn't let them loose yet. And he had some ideas on how to prod her along. Some intimate ideas.

"Let's go home," he said, his passion coming out in his tone.

She met his eyes and he caught a flash of response. Locked with him in silent communication, heat brewing between them, she nodded. A surge of satisfaction coursed through him. He hoped she didn't tear his heart out when this was all said and done.

Chapter 11

A tortuously sweet anxiety kept Lily's pulse heavy as she led Wes up the stairs. The house was quiet. At the top of the stairs, she walked slowly toward her room, wondering if she should stop and drag him with her. She was still upset that he'd gone behind her back with the victims' officer, but that didn't matter in the grand scheme of things. She could see that now. He hadn't meant to hurt her. He was only being what he'd always been. Careful with her and her well-being. That's what made her keep falling in love with him. How could she stay mad?

He took her hand when she started for her bedroom door. With a tug, she landed against him and met the intensity of his eyes. There was no mistaking his intent and the only answer in her heart was "yes."

She slid her arms around his shoulders, smiling her love. He kissed her and their passion erupted. He backed her into his bedroom and fell with her onto the bed.

She pulled his shirt up and he unbuttoned hers. He unclasped her bra and she threw it over the side of the bed. He got up to get out of his jeans and watched her shimmy out of hers while still on the bed. He pulled her underwear off and lay on top of her, holding himself up with his hands on the mattress. Both of them breathed heavy.

He didn't wait and she didn't want him to. He pushed into her with one smooth motion. Sensation burst into a ball of flame that spread from there. She couldn't get enough air, couldn't kiss him enough. She moaned.

He pulled back and slid inside, going slowly and not pulling back again until he was as deep as he could get. He did that several more times, torturing her with a maelstrom of sensation.

"Wes," she breathed. She felt hot and sweaty and shivery. The sensations made her tremble.

He groaned and began to move faster, impaling her with hard thrusts now. Her body jerked with each delicious pounding. Reaching above her head, she braced herself against the headboard, giving his thrusts more force.

She cried out her pleasure. He kissed her, taking the sounds into his mouth.

"Lily," he breathed her name as she had his.

"Oh, God." She was swept away on a tide of mind-numbing ecstasy.

Abandoning the headboard, she reached around him and grabbed his butt. She moved with him as he ground his hips against hers with each wet slide. He looked down at her, at her breasts as they jostled with his loving, and then lower. When he looked back up at her, he lowered his mouth to hers and kissed her. She ran her fingers into his hair, and then let her hands fall to the mattress, closing her eyes.

"Look at me," he whispered.

She opened her eyes and met the heat of his while he

pushed into her and withdrew. Another sound burst from her as a powerful release followed, endlessly pulsing. He groaned, going deep one last time and holding himself there as his orgasm joined hers.

"Lily." He kissed her cheek, her mouth. "I want you forever."

I want you forever, too. The words were in her throat, nearly making it to her tongue, but she stopped herself. This was the most gritty sex she'd had in more than fifteen years. She felt a little vulnerable, a little uncertain.

Wes lay on her, catching his breath along with her. It was an erotic feeling, lying beneath him with her knees still parted. Naked. Exposed.

Lifting his head, breathing more calmly now, he pressed a tender kiss to her mouth and then looked down at her.

"Are you okay?" he asked.

She nodded.

"I know. It was like that for me, too."

Powerful. Frightening.

"It's okay, Lily."

Was it?

He kissed her again and rolled to her side, pulling her back against him. They spooned. The sweetness of it warmed her. This was like nothing she'd experienced before. The urgency had some resemblance, but in all her wild encounters, none had held such poignancy. Relaxing in his arms, she let herself fall onto a cloud of love.

May waited for her mom to pick her up in front of the school, standing beside Levi. He made her feel so good. And everyone was starting to notice how much he liked her.

Yesterday, a girl on the cheerleading team had said hi to her. Today, she hadn't noticed any mean looks. How great it would be to have people start liking her!

"You think your mom will let me take you to dinner this Friday?" Levi asked.

"I don't know." She was grounded until then. "I can ask her." Maybe in her distraction she'd say yes.

"Text me when you find out."

"Okay."

He leaned toward her and her heart went like a rabbit when she felt him kiss her. Right in front of everybody!

But this morning her mom was acting different. And she was pretty sure it was because of Wes. They'd gone out to dinner or something and May heard them go into Wes's room together.

She swallowed all the heat swelling inside her and looked up into Levi's fantastic eyes. He smiled down at her.

"Wanna text all night?" he asked.

"Sure." She laughed and hoped it didn't sound too much like a girlish giggle.

She loved texting him. He was witty and cool.

"It sucks that you're grounded. I can't wait to take you out," Levi said. "I don't want to wait 'til Friday."

"Me neither."

"I gotta go. I'm supposed to drop some groceries off at my grandma's. But I'll text you as soon as I'm home, 'kay?"

"'Kay." She beamed.

He turned and walked away. She headed for the street, looking for her mom in Wes's Jeep. She wasn't here yet. A man standing outside a car caught her attention. Was he looking at her?

She couldn't see him from here. Was he a senior? His car was old and dented on the driver's door and the white paint was dull. She didn't know what kind of car it was. She stopped at the curb and waited for her mom.

The man didn't move. He was definitely looking at her. What for?

Spotting Wes's Jeep, she felt better. The guy gave her the creeps.

Getting into the Jeep, she shut the door.

"Hey, sweetie," her mom said. She looked really happy today.

"Hey. Did you and Wes make up?"

"What do you mean?"

"He said he made a mistake…and you're…I don't know… glowing."

Lily laughed briefly. "We aren't kids anymore, May."

"You did make up with him," May teased.

Her mom just kept smiling. May looked out the back window. The strange man had gotten into his car and now he had turned and driven the other way down the street. She'd see if he was there again tomorrow. If he was, she'd tell her mom. She faced forward and bolstered her nerve to ask her mom about Levi.

"Mom?"

"Yes?"

"Is it okay if I go out with Levi this Friday? He wants to take me to dinner."

Her mom looked at her dubiously.

"I promise that's all we'll do. I'm not lying this time. I swear."

"I'll think about it."

"I'm supposed to tell him tonight."

"Is he going to call you?"

"Text." All night! That just tickled her insides.

"Then tell him I have to think about it. He can wait a day."

May wanted to groan. She didn't want to wait. But she kept her mouth shut. Her mom might not let her go if she pushed too much.

* * *

The next day Lily still didn't know if she would let May go out with Levi. She handed a young woman her stack of books and saw Finn walk into the library. It was the middle of the afternoon. Was he here for a book or to see her? She was surprised when he came to stand at the counter.

"Hello, Lily."

"Finn?"

"I just wanted to stop by and tell you how glad I am that you and Wes are hitting it off."

Really?

"I didn't get a chance to tell you that the day before yesterday. When I said I'd heard a lot about you, I didn't mean…"

"It's okay. I'm used to it. It's nice of you to stop by and—"

"No. What I meant is that Wes has told me nothing but good things about you."

Oh. She perked up. "Really?"

"Yes. I mean, I've heard all the rumors like everyone else." He rolled his eyes. "How can you avoid it?" Then he smiled like a doctor who'd had a lot of face-to-face time with his patients. "But what he's told me about you just goes to show what a waste of energy all that is."

Lily felt her smile grow big. "Thank you."

"Don't mention it. I hope you and Wes make it as a couple. He's been alone too long. I'd like to see him happy."

A woman appeared behind Finn, checking out a rack of audio books located near the front counter. Finn saw her and went still. Lily wondered if he knew the woman.

She disappeared around the end of the rack and walked away, heading to another part of the library.

Finn turned away and faced Lily again.

"Someone you know?"

"Someone I haven't seen in years. Rachel Grant's cousin Carly."

"Oh, yeah. Bonnie Gene introduced me to Rachel once. How do you know her?"

"We went to school together." He got a faraway look, one tinged with what Lily could only call bitterness. "I'm glad she didn't see me."

"Don't want it getting back to Rachel that you're here, huh?" she teased. Clearly Rachel was a high-school love that he hadn't forgotten.

"I'd rather not have to deal with the drama."

Lily laughed lightly. "One of those, huh?"

He smiled, but it was full of derision. "I'll get out of your hair now. I just wanted to stop by and make sure you didn't misinterpret what I said."

"It's no trouble. Thanks for stopping by. I really appreciate it." Was it just her or were more and more people in town beginning to warm up to her?

Finn left and a few minutes later Wes came strolling in.

Lily shook her head, more from delight than amazement. "You just can't stay away from libraries, can you?"

"Only this one."

"It's a little early for dinner," she teased.

"I thought I'd make dinner for you tonight."

"It would be nice to see my daughter."

"Your dad, too."

That dimmed her spirit some. "He'd be happier having dinner with his nurse."

Wes chuckled. "Actually, I came here for a work-related reason."

There went the rest of her spirit. "Oh."

"But I'm not above using it for an excuse to see you."

She smiled.

"Someone came forward today about the flowers," he

said, growing serious. "A boy who lives in Karen Hathaway's neighborhood. He said she offered to pay him to buy the flowers and have them delivered to you."

What kind of person would put a kid up to that sort of thing? A disturbed one, that's for sure. The boy had probably carried his burden around, especially if he'd learned of the vandalized truck and the fire. "Did you confront Karen about it yet?"

He nodded. "And she confessed to the vandalism when I pressed her. She said finding out that you'd moved back upset her. It caused her to fight with her husband, even though when I questioned him he took her side. Just like the first time I talked to him."

"Jealousy can be so ugly."

"She denied trying to set the library on fire, though."

Lily stared at him as the implications of that sank in. "Do you believe her?"

"Yes. Sending flowers with a cryptic message and vandalizing someone's property are benign compared to trying to hurt someone."

Or worse. "Do you think whoever started the fire intended for me to die?"

"It had to cross their mind as a possibility. Yes, I think whoever started it was hoping you'd be trapped inside. Otherwise, why the library? They could have started your house on fire, but they singled you out. Your daughter and your dad would have been in the house. You were alone in the library. Somebody is mad as hell at you."

And Lily could think of only one person who had reason to be mad at her.

"Is there anyone else in town who might have the motive to hurt you?"

Lily shook her head. But then again…

"There are a lot of people who don't like me," she said.

"Yeah, but enough to start a building on fire?"

Lily turned, rubbing her arms. She felt sick to her stomach. "The victims' officer said Brandon moved to North Carolina."

"Yes, and I checked. He did move there."

She faced him again. What was going on?

"We don't have much to go on. The arsonist used a rock wrapped with rayon cloth, probably from a blouse. There's nowhere around here that sells that kind of thing, so the arsonist probably already had it with them when they came to throw it through the window."

Which could support the idea that Brandon had come from North Carolina, rayon cloth in tow.

"If it was Gates, I doubt he would have brought anything from his house or the house of any his relatives. Too much of a risk. If it was him, he probably bought the material, like a shirt, and picked up the rock on the way."

"It was him, wasn't it?" Lily felt numb inside. Was he going to try to hurt her again?

Wes sighed. "We don't know. I have someone checking to see if he left town. And let's not discount the possibility that it's someone in Honey Creek. Karen could be lying, too."

Maybe. But Lily wasn't comforted. She was going to start watching her back.

"What will happen to her?" Lily asked.

"She'll probably be fined and be forced to pay restitution and maybe serve some community service. She'll have to pay for your truck repair."

She nodded. Fair enough.

"I've got to go talk to Eileen Curtis now. What time do you get off?"

"I have to go pick up May from school."

"I'll meet you at home then."

Home. There was that word again. "Okay." She was warm and tingly everywhere.

He stepped closer, leaning in to kiss her. He moved his mouth over hers in a subtle but sexy caress, enflaming her in an instant. When he lifted his head, she was breathless and hot all over.

"Don't go anywhere else. Pick May up and go home, okay?"

She nodded, wanting him to kiss her again.

"I won't be long," he said.

He turned and left and Lily put her fingers over her lips, more in love than ever.

Wes walked into Curtis Real Estate and waited in the entry for Eileen to get off the phone. Several minutes later, she did and appeared in the doorway of her office.

"Sheriff." She sounded surprised. "Come in."

He went into her office and sat in a chair before her desk. She sat behind it, watching him warily. There was a vase of yellow roses on the desk and everything was tidy. Pictures on the wall were Mediterranean. Elegant. Didn't fit the profile of a killer.

But he had a job to do.

"I know your name isn't really Eileen Curtis," he said, knowing it would feel like a bomb dropping on her refined new world.

Her back stiffened, straightening her posture while her lips parted slightly. He saw her chest rise and fall faster.

"What do you mean?"

"You're real name is Tina Mueller. You left Atlanta after your stepfather was killed."

"That isn't my name."

He didn't argue with her. "I'm here to ask you where you were the night Mark Walsh was murdered."

"Wh-what…I don't understand. You think I killed him? Is that why you came here the last time?"

Last time he'd asked her about the first time Walsh had supposedly died. He hadn't asked her where she was when he was actually killed because he didn't want her to think she was a suspect. But the time was right now.

"I'm here to ask you some questions."

"I didn't kill anyone."

"You're wanted for murder in Atlanta."

"I am not."

"Eileen Curtis isn't, but Tina Mueller is."

"I told you, that isn't my name."

"Then you shouldn't have any problem answering my questions."

She didn't say anything and he wondered if she was contemplating whether to get a lawyer.

"Did Mark Walsh arrange for you to take over the identity of Eileen Curtis?"

Wes had spoken with her ex-husband over the phone and he'd never suspected a thing. She'd protected her identity very well. It only convinced Wes all the more how much she valued her freedom and her new way of life. But if she killed Walsh…

Still, she remained silent.

"Did he?" he pressed.

"I told you, I never met him."

"If your name is Tina Mueller, you did. I have a recording to prove it."

Her eyes were bright with clever processing. "I didn't kill anyone."

"Where were you on June 29 between seven and midnight?"

"I don't know. That was a long time ago. Are you accusing me of murder?"

"Not if you have an alibi." But then there was the issue of her stepfather's murder. The detective working the case wanted her extradited.

"I'll have to do some digging on that. Check my daytimer, and some receipts. My daytimer is in my purse. I'll go and get it."

She stood and went to another door off her office. She disappeared from view and Wes waited. When she didn't reappear, he felt a hunch and went after her. She wasn't in the adjoining room and the back door was open. Squealing tires and a roaring engine told him all he needed to know. He looked through the door and saw her white Lexus racing down the alley.

He ran to the front and jumped into his SUV, flipping on his siren and lights. Spotting her Lexus swinging onto Main Street, he wove around slower traffic to try and catch her. She turned a corner. He also turned there and saw her turn another one down the street. When he reached that he had lost her, but one of the turnoffs led to the highway. He headed there.

He saw her on the highway.

Racing after her, he closed the distance. She made it to Highway 90 and headed west.

Wes stayed on her bumper.

After five minutes, she must have realized she wasn't going to get away. She slowed and pulled off to the side. He drew his gun and approached her carefully.

She rolled her window down. Her cheeks were wet from tears.

"I didn't kill anyone," she said in a pathetic tone.

"Good. Let's fix it then. Will you get out of the car?"

She sniffled and opened the car door. Getting out, she didn't fight him as he handcuffed her and took her to the backseat of his SUV. He went back for her purse and then got behind the wheel.

"I'll have your car towed," he said.

But Eileen…or Tina just stared out the window.

He drove her to the sheriff's office and parked.

"Mark did give me all the papers I needed to start a new life," she said from the backseat. "In exchange, he made me… do things."

Wes didn't open his door to get out. Instead, he turned to look back at her. "What did he make you do?"

"He made me sleep with your father, Darius Colton."

Darius? Walsh had forced her to sleep with Wes's father? "Why?"

"He wanted me to try to find some bank account statements."

"Did you?"

"Yes, but they were nothing unusual. As far as I could tell it was a waste of time."

"Why did Mark want to see Darius's bank statements?"

"He never said, but knowing Mark, he wanted to find something to hold over Darius's head. Mark liked controlling people." Her shoulders quivered with a shudder. "He liked to control me, too, especially after I broke up with him."

"And he caught you stealing his wife's ring."

She wiped a tear that was rolling down her cheek. "Yes. Sometimes I wonder if he did it just to punish me."

"By making you sleep with Darius?"

"Darius is an… Sorry, I know he's your father, but he's not a very nice man, and Mark was angry that I broke up with him. It hurt his ego, so he needed to make me pay."

Wes didn't comment. Darius could be overbearing sometimes. But this whole idea of Walsh choosing Darius for Eileen to sleep with was peculiar. He must have had a reason to want to see the bank statements, but they'd shown nothing unusual. Had Walsh wondered if Darius was involved in money-laundering? That didn't make any sense. Darius had more money than he knew what to do with. Why would he want to get his hands dirty when he didn't even need to?

More likely Walsh wanted to find a way to control Darius, just as Eileen said. And to punish her.

"How many statements did you give Walsh?" he asked.

"A whole year's worth. And there was more than one account. I'm pretty sure it was everything Darius had. I slept with him twice. Once to get the statements and once to put them back after I made copies." Her shoulders shuddered again. "It was awful. He's a terrible lover. A selfish one."

Wes ignored her retrospection. This was his father they were talking about. "Did you keep any copies for yourself?"

"No. Are you kidding? Back then, all I wanted was for Mark to leave me alone. I was glad when I heard he'd been killed."

"Did he ever contact you?"

"No."

"Not ever? Not even when he came back to Honey Creek?"

"No. I never heard from him. And if I had, I don't know what I would have done."

"Would you have killed him?"

"I told you, I didn't kill anyone." She looked right at him in the rearview mirror and Wes had a creeping feeling that she was telling the truth.

"Who killed your stepfather, then?"

Her expression closed and she looked out the window.

Was she hiding something? He'd be sure to let Detective Isaac know what he thought.

Chapter 12

Lily parked in front of the school and watched all the kids climb into buses, walk, ride bikes or get into their parents' cars. When the crowds began to thin, she started to wonder where her daughter was.

The buses drove away and soon there were only one or two stragglers milling around. Lily got out of the Jeep and went inside the school. Finding the office, she asked the secretary to page her daughter. When that didn't produce May, Lily asked where her last class was. She went there, but it was dark and empty.

Her heart beat fast. She was getting scared. May. Where was she?

She called Wes's house. No one answered.

She called May's cell phone. Nothing. Wes's cell came next. No answer.

Her dad didn't have a cell phone.

Driving toward Wes's house, she tried to calm her trembling hands. What if something had happened to May?

Her cell rang, making her body jerk. She looked at the number. It was May.

"Oh, thank God." Relief washed through her as she pressed the button to connect the call. "May. Where are you?"

"Mom?" May sounded shaky. And she was crying.

Dread plunged to her core. "May? Where are you? Are you all right?"

"Lily, Lily, Lily," said a man's voice. He must have taken the phone away from May.

Oh God, oh God, oh God.

"I've been waiting a long time for this."

Brandon.

"If you so much as touch my daughter, I'll tear your eyes out with my bare fingers."

"Just outside town is an unmarked road. It's past an old cabin that's falling apart. You'll see it on the right."

She knew the one he meant.

"I want you to take that road until it forks. Take the left route until it dead ends. You'll see my camper."

"You let her go or I'll make sure you die before anyone can send you back to prison."

"You come here, sweet Lily, and you come alone, or the girl will take your place. If you call anyone for help, I'll kill her. Understand?"

Lily couldn't find her voice.

Brandon disconnected.

Swallowing, she breathed through her nausea. To think of him doing to May what he'd done to her...

She'd kill him.

Lily swung the Jeep around and floored it on the highway. She wasn't far from the cabin.

Should she call the cops? 911? No. He'd kill May if he heard sirens.

Wes.

She brought his number up in her cell phone address book and pressed Send. It rang and rang and he didn't pick up. Where was he? What was he doing?

His message system beeped. "Wes, this is Lily. Brandon has May. He's kidnapped her." She did her best to describe the area where he'd taken her. "He warned me to come alone. He said he'd kill May if I didn't do as he said. He said he'd kill her, Wes." She knew she sounded frantic, but she *was* frantic.

She came to the dirt road and flew down it. She had to reach May. She didn't want to leave her alone with that monster. But she didn't have a gun. Or a knife.

A pen would work. If she could stab one of his eyeballs maybe it would penetrate to his brain. She leaned over to the glove box and dug around. The Jeep swerved with her effort. She found a pen.

A camper came into view. She slid the Jeep to a halt and waited, leaving it running. She wanted him to come outside, hoping he'd have May with him.

The door opened and he stood there, curling his index finger, beckoning her to come to him. Damn it.

Tucking her cell in her back pocket, she got out of the Jeep, holding the pen at her side. Slowly she approached, seeing a gun tucked into the front of his jeans.

"Where is she?" Lily stopped walking. "Show her to me."

Brandon jerked his head at where May must be, and she stumbled next to him.

"Mom!" May shoved Brandon and raced for her. Lily caught her daughter against her and guided her so she stood behind her.

"Did he hurt you, baby?" she asked, watching Brandon step down the stairs of the camper. He looked a little unsteady. Had he been drinking?

"No." May was crying.

Lily reached behind her and took May's hand, pressing it against her back pocket.

Sniffling and beginning to regain control, May slipped the phone from the pocket as Brandon drew near.

"Run," Lily said. "Get to the Jeep." It was still running.

"I don't want to leave you."

"Do what I tell you. Run. Now."

Brandon pulled the gun from his jeans and aimed for the Jeep. He fired and one of the front tires blew.

Lily's heart crushed under the weight of apprehension. Now what?

Pushing off Lily's back, May started running. She went for the Jeep anyway.

"May!" Lily shouted. Then, to her horror, she saw Brandon aiming his gun at May.

She charged for him. He wasn't far from her now. The gun went off. She tackled him, landing on top of him on the ground. Her right leg felt funny and it took her a second or two to realize she'd been shot.

He punched her and then hit her with the gun. She got dizzy and disoriented and fell off him. The pen slipped from her fingers and fell to the ground. Brandon started to climb to his feet.

Determined, she pushed him the same time she swung her leg back over him, straddling him and stopping him from standing. He moved the aim of the gun toward her. She grabbed it with both hands and deflected his aim as he fired again. She picked up the pen and stabbed him, going for his eye but hitting his cheek.

He yelled and smacked her hand away. Lily stood and

kicked his wrist, the one that held the gun. It flew from his grasp.

Staggering, her leg not supporting her well, she kicked the gun so that it skittered across the gravel surface, out of his reach.

He sprang to his feet and bashed her head with his fist again. This time it knocked her to the ground and her vision fogged. She was vaguely aware of him going toward the Jeep.

"Run, May!" she yelled. "Get out of here!"

She was getting weak. Rolling to her butt, she saw blood soaking her jeans. She was bleeding. Badly.

May was fighting Brandon off, kicking at him from the driver's seat and struggling to keep him from taking the cell phone from her. She dropped the phone and Brandon picked it up. She tried to take it from him. When he smacked her, Lily saw red.

She rolled to her hands and knees and crawled toward the gun. Hearing May cry out, she looked back. Brandon was dragging her from the Jeep. But May bit his hand and he yelped. She got away.

"Run, May!" Lily screamed.

And she did. May bolted down the road.

Lily reached the gun and took hold of it. Rolling onto her backside, she started firing.

Leaving Eileen in the holding cell, Wes went back to his SUV for his phone. He checked the screen and saw Lily had tried him twice. A sense of extreme foreboding slammed him. And then he heard someone shouting.

"Sheriff! Sheriff!"

He looked up to see a boy running toward him. Levi Harrison, the boy May was seeing.

"You gotta come quick!" He waved his cell in front of him,

skidding to a stop in front of him. "It's May. Somebody's got her and her mom. She called me, but she got disconnected when he caught her. She tried to tell me where they were, but he cut her off."

"Get in."

In the SUV, Wes dialed his voice mail. Lily's voice streamed fast, telling him what he needed to know. He raced for the west end of town, lights and siren blaring for the second time today.

Damn it. He'd have gotten her call before now if he'd had his phone with him, but the drama with Eileen had preoccupied him.

The campsite wasn't far outside of town. He swerved onto the dirt road and saw May jogging wearily along the side. Wes stopped and Levi jumped out to help her. She was crying hysterically. Levi held her and guided her into the SUV, seating her in the middle and holding her to his side.

May babbled incoherently about what had happened. Brandon shooting out the tire, fighting her until she got away.

Shooting Lily….

Wes could hardly contain his fear. Or his fury. Minutes later he reached the dead end. He saw the Jeep and two bodies. His fear escalated until his head felt bloodless.

He faced the two teenagers. "You two stay here. Don't move."

Levi nodded.

May leaned forward, her hand on the dash, searching the scene in front of them. "Is my mom all right?"

"Stay here," Wes repeated. He handed the radio to Levi. "Tell Ryan to send an ambulance."

Levi took the radio and when Wes saw that he knew how to use it, he shut the driver's door and ran toward the bodies. One was Brandon Gates, shot in the chest and neck. He wasn't moving and looked dead. There was no gun on the ground next to him so he passed him and went to Lily.

She lay sprawled on the ground a little farther away, a gun close to her unmoving hand.

"Lily." He knelt beside her and checked for breathing. It was warm and glorious against his cheek. He felt for a pulse. Weak, but there.

He looked back to see a thumbs-up from Levi.

Help was on the way.

Chapter 13

Lily woke to bright lights and stabbing pain in her right thigh. Lifting the covers over her, she saw a bandage. It all came rushing back. She searched the room. Wes sat in a chair beside her, his head bowed in sleep. There were flowers everywhere. Who were they from?

She rolled her head to see Wes again. Watching him sleep took her mind off the pain.

As if sensing her stirring, his eyes opened and his head straightened, his gaze finding hers. In the next instant, he came alert and propelled himself from the chair to go to her, leaning over her, sliding one hand alongside her head and taking her hand with the other.

She smiled.

He kissed her. "I'm so glad you're awake."

"What happened?"

"You were shot in the right thigh and it nicked your femoral artery. You lost a lot of blood. The doctor was confident, but wouldn't say with any certainty that you were going to make it." He kissed her again. "We were so worried."

"We?"

"Your dad and May were here. They went home this morning to rest, but they'll be back soon. You had surgery last night. It was late when they finished."

"Lily."

She looked toward the door where the voice had come from. Her dad stood there, his face a contortion of relief and repentance. He walked into the room.

Wes stood, giving her hand a squeeze. "I'll give you two a few minutes."

And she realized he and Shay must have talked.

Wes left the room and her dad moved the chair closer to the bed and sat. He clasped his hands between his knees and took a moment before he began. Finally he looked up at her.

"Lily…I'm sorry. When Wes called and told me what happened, I thought of losing you before…" He got a little choked up.

"It's okay," she said, reaching her hand out.

He took it between both of his. "I don't want to leave this earth without knowing my daughter. Because I don't really know you, Lily."

Moisture burned her eyes. She'd wanted this for so long. Her dad.

"I can see you've changed," he continued. "And I also realize your mom and I could have done things differently with you when you were growing up. I should have been there for you more."

"I'm not looking back. I made a lot of mistakes. You aren't to blame for those decisions."

"You *are* different now, Lily. And it breaks my heart to know what happened to you is the reason you changed."

"I like to think I would have changed anyway." She smiled.

"Then that's the way I'll think of it, too." He looked toward the flowers on the windowsill and on the counter across the room. Color exploded everywhere.

"Between Wes and Levi, the whole town knows you're here," he said. "Mary and Jake Pierson sent flowers. So did Bonnie Gene and her husband. Finn, too."

Recalling what Finn had told her about Rachel, Lily wondered how long before the two ran into each other. It would be quite a spectacle. More gossip for the town, that's for sure. Something new to focus on.

"Maisie Colton even sent you something," Shay said. "It's the big bouquet of yellow roses."

"Maisie sent flowers?"

"Wes told her what happened. He also told her he was going to marry you so she'd better change her tune where you're concerned. So she sent flowers." Shay laughed wryly.

The words gave her a jolt. Marry her?

"Won't be long before the whole town sees what I do now," he said. "A strong woman who's full of integrity."

"Dad." She wiped the tear that slid down her cheek.

"You've done a great job with May. I can't wait to spend the rest of my days with the two of you. It'll take some time, but I want us to be a family."

"Oh, Dad." She cried and he got up to lean in for a hug. She couldn't ask for anything better.

A few days after coming home to Wes's house from the hospital, Lily was beginning to wonder if she was overstaying her welcome. Wes had brought her here, but now that Karen had been caught and Brandon was dead, there was really no reason for her to stay any longer.

Wes hadn't mentioned anything about what her dad told

her. Not that she was worried. She felt more like pinching herself. Having a man like him love her seemed surreal. Too good to be true. But why hadn't he said anything? Did he not want to marry her after all? Had he only said that to her father because of the drama surrounding her injury?

She hobbled downstairs after taking a late-afternoon nap. A news program played on the television. Stormy weather was on the way.

Wes was at the kitchen table, poring over his notes. He looked up and smiled.

"I was going to come up and wake you if you didn't come down soon," he said.

"Really?" She looked around the house. It was too quiet. "Where are Dad and May?"

"They went out for a while."

"Out?"

"Yeah. Grandpa-and-granddaughter time."

That made her smile. "Where did they go?"

"They didn't say."

"Huh." She supposed that wasn't odd. Maybe it was the way Wes told her, as if he were trying to be nonchalant.

He pushed his chair back and stood. "You hungry? How about we go out for dinner?"

"You want to go out?"

"Yeah. Let's go down to Kelley's. You feel up to it?"

"Uh…sure." Actually, she felt great. She was moving around without crutches now. She limped, but at least she was getting better. But he was acting funny.

"What's the matter?" she asked.

"Nothing. I just feel like going out. We've been cooped up in this house for days."

He'd gone to work, though.

"Okay." She looked down at herself. Baggy jeans and a

long-sleeved, ribbed, white T-shirt. All she needed were shoes and those were by the door.

She put them on and eyed Wes as she made her way out the door. He was smothering a grin.

"What are you up to?"

"Nothing. I'm hungry." He wiggled his eyebrows. "For more than food."

They hadn't made love since she'd been shot. It would hurt too much, according to him anyway. But maybe not now. After dinner, if…

Wes opened the passenger door of his SUV and helped her inside. His cell rang as he climbed onto the driver's seat. He answered and his mood sobered.

"Detective Isaac," he said, glancing at Lily. He seemed surprised.

She waited while he listened.

"Then Tina was telling the truth," he said after a few moments, and then more minutes passed while he listened again.

"Thanks for letting me know." Shortly thereafter, he ended the call.

"What happened?" Lily asked.

"That was the detective who worked the Tina Mueller case in Atlanta," he explained. "He said a woman came forward and confessed to killing Tina's stepfather. She was fifteen when he kidnapped her and kept her in the basement." Wes looked over at her, his face revealing what the detective must have told him about what Tina's stepfather had done to the girl. Kept her for a sex slave in his basement. "Tina managed to leave a butcher knife in the basement for the girl, and the next time the stepfather came down for one of his visits, the girl killed him. Just before that, that same night, he beat up Tina, who saw the girl kill him and helped her cover it up. They were afraid of being charged with murder."

"What happened to the girl?" Lily asked.

"She went back home and told her parents that she ran away. She didn't tell anyone about Tina's stepfather."

"What will happen to them now?"

"I don't know. They can probably prove self-defense. Tina gave the girl a knife so she could defend herself."

Lily wondered if Tina would come back to Honey Creek. Would the town support that? After what Lily had endured, she didn't hold much hope for the woman.

Wes parked down the street from Kelley's. There were a lot of cars out tonight.

"Everybody must have decided to go out for dinner tonight," she said, and then she eyed him and wondered again. What was he up to?

He opened the door for her and she entered. Kelley's was packed.

Bonnie Gene appeared, smiling from ear to ear. "It's good to see you up and about, Lily. Come here. We have a table ready for you."

Bonnie Gene led her to a table in the middle of the restaurant. Lily sat, but Wes remained standing. Only then did Lily notice the occupants of the tables surrounding her.

Finn. Damien. Mary and Jake. Maisie and her entourage of friends. Maisie smiled and waved but it appeared forced. She wasn't enjoying herself. Lily smiled back anyway. Then she saw May and her dad. May giggled and Lily slid her gaze up to Wes.

"Grandpa-and-granddaughter time?" she queried.

He grinned and reached into the front pocket of his jeans. "Lily Masterson," he said, loud enough for everyone in the now-quiet restaurant to hear. "There's no other woman for me."

He held out a ring. The elongated garnet center stone was flanked by two round diamonds. Simple but elegant.

She looked from it to Wes.

"Will you marry me?" he asked.

She sprang to her feet, putting most of her weight on her good leg, and wrapped her arms around him. Planting kisses on his mouth and all over his face, she could only laugh her joy.

"It took you long enough," she teased.

"Is that a yes?" he said between kisses to his mouth.

"Yes!"

Everyone in the restaurant cheered. It was a homecoming. At last she was accepted. There was nothing in her closet to hide, and nothing to run from. She was home.

* * * * *

Dear Reader,

Welcome to the next installment in the ongoing adventures of the Colton clan! It has been a delight to write about this feisty and fun bunch. I couldn't possibly write this letter to you without mentioning the real brown dog that is the inspiration for the canine hero in this story. Some years ago, a stray dog wandered up to our door, starved, injured and so frightened of humans he could hardly bring himself to ask for help. But ask he did. It took us months to touch him and two years to coax him into our house. With plenty of patience and love, he gradually regained his faith in humans.

I'm pleased to report that the real Brownie now lives a life of pampered ease as a member of my family and is known around here as the "love sponge." He is the most loyal, gentle and grateful dog I've ever had the pleasure of knowing. He had a rough start in life, but with courage and persistence he got his happy ending… just like Finn and Rachel.

May you and those you love be every bit as lucky in your lives.

Warmly,

Cindy Dees

DR COLTON'S HIGH-STAKES FIANCÉE

BY
CINDY DEES

This book is for all the generous and compassionate people who volunteer in animal shelters, rescue programs and animal protection programs everywhere. I am brought to tears often by your kindness and caring. All of our lives—both human and non-human—are made better by your loving work.

First published in Great Britain 2011
Harlequin Mills & Boon Limited,
Eton House, 18-24 Paradise Road, Richmond, Surrey TW9 1SR

© © Harlequin Books S.A. 2010

Special thanks and acknowledgment to Cindy Dees for her contribution to *The Coltons of Montana*.

ISBN: 978 0 263 88514 9

46-0311

Harlequin Mills & Boon policy is to use papers that are natural, renewable and recyclable products and made from wood grown in sustainable forests. The logging and manufacturing processes conform to the legal environmental regulations of the country of origin.

Printed and bound in Spain
by Litografia Rosés S.A., Barcelona

Chapter 1

Rachel Grant sighed down at her chipped and dirt-encrusted fingernails. What she wouldn't give to be at Eve Kelly's Salon Alegra right now, getting a manicure and not staring at a shelf of toilet parts in a hardware store. But such were the joys of home ownership on a shoestring budget.

Whoever said that men didn't gossip as much as women was dead wrong. But they would be right about one thing: Man-gossip left a lot to be desired in comparison to girl-gossip. Floyd Mason, owner of the hardware store, was gossiping with someone whose voice she didn't recognize the next row over in Paint, and, of course, she was shamelessly eavesdropping. Floyd drawled, "Seems like there's Colton boys all over town all of a sudden."

The customer replied, "I hear Damien Colton's back. The missus sent me over here to get a dead bolt for the back door because of 'im."

Bless Floyd, for he replied, "Why's that? Damien didn't

murder Mark Walsh the first time around or else the bastard wouldn't have turned up dead for real a few months ago."

"Yeah, but fifteen years in a penitentiary…that's gotta change a man. Make him hard. Mean. Maybe even dangerous."

She might have her own bone to pick with the Colton family, but she bristled at the suggestion that Damien had become a criminal. She'd never for a minute thought he was capable of murder, not fifteen years ago, and not now. She had half a mind to march around the corner and tell the guy so.

Thankfully, Floyd drawled, "Ahh, I dunno 'bout Damien bein' dangerous. Those Colton kids might'a been wild, but they was never bad. At least not that kind of bad."

"I hope you're right," the customer drawled. "Ever since Damien got outta jail, it's been like old-home week over at the Colton place. Wouldn't be surprised if they's all back in town by now to welcome home the prodigal son."

Rachel's heart skipped a beat in anticipation and then just as quickly thudded in dismay. Please God, let it not be *all* of the Coltons back home. She really, truly, never needed to see Finn Colton again as long as she lived. He'd been the best-looking boy in the high school. Maybe the entire town. Smartest, too. Was so effortlessly perfect that she'd fallen in love with him before she'd barely known what had happened to her. Oh, and then he'd broken her heart for fun.

The bell over the hardware store's front door dinged, jolting her from a raft of old memories. Very old. Ancient history. Water *way* under the bridge—

"Speak of the devil!" Floyd exclaimed. "Long time, no see, boy! You're looking great. All growed up…got the look of your daddy about you."

Rachel glanced toward the front of the store. It took

no more than a millisecond for certain knowledge to hit her that a Colton had just walked through that door. The brothers were all tall, broad-shouldered, hard men who dominated any room they entered. And one of them was here now. A wave of loss slammed into her. Its backwash was tempered by bits of humiliation, fear, and a few specks of nascent anger swirling around like flotsam. But mostly, it just hurt.

Rachel ducked, wishing fervently that the shelves were at least two feet taller than their five-foot-tall stacks. Which Colton was it? Several of them had left town after high school and gone on to bigger and better things than Honey Creek had to offer.

It didn't matter which Colton it was. She didn't want to see any of them. And she especially didn't want to see Finn. Her knees were actually shaking at the prospect. Lordy, she had to get out of here *now*. Preferably unseen. She randomly grabbed the nearest rubber toilet gasket and took off crawling on her hands and knees for the front of the store and the cash register. *Pleeease let me make it out of here. Let me be invisible. Let me make it to the front door—*

"Ouch!" She bumped into something hard, nose-first, and pulled up short. That was a knee. Male, covered in denim. And it smarted. She grabbed the bridge of her nose, which was stinging bad enough to make her eyes water.

"Lose something?" a smooth voice asked from over-head.

Oh. My. God. She knew that voice. Oh, how she ever knew that voice. It was dark and smooth and deep and she hadn't heard it in fifteen years. It had gained a more mature resonance, but beyond that, the voice hadn't changed one iota.

"I asked you a question, miss. Did you lose something?" the voice repeated impatiently.

Her mind? Her dignity? Definitely her pride.

She forced her gaze up along the muscular thighs, past the bulge that was going to make her blush fiercely if she dwelled on it, past the lean, hard waist beneath a black T-shirt, up a chest broad enough to give a girl heart palpitations, and on to a square, strong jaw sporting a sexy hint of stubble. But there was no way her gaze was going one millimeter higher than that. She was *not* looking Finn Colton in the eye. Not after he'd caught her fleeing the hardware store on her hands and knees.

"Uh, found it," she mumbled, brandishing the hapless gasket lamely.

"Rachel?" the voice asked in surprise.

Her gaze snapped up to his in reflex, damn it. She started to look away but was captured by the expression in his green-on-brown gaze. What was he so surprised at? That she was crawling around on the floor of the hardware store? Or maybe that she still lived in this two-bit town? Or that she looked like hell in ratty jeans and a worse T-shirt and had on no makeup and her hair half coming out of a sloppy ponytail? Or maybe he was just stunned that she'd dared to breathe the same air as he, even after all these years. She hadn't been good enough for him then; she surely wasn't good enough for him now.

Her gaze narrowed. She had to admit Finn looked good. More than good. Great. Successful. Self-assured. The boy had become a man.

For just one heartbeat, they looked at each other. Really *looked* at each other. She thought she spotted something in his gaze. Longing, maybe. Or perhaps regret. But as quickly as it flashed into his eyes that unnamable expression blinked out, replaced by hard disdain.

Ahh. That was more like it. The Finn Colton she knew and loathed. "Finn," she said coldly. "You're standing in my way. I was just leaving."

With a sardonic flourish of his hand, he stepped aside and waved her past. *Jerk.* Watching him warily out of the corner of her eye, she took a step. She noted that his jaw muscles were rippling and abruptly recalled it as a signal that he was angry about something. All the Coltons had tempers. They just hung on to them with varying degrees of success. Finn was one of the calmer ones. Usually. He looked about ready to blow right now, though.

Hugging the opposite side of the aisle, she gave him as wide a berth as possible as she eased past. She made it to the cash register and looked up only to realize that just about everyone in the store was staring at her and Finn. Yup, men were as bad as women when it came to gossip.

She had to get out of there. Give them as little fodder for the rumor mill as possible. She was finally starting to get her life together, she had a new job, and she didn't need some new scandal to blow everything out of the water when she was just getting back on her feet. She fumbled in her purse for her wallet and frantically dug out a ten-dollar bill. The clerk took about a week and a half to ring up her purchase and commence looking for a small plastic bag to put her pitiful gasket in.

She snatched it up off the counter, mumbling, "I don't need a bag," and rushed toward the exit. But, of course, she couldn't get out of there without one last bit of humiliation.

"Miss! Miss! You forgot your change!"

Her face had to be actually on fire by now. She was positive she felt flames rising off her cheeks. She turned around in chagrin and took the change the kid held out to her.

"Don't you want your receipt? You'll need it if you have to return that—"

She couldn't take any more. She fled.

She didn't stop until she was safely locked inside her car, where she could have a nervous breakdown in peace. She rested her forehead against the top of the steering wheel and let the humiliation wash over her. Of all the ways to meet Finn Colton again. She'd pictured it a thousand times in her head, and not once had it ever included being caught crawling out of the hardware store in a failed effort to dodge him.

Knuckles rapped on her window and she jumped violently. She looked up and, of course, it was *him*. Reluctantly, she cracked the window open an inch.

"If you're going to faint, you should lie down. Elevate your feet. But don't operate a motor vehicle until any light-headedness has passed."

He might be a doctor, but that didn't mean he needed to lecture her on driving safety. Sheesh. He didn't even bother to ask if she was feeling all right! She snapped, "Why, I'm feeling fine, thank you. It was so kind of you to ask. I think I'll be going now. And a lovely day to you, too."

She rolled up her window and turned her keys in the ignition. Thankfully, her car didn't choose this moment to act up and coughed to life. She stomped on the gas pedal and her car leaped backward. Finn was forced to jump back, too, or else risk getting his toes run over. It might have been petty, but satisfaction coursed through her.

She pulled out of the parking lot with a squeal of tires that had heads turning up and down Main Street. How she got home, she had no real recollection. But a few minutes later, she became aware that she was sitting in her driveway with her head resting on the steering wheel again.

Finn Colton. Why, oh why, did he have to come back

to Honey Creek after all these years? Why couldn't he just stay in Bozeman with his perfect job and a perfect wife, two point two perfect kids, and a perfect life? Heck, knowing him, he had a perfect dog and drove a perfect car, too.

All the joy had been sucked right out of this day. And she'd been so excited to cash her first paycheck and have a few dollars in her pocket to start doing some desperately needed repairs around the house. Cursing Colton men under her breath, she dragged herself into the house and got to work fixing the toilet.

The gossip network took under thirty minutes to do its work. She'd just determined that, although she'd miraculously managed to get the right-size gasket, her toilet was officially dead. She was going to have to replace all the tubes and chains and floaty things that made up its innards.

Her phone rang and she grabbed the handset irritably. "Hello."

"Hi, Raych. It's me."

Carly Grant, her sometimes best friend, sometimes pain in the ass, second cousin. They'd been born exactly one week apart, and they'd had each other's backs for their entire lives. Carly had stuck by her when no one else had after Finn dumped her, and for that, Rachel would put up with a lot of grief from her scatterbrained cousin. Rachel's irritation evaporated. "Hey. What are you doing?"

"I'm wondering why my home girl didn't call me to tell me she ran into the love of her life down at the hardware store. Why did I have to hear it from Debbie Russo?"

"How in the heck did she hear about it?" Rachel demanded.

"Floyd Mason told his wife, and she had a hair appointment at Eve's salon at the same time Debbie was having a mani-pedi."

Rachel sighed. Telephone, telegraph, tell a woman. Sometimes she purely hated living in a small town. Actually, most of the time. Ever since she'd been a kid she'd dreamed of moving to a big city. Away from nosy neighbors and wide open spaces…and cows. Far, far away from cows.

She'd have left years ago if it wasn't for her folks. Well, her mom, now that her dad had passed away. A sharp stab of loss went through her. It had been less than a year since Dad's last, and fatal, heart attack. Sometimes his death seemed as if it had happened a lifetime ago, muted and distant. And sometimes it seemed like only a few days ago complete with piercing grief that stole her breath away. Today was one of the just-like-yesterday days, apparently.

"So. Spill!" Carly urged.

"Finn Colton is *not* the love of my life!"

"Ha. So you admit that you did see him!"

"Fine. Yes. I saw him. I was crawling on my hands and knees, my rear end sticking up in the air, trying to make a break for it, and he walked right up to me."

Carly started to laugh. "You're kidding."

"I wish I were," Rachel retorted wryly. "I can report with absolute certainty that his cowboy boots are genuine rattlesnake skin and not fake."

"Oh, my God, that's hilarious."

Rachel scowled. She was *so* demoting Carly from BFF status. "I'm glad I amuse you."

"What did he say?" Carly asked avidly.

"Not much. He said my name, and I said his. Then I got the heck out of Dodge as fast as I could." She added as a sop to Carly's love of good gossip, "He did knock on the window of my car to tell me that I looked like crap—and that if I was going to faint, I shouldn't drive."

"What a jerk!" Carly exclaimed loyally.

Okay, she'd just regained her status as best friend forever.

"You'll have to fill me in on the details while we drive up to Bozeman."

Rachel groaned. She'd forgotten her promise to go with Carly to shop for a dress for the big celebration of the high school's hundredth anniversary, which was scheduled for next weekend in conjunction with the school's homecoming celebration.

"You forgot, didn't you?" Carly accused.

"No, no, I'll see you at three. But right now I have to go back to the hardware store and get more parts for my toilet."

"Hoping to see your favorite Colton brother again?"

"When they're having snowball fights in hell," she retorted. She slammed the phone down on Carly's laughter and snatched up her car keys in high irritation.

Finn threw his car keys down in high irritation. He remembered now why he hated Honey Creek so damned much.

His older brother, Damien, finished off his sandwich and commented, "Funny how you can want worse than anything in the world to get back home. And then you get here, and in under a week, you'd do anything to get away."

Finn rolled his eyes. Nothing like being compared to a recent ex-con and the analogy working. Especially since he'd been working like crazy for the last fifteen years to recover the family reputation from Damien's murder conviction. He dropped a brown paper bag from the hardware store onto the kitchen table. "Here are your fence fasteners. Need some help installing 'em?"

Damien shrugged. "Sure. If you don't mind getting those lily-white doctor hands dirty."

Finn scowled. "I grew up working a ranch. I didn't go completely soft in medical school."

"We'll see."

An hour later, Finn was forced to admit that compared to his massively muscled brother, he qualified as a bonified sissy. But the sweat felt good. They were restringing the barbed wire along the south pasture fence. His hands were probably going to be blistered and torn tonight, but he wasn't about to complain after the lily-white doctor-hand crack.

Seeing Rachel Grant again had rattled him bad. He needed to get out and do something physical. Something strenuous that would distract him from memories of her. He'd loved her once upon a time. Been dead sure she was the one for him. And then she'd up and—

"Hey! Watch it!" Damien exclaimed.

Finn pulled up short, swearing. He'd almost whacked off his brother's hand with the sledgehammer.

"How 'bout I take that?" Damien suggested warily. "In fact, why don't we take a break and go get a bite to eat? Maisie made chili this morning."

As a bribe, it was good one. His oldest sibling might be nosy and overbearing, but the woman made a pot of chili that could put hair on a guy's chest. He stomped into the mud room of the main house a few minutes later. The warmth inside felt good after the hint of winter in the air outside.

"Hey, boys," Maisie called. "Pull up a chair."

Damien led the way into the enormous gourmet kitchen. "Watch out for him—" he hooked a thumb in

Finn's direction "——Honey Creek's already getting on his nerves."

Maisie commented slyly, "The way I hear it, it's someone in Honey Creek who's getting on his nerves."

Finn's head jerked up. How did she do that? That woman knew more gossip faster than anyone he'd ever met. And she wasn't afraid to use it to get exactly what she wanted. Or to manipulate and hurt the people around her. She saw herself as the real matriarch of the clan in lieu of their reclusive and withdrawn mother and, as such, responsible for shaping and controlling the lives of everyone named Colton in Honey Creek. Maisie had been one of the reasons he'd bailed out of town as soon as he could after high school.

He moved over to the stove and served up two bowls of steaming chili. He plunked one down on the table in front of Damien and sat down beside his brother to dig into the other bowl.

He heard arguing somewhere nearby and looked up. Damien's twin brother, Duke, and their father, Darius, were going at it about something to do with the sale of this year's beef steers. Those two seemed to be arguing a lot since he'd gotten back two days before. Not that he had any intention of getting involved, but Duke seemed to have the right of it most of the time. But then, Darius always had been a dyed-in-the-wool bastard. A hard man taming a hard land.

Maisie sat down across from him. "So tell me. How'd your meeting with that Jezebel go?"

No need to ask who she was talking about. Maisie always had called Rachel "that Jezebel." He also knew Maisie would badger him until he told her exactly what she wanted to know.

He answered irritably, "We didn't have a meeting. I bumped into her in the hardware store." Amusement flashed through his gut at the recollection of her crawling for the door as fast as she could go. Her pert little derrière had been wiggling tantalizingly, and her wheat-blond hair had been falling down all around her face. Which was maybe just as well; it had partially hidden the sexy blush staining her cheeks.

"Come on. You know I'll find out everything anyway," Maisie said.

He sighed. Like it or not, she was right. "That's all there was to it. I saw Rachel, she saw me, she walked out. I bought Damien's fasteners and came home."

"You men. No sense of a good story. I swear, we'll never get on *The Dr. Sophie Show* unless I do all the work." She scowled and pressed, "What was she wearing? How did she look at you? Did she throw herself at you? Did she look like she's still scheming to land herself a Colton?"

Actually, Rachel had looked pissed. Although he didn't see why she had any right to be angry. She was the one who'd betrayed him and wrecked what they had between them. He supposed he did have Maisie to thank for finding out the truth about her before he'd gone and done anything dumb like propose to Rachel. How could she have—

He broke off the bitter train of thought. Her betrayal had happened a lifetime ago, when they were both kids. It was time to let it go. Beyond time. He was so over her. And as long as he was home in Honey Creek, he damned well planned to stay over her.

Chapter 2

Rachel's heart wasn't in shopping today. Not only was she still badly shaken after having seen Finn, but watching Carly spend money when she didn't have a dime to spare kind of sucked. Edna down at the Goodwill store had spotted a perfect dress for her a few weeks back and had offered to alter it to fit her slender frame, and for that Rachel was grateful. But she didn't dare dream of a day when she could waltz into a fancy department store like her cousin and buy a nice dress for a party. Not until her mother passed away and the nursing home bills quit coming. And as hard as it was to cover those bills, she dreaded them stopping even worse. Her mother was all she had left.

She felt guilty for secretly counting the days until her mother finally slipped away. But her mom was the only thing holding her in Honey Creek. Ever since they'd found out the summer after Rachel's sophomore year in high school that her mom had early-onset Alzheimer's disease, she'd been trapped here. Her dad had already had his first heart attack by then, and there was no question of Rachel going away to college. He needed her to stay home to help out with her mom.

Not that she was complaining. Well, not too much, at any rate. She loved her folks. They'd been a close-knit trio, and she'd been willing to set aside her big dreams of seeing the world for her parents. And after Finn had left, taking their dreams of escaping Honey Creek together with him, it had been easier to reconcile herself to sticking around.

But sometimes she imagined what it would have been like to travel. To see Paris and Rome and the Great Pyramids of Egypt. Heck, at this point, she'd be thrilled to see Denver or Las Vegas.

If only she knew why he'd dumped her like he had, so publicly and cruelly. The worst of it was that everyone else in town followed his lead and blamed her for whatever had broken them up. Nobody seemed to know exactly why Finn did such an abrupt one-eighty about her, but she was a girl from the poor side of town, and he was Honey Creek royalty. Clearly the whole thing must have somehow been her fault.

It was no consolation knowing that it wouldn't be much longer before she was free to leave. Her mother's health was fragile, and truth be told, her mother was so far gone into Alzheimer's she usually had no idea who Rachel was. She could probably leave town and go start a new life somewhere else and her mother wouldn't know the difference. But *she'd* know. And unlike Finn Colton, she wasn't the kind of person who turned her back on the people she loved.

"Oh!" Carly exclaimed. "There it is!"

Rachel looked up, startled. Her cousin was making a beeline for the far display case. Must've spotted the perfect dress. Carly might be a ditz, but the girl had impeccable taste in clothes. Rachel tagged along behind, wondering if it were the little black number or the dramatic red dress that had caught Carly's eye.

Another woman was closing in from their right, and Rachel watched in amusement as both Carly and the other woman reached for the black dress at the same time.

"You take it."

"No, you take it."

Rachel finally caught up and suggested diplomatically, "Why don't you both try it on, and whoever it looks best on can have it?"

Laughing, the other two women dragged her into the dressing room to act as judge. Like she'd know fashion if it reached out and bit her. Her whole adult life had been a financial scramble, first to work herself through college online and have enough left over to give her folks a little money, then to help her folks fix up the house and now to pay for her mom's medical bills. What clothes she didn't make for herself she picked up at the Goodwill store, mostly. Of course, because she was a volunteer, she got dibs on the best stuff before it went out on the sales floor. Still. Just call her Secondhand Rose.

Carly disappeared into the dressing room first. The other woman turned out to be the chatty type and struck up a conversation. "Do you live here in Bozeman?"

"No. We live in Honey Creek. It's about twenty miles south of here as the crow flies."

"Oh!" the woman exclaimed. "I've heard of it! One of the doctors at the hospital is from there. I'm a nurse down at Bozemen Regional."

Rachel's stomach dropped to her feet. She had an idea she knew exactly which doctor her impromptu companion was talking about. Desperate to distract her, Rachel asked, "So, what's the special occasion you're shopping for?"

"A first date. With this cute radiologist. He just divorced his wife and is *very* lonely, if you catch my drift."

Rachel smiled. "Sounds like fun."

"So. Do you know Dr. Colton? I mean, to hear him talk about it, Honey Creek's about the size of a postage stamp. He says everyone knows everyone else."

Rachel nodded ruefully. "He's right. And yes, I went to school with Finn."

"Oh, do tell! He's so private. None of the nurses know much about him. Gimme the dirt."

Rachel winced. Nothing like being the dirt in someone's past. "There's not much to tell." She paused, and then she couldn't resist adding, "So, what's he up to these days? Is he married? Kids?"

"Lord, no. If he wasn't so…well, manly…we'd all think he was gay. He never dates. Says he has no time for it. But we nurses think someone broke his heart."

Great. She was dirt *and* a heartbreaker. But something fluttered deep inside her. He'd never gotten seriously involved with anyone else? Funny, that. She commented lightly, "Huh. I'd have thought the girls would've been hanging all over him. He was considered to be a good catch in Honey Creek."

The nurse laughed gaily. "Oh, he's got women hanging all over him, and he's a good catch in Bozeman, too. Thing is, he just doesn't seem interested. That is, assuming he doesn't have some secret relationship that none of us know about. But, it's pretty hard to hide your personal life in a hospital. We spend so much time working together, especially down in the E.R., you pretty much know everything about everybody."

So. No perfect wife and no two point two perfect kids

yet, eh? What was the guy waiting for? He'd talked about wanting a family of his own when they'd been dating. Of course, in his defense, she'd heard that medical school was grueling. Maybe he just hadn't had time yet to get on with starting a family. Well, she wished him luck. With someone emphatically not her. She'd had enough of Colton-style rejection.

"What do you think?" Carly asked. She came out of the changing room and twirled in the clingy black dress.

The nurse laughed. "It's not even a contest. That dress was made for you. I'm not even trying it on. I'll go find another one."

Carly hugged the woman. "C'mon. I'll help you. I have a great eye for fashion. I saw a red satin number that would be a knockout with your hair color…"

Rachel sat in the deserted dressing room. A few plastic hangers and straight pins littered the corners. Why was she so depressed to hear about Finn's single state? Maybe because it highlighted her own lack of a love life. At least he was still a good catch. Truth be told, she'd never been a good catch, and everyone had thought their dating in high school was an anomaly to begin with.

His older sister, Maisie, had called her a phase. Said that Rachel was Finn's rebellion against what all his family and friends knew to be the right kind of girl for him. Yup—dirt, a heartbreaker and the anti-girlfriend. That was her.

"Raych? You gonna sit there all day?"

She looked up, startled. "Oh. Uhh, no. I'm coming."

"So when do I get to see this secret dress you've found for the homecoming dance?" Carly asked as they walked out of the mall.

Rachel rolled her eyes. "We're not in high school anymore, you know."

"Aww, come on. Don't be a spoilsport. With the hundredth anniversary of the school and all, *everyone's* coming back for homecoming."

Rachel grimaced. At the moment, a party sounded about as much fun as a root canal. She replied reluctantly, "My dress is a surprise."

"Fine. Have it your way. Maybe if you're lucky, Finn will stick around long enough to go to the dance."

"Oh, Lord. Can I just slit my wrists now?"

Carly laughed. "You've got it all wrong. This dance is your chance to show the jerk what he's missing. It's all about revenge, girlfriend."

She sighed. "If only I had your killer instinct."

"Stick with me, kid. We'll have you kicking men in the teeth in no time."

There was only one man she wanted to kick in the teeth. And now that Carly mentioned it, the thought of sashaying into that dance and telling him to go to hell made her feel distinctly better.

But by Monday morning, Rachel's bravado had mostly faded. Another set of bills had come in from the nursing home and she'd had to empty her bank account to cover them. Thank God she'd landed this job at Walsh Enterprises. Craig Warner, the chief financial officer, had actually been more interested in her accounting degree than her tarnished reputation and past association with the Coltons. Her next paycheck would arrive this Friday, and then, good Lord willing, she'd be able to start digging out of the mountain of medical bills.

"Good morning, Miss Grant."

She looked up as Craig Warner himself walked through the cubicle farm that housed Walsh Enterprises' accountants and bookkeepers. He paused beside hers. "Good morning, sir."

"How's the new job coming?"

"Just fine. I'm so grateful to be here."

The older man smiled warmly. "We're glad, too, Miss Grant. Let me know if you have any questions. My door's always open."

Enthusiastically, she dived into the financial records of Walsh's oil-drilling venture. Craig had asked her to audit the account with the expectation that she would take over responsibility for it afterward.

She'd been working for an hour or so when she ran into the first snag. Several of the reported numbers didn't add up to the receipts and original billing documents. Who'd been responsible for maintaining this account? She flipped to the back of the file and frowned. Whoever had signed these papers had done so in a completely illegible scrawl. No telling who'd managed the account. She flipped farther back into the earlier records. Still that indecipherable scribble. Until fifteen years ago. Then a signature jumped off the page at her as clear as a bell. Mark Walsh.

Walsh, as in the founder of Walsh Enterprises. The same Mark Walsh who'd been found murdered only weeks ago. A chill shivered down her spine. How creepy was that, looking at the signature of a dead man? His hand had formed those letters on this very paper.

She went back to the more recent documents and corrected the error. Good thing she'd spotted it before the IRS had. It was the sort of mistake in reporting profits that could've triggered a companywide tax audit. Relieved, she moved on with the review.

By the time she found the third major discrepancy, she was certain she wasn't looking at simple math errors. Something was *wrong* with this account. She double- and triple-checked her numbers against the original documents. There was no doubt about it. Somebody had lied like a big dog about how much money this oil-drilling company had made. Over the years, *millions* of dollars appeared to have been skimmed off the actual income.

What to do? Now that he was tragically dead, was Mark Walsh a sacred cow? Would she be fired if she uncovered evidence that maybe he'd been involved in embezzlement? Who had continued the skimming of monies after he'd supposedly died the first time? Had someone within Walsh Enterprises been in league with Mark Walsh to steal money for him? Had this been where Walsh had gotten funds to continue his secret existence elsewhere for the past fifteen years?

His family had already been through so much. And now to heap criminal accusations on top of his murder? Oh, Lord, she needed this job so bad. The last thing she wanted to do was rock the boat. And it couldn't possibly help that for most of her life her name had been closely associated with the Coltons. There hadn't been any love lost between the Walshes and Coltons since even before Mark Walsh's first murder, the one supposedly at the hands of Damien Colton.

But what choice did she have? She would lose her CPA license if she got caught not reporting her findings. She scooped up all the documents and the printouts of her calculations and put them in her briefcase. Her knees were shaking so bad she could hardly stand. But stand she did. Terrified, she walked to the elevator and rode upstairs to the executive floor. Craig Warner's secretary looked surprised to see her, almost as surprised as Rachel was for being here. The woman passed Rachel into the next office, occupied by Lester Atkins, Mr. Warner's personal assistant. Rachel wasn't exactly sure what a personal assistant did, but the guy looked both busy and annoyed at her interruption.

"Hi, Mr. Atkins. I need to speak with Mr. Warner if he has a minute."

"He has an appointment in about five minutes. You'll have to schedule something for later."

Disappointed, she turned to leave, but she was intercepted by Mr. Warner's secretary standing in the doorway. "If you keep it quick, I'm sure Mr. Warner won't mind if you slip in."

Rachel felt like ducking as the secretary and Lester traded venomous looks. She muttered, "I'll make it fast."

Actually, she loved the idea of not getting into a long, drawn-out discussion with Mr. Warner. She'd just float a teeny trial balloon to see where the winds blew around here and then she'd bail out and decide what her next move should be. In her haste to escape Lester's office, she ended up barging rather unceremoniously into Mr. Warner's.

He looked up, startled. "Rachel. I didn't expect to see you this soon."

She smiled weakly. "Well, I've hit a little snag and I wanted to run it by you."

Craig leaned back in his chair, mopping his brow with a handkerchief before stuffing it in his desk drawer. "What's the snag?"

"I was comparing the original receipts against the financial statements of the oil-drilling company like you asked me to, and I found a few discrepancies. I'm afraid I don't know much about Walsh Enterprises' procedure for handling stuff like this. Do we just want to close the books on it and move on, or do you want me initiate revising the financial statements?"

Craig frowned and she thought she might throw up. "How big a discrepancy are we talking here?"

She squeezed her eyes shut for a miserable second and then answered, "Big enough that the one person whose signature I can read would be in trouble if he weren't already dead."

"Ahh." Comprehension lit Craig's face. She thought she heard him mutter something under his breath to the effect of, "The old bastard," but she couldn't be sure.

The intercom on his desk blared with Lester announcing, "Mr. Warner, your eleven o'clock is here."

Rachel leaped to her feet with alacrity. Her need to escape was almost more than she could contain. She had to get away from Warner before he fired her.

He stood up. "I've got to take this meeting. We'll talk later."

She nodded, thrilled to be getting out of here with her job intact.

"And Miss Grant?"

She gulped. "Yes, sir?"

"Keep digging."

He was going to support her if she found more problems. Abject gratitude flooded her. God bless Craig Warner. Weak with relief, she stepped into Lester's office. And pulled up short in shock. The last person she'd ever expect to see was standing there. And it was *not* a nice surprise. "Finn!" she exclaimed. "What on earth are you doing here?"

He arched one arrogant eyebrow. "Since when is what I do any of your business?"

Good point. But had she not been standing well within earshot of her boss, she might have told him to take his attitude and shove it. As it was, she threw him a withering glare and said sweetly, "Have a nice day." *And go to hell,* she added silently.

"Finn. Thanks so much for coming," Craig Warner said from behind her. "I know it's strange in this day and age to ask a doctor to make a house call—"

Lester pulled the door discreetly closed and Rachel heard no more. Was Craig Warner sick? He looked okay. Maybe he was a little pale and had been perspiring a bit, but the guy had a stressful job. And why call a specialist like Finn? Last she heard, he was an emergency internist—not a family practitioner.

She started back to her desk, her thoughts whirling. *Keep digging.* What exactly did Warner expect her to find? And why *had* Finn agreed to see Craig in his office? Why not tell the guy to call his own doctor? Maybe Finn had come over here to wreck her new job. After all, he'd successfully wrecked just about every other part of her life. Without a doubt, the worst part of living in a small town was the insanely long memory of the collective populace. You made one mistake and it was never forgotten, never forgiven.

She worked feverishly through the afternoon and found more and more places where money had been skimmed off of the profits of the oil-drilling company and disappeared. She'd have stayed late and continued working if tonight she hadn't volunteered down at the senior citizens' center. It was bingo night, and the retirees didn't take kindly to any delays in their gambling.

Finn rubbed his eyes and pushed back from the computer. He'd been searching various medical databases for symptoms that matched Craig Warner's but so far had come up with nothing. The guy was definitely sick. But with what? His symptoms didn't conform to any common disease or to any uncommon diseases that he could find, either. He'd begged Craig to go to Bozeman and let him run tests there, but Craig had blown off the suggestion. He'd said he just needed some pills to calm his acid stomach and wasn't about to make a mountain out of a molehill.

But in Finn's experience, when a non-hypochondriac

patient thinks he's sick enough to seek medical advice, it usually isn't a molehill at all.

He dreaded going home to face more of Maisie's grilling over his latest encounter with his ex-girlfriend. For she'd no doubt heard all about it. She had a network of informants the FBI would envy.

It had been a nasty shock running into Rachel like that today at Walsh Enterprises. The woman was sandpaper on his nerves. As if he fell for a second for that syrupy-sweet act of hers. He knew her too well to miss the sarcasm behind her tone of voice. Once it would've made him laugh. But now it set his teeth on edge. He'd been prepared to act civilized toward her when he'd come back to Honey Creek, but if she was determined to make it a war between them, he could live with that.

Muttering under his breath, he pushed to his feet and headed out of Honey Creek's small hospital.

"What're you doing here, bro?"

Finn pulled up short at the sight of his brother, Wes. It still looked funny to see him in his sheriff's uniform and toting a pistol. Wes had been as big of a hell-raiser as the rest of the Colton boys. Finn supposed there was a certain poetic justice in Wes being the guy now who had to track down wild kids and drag them home to their parents.

Belatedly, Finn replied, "I was just using the hospital's computer to look up some medical information on their database."

"Trying to figure out how to poison certain of the town's females, maybe?"

Finn snorted. "Yeah. Maisie. That woman gets nosier every time I see her."

Wes shook his head. "Sometimes I wonder if they switched her at birth and Mom and Dad brought home the wrong baby. I stopped by to see if you'd want to get a bite to eat?"

"Yeah, sure. Lily working late tonight?"

"Mother-daughter Girl Scout thing. I'm baching it for supper. I saw your truck in the parking lot."

Finn walked out onto the sidewalk with Wes. It was strange enough thinking of his older brother as sheriff. But a family man, too? That was downright weird. It made Finn a little jealous, though. He'd been so sure he and Rachel would have a passel of towheaded ankle-biters by now. Funny how things turned out.

The sun was setting, outlining the mountains in blood red and throwing a kaleidoscope of pinks and oranges and purples up into the twilight sky. His thoughts circled back to Wes's comment about Maisie not belonging to the family. He commented reflectively, "I dunno. Sometimes I see a bit of Dad in Maisie. The two of them get an idea stuck in their craw and they won't let it go."

Wes laughed. "Right. Like the rest of us Coltons aren't that same way? Stubborn lot, we are."

Finn grinned. "Speak for yourself, Sheriff. I'm the soul of patience and reason."

Guffawing, Wes held the door to his cruiser open for him. "Then you won't mind paying for supper, will you, Mr. Patience and Reason?"

Finn cursed his brother good-naturedly. He didn't mind, though. He made decent money as a physician, and public servants didn't rake in big bucks. He did roll his eyes, though, when Wes drove them to Kelley's Steakhouse, which was without question the most expensive restaurant in town. They ordered steaks with all the trimmings, and then Finn picked up the conversation. "How's the murder investigation coming?"

Wes shrugged. "Frustrating. There are damned few

clues, and everywhere I look I find another suspect with a motive for killing Walsh."

"No surprise there," Finn commented. "He wasn't exactly cut out for sainthood."

"No kidding. It just stinks that Damien had to pay for something he didn't do."

They fell silent, both reflecting on the bum deal life had dealt their brother. Finn had visited Damien regularly in jail and tried to be supportive, but a little worm of guilt squirmed in his gut. Damien had always sworn he didn't kill Walsh. Turned out he'd been telling the truth all along. They all should've tried harder to get him exonerated.

Fifteen years was a hell of big chunk of a person's life to throw away. It hardly seemed like that long to him, but he imagined it had felt like twice that long to Damien.

It seemed like only yesterday Finn had been in high school, excited to play in the district football championship, dating the prettiest girl in the whole school, and counting the days until he was going to blow this popsicle stand for good. Of course, Rachel had a couple more years of high school to go before she could join him, but then…then they were going to run away together and see the world.

And it had all changed with a single phone call. He'd never forget his sister Maisie's voice, delivering the news that had shattered his world—

"Earth to Finn, come in."

He blinked and looked up at his brother. "Sorry. Was just remembering stuff."

"Yeah, Honey Creek has that effect on a soul, doesn't it? Want go down to the Timber Bar and get a beer? I'm off duty."

"Sounds great. But you're paying, cheapskate."

Chapter 3

It was nearly midnight when Rachel pulled into her driveway. The bingo had ended at ten, but the usual volunteers who cleaned up hadn't shown up tonight. Folks knew she was single and had no life of her own, so they didn't hesitate to recruit her for the crap jobs that required sticking around late. And of course, she was too much of a softie to say no.

She got out of her car and locked it. The weather had turned cold and it felt like snow. Soon, winter would lock Honey Creek in its grip and not let go until next spring. She made a mental note to get out the chains for her tires and throw them in the trunk of her car.

She headed across the backyard under a starry sky so gorgeous she just had to stop and look at it. But then a movement caught her attention out of the corner of her eye and she lurched, startled. That was something or someone on her back porch!

She fumbled in her purse for the can of mace that swam around in the jumble at the bottom of it. Where was that can, darn it? Whoever it was could rob her and be long gone before she found it at this rate! She ought to keep the thing on her keychain, but it was bulky, and this was Honey Creek. Nothing bad ever happened here. Not until Mark Walsh's murder. Why hadn't it occurred to her before now that she ought to be more careful?

Whoever was on the porch moved again slightly. The intruder appeared to be crouching at the far end of the porch near the back door.

"I see you!" she shouted. "Go away before I call the police!"

But the intruder only slinked back deeper in the shadows. Her eyes were adjusting more to the dark, and she could make out the person's shape now. There. Finally. Her fingers wrapped around the mace can. She pulled it out of her purse and held it gingerly in front of her like a lethal weapon.

"I swear, I'll use this on you. Go on! Get out of here!"

But then she heard something strange. The intruder whimpered. She frowned. What was up with that? Surely she hadn't scared the guy that bad. She heard a faint scrabbling sound…like…claws on wood decking.

Ohmigosh. That wasn't a person at all. It was some kind of animal! She was half-inclined to laugh at herself, except this was Montana and a person had to have a healthy respect for the critters in this neck of the woods.

She peered into the shadows, praying she wasn't toe to toe with a mountain lion. She wasn't. Actually, the creature looked a little like a wolf. Except he was too fuzzy and too broad for a wolf. They were leaner of build than this guy. Nope, she was face-to-face with a dog.

She lowered the can of mace and spoke gently, "What's the matter, fella? Are you lost?"

Another whimper was the animal's only reply.

She squatted down and held out her hand. Okay, so a stray dog wasn't exactly the safest thing in the world to approach cold, either, but she was a sucker for strays. Heck, she'd been collecting them her whole life. *Yeah, and look where that had gotten me,* a cynical voice commented in the back of her head.

The dog took a step forward, or rather hopped. He was holding his right rear leg completely off the ground. "Oh, dear. Are you hurt? Let me go inside and put down my purse and turn on a light and then we'll have a look at you."

She hurried into the kitchen and dumped her purse and mace canister on the table. She turned on the lights and opened the back door. "Come here, Brown Dog. Come."

The dog cringed farther back behind an aluminum lawn chair. She squatted down and held out her hand. The dog leaned like it might take a step toward her and then chickened out and retreated even farther behind the chair. If she knew one thing about frightened animals, it was that no amount of coaxing was going to get them to go where they didn't want to go. Looked like she had to go to the dog.

"Hang on, Brown Dog. Let me get some more light out there and then just have a look at you on the porch. Would that make you feel better?"

She kept up a stream of gentle chatter as she went inside, opened all the blinds and flooded the back porch with light. She stepped back outside. And gasped. The entire far end of her porch was covered with blood. As she watched, the dog staggered like it was nearly too weak to stay on its feet. Even though the dog had a thick, shaggy coat, she could still see hip bones and shoulder blades protruding. The creature was skeletal, his eyes sunken and dull in his skull.

And then she caught sight of his right hind leg. It was a bloody, mangled mess with white bone sticking out of a gaping wound she could put several fingers into. For all the world, it looked like he'd been shot. And the bullet looked to have nearly ripped his leg off.

Oh, God. This was way beyond her paltry skills with antibiotic cream and bandages. The sight of the wound nearly made her faint, it was so gory. She had to call a vet, and *now*. Dr. Smith, Honey Creek's long-time veterinarian, retired a few months back, and the local ranchers had yet to attract another one to town. She'd have to call someone in Bozeman. She raced into the house and pulled out the phone book, punching in the first number she found.

"Hello," a sleepy female voice answered the phone.

She blurted, "Hi. A dog is on my back porch. He's been shot and he's in terrible shape. I need a veterinarian to come down to Honey Creek right away!"

"I'm sorry, dear, but my husband doesn't cover that far away. And besides, he's out on a call. Said he'd be gone most of the night."

Oh God, oh God, oh God. *Breathe, Rachel.* "Is there another vet in the area I can call?"

"I'm sorry. I don't know any small-animal vets who'll go to Honey Creek. You'll have to bring the dog up to Bozeman. Can I take your number and have my husband call you? He may have a suggestion."

No way could she pick up that big dog by herself and hoist him into her car. And even if she did manage it, she suspected the dog on her porch wasn't going to live another hour, let alone through a long drive over mountain roads.

It might be twenty miles as the crow flew to Bozeman, but the drive was considerably longer. Especially at night, and especially when it got cold. Even the slightest hint of moisture on the roads would freeze into sheet ice in the mountains. "Thanks anyway," Rachel mumbled. "I'll figure out something else."

She hung up, thinking frantically. Now what? She needed someone who could handle a gunshot wound. A doctor. Maybe she could take the dog down to the local emergency room—

No way would they let her in with a stray dog carrying who knew what diseases. She swore under her breath. She got a bowl of water for the dog and carried it outside. Tears ran down her face to see how scared and weak he was and how voraciously he drank. He was *dying*. And for who knew what reason, he'd wandered up to *her* porch. She *had* to get him help.

Without stopping to think too much about it, she pulled out her cell phone and dialed the phone number that hadn't changed since she was in high school, and which she'd had memorized for the past decade and more.

"Hello?" a gruff male voice answered.

She couldn't tell which Colton it was, but it definitely wasn't Finn. She spoke fast before her courage deserted her. "I need to speak to Dr. Finn Colton. This is a medical emergency. And please hurry!"

While she waited a lifetime for him to come to the phone, the dog lay down on the porch, apparently too weak to stand anymore. Panic made her light-headed. He was dying right before her eyes!

"This is Dr. Colton."

"Oh, God, Finn. It's Rachel. You have to come. I tried to call a doc in Bozeman but he can't come and there's so much blood from the gunshot and I don't know what to do and I think I'm going to faint and please, there's no one else I can call—"

He cut her off sharply. "Unlock your front door. Lie down. Elevate your feet over your head. And breathe slowly. I'll be right there."

The phone went dead.

Why would she put her feet up? Time was of the essence right now. She ran into the kitchen and grabbed all the dish towels out of the drawer. The dog let her approach him and press a towel over his bloody wound, indicating just how close to gone he was. Pressure to slow the bleeding. That's what they said in her Girl Scout first-aid training about a century ago.

The dog, which she noted vaguely was indeed a boy, whimpered faintly. "Hang on, fella," she murmured. "Help is on the way." She stroked his broad, surprisingly soft head and noticed that his ears were floppy and soft and completely out of keeping with the rest of his tough appearance. His eyes closed and he rested his head in her hand. The trust this desperate creature was showing for her melted her heart.

Oblivious to the pool of blood all over her porch, she sat down cross-legged beside the dog and gathered the front half of his body into her lap. He was shivering. She draped the rest of the towels over him and cradled him close, sharing her body heat with him. "It'll be all right. Just stay with me, big guy. I promise, I'll take care of you."

The dog's jaw was broad and heavily muscled, somewhat like a pit bull. Maybe half pit bull and half something fuzzy and shaped like a herding dog. Underneath the layer of blood he was brindled, brown speckled with black.

"Hang in there, boy. Help is on the way. Finn Colton's

the one person in the whole wide world I'd want to have beside me in an emergency. He'll fix you right up. You just wait and see."

Finn tore into his bedroom, yanked on a T-shirt, grabbed his medical bag and sprinted for the kitchen. He snatched keys to one of the farm trucks off the wall and raced out of the house, ignoring a sleepy Damien asking what the hell was going on.

He peeled out of the driveway, his heart racing faster than the truck. And that was saying something, because he floored the truck down the driveway and hit nearly a hundred once he careened onto the main road.

"Hang on, Rachel," he chanted to himself over and over. "Don't die on me. Don't you dare die on me. We've got unfinished business, and you don't get to bail out on me by croaking," he lectured the tarmac winding away in front of his headlights.

He'd followed her home from the hardware store this morning—at a distance of course, where she wouldn't spot him. He'd been worried at how she looked in her car in the parking lot. It was nothing personal, of course, just doctorly concern for her well-being. Good thing he had followed her, because he knew where she lived now. Turned out she was living in her folks' old place. On the phone, she'd sounded on the verge of passing out from blood loss. And a gunshot? Had there been an intruder in her house? An accident cleaning a weapon? What in the hell had happened to her? First Mark Walsh, and now this. Was there a serial killer in Honey Creek?

He'd call Wes, but he'd left his cell phone back on his dresser at home, he'd been in such a rush to get out of there. He'd have to call his brother after he got to Rachel's place. And after he made sure she wasn't going to die on him.

"Hang on, baby. Don't die. Hang on, baby. Don't die—" he repeated over and over.

In less time than Rachel could believe, headlights turned into her driveway and a pickup truck screeched to a halt behind her car. Finn was out of the truck, medical bag in hand before the engine had barely stopped turning.

"Rachel!" he yelled.

"I'm right here," she called back more quietly. "No need to wake the entire neighborhood."

He raced up to her, took one look at the blood soaking her clothes and flipped into full-blown emergency-room-doctor mode. "Where's the blood coming from? How did you get hurt? I need you to lie down and get these towels off of you—"

"Finn."

"Be quiet. I need to get a blood pressure cuff on you. And let me call an ambulance. You're going to need a pint or two of blood—"

"Finn."

"What?"

"I'm not hurt."

"Are you kidding? With all this blood? Shock can mask pain. It's not uncommon for gunshot victims not to be aware that they've been shot for a while. Where did the bullet hit you?"

"I wasn't shot. He was."

She pulled back the largest towel to reveal the dog lying semiconscious in her lap.

"What the—"

"I'm not hurt. The dog was. Please, you've got to help him. He's dying."

Finn pulled back sharply. "I don't do animals."

"But you do bullet wounds, right?"

"On humans."

"Well, he's a mammal. Blood, bone. Hole in leg. Pretty much the same thing, if you ask me."

Finn rose to his feet, his face thunderous. "You scared ten years off my life and had me driving a hundred miles an hour down mountain roads in the middle of the night, sure you were dying, to come here and treat some *mutt?*" His voice rose until he was shouting.

Oh, dear. It hadn't occurred to her that he'd think she was shot. And he'd driven a hundred miles an hour to get to her? Something warm tickled the back side of her stomach.

"Finn, I'm sorry if I scared you. I was pretty freaked out when I saw all the blood. I called a vet in Bozeman. But he's out on a call that's supposed to take all night and his wife said no small-animal vet would make a house call to Honey Creek anyway. And it's not like I could take the dog to the Honey Creek hospital. You're the only person I know of in town who can take care of a serious gunshot wound and make a house call."

"I'm going home." He picked up his bag and turned to go.

"Wait! Finn, please. I—" she took the plunge and bared her soul "—I've got no one else."

He turned around. Stared down at her, his jaw rigid. Heck, his entire body was rigid with fury.

"I'm sorry for whatever I've done in the past to treat you badly. I'm sorry I did whatever I did that broke us up. If it makes you feel better, I'll take full responsibility for all of it. But please, please, don't take out your anger at me on a poor, defenseless animal who's never done anything to you."

Finn stopped. He didn't turn around, though.

"Please, Finn, I'm begging you. If you ever had any feelings for me, do this one thing."

He pivoted on his heel and glared down at her. "If I do this you have to promise me one thing."

"Anything."

"That you'll never call me again. Ever. I don't want to see you or speak to you for the rest of my life."

She reeled back from the venom in his voice. Did he truly hate her so much? "But you'll take care of Brown Dog?"

His gaze softened as he looked down at the injured animal. "I'll do what I can."

She nodded. "Done."

"We've got to get him inside. Although the cold has probably slowed his metabolism enough to keep him alive for now, he'll need to warm up soon."

Working together, they hoisted the big dog and carried him inside, laying him on her kitchen table. It made her heart ache to feel how little the animal weighed given his size and to feel the ribs slabbing his sides. He was skin and bones.

Finn gave the dog a critical once-over. "This dog's so emaciated that treating his gunshot wound is only going to delay the inevitable. I've got a powerful tranquilizer in my bag. It should be enough to put him down."

"Put him down as in kill him?" she squawked.

"Yes. Euthanasia. It's the humane thing to do for him."

"Since when did you turn into such a quitter?" she snapped. "Our deal was that you'd do your best to save him, not kill him."

Finn glared at her across the table. "Fine. But for the record, you're making this dog suffer needlessly. I can't condone it."

"Just shut up and fix his leg."

"Make sure he doesn't move while I wash up," Finn ordered. He moved to the sink and proceeded to meticulously scrub his hands. He hissed as the soap hit his palms and Rachel craned to see a series of raw blisters on his palms. Where had he gotten those?

Finally, he came back and laid out a bunch of stainless steel tools on the table beside Brown Dog. "You'll assist," he ordered.

Great. She never had been all that good with blood. A person might even say she was downright squeamish. And surely he remembered that. A suspicion that he was doing this to torture her took root in her mind. But if it meant he took care of the dog, so be it. "As long as I don't have to look," she retorted.

"Hand me both pairs of big tweezers." He held out one hand expectantly.

She gasped as she got a better look at his bloody blisters. "What happened to your hands?"

"I helped Damien string fence today. Wasn't expecting to have to scrub for surgery tonight. Had to take the skin off the blisters while I scrubbed up so no bacteria would hide underneath."

She stared. He'd torn up his hands like that for the dog? Awe at his dedication to his work flowed through her.

For the next hour, the kitchen was quiet. Finn occasionally asked for something or passed her a bloody gauze pad. His concentration was total. And she had to admit he was giving it his best shot at saving this dog. He murmured soothingly to the animal, even though it was clear the dog was out cold from the injection Finn had given him.

She couldn't help glancing at the surgical site now and then. It appeared Finn was reconstructing the dog's leg. He set the broken femur and then began a lengthy and meticulous job of suturing tendons and muscles and whatever else was in there that she couldn't name and didn't want to.

Finally, when her head was growing light and she thought she might just faint on him in spite of her best efforts not to, Finn started to close up the wound. He stitched it shut in three different layers. Deep tissue, shallow tissue, and then, at long last, the ragged flesh.

Her stove clock read nearly 2:00 a.m. before Finn straightened up and stretched out the kinks in his back. He rubbed the unconscious dog's head absently. "All right. That's got it. Now we just have to worry about blood loss and infection and the patient's generally poor state of health. I'll leave you some antibiotic tablets to get down him by whatever means you can. If he wakes up, you can start feeding him if he's not too far gone to eat."

Although he continued to stroke the dog gently, Finn never once broke his doctor persona with her. He was cold and efficient and entirely impersonal. If she weren't so relieved that he'd helped her, she'd have been bleeding directly from her heart to see him act like this. Again.

She would never forget the last time he'd been this angry and cold and distant. It had been the night of his senior prom. She'd been waiting for him in the beautiful lemon-yellow chiffon dress her mother had slaved over for weeks making. She'd had a garland of daisies in her hair, the flowers from their garden woven with her father's own hands. Finn had been acting strangely when he came to the door but was polite enough to her parents. Then he'd taken her to the dance, waited until they were standing in front of the entire senior class of Honey Creek High and told her in no uncertain terms how she was worthless trash and vowed he never wanted to see her again.

He'd kept that promise until today. Well, and tonight, of

course. Strange how he'd renewed his vow never to see her again within twenty-four hours of seeing her for the first time. She'd never known what had caused him to turn on her then, and she darned well didn't know why he was so mad at her now. He was like Jekyll and Hyde. But mostly the monstrous one. Were it not so late, and she so tired and stressed out and blood covered, she might have asked him. But at the end of the day, it didn't matter. They were so over.

He plunked a brown plastic pill bottle on the counter. "Based on his weight, I'd say half a tablet every six hours for the next week or until he dies, whichever comes first."

She frowned at him. "That was uncalled for."

"I said I'd treat the damned dog. Not that I'd be nice about it."

"Well, you got that right. You're being a giant jerk," she snapped.

Finn scooped the rest of his surgical instruments into his bag and swept toward the door. "Goodbye, Rachel. Have a nice life."

All of a sudden everything hit her. The shock and terror of the past few hours, the stress of the surgery and its gory sights, but most of all, the strain of having to be in the same room with Finn Colton. All that tension and unresolved anger hanging thick and suffocating between them. Watching him walk out of her life *again*. She replied tiredly, "Go to hell."

She thought she heard Finn mutter, "I'm already there."

But then he was gone. All his energy and male charisma. His command of the situation and his competence. And she was left with an unconscious dog lying in the corner of her kitchen, a bottle of pills, and a bloody mess to clean up.

So exhausted she could barely stand, she mopped the

kitchen and the porch with bleach and water. How Brown Dog had any blood left inside his body, she had no clue. She was pretty sure she'd cleaned up an entire dog's worth of blood.

Just as she was finishing, he whimpered. Now that his surgery was over, Finn had said it was safe for him to eat. Maybe she'd better start him off with something liquid, though. She pulled out a can of beef consommé that had been in the back of her cupboard for who knew how long and poured it into one of her mixing bowls. She thinned it with a little water and warmed it in the microwave before carrying it over to the groggy animal.

"It's just you and me now, Brownie boy."

She sat down on the floor beside him and used her mother's turkey baster to dribble some of the broth into his mouth. At first he swallowed listlessly, but gradually he grew more enthusiastic about licking his chops and swallowing. By the time she finished the soup, he was actually sucking at the tip of the baster.

"We'll show Finn, won't we, boy? We're survivors, you and me."

Chapter 4

Rachel came home at lunch to change the newspapers under Brownie, give him his antibiotics and use the turkey baster to squirt canned dog food puréed with water down his throat. He was still too weak to do much but thump his tail a time or two, but gratitude shone in his eyes as she tenderly cared for him.

"What's your story, boy? Where'd you get so beat up? Life sure can be tough, can't it?"

She settled him more comfortably in the corner of her kitchen in his nest of blankets and headed back to work. The afternoon passed with her finding more and more discrepancies in the Walsh Oil Drilling Corporation records. She'd be worried about it if she weren't so tired from last night and so concerned about the wounded animal in her kitchen. So when Lester Atkins called her and asked her to come to Mr. Warner's office, she merely grabbed her latest evidence of the embezzlement and headed upstairs.

But when she stepped into the office, she pulled up short. Wes Colton, in full sheriff garb, was standing beside Craig Warner's desk. Wes's arms were crossed. And he was glaring at her. Good lord. What had Finn told him when he'd gone back to the ranch last night? Had Finn sicced Wes on her to get her fired?

"Good afternoon, gentlemen," she managed to choke past her panic.

"Have a seat, Miss Grant," Craig started.

Oh, God. This *was* an exit interview. Wes was here to escort her out of the building. The sheriff parked one hip on the corner of Warner's massive desk, but he still loomed over her. The guy was even bigger and broader than Finn.

"How are you feeling today, Miss Grant?" Wes rumbled.

"Tired, actually. I'm sure Finn told you about my rather adventurous evening last night."

"He did. Any idea who shot your dog?"

She shook her head. "I've got no idea. He just wandered up to my porch already shot. I never saw the dog before last night."

"Kind of you to go to all that trouble to help him," Wes murmured.

Was that skepticism in his voice, or was she just being paranoid? She shrugged and waited in resignation for this travesty to proceed.

On cue, Craig spoke quietly. "Miss Grant, I'd like you to tell Sheriff Colton what you told me on Friday."

She blinked, startled. "You mean about the Walsh Oil Drilling accounts?"

He nodded.

Okay. She didn't see what that had to do with her getting fired, but she'd play along. She turned to Wes. "Mr. Warner asked me to do an internal audit of the financial records of Walsh Oil Drilling Corporation for the past several years. Walsh Oil Drilling is a wholly owned subsidiary of Walsh Enterprises so we have legal purview over—"

Wes waved a hand to cut her off. "I'm not interested in the legal ins and outs of corporate structure. I'm confident that Craig is operating within the law to do the audit."

She adjusted her line of thought and continued. "Yes, well, I looked at last year's records first. I compared the original receipts, billing documents and logged work hours against the financial reports. And I found several major discrepancies. Based on that, I started going back further and looking at previous years."

"And what did you find, Miss Grant?" Wes asked.

"More of the same. Somebody's been skimming funds from this company over at least a fifteen-year period. Maybe since the founding of the company itself seventeen years ago."

Wes definitely looked interested now. "How much money are we talking?"

"Millions. As much as two million dollars the year the company made a major oil strike and had a windfall income spike."

Wes whistled low between his teeth. "Any way to tell who was taking the cash and cooking the books?"

She shrugged. "Mark Walsh himself signed off on the earliest financial reports. If he wasn't taking the initial money himself, he was certainly aware of who was and how much he was taking. After his first death…" The phrase was weird enough to say that it hung her up for a moment. But then she pressed on: "…somebody kept taking it. I can't read the handwriting of whoever was signing off on the financial documents, but it appears to have been the same signature for the past fifteen years."

Wes glanced over at Warner. "You weren't kidding when you said I'd want to hear this." To Rachel he said, "Who else knows about this?"

"Nobody. Just me and Mr. Warner."

Wes nodded, thinking. "I'd like to keep it that way for a while. This may be just the break we're looking for."

She frowned. "Huh?"

"In the Walsh murder investigation."

"You think whoever killed Mark was helping him skim money from his companies and killed him over it?" she asked in surprise.

Wes shrugged. "I wouldn't want to speculate. I just know that Mark Walsh was damned secretive, and it's been nearly impossible to learn much about his life over the past fifteen years. If nothing else, you may have just answered how he was able to pay for his ongoing existence without his family knowing anything about it. Can you give me a complete rundown of how much money went missing and when, Rachel?"

He was using her first name now? Was that a good sign? "Uhh, sure. I can have it for you in a day or so. I've got a few more years' worth of records to review and then I'll be able to compile a report."

"That would be great. And, Craig, thanks for calling me."

The two men shook hands and Wes turned and left. Craig sat down quickly, mopped his forehead with a tissue and then tossed the tissue in the trash. He didn't look good. His skin was pale and pasty and he had that uncomfortable look of someone who was contemplating upchucking.

"Can I get you a glass of water, sir?" she asked in concern.

"Yes, thank you."

She went over to the wet bar on the far side of the room

and poured him a glass of water. She carried it to his desk. "Are you feeling all right, Mr. Warner?"

"It'll pass. I've been having these spells for a couple of weeks." He smiled wanly at her. "I'm a tough old bird. I'm not about to go anywhere."

She smiled back at him.

"What's this about a shot dog?" he asked.

Likely he was just looking to distract himself from throwing up. She told him briefly about Brownie and his injuries and Finn coming over to perform surgery on him. She left out the part about Finn's bitter anger toward her.

"You've got a good heart, Miss Grant."

She smiled at her boss. It was a rare moment when anyone in this town said something nice to her. She savored it.

"As soon as you're done with those last financial reports, why don't you take the rest of the day off and go look after your four-legged houseguest?"

She nodded, touched by his kindness. "Thank you, sir."

He waved her out of the office. She suspected he was losing the battle with his stomach and wanted a little privacy to get sick into his trash can. Poor man. She hoped he felt better soon.

Finn helped Damien string barbed wire all day. The hard labor felt good and helped him burn off a little bit of the residual stress from last night. He still wasn't entirely recovered from that panicked call from Rachel Grant. The woman had about given him a heart attack. Good thing she'd agreed to stay the hell away from him forever. He couldn't take much more of that from her.

"Anything on your mind?" Damien finally asked late in the afternoon.

Finn looked up surprised. "Why do you ask?"

"You're working like a man with a chip on his shoulder."

"What? I can't come out here and help string a fence out of the goodness of my heart?"

Damien cracked a rare smile at that. "Not buying it."

"When did you get so perceptive?" Finn grumbled.

Damien shrugged. "Prison's a tough place. Gotta be good at reading people if you want to stay out of trouble."

Finn was startled. To date, Damien hadn't said more than a few words about his time in jail. "Does it feel strange to be out?" he ventured to ask.

Damien shrugged. He pounded in a metal stake and screwed the fasteners onto it before he finally answered. "It's surreal being back home. Didn't think I'd ever see big open spaces like this again. I missed the sky. It goes on forever out here."

Finn looked up at the brilliant blue sky overhead. Yeah, he might go crazy if he never got to see that. "How'd you do it? How did you keep from losing your mind?"

"Who says I didn't lose it?" Damien retorted.

Finn didn't say anything. He just waited. And sure enough, after two more posts, Damien commented, "About a year in, I beat the shit out of guy who chose the wrong day to cross me. Growing up with all you punks for brothers served me well. I knew how to handle myself in a fight."

Finn grinned and passed Damien another fastener while he started in on the next post.

Damien continued reflectively. "I got thirty days in solitary. A month in a box broke something in me. It was like I lost a piece of myself. The fight went out of me. It became about just surviving from one day to the next. I played a game with myself. How long could I live in there without losing it again? I made it 4,609 days. And that was when I got word that Walsh had been found dead for real this time and I was going to be released."

Finn shuddered. "God, I'm sorry—"

Damien cut him off with a sharp gesture. "What's done is done. If I learned nothing else in the joint, I learned to keep moving forward. Don't look back. I live my life one day at a time. No apologies. No regrets. It's over."

Finn nodded. His brother was a better man than he. No way could he be so philosophical about a miscarriage of justice costing him fifteen of the best years of his life.

They knocked off when the sun started going down. It got cold fast, and by the time they got up to the main house, he was glad for the fleece-lined coat his brother had tossed him across the cab of the truck.

As beautiful as the log mansion their father had built was, Finn was restless tonight. The heavy walls felt confining and the massive, beamed ceilings felt like they were closing in on him. Hell, Honey Creek was closing in on him.

If his old football coach hadn't extracted a promise out of him to stay for the big homecoming dance this coming Saturday night, he'd be on his way back to Bozeman already. But Coach Meyer was losing his battle with cancer, and he'd asked all his players to come back for one last reunion. It was damned hard to say no to a dying man's last request.

He had to get out of the house. He grabbed his coat and a set of keys and stormed out. As he stomped through the mud room intent on escape, Maisie's voice drifted out of the kitchen. "What's his problem?"

Damien's voice floated to him as he opened the back door. "Woman trouble."

Finn slammed the door shut so hard it rattled in the frame. Woman trouble? Ha!

* * *

Rachel raced home from the office to check on Brownie. He seemed more alert and had a little more appetite. He even gave several thumps of his thick, long tail whenever she walked into the kitchen. After both of them had eaten, she signed onto the Internet to do some research about care of injured animals. She browsed various veterinary advice sites for an hour or so and then, following the recommendation of several of them, went into the kitchen to check the color of Brownie's gums. Supposedly, pink was healthy and dark red or pale white was bad.

Gingerly, she took hold of his lip and raised it to take a peek. He pulled his head away weakly but not before she glimpsed pasty white gums. She laid her hands on his side and he definitely felt hot to the touch. Oh, no. Finn had warned her that infection and fever were a major risk to Brownie's survival.

She headed for the phone and dialed the same veterinarian from the night before. "Hi, this is Rachel Grant. I called last night."

"Ahh, yes. The injured dog. How's he doing?"

"I think he's developing a fever."

"If you want to bring him up to Bozeman, I'll meet you at my office."

She winced. The dog had to weigh seventy pounds, even in his emaciated state, and even if she could lift him herself, she doubted Brownie would cooperate with getting into her compact car. At least not without doing even more damage to his injured leg. "I don't think I can get him up to Bozemen by myself."

"You can try giving him some acetaminophen for the fever," the vet suggested.

She forced the suggested medication down Brownie's throat and hovered nervously over him for the next hour.

He was getting worse quickly. He stopped wagging his tail at her, and then his eyes went dull and finally he couldn't even raise his head anymore. She eyed the heavy bandage wrapping his leg. Should she take it off and check the wound? Or would that introduce even more chance of infection? If only she knew more about caring for a wound like this!

But she knew someone who did. Small problem: She'd promised never to cross his path again.

Over the next hour, Brownie's breath grew raspy and shallow. She was losing him. What the heck. Finn could get over it. She dialed the Colton phone number. The good news was that Duke answered the phone and was reasonably pleasant with her. The bad news was that Finn wasn't home and Duke didn't know where he was. But he did give her his missing brother's cell phone number. Finn was going to have a fit when he found out Duke had done that.

She hung up and dialed Finn's cell phone.

"Yeah?" he shouted. From the noise in the background, it sounded like he was at a party. Or maybe a bar.

"It's me. Brownie's got a bad fever and he's struggling to breathe."

"Tough shit."

Rachel gasped. "Do you torture small children, too, Doctor?" she asked sharply. "This dog has never done anything to hurt you, and you'd turn your back on him?"

"He's just some mutt."

"Oh, and he's not worthy unless he's a purebred? Kind of like being a Colton or a Kelley or a Walsh in this town? The rest of us are lesser life forms to you purebreds? Is that it? You know, I'm glad whatever happened between us happened. You really are a bastard."

She slammed her phone down and took deep satisfaction

in doing so. What a *jerk*. She glanced down at the dog suffering in the corner. "I'm sorry, boy. I may have just driven away your best chance at pulling through." There had to be something she could do. This was the kind of stuff her mother had always been able to handle. *Think, Rachel. What would Mom do?*

Her mother probably would have trotted down the street to visit old Harry Redfeather. He was some sort of medicine man among the local Lakota Sioux. As soon as the idea occurred to her, Rachel knew it to be a good one. If nothing else, the man had a lot more life experience than she did. Maybe he knew of some remedy for a fever.

She grabbed her down ski jacket and gave Brownie a last pat. "Hang in there, buddy. We don't need any nasty old Coltons anyway."

She jogged three houses down to Harry's place and banged on the front door. He was known to be a little hard of hearing. After a minute, his front door opened.

"Rachel, come in and be warm by my fire. Old Man Winter's blowing in tonight. Snow before morning."

She frowned. "I don't think any is in the forecast."

He smiled serenely and said nothing.

"Harry, a dog showed up on my back porch last night. He was starving and shot and half dead. Finn Colton operated on his hind leg to remove the bullet, but tonight the dog's got a terrible fever. Do you know of anything I can do to bring his temperature down? He's burning up. I'm worried that he's got an infection."

Harry nodded. "Come. You can help get my herbs."

He led her to a disreputable-looking wooden shed out behind his house. She ducked inside the low door after Harry and was surprised to find it stuffed with dried plants hanging in bundles from the nearly every square inch of the walls and rafters.

"Get me a sprig of that one over there." Harry pointed at a bundle on the wall. She did as he instructed, pulling various branches and bundles of herbs down for him. "And one stalk only of that one with the purple flowers."

"What is it?" she asked as she handed him the stem of dried flowers.

"Wolfsbane," Harry muttered as he ground leaves together.

She frowned. "Isn't that poisonous?"

"Yes. But a little of it will strengthen the spirit of your dog." In a few minutes, Harry handed her a plastic bag full of ground herbs. "Steep a spoonful of this in warm water and pour the tea down his throat every hour until his fever breaks. And burn this smudge stick around him to help cleanse his spirit. Do you know how to do that?"

Rachel nodded. Ever since she'd been a little girl, she'd seen Harry light up the tightly tied bundles of herbs and waft the smoke around with his free hand. She took the medicines and headed back to Brownie. Over the next several hours she dutifully fed the dog the healing tea. He didn't seem to get any better, but he didn't get any worse, either.

As the hour grew late, the wind began to howl outside, sweeping down out of the high Rockies. She set an alarm for herself and laid down on the couch under a quilt to rest until it was time for Brownie's next dose. It certainly did feel like snow in the air.

She'd dozed off and was warm and cozy when a loud pounding noise dragged her unwillingly from her nap. She glanced at her watch. Not time for the next dose. She rolled over to go back to sleep when the pounding started up again. And this time it was accompanied by shouting. What the heck?

She stumbled upright and headed for her front door. She

pulled back the lace curtain to peer through the glass. Her jaw dropped. She had to be hallucinating.

A massive eighteen-wheeler was just pulling away from the curb in front of her house, and a man was standing at her door. Stunned, she opened the front door on a gust of frigid air and icy particles that stung her skin, and the storm blew Finn Colton into her living room.

Chapter 5

Finn didn't know what the hell he was doing standing here, freezing his butt off. But he'd been drinking and chewing on Rachel's phone call ever since he'd gotten it. Despite his tough words to the contrary, he really was worried about that damned dog of hers. He always had had a big soft spot for animals. Truth be told, he'd wanted to be a veterinarian and not a human doctor. But when Damien went to jail, his father got all obsessive about redeeming the Colton name and had pushed him mercilessly to become a physician.

Finn was royally pissed when Rachel called him. She'd broken her promise, and after a few more beers that had ticked him off worse than the fact that she'd called him. Not to mention she'd accused him of being cruel to animals and small children. He was a doctor, for God's sake. A healer.

One thing had led to another, and he'd moved on to slamming down shots of whiskey. Somehow a trucker at the

Timber Bar had volunteered to drive him over to Rachel's place, and he'd actually taken the guy up on the offer. The last time a woman had driven him to drunkenness at the bottom of a bottle, it had been Rachel, too. At least he was fairly sure he was drunk. Why else was his head swimming and his feet not attached to his body?

"What on Earth?" Rachel exclaimed. "Where's your coat?"

"What? My…I dunno." He'd remembered to grab his medical bag out of his truck but apparently not his coat. Must be drunker than he'd realized.

"Oh, get in here before you freeze to death." She closed the front door behind him.

With the amount of alcohol in his blood, he doubted any part of him would be freezing anytime soon.

"What are you doing here, Finn?"

He squinted at her, trying to make out her facial features in the dark. "The dog. Came to see the dog. I don't torture little kids, you know."

She frowned for a moment. "Are you fit to see a patient?"

He gave her a bleary glare. "I can do a fever in my sleep. I think I have treated 'em in my sleep." He strode past her toward the back of the house. "Where's my hairy patient?"

As toasted as he was, something made him pause in the kitchen door and proceed more quietly. He moved slowly over to the corner and knelt down beside the motionless dog. "Hey, old man," he murmured. "I hear you're feeling a little under the weather." He stroked the dog's thick fur gently and came away with a handful of dry, coarse hair. The dog was burning up. It didn't take a fancy medical degree, human or otherwise, to know that this animal was in big trouble.

"Get me a bunch of towels and fill your sink up with cold water." He dug in his medical bag and came up with a vial and a syringe. Doing the math on a dosage started a faint headache throbbing at the back of his skull. He did the math a second time to be sure and pulled the antibiotic into the syringe. The dog's skin was dry and pinched as he injected the medication into his unprotesting hip.

"Here they are," Rachel panted. She sounded out of breath like she'd sprinted full out for the towels. The girl sure did seem attached to this mongrel for only having known him a day. Almost made a guy a little jealous.

"Soak those in the sink and then lay them over the dog. Keep his bandage dry."

Rachel followed his directions, bending over so close to him he could smell her vanilla perfume. He remembered the scent well and drew in an appreciative sniff of it. Nothing and no one else in the world smelled quite like that intoxicating combination of homey sweetness and Rachel.

In a matter of seconds the towel was warm to the touch. He passed it up to her and took the next one. They worked for close to an hour in silence. The edge of his buzz was wearing off and he moved automatically in fatigue. And then the dog started to feel a little cooler.

"The fever's breaking," Finn murmured.

Rachel sagged, supporting herself against the edge of the sink. He thought he spied tears tracking down her face.

"Without getting another lecture on my lack of concern for animals and children, why are you so attached to this beast?"

Rachel turned, dashing the tears from her cheeks. "He came to me for help, and that makes me responsible for him. Unlike some people in this town, I don't leave my own behind."

He flared up. "We did what we could for Damien. But there wasn't enough evidence to clear him once he was convicted."

Rachel shrugged. An awkward silence developed between them. He spent it checking the dog's bandages. "What are you calling this mutt, anyway?"

"He started out as Brown Dog. Then it became Brownie Boy and now it's just Brownie."

Finn frowned. "He's a big, macho dog. That's too girly a name for him."

"He chose a girl's porch to nearly die on. He's stuck with whatever name I give him."

"Were you always this bitchy?"

She glared at him. "No, it's your special talent to bring out this side of me."

"Figures. You got something to drink?"

"I've got coffee or water for you. Oh, and milk."

He scowled. That wasn't what he had in mind. If he was going to have to deal with this woman, he definitely needed alcohol and lots more of it. Barring that, he had to find some way to shut her up. The sound of her voice was doing weird things to his gut, and he had to make it stop. He didn't want to feel this way. It was too damned much like old times. Like before she ripped his heart out, when things had been so sweet between them that the joy of it had been nearly unbearable.

She took him by the elbow and steered him into her living room. The light from the kitchen was dim in there and the room was wreathed in shadows. Their silhouettes danced upon the walls, ghostlike. Maybe it was the booze, or maybe it was being up half the night last night and working hard all day today, but the years fell away from him and the two of them were sneaking into her parents' house late from a date, he eighteen, she barely sixteen, both of them innocent and crazy in love.

Regret for the loss of those two carefree kids stabbed him.

"What happened to us?" he whispered.

Rachel turned in surprise to stare at him. The line of her cheek was as pure and sweet as ever. He reached up to touch that young girl one more time before she slipped away from him into the mists of time and bitterness.

She made a soft sound. Whether it was distress or relief, he couldn't tell. But he stepped forward and wrapped her protectively in his arms, hushing her in a whisper.

"Don't leave me, Blondie. Stay with me a little longer. I've missed you so damned much."

Her head fell to his chest and all the tension left her body as she gave in to the magic of the moment. He touched her chin with one finger and raised her face to his. He kissed her closed eyelids and then her cheeks, lifting away the tears. He moved on to her jaw and finally her honeyed mouth. And it was like coming home after many long years away. His relief was too profound for words, his only thought to wonder if this was how Damien had felt when he'd walked out of that prison a free man.

And then she kissed him back. Like always, she was shy at first. But he was patient and slowly, gently, drew her out of herself and into the moment. Before long her slender arms came around his neck and her graceful body swayed into his. And then they were really kissing, deeply, druggingly, with heat building between them that would drive back the night outside and chase away all the old hurts.

He ran his fingers through her silky hair, still as golden and blond and full of light as it had always been. Her skin was still smooth, gliding beneath his fingertips like satin. And that little noise she made in the back of her throat—part moan and part laugh—was exactly the same. Everything about her, how he reacted to her, how he felt about her, was exactly the same.

The realization was like the sun rising in his unguarded eyes, blinding him with its undeniable presence. He turned, spinning her with him on invisible currents of air and light and carried her down to the couch, pulling her down on top of him as he sprawled. The sofa creaked and he chuckled as he threw aside a bunched quilt. And then he kissed her until he thought his heart might burst with the joy of it. His whole world spun around him dizzily and he laughed up at her.

"It's not just me, is it?"

She looked at him questioningly.

"How good this feels. As good as it ever did. We were great together. Could be great together again."

She stared at him in undisguised shock. Finally, she announced, "You're drunk."

"Yup. Ain't it grand?"

She smiled, although regret was thick in her sad gaze. She shook her head. "Mark my words. You're going to regret this in the morning."

"What the hell. You only live once. Damien's a good case in point. You never know what's going to happen tomorrow, so you'd better enjoy today."

"I'll be sure to tell your hangover that," she commented wryly.

"Kiss me some more."

"How about I go get you that cup of coffee so you can make an informed decision here?"

"Stay."

But she nimbly disentangled herself from his clumsy embrace and disappeared. He kicked off his shoes and stretched out, deliciously content. Damn, life was good. He'd have to thank that dog in the morning for getting sick and forcing him to come over here…

Rachel stood over the couch, coffee mug in hand, and looked down at Finn sleeping like a baby on her couch. And now the $64,000 question was, how much would he remember in the morning? How much did she *want* him to remember? Her rational self prayed he had a total blackout. But something tiny and stubborn in the back of her head wished that he would remember it all.

His kisses had brought it all back. Everything. How desperately she'd loved him. How they'd planned their escape from Honey Creek, sure they'd be together forever. How innocently and completely she'd given him her heart.

For a little while there, he'd kissed her like he remembered it all, too. They really had been great together. Right up until the moment he turned on her.

She covered him with a quilt, stunned at the direction his thoughts had gone when his inhibitions were removed by the Johnny Walker Red she'd tasted on his mouth. He'd wanted her. Asked her to remember how good it had been between them. Had even suggested they'd be that good together again. For a moment there, he'd been her old Finn. The one she'd never really gotten over. Who was she kidding? No matter how mad at him she'd been for dumping her and treating her so badly, there was still something about him…something irresistible between them.

And those kisses of his! Her toes had yet to uncurl from them. If he'd acted like a drunken lout and pawed at her and tried to shove his tongue down her throat, it would have been easy to resist him. But, no. He had to go and be all gentle and tender and caring, like she was made of fine porcelain and was the most beautiful and fragile thing he'd ever seen.

She pressed the back of her hand to her mouth to suppress a sob. Nobody had ever made her feel like that since him. And that was a big part of why she was still single and heading fast for a lonely middle age. Damn him! Why did he have to go and ruin her for anyone else? Worse, he had the gall to come back to Honey Creek and remind her why she couldn't settle for anyone less than him.

She turned and ran for her bed. Her lonely, cold bed. But at least it had fluffy down pillows into which she could cry out all her grief and loss and remembered pain. She'd thought that part of her life was over. She hadn't thought there were any more tears left to shed for Finn Colton. But apparently she'd been wrong.

When the alarm clock dragged her from sleep two hours later to check on Brownie, she stepped into the living room gingerly. Had it all been a dream? An exhaustion-induced hallucination, maybe?

Nope. A long, muscular silhouette was stretched out under her grandmother's quilt, one arm thrown over his head. She paused to examine his hand. A surgeon's hand with long, capable fingers. And then there was the fresh row of blisters not quite scabbed over on his palm. She tucked the quilt higher over his shoulder and tiptoed into the kitchen.

Whether it was Harry Redfeather's tonic or Finn's antibiotics or the cold towels, or some combination of the three, she didn't know. But Brownie seemed to be sleeping more comfortably and even thumped his tail a little for her. She changed the newspapers under him and tucked a blanket around him more securely. She even managed to get a little liquefied dog food down him. Miraculously, he seemed to have turned a corner for the better.

She stood up and reached out to close the kitchen blinds. An odd light was streaming through the window, too bright for moonlight. She stared in delighted surprise. Snow was falling. Big, fat, lazy flakes, drifting down in silent beauty. The entire world was blanketed in white, fresh and shining and clean. She loved new snow better than just about anything on earth.

How appropriate for this night. Brownie had been given a new chance at life. And her and Finn? She didn't have a clue what had happened between them, but it was certainly new and different. Tomorrow morning would tell the tale, she supposed.

She closed the blind quietly and reached down to pet Brownie. "Sleep tight, fella. Enjoy being warm and dry and safe, eh?"

It must've been a trick of the moonlight because for a moment she could swear he'd smiled at her. Then he shifted and settled down, deeply asleep once more.

Yes, indeed. The morning would tell the tale.

Finn blinked awake into light so blinding he thought for a moment he was lying on a surgical table. "What the hell?" he mumbled.

His feet were hanging off the end of his bed, which was barely wide enough to hold him. Something heavy and warm lay across him. Where in blue blazes was he? He squinted and sat up, swinging his feet to the floor. A living room. On someone's sofa. Man, he must've really tied one on last night. He couldn't remember the last time he'd done that. He was the respectable Colton. The good son. He didn't go out and get ragingly drunk.

He did vaguely remember being severely pissed off at

something. No, some*one*. He'd tossed back a whole lot more whiskey than he usually did. And then…he frowned. He remembered a semitruck. And getting a ride to somewhere. But where?

He looked around and spied lace curtains at the windows. He reached up to rub his face and caught a whiff of something familiar on his shirt sleeves. *Vanilla.* This was Rachel's couch!

It all came back to him, then. The dog. She'd chapped his butt but good for failing to help her dog get over his fever. He'd tried to drink away the memory of the animal's sad brown eyes and failed. Not to mention the dog's new mistress. He'd ended up piling in that truck and hitching a ride over here while some trucker laughed at him the whole time about being in love. He was *not* in love with Rachel Grant!

He remembered her letting him inside and the two of them working on the dog together for a long time until the fever had finally broken. He frowned, glancing down at the couch, and the rest of it came rushing back. He had pulled her down on top of him and kissed Rachel's lights out…or maybe more accurately they'd kissed each others' lights out.

And he'd said he missed her. That they'd been good together. Could be good together again.

He swore long and fluently. That was possibly the dumbest thing he'd ever done in his entire life. And he'd done some pretty stupid things over the years. He vowed then and there never to mix booze and women again as long as he lived. He should probably be grateful he'd only ended up on her couch and not in her bed. Talk about complicating things!

But then insidious images of what she would look like and feel like, naked and silky and willing in his arms, invaded his mind. His body reacted hard and fast, pounding with lust. Damned, traitorous flesh.

"Hi, there. I thought I heard you moving around," Rachel said from the doorway.

He yanked the quilt across his lap to hide his reaction to thinking about being in bed with her. "G'morning," he grumbled. "How's the mutt?"

"The mutt is doing great. He went out in the backyard under his own steam to pee and hopped back inside all by himself."

"Could you dial down the chipper meter a bit?" he groaned.

"Headache, pukey gut, or both?" she asked sympathetically.

"If the guys jackhammering my eyeballs out of my skull are a headache, let's go with that."

"A pile of aspirin coming right up." She brought the pills along with a big pitcher of cool water. He drank several glasses down, and although his head still throbbed, the jackhammers went on break.

She asked sympathetically, "Do you think you could eat? You might feel better if you got some food into your stomach."

"Something starchy, please."

"Pancakes?"

"Perfect."

"If you want to take a shower while I make you a stack, that's okay."

He nodded wearily and hauled himself to his feet. He glanced across the living room at the shadow he cast on the far wall. Memory of a slender, feminine shadow moving sinuously there last night came to mind. He ought to apologize. Tell her it had all been a terrible, alcohol-induced mistake. But his throat closed on the words and his tongue stayed stubbornly silent. He shook his head to clear the memory—and groaned. Big mistake. It felt like he'd just thrown his brain in a blender. Ugh.

He made a beeline for the bathroom and the hottest shower her house could serve up.

Rachel looked up from the table where she was just setting down two glasses of orange juice and was mortified to see Finn holding the mystery piece from her latest attempt at toilet repair.

He said casually, "You didn't need this, so I took it out and hooked up the handle properly. You're flushing like a champ, now."

Her face heated up. "Surgery on my dog and now surgery on my toilet. How will I ever repay you?"

He grinned, a self-conscious little thing that looked strange on him. Was he actually embarrassed? About what? She was the one who couldn't fix a toilet. He slid into the chair across from hers, and suddenly her kitchen shrank from cozy to itty-bitty.

He bit into the pancakes cautiously. She hoped it was because he was being respectful of his stomach's propensity to revolt and not because he thought her cooking was that bad. In fact, she was a pretty decent cook when she bothered to do it. It was just that she lived alone and most of the time it was easier to toss something into the microwave.

"Mmm. Good," he murmured.

Relieved, she dug into her own breakfast.

"Don't you have to be going to work?" he asked.

"I have an appointment this morning," she replied. With his brother. To turn over the copies of the financial records Wes had asked for. The same records he'd asked her not to talk to anyone about. So of course, Finn asked the obvious question.

"Who's the appointment with?"

"Nobody," she answered evasively.

"Nobody who? Must've moved into town after I left."

"Ha, ha. Very funny."

"Who's it with?" he pressed.

She sighed. "You're not making it easy to tell you tactfully that it's none of your business."

The open expression on his face snapped into something tight and unpleasant in the blink of any eye. Dang it! And they'd been getting along so well.

She frowned. And she was desperate to get along with him well, *why?* She was the ex. The very-ex ex. There was no way he'd ever contemplate getting back together with her. At least not sober. He'd had going on fifteen years to get around to it and never had. Last night had been a whiskey-induced anomaly. Nothing more. She could only pray that the fact he hadn't mentioned their kiss this morning meant he didn't remember it.

He pushed his plate back. "Thanks for breakfast. I seem to have left my cell phone in my coat pocket, and I have no idea where my coat is at the moment. Could I use your phone to call a cab?"

"I've got some time before my appointment. I can drive you wherever you need to go."

"I've put you out too much already."

She rolled her eyes. "You saved my dog's life. I definitely owe you a ride. Is your truck over at the Timber Bar?"

"Not anymore. Damien and Duke picked it up last night so I wouldn't try to drive it drunk."

"So you need a ride to the ranch?" Internally, she gulped. It was bad enough having to face him again. But the whole Colton clan? Yikes!

He sighed. "I can see from your face you're not thrilled at that prospect. Really. I'll call a cab."

"Really. I'll drive you home." He glared, and she glared back. The same fire that had zinged back and forth between them last night flared up again, and her kitchen went from itty-bitty to minuscule. Even Brownie lifted his head in the corner to study them.

"I'm calling—"

She cut him off. "I'm not some impressionable fifteen-year-old sophomore that a big, bad senior can push around anymore. I'm taking you home and that's that. Now hand me your plate."

A grin hovered at the corners of his mouth as he passed her his plate in silence. She rinsed off the syrup quickly and popped the dishes and utensils into the dishwasher. Maybe later she'd take them back out and put her lips where his had been. Goodness knew, she was all but drooling over him already.

Finn surprised her by going over to Brownie and squatting down beside him. He held his hand out and let the dog sniff it, then scratched him gently under the chin.

Whoever said men weren't capable of being as tender as women was dead wrong. And furthermore, it was as sexy as hell when a man was gentle and sweet. Her racing pulse was proof enough of that.

Finn murmured to the dog, "How're you feeling this morning, buddy?"

Brownie whimpered as if in response.

Finn glanced up at her. "Sounds like he's conscious enough to be in pain, now. We've got some tramadol out at the ranch I can give you."

"What's that?"

"A painkiller. Wouldn't want the big guy to be uncomfortable now, would we?"

The whole time he spoke, Finn was petting the dog easily, trailing his fingers through the dog's thick coat.

Rachel could hardly tear her eyes away from the magic his hand wove. What would it feel like if he did that across her skin? The idea made her shiver.

Finn glanced up and caught her red-handed staring at him like he was a two-inch-thick, sixteen-ounce prime rib cooked to perfection. She ripped her gaze away hastily. "Uhh, ready to go?" she mumbled.

He stood up leisurely, which put him about a foot from her in her little kitchen. "Yeah," he murmured. "I'm ready if you are." His voice rolled over her, smooth and masculine. And it didn't sound at all like he was talking about leaving. He sounded distinctly like he was talking about *staying*.

Her breath hitched. Then her heart hitched. And then her brain hitched. Was it possible? In a fog of lust and disbelief, she grabbed her keys and her briefcase and led the way out the back door. Last night's snow was mostly gone, but patches of it remained in the grass.

"Winter's coming," Finn commented.

"My favorite time of year," she commented back.

"I remember that about you. You like the holidays and curling up under a blanket with a cup of hot chocolate and watching it snow."

She all but dropped her keys. He remembered that about her? After all these years? What did it mean? In a lame effort to cover her shock, she said, "Yeah, but now that I have to drive in it, the romance of snow has worn off somewhat."

He grimaced at her compact car. "You need to get yourself something bigger and heavier. With four-wheel drive. You live in Montana, after all."

Like she could afford something like that. Maybe in a year or two after she'd dug out from under the bills. Finn looked comical folded into the passenger seat of her little car. The roads in town were wet, and as they headed east into the hills toward the Colton spread, the pavement started to get slippery.

To distract herself from visions of driving off the side of a mountain and killing them both, she asked, "Did you get roped into going to the Honey Creek High anniversary celebration next Saturday?"

"Only reason I'm sticking around town this week. Couldn't let Coach Meyer down."

Rachel swallowed hard. She should've put it together that he'd be at the dance. The daring gown that was being altered for her right now flitted through her mind. *Ohmigosh.* She'd fallen in love with the dress precisely because it was a defiant statement of sensuality. She'd tried for years to be the person everyone in Honey Creek wanted her to be, and the gown was a big, fat announcement that she was done chasing respectability—or paying penance for a crime they'd never bothered to tell her about. If they thought she were a tart, why not be one? Surely tarts had more fun than she'd had for the past fifteen years.

Maybe she could find a burlap sack at the Goodwill store before Saturday.

Or maybe she'd just skip the dance. Although she'd promised Carly she'd go. No way would her cousin let her back out of it without raising a huge stink. Crud.

She fell silent, contemplating ways to duck both the dance and Carly but coming up empty. Finn stared out the window as the mountains rose around them. The high peaks wore their first caps of snow and wouldn't lose them again until next spring. As the roads grew narrower and steeper, she concentrated carefully on her driving. She might not have a fancy truck like Finn, but she knew how to handle winter road conditions. She took it easy and finally turned into the familiar driveway. The big, wrought-iron arch over the entrance still held up the elaborately scrolled letter *C*. Yup, the Coltons were royalty in this town.

A wash of old memories swept over her: amazement that someone who lived in this palatial place could be interested in her; the excitement of imagining herself a member of the Colton clan someday, dreaming of living in the magnificent log mansion that sprawled forever along a mountaintop; her intimidation at meeting Finn's parents for the first time. She'd so wanted to make a good impression on them. But then Maisie had been nasty to her, and she'd gotten tongue-tied and ended up standing in front of Finn's family red in the face and unable to form complete sentences. It had been the most humiliating experience of her life…until the night of prom, of course, when Finn had dumped her.

"Pull around back by the kitchen entrance," he directed.

She nodded and to make conversation added, "This place is still as beautiful as ever."

He shrugged. "It's a house." She didn't think he was going to say anything more, but then he added, "You know what they say. A house isn't necessarily a home."

"Your home's in Bozeman for good, then?"

Another shrug. "I haven't found a home yet."

Now what did he mean by that? She was fairly certain he wasn't talking about finding a house. Her impression was that he was talking about having found love. Companionship. Family. Roots. Her father might be gone and her mother gone in all but body, but at least they'd been a close family. They'd stuck together through thick and thin and been there for each other. Heck, they'd had fun together.

Finn interrupted her thoughts. "Come in while I get the pills for you."

"No, that's okay. I'll wait in the car."

His head whipped to the left. "You scared, Blondie?"

Her spine stiffened. "No, I'm not!"

"Yes, you are. You're chicken to face my family," he accused. He looked on the verge of laughing at her.

"Wouldn't you be?" she shot back.

That wiped the grin off his face. "Yeah, I suppose I would be."

"All right then. So, I'll come inside and show you I'm braver than you ever were. I'm not scared to face the mighty Coltons."

Except she *was* scared. And for some reason, Finn went grim and silent as he climbed out of the car. Had he caught her veiled barb about being afraid to stand up to his family? She didn't like the practice of taking pot shots at other people, but it was hard not to take a swipe or two at him after all the years of pain and suffering he'd caused her. Vaguely nauseous, she marched toward the back door behind him, praying silently that none of the other Coltons would be around.

Her prayer wasn't answered, of course. Finn held the back door for her and she stepped through a mud room the size of her living room and into a giant rustic kitchen that could grace the pages of a home-decorating magazine. A big man sat on a bar stool with his back to her, hunched over a mug of something steaming. He turned at their entrance and she started. Although he'd changed a great deal, he was still clearly Finn's older brother.

"Hi, Damien. Welcome home," she said.

"Thanks," he muttered.

"It's good to have you back," she added sincerely.

He glanced up again, surprise glinting in his hard gaze for a moment. "It's good to be back."

"I'll go get the drugs, Rachel. Stay here," Finn ordered.

He strode out of the kitchen for parts unknown in the mansion.

"You two dealing drugs now?" Damien asked wryly.

"Yup. Thought we'd corner the market on doggie painkillers."

"Come again?"

Rachel grinned. "A stray dog wandered up to my house night before last. He'd been shot and was bleeding and half starved. I couldn't get him to a vet, so Finn came down to town to help him. Did surgery on my kitchen table to remove the bullet and repair his leg."

"Finn did that for you?" Damien asked in surprise. She nodded and he gestured at the bar stool beside her. As she slid onto it he asked, "Coffee?"

"Yes. Thanks."

He poured her a mug and sat back down beside her. Great. Now what were they supposed to talk about? The guy had never been the chatty type, even before he went to jail for half his adult life. She resorted to, "Finn says you've been doing a lot of work around this place."

He shrugged.

"Do you know what you're going to do next?"

He looked at her questioningly.

"I mean, are you planning to stick around Honey Creek long term?"

He raised his mug to her. "You're the first person with the guts to ask me that outright."

"It's not about guts. I'm just interested. I can speak from experience that it sucks to be an outcast among people you thought were friends."

"Yeah?"

"Yeah," she replied, warming to the role of advice giver about something she was an expert in. "You stick by your guns, Damien, and do exactly what you want to do. Ignore the funny looks and snarky comments. I wish I had done it sooner."

He surprised her by mumbling, "Do they ever stop? The looks and the comments?"

She looked him dead in the eye and answered candidly, "I'll let you know when they do."

He grunted. She wasn't sure what the sound meant. Maybe agreement. Maybe disgust.

She said reflectively, "The thing about small towns is no one ever forgets."

He muttered into his mug, "Don't need 'em to forget. Just need 'em to forgive."

She laid her hand on his arm and it went rock hard under her palm. "You don't need anyone's forgiveness. You did nothing wrong. You hold your head high in this town, Damien Colton."

"Maybe before I take off I'll stick around long enough to see Walsh's real killer caught."

"I sincerely hope Wes catches the killer for you. And soon."

An actual smile lit Damien's eyes. "You're not so bad, you know. Finn was a fool to—"

A female voice cut sharply across his words. "What in blue blazes are *you* doing in my house? We don't cotton to white trash sluts around here."

Rachel looked up, stunned at the attack, and her heart fell to her feet. *Maisie.* The woman had always hated Rachel's guts for no apparent reason.

Damien surprised her by cutting in. "Don't be a bitch, Maisie. Rachel brought Finn home."

"Are you telling me he was with her all night last night?" Maisie screeched. "Just couldn't wait to get your hooks back into him, could you? After all these years you still don't get it, do you? You'll never be good enough to be a

Colton, missy. You leave my brother alone. You broke his heart but good the last time, and I'll not stand for you doing it to him again, you hear me?"

Rachel eyed the back door in panic. If she was quick about it, she could make the mud room and be outside before the other woman could catch her.

Damien spoke up mildy. "Shut up, Maisie. What Finn and Rachel do or don't do is none of your business." There was steel behind his words, though. Rachel blinked. At the moment, he didn't sound like a guy she'd want to cross in a dark alley.

"Here they are—" Finn burst into the kitchen, took in the scene of Rachel eyeing the back door, Maisie glaring at Rachel and Damien glaring at Maisie, and fell silent.

Hands shaking, Rachel took the brown plastic bottle from Finn and slid off the stool. "Thanks for everything, Finn. I don't know what I'd have done without you." How she got the words out with any semblance of composure, she had no idea.

"Any time," he replied. Whether he actually meant that or just said it out of automatic politeness, she had no idea. If only she could get out of here without any more collateral damage from Maisie Colton. Folks in Honey Creek were about equally split over whether she was just a spoiled bitch or a little bit crazy. Either way, Rachel usually steered well clear of her. And it was time to do that now.

"Nice talking with you, Damien," Rachel said.

"You, too."

She didn't know how to say goodbye to Finn, so she just nodded at him and turned to leave.

"Be careful driving home, Blondie," he murmured quietly enough that she doubted Maisie heard.

For some inexplicable reason, tears welled up in her eyes. She just nodded mutely and fled like the big, fat chicken she was. So much for being braver than Finn Colton.

Chapter 6

The next few days were busy ones for Rachel. She visited her mother at the nursing home and cried in her car afterward at how delighted her mother had been that the nice young woman had brought her a cup of chocolate pudding. Her mother was continuing to lose weight and looked so frail that a strong wind might blow her away.

Rachel did a volunteer shift at the Goodwill store and was dismayed to discover the place was plumb out of burlap sacks. It didn't even have any conservative dresses that would remotely fit her, either. She was stuck with the one Edna was nearly done altering.

At work, she commenced revising the Walsh Oil Drilling financial statements, a job that was going to take her weeks to complete. Craig Warner was out of the office for a couple of days but had stopped by to say hello to her on Thursday morning. She took that as a sign that maybe she wasn't going to lose her job over exposing the company founder's embezzlement, after all. At home, she slept and ate around caring for Brownie, who was gradually recovering. She thought he might be putting on a bit of weight, too.

The weather was strange all week. After the snow, the next day the temperature went up to nearly eighty degrees. Mother Nature was as unsettled as Rachel felt.

She didn't run into Finn around town again, but she was vividly aware of his presence. It was as if she felt him nearby. Every now and then she got a crazy notion that he was within visual range. But whenever she turned to look for him, he wasn't there. It was probably the lack of sleep making her hallucinate. Either that, or she was as big a lovesick fool as she'd ever been. She tended to believe it was the latter.

Her rational mind argued that she was insane to entertain any thoughts of Finn at all. Maisie was right. Hadn't she learned her lesson the first time around? She would never be good enough to be a Colton. But her heart stubbornly refused to listen to reason. She dreamed of him. The kinds of dreams that made her wake up restless and hot and wishing for a man in her bed. Finn Colton, to be exact.

Why, oh why, did he have to come back to Honey Creek?

She rushed home after work on Thursday to take care of Brownie and change clothes. Walsh Enterprises was throwing a barbecue to kick off the centennial homecoming weekend celebration, and as a Walsh employee, she was invited.

She'd never been out to the Walsh spread other than to drive by at a distance. It looked homey and charming from the main road. The Walsh house turned out to be deceptive, though. It looked like a fairly normal country-style home with a broad front porch and dormer windows in the steep-pitched roof. But when she stepped inside, she was startled at the size of the place. Nothing but the best for one of the town's other royal families, she supposed. These people lived in a world different from hers entirely.

Lucy Walsh, who was only a couple of years older than Rachel, ushered her out back to where easily a hundred people milled around the swimming pool balancing plates of food and drinking tall glasses of beer from the Walsh brewery.

He was here. She knew it instantly. Finn's presence was a tingling across her skin, a sharp pull that said he was over by the bar. She looked up, and there he was. Staring across the crowd at her like he'd felt her walk into the party the same way she'd felt him.

He was, of course, the only Colton at this Walsh barbecue. Frankly, she was surprised he had come. The two families weren't exactly on friendly terms. But then, Finn always had been the *good* Colton. The diplomat. The one who smoothed things over.

He wore a pale blue polo shirt and jeans and looked like a million bucks. It was all she could do to tear her gaze away from him. But in a gathering like this, she dared not look like she bore any interest at all in him. The rumors would fly like snowflakes in January if she did.

In fact, she assiduously avoided him for the next hour. Thankfully, Carly arrived and took her in tow. Her cousin was outgoing and popular and made lively conversation with dozens of people. It allowed Rachel to nod and smile and act like she was having fun, when mostly she was concentrating on keeping tabs on Finn and forcing herself not to look at him. When the strain became too much for her, she went inside in search of a restroom and found a long line of people waiting to use one.

Jolene Walsh, Lucy's mom, stopped to speak to Rachel

in the hall. "Why don't you go upstairs, dear? There are several bathrooms, and you won't have to wait."

"Thanks, Mrs. Walsh."

"Call me Jolene, dear."

She thought she detected a hint of sadness in the woman's voice. She'd had a rough go of life, too. It was no secret that Mark Walsh had cheated on his wife and been a rotten husband until his first death. By all accounts, Jolene had kept to herself for years afterward and let Craig Warner mostly run Walsh Enterprises. Then Mark had shown up dead for real and plunged Jolene into yet another scandal. Poor woman.

"Thanks, Jolene," Rachel murmured. She headed upstairs and went in search of a bathroom. She ducked into a bedroom and saw a door that looked promising. She headed toward it and started when it opened.

Finn stepped out.

"Oh! Hi," she murmured, flustered.

"Hi. Enjoying the party?" Finn asked. He glanced warily toward the open bedroom door.

"Uhh, yeah. Food's great."

"How's Brownie?"

"Getting better slowly. He's started trying to put weight on his leg, but he cries every time he tries it."

Finn frowned. "Femurs are intensely painful bones to break in humans. I suspect it's similar in dogs. Let me know if the pain doesn't seem to subside in a few days."

"Okay. Thanks."

He took a step closer and asked quietly, "How are *you* doing, Blondie?"

She looked up at him, startled. "Tired, actually. Taking care of Brownie around the clock is hard work."

He nodded and reached out to trace beneath her eye with the pad of his thumb. She froze, stunned that he would touch her voluntarily. "Get some rest. He's depending on you."

She nodded, her throat too tight to speak. He *was* talking about the dog, right?

Finn took a step forward, his fingers still resting lightly on her cheek. His head bent down toward hers slightly. *Ohmigosh*. He was going to kiss her!

Someone burst into the room in a flurry of noise and movement. "Finn, come quick! We need a doctor—" Lucy Walsh broke off, looking back and forth between them. "Oh!"

Finn jumped back at about the same instant Rachel did, but he was first to speak. "What's wrong?"

"Craig has collapsed. Hurry!"

Finn spared Rachel an apologetic glance, then raced out of the room after Lucy. Rachel sat down on the edge of the bed, breathing hard. Holy cow. Finn Colton had been about to kiss her. And he wasn't drunk this time. At least, she was pretty sure he wasn't.

As worried as she might be about her boss, she couldn't exactly go busting downstairs immediately after Finn with her cheeks on fire. Not if she didn't want to be the stuff of gossip for weeks to come. She stumbled into the bathroom and splashed cold water over her face until her cheeks had returned to a normal pink in the mirror. Her brown eyes were too big, though, too wide, and her hands were shaking. There was no way she was going to hide the fact that something had happened between her and Finn up here.

Crud. She seemed to have a knack for doing practically nothing yet managing to put herself into prime rumor position. She really wished she would stop doing that. Reluctantly, she walked downstairs. An ambulance siren screamed in the distance. Oh, dear. Craig must be seriously ill. She hoped it was nothing like a heart attack.

She stepped out onto the back patio. A crowd of people was clustered around the far end of the pool, and she spotted Finn kneeling next to a prone figure. At least he wasn't doing CPR on Craig. That was good news, right? A pair of paramedics raced around the side of the house, pulling a stretcher. She watched in dismay along with everyone else while they loaded Craig onto it and, with Finn jogging beside them, rushed Craig out to the ambulance.

Lucy Walsh, who happened to be standing next to Rachel, turned blindly to her, her face pale. "I've got to take my mom to the hospital. She's too upset to drive. Could you keep an eye on things around here? Everyone can stay if they like, but we've got to go."

Rachel nodded, stunned. In moments, the Walsh party was nearly devoid of Walshes. Lester Atkins made an announcement that people should feel free to stay and enjoy the barbecue. But the life had gone out of the evening. People trickled out steadily over the next hour until the place was deserted.

Rachel stepped in to supervise the caterers when Lester got a call from the Walshes and had to race off to the hospital. That couldn't be a good sign. She said a prayer for Craig and turned to the daunting task of cleaning up after two hundred people. After all, she was the town's resident pitch-in-and-volunteer girl. Thankfully, the caterers were efficient, and it only took an hour or so for them to pick up the mess, pack the tents and tables and leave the remaining food in coolers in the kitchen.

Rachel climbed into her car a little after midnight and started the long drive back to town. Finn was a great doctor and he was looking after Craig. Everything would turn out okay. Except an ominous rumbling in her gut said that everything was not okay in Honey Creek.

Finn parked his truck behind his family's mansion and sat there for a while staring at nothing. What on earth was wrong with Craig Warner? He understood why the local chief E.R. doctor had recruited him to consult on this case. But even as a specialist in gastrointestinal disorders, he was stumped. He'd seen a lot of strange cases in emergency rooms before, but this one was baffling. He'd ordered up a raft of tests, but the nearest lab was in Bozeman and he wouldn't have any results on most of the lab work until morning. He'd considered ordering a helicopter to transport Craig up to Bozeman, but frankly, he didn't think the man would survive the flight.

Damn it, the guy couldn't die on him! Besides the fact that he took pride as a physician in hardly ever losing a patient, how ironic would it be for one of the mainstays of the Walsh family to die on the watch of a Colton?

He climbed out of the truck, shrugging deep into the jacket he'd snagged from the mud room earlier. He didn't feel like going inside. The weather had swung back from summer warm to cold tonight, and the temperature fit his mood. He strolled out toward the back acreage and spied a light on in the main barn. What was going on out there? He headed for the light.

The dew soaked through his docksiders and the night air bit sharply at his nose. The warmth of the barn was tangible as he stepped inside. A rich smell of cattle and disinfectant washed over him. This always had been his favorite place on the whole ranch. Damien leaned against a stall door at the far end of the cavernous space.

He joined his brother and glanced into the stall. A

cow lay on her side, straining in the distinctive spasms of delivering a calf. "Everything okay?" Finn asked.

Damien shrugged. "First calf. She's struggling with it. Thought I'd keep an eye on her in case she needs help."

"Late in the year to be calving, isn't it?" Finn murmured.

Damien shrugged. "I wasn't around ten months ago to know how she got in with the bull."

Finn fell silent. They watched the cow stand, pace around a bit, then lay back down and strain again. Finn asked, "You check the calf's position?"

"Yeah. Presentation's normal."

Funny how both of them had been gone from the ranch for over a decade, but the knowledge of ranching and cattle husbandry came back unbidden. The rhythm of life out here got into a man's bones and never left him.

Damien commented, "I figure we give her another push or two, and if she doesn't make any progress, we go in and help."

"Want me to call a vet?"

Damien replied, "I hear Doc Smith retired. There's no vet in town these days, so we're on our own. But you're a doctor. Some of that fancy medical stuff has to apply to cattle, doesn't it?"

Finn nodded. Something in his gut ached with longing to go to veterinary school and take Doc Smith's place as the local vet. But, no. He had to become a "real" doctor. Respectable. Successful. Distinguished.

Damien looked over at him with that disconcertingly direct stare he'd developed in prison. "What brings you out here at this time of night? I thought you were going to the Walsh barbecue."

"I went. Craig Warner collapsed and had to be rushed to

the hospital. I spent most of the evening in the emergency room with him."

"He gonna be okay?"

Finn shrugged. "Don't know. We can't figure out what's wrong with him. He's in critical condition."

Damien frowned. "Can't say as I wish anyone associated with the Walshes well, but I don't wish death on the guy."

Finn nodded. Once upon a time, Damien had been crazy in love with Lucy Walsh until her father ran Damien off. That was what the prosecutors used as Damien's motive for supposedly murdering Mark Walsh. *Women. The root of all evil.*

"You think?" Damien murmured in surprise.

Finn glanced over at his brother. Had he said that out loud?

"You got woman trouble, Finn?"

He frowned. Did he have woman trouble? He wasn't sure. He'd been on the verge of kissing Rachel again at the barbecue before Lucy burst in to announce that Craig had collapsed. And that would've been a colossal mistake.

"Only trouble I'm having with women is staying away from them. Or rather getting them to stay away from me."

"Rachel's not stalking you, is she? She didn't strike me as the type."

"Hell, if anything I'm the one stalking her." He jammed a hand through his hair. "But I know better. The woman's poison. She reeled me in the last time and then betrayed me."

"You mean back in high school?" Damien asked. He sounded surprised again.

"Yeah," Finn answered impatiently.

"You still carrying a torch for her after all this time?"

"I'm not carrying a torch for Rachel Grant!"

"Dunno. From where I stand, it sure looks like you are. Helping her with that dog and spending the night at her house. Were you really only on her couch?"

Rage exploded in Finn's chest. It boiled up within him until his face was hot and his fists itching to hit something. What the hell? He checked the reaction, stunned at its violence. Where had that come from? Was he really so defensive of Rachel? Or was it maybe that it just pissed him off to have someone else see the truth before he did?

The cow laid down abruptly and commenced another contraction.

"Crap," Damien exclaimed softly. "The calf has turned. Those aren't front hooves."

Finn followed his brother into the pen. "I'll hold her down. You're stronger than me. You pull the calf."

They went to work quickly. Finn put a knee on the cow's neck, leaning on it just enough to keep her from getting up. As another contraction started, Damien wrapped a towel around the calf's back legs, braced himself with his boots dug deep into the sawdust and commenced pulling for all he was worth.

"Ease up," Finn said as the contraction ended. Damien and the cow had the calf's entire hind legs out. Damien tore back the silver-white amniotic sac to get better purchase on the slippery calf.

"Big calf," Damien commented, breathing hard.

"Here comes the next contraction," Finn replied.

Damien nodded and commenced pulling again. It took maximum effort from cow and human, but a few moments later, the calf popped out in a rush of fluid. Finn and Damien pulled the sac back from the calf's face and cleaned out its nose. The calf shook his head and snorted, breathing normally. The cow lowed to her baby and after passing the afterbirth got to her feet to examine her offspring. While mother administered an energetic bath to her baby, Finn got a barn shovel, took the afterbirth out of the stall and checked it make sure it was intact and whole.

He and Damien leaned on the stall wall and watched as the calf started struggling to get to its feet. Mom's enthusiastic licking wasn't helping, and she knocked the little guy over a few times. There was something miraculous to watching new life unfold like this. It put everything else in the world into perspective.

Damien murmured, "Rachel seems like a decent woman. Why is it you hate her guts, again?"

Finn was startled. Why had Damien circled back to this subject? "You know why. She slept with some other guy. Hell, she ripped my guts out and stomped on them."

Damien shrugged. "Yeah, yeah. I remember. I was there when Maisie told you." He paused. "But it's been fifteen years. That's a long time. People change."

"Yeah, but just because people change, that doesn't mean it's always for the better."

"They don't always change for the worse, bro."

Finn looked over at Damien in surprise. "When did you become such an optimist about the human race?"

"I'm no great optimist. It's just that…" Damien seemed to search for the right words and then settled on "…life's too short. You gotta do what makes you happy. If you want to give things with Rachel another go, then you should do it."

Finn reared back. "I don't want to give things with Rachel another go!"

"Why the hell not? She's a beautiful woman, and she's plumb tuckered in love with you. If I had a woman like that who wanted me like she wants you, I wouldn't think twice about going for it."

"In love? With me? You're nuts. She hates my guts!" His outburst startled the cow into turning defensively and banging into her calf, who stumbled and fell over.

"Shh," Damien hushed him. "You're upsetting momma and interfering with junior's first meal."

Finn subsided, but his brain was in a whirl. Why on earth did Damien think Rachel still had a thing for him? She might have turned to him for help with her injured dog, but she'd made it plenty clear that she wished he'd leave town and stay gone. Except she'd kissed him back last night when she thought he was too drunk to remember the kiss today. And earlier this evening at the barbecue, she'd definitely leaned toward him when he'd leaned toward her—

Cripes. Was he so desperate that he was analyzing *leaning,* now?

The sound of sucking pulled his thoughts back to the moment. He smiled as the calf butted his mother's udder and sucked some more.

"Nice-looking calf," Damien commented. "Maybe I'll ask the old man to give him to me as a starter bull for my new ranch."

"You still planning to move to Nevada and start your own place?" Finn murmured.

"Nothing to hold me around here anymore," Damien retorted. "Just a whole lot of bad memories and bad blood."

It hurt to hear the pain in Damien's voice. The guy'd been through so much and gotten such a raw deal. Finn really wished there was something he could do to put a smile back into his brother's eyes.

"Things sure didn't turn out how either of us planned, did they?" Finn muttered. "I thought I was going to marry

Rachel, go to vet school and live happily ever after, and you were going to run the ranch and marry Lucy."

Damien's gaze went glacial. Finn froze as actual violence rolled off his brother's massive shoulders. For the first time since he'd gotten home, Finn was a little afraid of his older brother. By slow degrees, Damien's bunched muscles relaxed and the violence pouring off of him ebbed. Finn released a slow, careful breath.

Damien glanced wryly over at Finn. "It's not too late for you. You can still have it all."

Finn wanted to shout that he didn't want Rachel Grant, but once again, the words wouldn't come out of his throat. They stuck somewhere in his gut and refused to budge.

Damn, that woman messed him up like no other female ever had. Coming back to Honey Creek had been a big mistake. A huge one. To hell with the homecoming dance. He'd pay his respects to Coach Meyer in the morning and get the hell out of town.

Chapter 7

Rachel dragged herself into work the next morning as exhausted as she'd ever been in her life. Brownie had been restless and uncomfortable last night, and what with worrying over Craig Warner and replaying that almost-kiss with Finn Colton over and over in her head, she'd barely slept at all.

After hours and hours of wrestling with the decision, she'd determined that no matter how much attraction still lingered between the two of them, she and Finn were better off going their separate ways and living their own lives. Too much time had passed and they'd both changed too much. Even if they had been wildly attracted to one another as kids, teen lust was no basis for a long-lasting relationship.

Only a few minutes after she'd sat down at her desk, Lester Atkins summoned her to his office. Alarm coursed through her. What could he possibly want with her? As

Craig's personal assistant, he had a great deal of unofficial power at Walsh Enterprises. And some of his power was entirely official. She gathered from her coworkers, for example, that he had the power to fire people at her pay grade.

Craig Warner's secretary wasn't at her desk when Rachel got to the woman's office, so she stepped through into Lester's. He wasn't there. Strange. She glanced into Craig's office and was startled to see Lester sitting at Warner's desk. His palms were spread wide on the leather surface, and a look of satisfaction glutted his features.

Rachel stepped back hastily into the doorway to the secretary's office and cleared her throat loudly. Lester came out of Warner's office immediately, the look in his eyes one of suspicion now.

"Ah. There you are, Miss Grant. I have some paperwork I need you to take over to the hospital and get signed."

"Does that mean Mr. Warner's doing better?" she asked hopefully.

"No. He's still in critical condition. I need Mrs. Walsh's signature."

Rachel frowned. From what she gathered, Craig Warner and Jolene Walsh had quietly been an item for the past year or two. She hardly imagined that Jolene would want to deal with business matters when her lover was fighting for his life.

Lester must've caught the frown, because he snapped, "I wouldn't bother her with trivial matters. This paperwork is vitally important and has to be signed right away." He picked up a thick manila folder off his desk. "I've marked the spots that need signing with sticky notes. Jolene doesn't need to read any of it. You can tell her I've reviewed it all and she just needs to sign it. Bring it back to me when she's done it."

Rachel nodded and took the file he thrust at her. As she drove to the hospital, she couldn't get the sight of that gloating pleasure on Lester's face out of her mind. She glanced down at the folder resting on her passenger seat several times. What was he up to? She pulled into a space in the hospital parking lot and turned off the ignition. It was none of her business. But the Walshes were bound to be distracted. And she neither liked nor trusted Lester. She picked up the file.

There had to be a hundred pages of dense legal papers in the folder. She tried to read the first few pages but got bogged down in the language so fast that she shifted into merely scanning the pages superficially.

And then the words *Walsh Oil Drilling Corporation,* leaped off a page at her. She stopped and went back to it. She appeared to be in the middle of some sort of contract. She backed up a few pages and read more closely. The contract appeared to be fairly innocuous. Walsh Oil Drilling was leasing mineral rights to several large tracts of land on the West Coast for exploration and possible development. The other party in the deal was a corporation she'd never heard of before—Hidden Pines Holding Company. She plowed through a dozen pages of clauses before she reached the end of the agreement and a sticky note marking where Jolene was supposed to sign the contract.

Rachel jolted as she looked down at the signature blocks on the page before her. She recognized one of the signatures of a Hidden Pines official. Or, more accurately, one of the illegible scrawls. It looked an awful lot like the scrawls on the fraudulent Walsh Oil Drilling financial records she'd been poring over for the past week. She studied the scribble. It had a different loop at the beginning and trailed off a little more horizontally than the one on the financial records, but the rest of it—the way it floated above the line, the aggressive slash of it—was nearly identical.

She needed to show this to Wes Colton. Except Lester would get suspicious if she didn't get Jolene's signature and bring it back to the office right away. Not only would Wes not want the guy involved with this, but Lester had the power to fire her, and she really couldn't afford to lose this job. Maybe she could find a copy machine in the hospital and make a copy of the page.

Who was the owner of Hidden Pines Holding Company? And how was he or she involved with skimming Walsh Oil Drilling monies? It seemed awfully fishy that the two companies were doing business together like this.

She closed the folder and headed into the hospital. It wasn't a big place and she had no trouble finding the Walsh clan. They all but filled the main waiting room.

Jolene Walsh greeted her warmly, if wanly. "Rachel, dear. How kind of you to stop by."

"How's Mr. Warner? He's been so kind to me."

"There's no change. Finn says that's good news. He went down fast last night, but he seems to be holding his own now. He's still having trouble breathing, though, and they can't make heads nor tails of his blood work."

Rachel expressed her sympathy and prayers for Mr. Warner's recovery. Then she winced and said, "Actually, Mrs. Walsh. I'm here on business. Lester Atkins sent me over with some documents for you to sign. But I need to make copies of them before you do."

"Oh!" Mrs. Walsh looked surprised.

Rachel added hastily, "If you'd rather wait on signing these, I'll be glad to tell Lester that. Really, this is no time to be thinking about contracts and the like."

Mrs. Walsh blinked and then examined Rachel more closely. For a moment, Rachel got the impression of acute perceptiveness behind the woman's gaze. Like she'd heard the layers of hidden warning behind Rachel's words. "Yes. Yes, you're right. Now's not the time. Who knows what I might end up signing. Tell Lester I'll take a look at the documents in a few days, when Craig's feeling better."

Rachel nodded, deeply relieved, and turned to leave. And she all but ran into Finn Colton's chest. She didn't need to look up to know those broad shoulders, even if they were covered in a white lab coat this morning.

"Sorry," she mumbled. "I was just leaving."

"Hey," he murmured. "Aren't you even going to say hello?"

Her gaze snapped up to his. "In front of all these people?"

"There's no reason for us not to act civil to one another in public," he replied evenly.

It wasn't the civil bit that worried her. It was the incendiary attraction that flared up between them any time they got into close proximity that had her nervous. It was flaring up, now, in fact, if the heat in her cheeks was any indication. She took a step back from him. "Uhh, hi, Finn. I was here on business, but I'm just leaving. Unless you can tell me where to find a copy machine in this hospital."

"Try the nurse's station. They handle massive amounts of paperwork."

"Thanks." She turned and walked away from him even though every fiber in her body wanted to turn around and fling herself into his arms. But when she heard him murmur, "The blood work is coming back from Bozeman, and it's not good," she did turn around.

Mrs. Walsh collapsed into a vinyl-covered chair and Lucy sank down beside her, holding her mother's hand.

Finn continued gently. "His liver is failing. We don't know why. It seems to be accumulating toxins at a rapid rate, and they're poisoning his body. I'm going to start him on a course of chelation using specially engineered cell salts."

"Cell salts?" Jolene Walsh repeated faintly.

Finn explained. "It's an experimental treatment. I'll introduce specially designed salts into Mr. Warner's body. If all goes well, the salt molecules will bind to the toxins in his liver. And because the body readily flushes salt out of itself, the idea is for his body to flush the salts and take the poisons with them. But we don't have time to do lengthy studies and create a salt specifically for the toxins in Mr. Warner's system. We're going to have to make our best guess at which salt complex to use."

Rachel was impressed by Finn's reassuring calm with Jolene. His explanation had also been clear and easy to follow. Who'd have guessed that the fun-loving teenager she'd once known would have developed into a doctor like this? Of course, the wild recklessness wasn't entirely gone. It had been dangerous in the extreme for him to contemplate kissing her at the Walsh barbecue.

Finn was speaking again. "…need your signature on some releases before we start the treatment, since it's still experimental."

Jolene glanced up at Rachel, and she smiled at the older woman. These were the sorts of things she needed to be signing right now. Not oil-drilling contracts for Lester Atkins. And on that note, Rachel slipped quietly from the waiting room.

When she approached the nurse's station, the place was in chaos, with nurses rushing every which way. Apparently, there'd been a car accident outside of town and several victims were in the midst of being admitted. Rachel decided to go to the library and make her copies there. She started toward the parking lot but stopped in surprise as she spied

Wes Colton standing in front of the hospital. Alarm jangled in her belly. Did his presence have something to do with Craig Warner's mystery illness?

She walked up to him and waited while he finished a call on his cell phone.

"Hi, Rachel. What can I do for you?"

"It's what I can do for you. I've found something I think you might want to take a look at."

"Regarding?"

"Those financial records I gave you. I may have found another place where that one mysterious signature was used. Recently."

"How recently?"

"It's dated two days ago."

Wes glanced around the parking lot and then leaned close to murmur, "Meet me in my office in an hour. And don't say anything about it to anyone."

She nodded, feeling very James Bond-like, and headed for her car. She used the hour to run home and check on Brownie. He was still restless, and she gave him another dose of the painkiller Finn had given her.

Wes was waiting when she arrived at his office. She opened the folder and showed him the signature, and he pulled out his copies of the financial records and compared the two.

"Good eye, Rachel. I'll send these off to a handwriting expert and see what he can make of it."

In short order, Wes had copied the contents of the entire file. As he handed the documents back to her, he asked, "Atkins likely to hassle you over not getting these signed?"

She looked up at Wes in alarm. "I hope not."

"If he gives you any trouble, you let me know. Jolene won't stand for an employee being fired for looking out for her best interest. I'll have a word with her if Lester tries to mess with you."

She smiled her gratitude at him. Who'd have guessed a Colton would look out for her like this? And with a Walsh, no less. *Too bad it wasn't Finn showing such concern.*

As she stood up to leave the sheriff's office, the bell on the outer door rang behind her. A large, familiar shadow filled the doorway. Her heart tripped and sped up.

"Finn!" Rachel exclaimed. "Are you following me?"

"Gee. I was just about to accuse you of the same thing," he retorted, grinning.

Wes looked back and forth between them shrewdly. Rachel squirmed. At this rate, everybody in town would know there were sparks flying between the two of them. But nobody seemed to believe her avowal that even though there might be sparks, she had no intention of starting any fires.

Wes gathered up the papers on the desk. "Let me just put these in the safe and then I'll be ready to go."

Rachel picked up her briefcase and headed for the door. Small problem: the only way out of the sheriff's office was right past Finn. And he wasn't moving. She approached him warily. "Any change in Craig Warner's condition?"

Finn shrugged. "We've started the cell salt therapy. It's too early to tell if it's going to do any good."

"And if it doesn't?"

Finn's jaw tightened and he didn't answer. Which was answer enough.

"I'll say another prayer for him."

"Thanks, Rachel."

"How are you doing? Did you get any sleep last night?"

He shrugged. "Medical school teaches you how to go without sleep. I'm okay. I just wish—"

"Wish what?" she asked quietly.

"I just wish I knew what in the hell is wrong with Craig," he burst out.

"You'll figure it out. I know you will." On impulse, she laid a hand on his chest and sucked in her breath at the heat and hardness of him. She'd meant the spontaneous gesture as a sympathetic one, but in the blink of an eye, tension thrummed between them, hot and thick. She glanced fearfully toward Wes's office and very carefully removed her hand from his chest. *Whoa. Note to self: do not touch Finn even under the most innocent of circumstances.* Not unless she had a burning desire to scorch herself silly.

Finn let out a slow breath. He tried to smile, but the expression seemed more of a grimace to her. "I'll do my best not to let the Walsh family down."

If he could manage normal conversation, she could, too. "Take care of yourself, okay?"

She felt anything but, normal, though. Her stomach was by turns heavy and floating, and her entire body tingled. Why did she only feel this alive when she was around him? Should she ride the wave and enjoy it while it lasted, or maybe she'd be wiser to try to wean herself off the addiction now before it got too bad.

She moved to pass him, but he reached out and stopped her with a hand on her arm. "I—"

She froze, waiting to see what came next.

"I'm sorry we didn't get to finish our conversation at the Walsh barbecue."

She stared, shocked. Okay. Not what she'd been expecting. He wanted to finish that kiss they'd almost started but had never gotten around to? Her gaze ducked away from his. "I'm, uh, sorry, too."

"Give me a rain check?"

"Uh, sure." Positively stunned now, she stumbled as

she heard Wes coming back out into the main room. Finn steadied her, a smile playing at the corners of his mouth.

"Thanks," she mumbled. And then she all but ran for the door, her cheeks on fire.

"She okay?" Wes asked.

Finn looked up at his brother, doing his damnedest to hide how shaken he was. He couldn't even be in the same room with Rachel without thinking about pulling her into his arms and kissing her senseless. Who was he kidding? He wasn't leaving town on her account anytime soon. And then she had to go and lay her hand on his chest. He'd thought he was going to come out of his skin when she touched him like that.

Belatedly, Finn answered, "She's great. She just doesn't know it yet."

"Huh?"

"Never mind."

"You thinking about getting back together with her?" Wes asked as they headed out the front door and Wes locked up.

Finn opened his mouth. Shut it. His first impulse was to reply that hell yes, he was getting back together with Rachel. But the inevitable reaction he would get from Wes made him pause.

It was a stupid idea. Hooking up with Rachel would bring him nothing but trouble. If he knew what was good for him, he'd leave well enough alone. Hell, if he really knew what was good for him, he'd get out of Honey Creek as soon as possible. Except he couldn't walk out on Craig Warner right now. No, he definitely had to stick around town until the crisis passed for Warner one way or the other. He didn't know whether to curse the man or bless him.

Rather than try to field any more uncomfortable questions from Wes that had no easy answers, Finn guided the talk into safer waters. "Any progress on the Walsh murder?"

"Maybe."

"Can you talk about it?"

"Nope."

Finn eyed his brother speculatively. Did Rachel have anything to do with the possible break in the case? Why else would she be in the sheriff's office? What did she know? He asked abruptly, "Is Rachel in any danger?"

Wes glanced over at him, startled. "Why do you ask that?"

"Umm, well, with that dog showing up on her porch shot and all…" It was a lame response but the best he could do on short notice.

"Nah. The dog's just one very lucky mutt to have found someone as soft-hearted as Rachel."

"What about whoever killed Walsh?"

"I don't think we have a serial killer on our hands, if that's what you're implying. Whoever killed Mark Walsh wanted him dead and him alone."

Finn exhaled heavily. "Maybe not."

Wes looked over sharply. The squad car slowed and Wes guided it over to the side of the road. When it was parked, he said, "You never did tell me why you called me earlier. That's why I swung by the hospital. But you were tied up with Warner. So talk. Now."

Finn frowned. "There's a chance—a small one, but a chance—that Craig Warner is the victim of foul play."

"How's that?"

"It's too early to be sure, but I've ruled out just about everything else. I think it's possible that Craig has ingested poison."

"Have you got any evidence?"

"Not yet. I wouldn't have said anything at all if you weren't my brother, and I know you won't go off half-cocked."

"When will you be able to say for sure?"

Finn shrugged. "I've sent blood and tissue samples to the crime lab upstate to look for various toxins. It may be a few days before all the results come back."

"Let me know what you find. And I'm saying that in my official capacity."

Great. Another reason he was trapped here in town with Rachel. Part of him was secretly thrilled, and part of him hovered between dismay and disgust. Finn nodded unhappily as Wes muttered to himself. "Different M.O. than the Walsh murder…but, the second Walsh father figure…who'd want to see the head of the family dead?"

Finn had a bad feeling in his gut. First Walsh and now Warner. What was going on in Honey Creek?

Chapter 8

Rachel stared at herself critically in the mirror, remembering another night long ago standing in front of this mirror preparing carefully for prom. The butterflies in her stomach were the same, the nervous anticipation, the worry that she had put on too much makeup and then that she hadn't put on enough—all of it the same. Even the man on her mind was the same.

Finn. Just thinking his name made her sigh. Although she couldn't say exactly what the sigh meant. Maybe it was nostalgic, maybe wistful. Surely it didn't have anything to do with being love struck, though. She knew better. Right?

Twelve years ago, she'd piled her hair on top of her head in a mass of curls and worn a coronet of daisies. Tonight, she pulled it back into a loose French twist that was more sophisticated. More appropriate to her age. After all, she was thirty years old now—a mature woman. She snorted. *More like a desperate one settling unwillingly into spinsterhood.*

Her prom dress had been a frothy yellow affair with ruffles and bows. This gown, although yellow as well, was anything but little-girly. Edna had done a magnificent job on it. The pale yellow silk draped around her in a smooth sheath, melding with her skin and hair tones until it was barely there. Whisper light, it moved like water against her skin. The long skirt was slit practically to her hip, so its narrow, hourglass cut didn't impede her movement at all. She slipped on the gold and crystal strappy high heels that completed the ensemble. She wore no jewelry at all. The dress didn't need it.

The doorbell rang. That would be Carly, but Rachel couldn't help the moment of flashback as she remembered how excited she'd been the night of prom. She'd had a surprise for Finn. She'd decided she was ready to make love to him, and that night was the night. He'd been sweet and patient and never pushed her, but she knew he'd be thrilled to take their relationship to the next level.

Finn had even hinted that he might be asking her to wait for him while he went off to college, and he'd even not so subtly found out what her ring size was. Had he planned on asking her to marry him? Her heart had told her that was exactly what he had in mind. And the thought made her so happy she could barely contain the joy bursting out of her. She would graduate and join him in college, and then the two of them would start a new life far away from this tiny corner of nowhere. Ha. How terribly wrong she'd been.

She picked up the crystal-encrusted clutch that had come with the shoes and headed for the front door. She flung it open and Carly stepped inside.

"Oh my God!" Carly exclaimed. "You did it! You finally picked out an outfit all by yourself that I approve of!"

Rachel laughed. "You like it?"

"Like it? I love it! You look practically naked! Finn is not going to be able to take his eyes off you."

"That's not the point," she protested. But then her conscience kicked in. *Okay, so that is secretly exactly the point.*

"Regardless. Every man in the room's going to be drooling over you, girlfriend. *Hoo wee!* Honey Creek isn't going to know what hit it!"

"Carly, I'm not trying to look like a slut. Be honest. Do I look cheap?"

Carly answered with uncharacteristic seriousness. "Rachel, you look like a million bucks. Honest. I've never seen you look more beautiful or classy."

She hugged her cousin. "You look pretty terrific yourself."

Carly twirled in the black cocktail dress and the skirt flared out. "Like it?"

"Yeah. Expecially the part where you twirl and flash your panties at everyone."

Carly grinned. "Not wearing any."

They headed out the front door and Rachel looked up. "You're going commando?"

"I'm thonging it. Makes me feel daring and naughty. How 'bout you? Is there any room under that dress for lingerie?"

Rachel laughed across the top of Carly's red Mustang. "I could never go out in public without underwear."

"Chicken."

"Tart," Rachel retorted as she slipped into her seat.

Carly kept glancing over at her as they headed for the

high school. Finally, Rachel asked, "What's wrong with me? Do I have lipstick on my teeth?"

Carly laughed. "No. I'm just thinking about walking into that dance with you. This is going to be fun."

Tonight was going to suck rocks. Finn glared into the mirror as he tied his tie. No way to get out of it, though. The whole Colton clan was going to the dance. Even his younger brothers, Brand and Perry, were going to be there. Darius had decreed it. Only Damien had been excused from the edict to go. He didn't need to become a circus sideshow in front of the entire town. Not to mention Darius had always been so hellbent on Colton respectability. The old man surely wouldn't want to parade his ex-con son in front of everyone. The young doctor in the family, though—that was a different matter. Finn had a sneaking suspicion he'd be on display tonight like some kind of damned trophy.

He shrugged into his suit coat and tugged it into place. An image of prom night all those years ago flashed through his mind. He'd had an engagement ring in his pocket and had been positive that Rachel would say yes. Sure, they were young. But true love was true love. From the moment he'd first laid eyes on her in biology lab, he'd known. She was the One.

He supposed she'd be at the homecoming dance tonight. No reason for her not to be there. But he mentally cringed at the idea. Another dance. The high school gym. Him and Rachel. Both there. But thankfully, not together this time.

Yup, tonight was definitely going to suck.

When they got to the high school, Carly declared the parking lot not full enough for their grand entrance and took a lap around town before coming back to the dance.

Rachel's nerves, which were stretched thin already, didn't need the delay. As she glanced down at her gown's plunging neckline and the way her push-up bra all but dumped her out of the top of it, she began to think better of this getup. She'd been feeling unappreciated and defiant the day the dress had come in to the Goodwill store and she'd impulsively bought the thing. But maybe that hadn't been such a good idea. She had the black dress she'd worn to her father's funeral at home…

"I can't do it, Carly. Run me home fast, will you? You can drop me off and come back here while I change."

"Change? Whatever for?" Carly squawked.

"I'm chickening out."

"Oh, no you're not, young lady." The Mustang swung into the high school drive and Carly accelerated threateningly. "You're going into that dance just as you are even if I have to drag you in there by the hair."

Rachel grimaced. She knew her cousin well enough to take the threat seriously. "This is a bad idea."

"This is a great idea. It's high time Finn Colton realized what he's missing. And when he begs you to take him back, you take that stiletto heel of yours and stomp on his heart. You hear me?"

Rachel winced. She hadn't been exactly forthcoming with Carly about her recent encounters with Finn. Carly wasn't known for her ability to keep a secret, and Rachel really hadn't wanted to be the gossip topic of the whole town again. As it was, enough people were throwing her and Finn speculative looks that rumors had to be swirling behind her back.

"Want me to drop you off in front?" Carly asked.

"No!" Rachel blurted. She flashed back to standing under the porch outside the gym, waiting for Finn to park his truck. He'd been so handsome striding toward her in his tux she'd actually cried a little. He'd been wearing a strange expression as he'd joined her that night, but she had put it down to his nerves at proposing to her. She couldn't have been more wrong!

Carly shrugged and pulled into the parking lot. "There's one of the Colton trucks over there. I wonder how many of them showed up tonight."

"Oh, Lord. If you're trying to make me run screaming from this stupid dance, you're doing a great job."

"C'mon, Raych. Let's go show all those fuddy-duddies just how amazing we Grant women are." Carly linked an arm through hers and marched toward the gym in a fashion that gave Rachel no choice but to go along.

This was dumb. Really dumb. She was going to walk in there and cause a scandal she'd spend another fifteen years living down. What *had* she been thinking to choose this dress? The doorway loomed and two ridiculously young-looking teenaged boys reached for the double doors.

"I can't do this," Rachel wailed in a whisper.

The doors swung open before them.

"Too late," Carly announced cheerfully. "Smile."

What the heck. If she were going to go down in flames, she might as well pretend to enjoy the ride. Rachel pasted on a smile and stepped inside. The wash of memories that came over her was almost unbearable. A mirrored disco ball spun slowly above the dance floor, and she swore the exact same hand-painted banners and crepe paper streamers decorated the walls. Even the bunches of helium balloons were the same.

She glanced around the room and was shocked to realize that it did, indeed, appear that she had stopped the dance. Every face in the room was turning her way, with varying degrees of amazement and appreciation painted upon them all. She spied the cluster of Coltons in the corner but didn't see Finn among the broad-shouldered group.

Her stomach fell. But then relief kicked in.

"C'mon. Let's turn this town on its head," Carly murmured, dragging her forward into the room. They just about reached the mob of people dancing in the middle of the gym floor when Rachel felt a presence behind her.

She paused. Half turned. And stared.

Whoever said men didn't know how to make a grand entrance had obviously never seen Finn Colton walk into a room. In a tuxedo. With one hand carelessly in a pants pocket like an Italian model. Or a movie star.

He stopped just inside the door, much as she had. And likewise, every head in the place turned his way. But then his gaze locked on her, and everything and everyone else in the room faded away. His gaze traveled slowly down her body to her toes and all the way back up to her face. It was hard to see his eyes in the dim half-light, but the expression on his face came darn near to open lust.

Carly cackled beside her. "Take that, Finn Colton! Now go for the kill, cuz."

"Uhh, how exactly do I do that?" Rachel mumbled back. Not only was her entire face on fire, but it felt like her neck, shoulders and arms were blushing, too.

"Easy. Flirt with him like crazy. Then leave with another guy. He'll never live it down."

"Another guy?" Rachel squeaked. "I don't do that sort of thing. My reputation would be ruined—"

"Like it's not already?" Carly shot back.

Her cousin's flippant remark stopped her cold. Sometimes she forgot what everyone else in town thought of her. She supposed they must be right if they all still believed she was a coldhearted heartbreaker after all these years.

After all, she had managed to drive Finn away from her even though he'd been crazy about her.

Rachel's gaze slid in his direction whether she willed it to or not. He had just reached his family and turned. And, oh Lordy, he was looking back at her, a tea cup of punch paused halfway to his mouth. She tore her gaze away from him hoping desperately that the move looked casual. Disinterested.

"Wow!" A male voice exclaimed from nearby. "You two look hot!"

Rachel glanced over at a cluster of young men who didn't look to be much older than college age. As a group, they were big and burly. Had to be some of the recent football players back in town for Coach Meyer's last hurrah.

Carly purred and preened as several of them came over to introduce themselves. Rachel nodded and smiled but couldn't have repeated any of their names if her life depended on it. One of them offered to go get her a drink and she nodded numbly.

A disk jockey was on a platform at one end of the gym spinning a combination of old and new music, most of it with a good dance beat. Back in the day, Rachel had loved to dance. The last time she'd danced in this room, Finn had held her in his arms…and called her the worst kind of human being. Loudly. In front of everyone. And then he'd walked out on her and left her standing in the middle of the dance floor with the whole school staring at her. And then, as she'd stumbled off the floor in a flood of tears that nearly blinded her, they'd laughed at her.

"Here's your punch," one of the nameless college students announced cheerfully. "We spiked it for you, seeing as how you're of legal drinking age."

She smiled ruefully. "Do I look that old?"

The young men laughed. "You look fantastic," one of

them retorted. It was gratifying when the others nodded vigorously in agreement.

"You guys are good for a girl's ego," she teased.

"Wanna dance?" one of them asked.

"Will you tell me if I look dopey? It has been a while since I've done it."

"I'll teach you all the latest moves," the one who'd brought her the punch promised.

"You wish," a smooth, deep voice muttered from behind her.

Rachel turned fast and nearly killed herself as she pivoted on the tall heels in her narrow skirt and proceeded to lose her balance. Strong hands caught her and steadied her. Hands whose touch thrilled her to the marrow of her bones.

She murmured to Finn, "It's not nice to sneak up on someone from behind and startle them."

"Sorry."

"Hey, buddy. She and I were just going out for a dance," the college student complained.

Finn sent the kid a quelling look that had the student slinking away in a moment.

"Finn! I was going to dance with him and you just chased him away!"

"He's too young for you."

She stood up to her full, heel-enhanced height. It still was only enough to bring her up to approximately his chin. "Are you calling me old?"

"No. I'm calling you a gorgeous woman in her prime, and he's a snot-nosed kid who wouldn't have the slightest idea what to do with a woman like you."

"Oh, and you do?" Rachel couldn't help retorting.

Finn's gaze went dark and lazy and smoky. "Yeah, I do."

She actually took a step back from all that sexual intensity rolling off of him. "It just so happens that that boy promised to teach me some new dance moves. And I plan to take him up on the offer."

Finn stepped closer and murmured, "Over my dead body. I'm not letting anyone else—boy or man—lay a hand on you, with you looking like that."

Rachel glanced down at her gown in surprise. Everything was where it was supposed to be. "What's wrong with my dress?" she asked defensively.

"Nothing. You look sensational. And that's the problem."

She gazed up at him steadily. Despite Carly's advice to stomp on his heart, she spoke gently. "You're not in any position to dictate who I do or don't dance with, Finn. I don't belong to you."

His jaw rippled and frustration glinted in his eyes.

She continued lightly, "In fact, you made that crystal clear to me in this very room. Or don't you remember?"

"I remember it perfectly well," he gritted out from between clenched teeth.

She nodded and smiled politely at him. "If you'll excuse me, then, I'm going to go collect my dance lesson."

It was hard—really, really hard—but she turned away from Finn and strolled across the room to where the college gang had congregated near the hors d'oeuvre table. And that was how she ended up spending the next hour dancing with a series of college students ten years her junior while Finn furiously avoided looking in her direction. Her heart broke a little every time she spied him across the gym with his back stubbornly turned to her.

The whole Colton clan had come to the dance, with one exception. There was no sign of Damien. Too bad. He was her favorite of the lot of them. But she could see how he might not like a gathering like this, where he might very well become a spectacle. Oh, wait. That was her job.

Another hour later, Rachel was running out of steam at keeping up the charade of enjoying herself. Were it not for the fact that Carly was her ride home, she'd have left already.

As if she wasn't miserable enough, the DJ got the bright idea to ask for all the former homecoming kings and queens to come out onto the dance floor for a spotlight dance. Rachel moved to the side of the room along with everyone else, relieved to get a moment to herself to hide in the shadows.

Then the cursed DJ announced, "Okay, kings and queens. Look around the room. If your date from homecoming is here, go get them and bring them out onto the dance floor. Don't worry spouses...you get the next dance."

Amid the laughter, Rachel's gaze snapped to Finn in horror. He'd been the homecoming king his senior year. And *she'd* been his date. She shrank back behind the biggest of the college students and did her best to fade into the wall. But it was no good. Finn, grim faced and tight jawed, was looking around the room for her.

She swore under her breath as he strode purposefully in her direction. He'd spotted her. In seconds he loomed in front of her. Rachel dimly noted silence falling nearby as locals watched with avid interest to see what happened next between the two of them.

"Well?" Finn muttered, looming in front of her. "Are you going to dance with me or not?"

Chapter 9

Finn was appalled by the look of horror on Rachel's face. Did she despise him so much? He'd thought they had something between them. Had felt it. But she looked as if she'd rather face a firing squad than dance with him.

"C'mon," he said. "People are starting to notice your hesitation. Let's just do this and get it over with."

She squared her bare, slender shoulders…which he'd give a year's salary to kiss right now. Damn, she looked incredible in that gown. She'd been wearing yellow the night of prom, too. It had suited her sunny personality. He'd never believed it possible that she would betray him so completely like she had. He'd loved her, for God's sake. Been sure she felt the same way about him. How could she have cheated on him with some other guy? And then, as if that wasn't bad enough—

"All right. Fine. Let's just get this over with." Rachel stepped forward resolutely.

He held out his forearm to her automatically and led her onto the floor.

The flood of memories was overwhelming. High school dances with her. Looking up into the stands at football games and wanting to play his best for her. Meeting her in the hallway between classes to steal a quick kiss and put a fiery blush on her cheeks. God, the laughter. She'd made him so damned happy. They'd been the two halves of a whole. When he was down, she'd cheer him up. When she was upset about something, she came to him to make it right. And he always did. They'd been magic.

The music wailed around them and she swayed in his arms, bringing back another entire flood of memories. Imagined mostly, but vivid nonetheless of what it would be like to finally make love with her, to become one body and one soul for real. He'd thought about it a lot when they'd been dating but had never pushed. After all, they'd had all the time in the world. The rest of their lives together. No matter how bad he'd wanted to be with her, she was worth the wait.

And then that last night had happened. That last dance. Images came rushing back unbidden, a bitter dessert that ruined the rest of the meal of memories and left a terrible taste in his mouth. His hurt. His disbelief. And ultimately his fury. He must have tensed because Rachel murmured, "Never fear. It will be over soon."

"You don't have to make it sound like I'm torturing you," he muttered back.

"You have no idea," she retorted.

He frowned down at her and words sprang from his lips before he could think better of them. "You could do a whole lot worse than me, you know."

Her gaze snapped up to his. "Is that an offer?"

"I—uhh—" Her question took him completely by surprise. His mind went blank. Was it an offer?

"Please don't hold me so close," she murmured through a patently plastic smile.

He loosened his arms fractionally. "Why? Do I make you uncomfortable? Remind you of how things used to be between us?"

Her light brown eyes went dark. Troubled. "You can't have it both ways, Finn. You can't flirt with me and try to get into my bed while you continue to throw the past in my face."

That made him pull back. Sharply. "I'm not trying to have it both ways. I'm here for a few weeks to welcome my brother home and then I'm leaving again. And in the meantime, I figured we might as well act civilized with each other."

"Is that what the other night in my living room was? Civilized?"

Ah-ha. So their kiss had had as big an effect on her as it had on him! He studied her closely. "I'm not sure that's the word I'd use to describe it, but it wasn't bad, was it?"

"I think I'd better not answer that question."

He glanced up and wasn't surprised to see that they were the center of attention. And then he spied his family. His brothers mostly just looked concerned. Maisie looked about ready to march out here and commit murder. But it was his father's expression that stopped him in his tracks. The man looked nearly apoplectic. Of course, Maisie and his father knew the whole story of what Rachel had done to him. They were the only ones who did. He'd made them swear fifteen years ago never to tell a soul what they'd learned about Rachel. He might have hated her for her betrayal, but he'd still loved her enough not to want to see her reputation publicly dragged through the mud. To his knowledge, neither of them had ever broken their promise.

But they were a stark reminder of just how treacherous a woman Rachel Grant truly was. Her right hand rested on his shoulder, and her left hand rested lightly on his waist. Where a moment ago her touch had felt like heaven, all of a sudden, her arms felt like a spider's web, sucking him in, luring him into her trap. Again. All the old hurt and betrayal flared up anew. She'd ruined all his dreams for the two of them. And damn her, she seemed to have ruined him for any other woman.

In all the years since he'd left Honey Creek, he'd never been able to trust another woman enough to give away his heart. What if someone else hurt him like she had? He didn't think he could stand it a second time.

They had finished another slow revolution and his family was about to come into sight again. His family, who'd stood by him when he'd wanted to turn down his college scholarship and just run away from Rachel, who'd kept him from falling into a bottle to drown his sorrows. The Coltons might have their problems, but at least they'd stuck by him when his life had fallen completely apart. Or, more accurately, when Rachel Grant had blown it completely apart.

He was being torn in two. And it was killing him.

"You're right," he announced abruptly. "I can't have it both ways. And I don't want it both ways." His arms fell away from her. "I'll never forget or forgive what you did to me, Rachel. No pretty dress or demure charm or injured dog is going change that. I can't do this anymore."

He pivoted on his heel and strode off the dance floor. He headed for the door and some cool air outside. He felt like she'd stuck a knife in his chest all over again. He'd known coming to this dance was a bad idea. That it would dredge up too many old memories and open up too many old wounds.

He burst outside into humid night air that clung heavily to his skin. He tore off his tie and shrugged out of his jacket, but he still felt like he was about to suffocate. He had to get away from there. From her. Far, far away. He'd head back to Bozeman this very minute were it not for Craig Warner lying near death in the hospital. Damn him.

But he could get away from Rachel. He fished the keys out of his pocket and marched into the parking lot. He climbed in his truck, hit the gas and peeled out of the parking lot as fast as he could.

Rachel stood in the door of the gym, tears flowing down her face, and watched him go—again. And he never looked back—again.

"Oh my God. I can't believe he did that to you!" Carly exclaimed. "Let's go to his house and trash his truck."

Her cousin's arm went around her waist; but like the last time Finn had humiliated her and abandoned her in this very spot, Rachel dared not accept the comfort. If she did, she would shatter into a million pieces. She had to hold it together until she could get out of there. Go somewhere far away by herself. And hide. And cry. And if she were lucky, she wouldn't get to the raving and screaming part until she was safely alone.

"Take me home, Carly," she ground out.

"I don't think you should be alone right now. Besides, I think you should go back in there and show them all that he doesn't—"

"No!" She cut off her cousin sharply.

"Rachel. Do you still have a thing for him? After everything he's done to you? Are you nuts?"

"No!" she snapped a second time. "Of course I don't

have a thing for him. I know better than to want Finn Colton. He's poison."

But a poison she was addicted to as surely as she was standing here.

"C'mon, Raych. We'll go to your place, open up a bottle of wine, and drink to what bastards men are!"

"No, thanks. Just take me home," she replied tiredly.

"You sure?"

Sympathy was something she couldn't handle right now. Carly's concern was threatening to break down her last remaining ounce of strength. "Let's just go."

It took determined effort on her part; but when they got to her place, Rachel managed to send Carly on her way without the threatened bottle of wine and man-bashing session.

Finally alone, she hung up the disastrous yellow gown carefully in her closet—no sense taking out her grief and anger on a dress, and besides, she could probably sell it for a little money in Bozeman. She checked in on Brownie, who looked alarmed and licked her hand in concern. Intuitive creatures, dogs.

"Don't worry about me, boy. You just get better. At least you're on the mend. I got one thing right this week at any rate."

The dog whimpered quietly as if mirroring her distress.

She lay down in her bed but felt numb. She paced her bedroom for a while and experienced alternating bouts of grief and humiliation. She kept waiting for the storm of tears, but it wouldn't come. Shockingly, what finally came was not self-pity at all. It was anger. She was even forced to move her pacing to the living room where she could work up a good head of steam.

She could not believe he'd done it to her again. He'd

walked out on her in front of the whole town and left her standing all alone in the middle of the dance floor again. She supposed she ought to be grateful that this time he hadn't reamed her out before turning on his heel and marching away from her. But it was hard to work up much gratitude for that. Her current frame of mind hovered closer to homicidal.

She was a grown woman. She lived a decent life. She was a nice person. There was no reason for her to put up with anyone treating her like this. She'd pack up her things and leave this two-bit town tomorrow were it not for her mother. As soon as Mom passed away, she was out of here forever.

But the moment the thought entered her mind, she shoved it away in dismay. She loved her mother. No reason to wish for her mom's death out of her own selfish anger.

How dare Finn act like that? She hadn't asked him to come back to town. To come to her house and kiss her and make her think they might actually have a chance. He had no right to play with her heart like this!

Who was he to judge her anyway? Just because he was a Colton didn't give him the right to treat other people like dirt. And especially when he couldn't even be bothered to tell them what they'd done to deserve it!

Why had he walked out on her tonight? She went over and over what they'd said; and while she'd called him on his mixed messages, that wasn't the sort of thing that made a person storm out of a room like he had.

And speaking of storming out of gyms, she was sick and tired of him accusing her of all sorts of bad things but refusing to tell her exactly what those bad things were. The guy had owed her an explanation for fifteen years and never had bothered to give it to her. After this latest fiasco, she expected it would be at least fifteen more years before he bothered to show his face around this town again. And by God, after waiting that long already, she wasn't about to wait that long again for some answers!

She was going to go out to that cursed ranch and demand some explanations once and for all. She had grabbed her car keys and stepped out onto the back porch before it dawned on her that it was three o'clock in the morning. Okay, fine. She'd go out there and demand answers when daylight broke.

But when daylight came, she was passed out across her bed, sleeping off the exhaustion and emotional rollercoaster of the night before. It was close to noon before she woke up, and were it not for Brownie whimpering to go out, she might have slept longer.

She stumbled into the kitchen and opened the back door for the dog. A wave of muggy warmth hit her in the face. Indian Summer was late this year. The air was turbulent, and ominous clouds were already building in the west. Looked like a storm brewing. Perfect weather to fit her mood.

Grimly, she fed the dog and moved his bed out to the back porch so he could enjoy the day's unseasonable warmth. She dressed in jeans and a T-shirt, stomped into a pair of cowboy boots and threw on a little makeup for confidence. Her eyes snapping and her cheeks unnaturally ruddy, she headed for the Colton ranch and a showdown with Finn. If she'd owned a six-shooter gun, she'd have strapped it onto her hip in her current state of mind.

Her bravado wavered as she turned into the Colton drive and passed under the big arch, but she took a deep breath and wrapped her righteous indignation more closely around herself. She drove around to the back of the main house.

She knocked on the back door.

No one answered. Cursing under her breath, she knocked again. Still nothing. She looked around for any sign of humans and noticed a barn door open up the hill. She headed for it. She was not leaving this place until she found out what in the hell was going on.

What in the hell was going on? Finn stared down at Craig Warner's latest blood work in dismay. The cell salts had been working. The guy was getting better. He'd even kept a little food down last night. And then this morning he had crashed worse than ever. His heart had stopped an hour ago, occasioning the call from the E.R. asking him to come in to the hospital to watch Warner so the on-call doctor could cover the emergency room.

"Get me a list of everything he ingested last night," he told the nurse hovering beside him.

"Already got it," the woman replied grimly.

Obviously, her thoughts were running in the same direction his were. He smiled his appreciation for her efficiency and took the sheet of paper she thrust at him. Four ounces of chicken broth. Five saltines. Two ounces of strawberry gelatin. Seven ounces of apple juice. Nothing there to explain Warner's cardiac arrest and respiratory distress.

"Double the cell salts," he told the nurse quietly.

"You already have him on a pretty high dosage."

"He'll die if we don't do something."

"Yes, sir."

He jammed a hand through his hair in frustration. What was he missing?

Missing? That would be Rachel.

Oh, for God's sake. He was not missing her. He'd done the right thing. Protected himself from another disaster at her hands. If they had gotten together, how long would it be this time before she turned to someone else? Before she broke his heart for good?

Rachel paused in the dim doorway of the barn while her eyes adjusted. Down the broad alley she saw a big, male figure enter a stall. She marched toward him, battle ready.

She got to the stall and looked inside. A man squatted in the corner, holding a bottle for a red-and-white calf who was noisily and messily drinking from it. He glanced up. *Damien.* Disappointment coursed through her.

"Hey, Rachel. What brings you out here? Looking for Finn?"

"Looking for answers," she replied grimly. "And Finn's the one who can give them to me, yes."

"He's not here. He got called to the hospital a while ago. Craig Warner had a setback, apparently."

"Oh. Too bad. He's a nice man."

Damien shrugged.

"Well, I'll be going, then."

"Before you leave, could you pass me that second bottle and the bucket on the floor beside the door?"

She looked down at her feet at a mash that looked like cracked-wheat cereal in a bucket. "Sure." She picked up bottle and bucket and opened the stall door. She eyed the momma cow warily. "She going to be okay with me?"

Damien glanced up at the gigantic creature casually. "Yep, she's pretty mellow for a first-time mom."

Despite his assurances, Rachel still gave the cow wide berth as she moved slowly across the stall to Damien's side. "What's the mash for?"

"Trying to get this little fella to start eating some solid food."

She gave the calf a critical glance. "He looks a little young for that."

Damien shrugged. "His mother's not making enough milk. Probably the weird time of year he was born. Mother Nature is telling her to preserve energy to get through the winter herself, and she can't spare much for junior. I'm bottle-feeding him until I can get him eating solid food, and the sooner I can do that, the better for his health."

She watched as the calf butted at the nearly empty bottle. "He's a cutie. Looks like he's playing you to get you to give him more milk."

"Animals are honest. They don't play games with you."

Rachel snorted and the cow flung her head up in alarm. "Sorry, momma," she murmured.

"Who's playing games with you?" Damien asked quietly.

"Your brother."

"Finn? That's never been his style. 'Course, I've been gone a long time, and maybe he's changed."

Rachel replied bitterly, "He did the same thing to me fifteen years ago. He hasn't changed his stripes at all."

Damien took the bottle away from the calf—much to its displeasure—and substituted his fingers, dipped in the mash, in the calf's mouth instead. The little guy sucked for a moment but then spit out Damien's fingers in disgust.

Rachel smiled. Damien patiently repeated dipping his fingers in the mash and putting them in the calf's mouth. "You're good with animals," she commented.

He shrugged. "Finn's the one with real magic where animals are concerned. Too bad he never followed his dream to become a vet. He'd have been a great one."

"At least animals would've forced him to be honest with them."

Damien glanced over at her. "You need me to beat him up for you?"

Startled, she looked at him full on. Humor glinted in his eyes. "No, but I'd sure as hell like you to tell me what happened fifteen years ago that turned him against me so suddenly and completely."

Damien blinked, startled. She swore that was guilty knowledge flashing in his gaze before he looked away, busying himself with feeding the calf.

"You know, don't you?" she accused.

He offered the calf the bottle once more and the hungry baby latched on, sucking eagerly. At length, he looked up at her grimly. "Yeah, I know what happened."

Chapter 10

Finn turned at the sound of a male voice calling his name. Wes. "Hey, bro. What brings the sheriff to the hospital on a Sunday morning?"

"How's your patient?"

Finn shrugged. "Had a setback between last night and this morning. Crashed on us about two hours ago. It was a near thing to get his ticker going again."

Wes lowered his voice. "Any idea what caused the crisis?"

Finn frowned. "No. He even was able to eat a little last night. We've tested for food allergies, and nothing he ate should've caused him to nearly die on us this morning. His blood stats are as bad as they ever were, too."

Wes lowered his voice even more. "Who was with him last night? Particularly at or near the time he was eating?"

Finn blinked. "You think one of the Walshes is trying to poison him? A business associate?"

Wes shrugged. "I need a nurse to pull the visitor logs and see who visited Craig last night. Can you arrange that?"

"Yeah, sure," Finn replied, startled. Wes wasn't kidding. He seriously seemed to think one of the Walshes might have poisoned Craig. Why on Earth would one of them do that? Craig was practically a member of the family. He and Jolene were obviously deeply in love, and her kids treated him like a father.

Wes murmured, "Are those blood tests we talked about back yet?"

"Yeah." Finn grimaced. The results weren't going to please his brother.

"And?"

"His arsenic levels are through the roof," Finn said quietly. Wes stared, and Finn continued, "I've ordered another round of tests to determine if his body has been storing up too much of it for a very long time for some reason, or if he has recently ingested massive quantities of the chemical—either by accident or foul play." As his brother's frown deepened, Finn reminded Wes, "It's possible he was exposed through some natural source, like a tainted water source at his home."

"But not damned likely," Wes muttered grimly.

"No. Not likely," Finn agreed. "I'll let you know what the tests show. The tox panel should be back in a day or two."

"Ever heard of an outfit called Hidden Pines Holding Company?" Wes asked abruptly.

"No. Should I have?"

"No." Wes shrugged. "I'm working on a subpoena to get the state of California to release the names of the company's officers to me. In the meantime, if you happen to overhear any of the Walshes mention it while they're hanging around here, let me know, okay?"

Finn frowned. "You want me to spy on a patient's family?"

"I want you to assist me in a murder investigation and a possible attempted murder investigation."

"I don't think there's anything in the Hippocratic oath to prevent me from doing that." Finn sighed heavily. "All right. I'll do it."

Rachel followed Damien out of the stall like a burr stuck to his back. No way was he getting away from her without spilling his guts. He went to a work area and rinsed out the bottles and bucket, and she waited nearby. Finally, he turned to face her.

"Why are you asking me about all this?" he murmured. "You know what happened as well as I do."

"All I know is that the boy I was crazy in love with turned on me for no reason, dumped me, humiliated me, and didn't come back to town for fifteen years. And I never found out why."

Damien blurted, "The abortion, of course."

Rachel stared. "What abortion?"

"Your abortion."

"What?" Her mind was a complete blank. What on Earth was he talking about? "You mean me? An abortion? I've never been pregnant, let alone had an abortion. Who are you talking about?"

Damien frowned. "I was there. I heard it all."

"Heard what? Tell me what happened, Damien." An awful suspicion was taking root in her head.

He exhaled hard. "It was the night of Finn's senior prom. I was just coming into the kitchen when Maisie told Finn about it. She saw you in Bozeman at an abortion clinic.

You were terribly upset. She went in and told them she was your friend who'd come up to be with you. They said you were in having the procedure done, but she could wait for you. She didn't stick around."

"And then she told Finn I'd had an abortion?"

"Yeah."

Rachel didn't know whether to laugh or cry. "Good God, Damien. I was still a virgin the night of prom. I couldn't possibly have had an abortion."

Damien frowned. "Maisie took a picture of you there in the clinic with the snazzy digital camera she'd bought that day. She showed it to Finn."

Rachel frowned. How could that be? She thought back to the spring of her sophomore year in high school. That was right about when her mother was first diagnosed with Alzheimer's. Her mom had only been in her mid-forties and the diagnosis had taken the doctors a while to make. They'd told the family that early-onset Alzheimer's had a tendency to be inherited and had offered Rachel genetic testing—

And then it clicked in her mind.

"Of course. That must have been the day we went to the pregnancy counseling center in Bozeman to get me genetically tested for early-onset Alzhemier's. My mother has that, you know. I had a fifty percent chance of having it, too. And I wanted to know…for my own peace of mind and because of Finn…didn't want to saddle him with me if I was going to lose my memory young…but I don't have the gene and everything was okay…" She trailed off.

Damien stared at her. "So there was no abortion?"

"No."

Eventually he murmured, "Accused of something you didn't do. Been there, done that. It sucks."

"Ya think?" she retorted. Panic was starting to build

somewhere deep inside her. Finn had believed all these years that she'd had an abortion? And then the other shoe dropped in her mind. She and Finn had never slept together. They'd agreed to wait until she felt ready. But if he thought she'd had an abortion, he also thought she'd slept with some other guy!

"How could he think that of me?" she exclaimed.

Damien shrugged. "If a woman were carrying my baby and got rid of it without even talking to me, I'd be pretty pissed off."

No kidding. "Not to mention he thinks I slept with someone else. I loved him with every bit of my being. I was dead sure he was my soul mate! Heck, I told him so over and over. How could he possibly think I would have betrayed him?"

"You'd have to ask him that."

Her gaze narrowed. "I will. He's at the hospital?"

"Yeah," Damien answered cautiously. "Should I call him and warn him you're coming down to kill him?"

"Nah," she retorted sarcastically. "It'll be more fun if I surprise him when I do the deed." She spun and headed for the exit with long, angry strides.

Finn frowned at his cell phone as he put it away. That had been a rather strange phone call from Damien. His brother had mentioned in a weird enough tone of voice that Rachel was coming over to the hospital to talk to him that it almost sounded like a warning. And then Damien had dropped that random comment about listening to people with an open mind. What the hell had that been all about?

As if that wasn't enough, Damien had ended the phone call with some cryptic remark about how he felt a storm coming. A big one. Had the guy been talking about the weather or Rachel? Finn couldn't tell.

He glanced out the window. The sunny day had gone an ominous color outside. He stepped closer to the glass to peer out. Thunder clouds roiled on the horizon, black and menacing. They blocked enough sunlight that the day had taken on a premature twilight cast, but not the cast indicating the serene ending of a day sinking into night. Rather, this greenish twilight presaged violence. Chaos. Storms, indeed.

Everything was big in Montana, including the weather. And it did, indeed, appear that they were in for a severe late-season thunderstorm. He went over to the nurse's station. "If we lose power, I'll need you to check Mr. Warner's ventilator immediately to make sure it switched to the backup power source."

The nurse glanced toward the windows across the waiting area and nodded. "Looks like we're in for a bad one."

Rachel was furious and growing more so by the second. She kept having to take her foot off the accelerator as her speed crept up again and again on her way down the mountain. Oh, yes. She was going to kill Finn. Slowly. And painfully.

The sky overhead grew darker and darker until she was forced to turn on her headlights to see the road. Bizarre. It was still late afternoon. She glanced up at the sky and gasped at the ugly mass of clouds overhead. It was a sickly counterclockwise swirl of purple and yellow, like a spinning bruise. Not good. Her gut told her to get down off this mountain fast and seek shelter before the full fury of this storm broke. As the road straightened out close to town, she stepped on the accelerator. Trash blew in front of her as the sky grew even darker and more ominous. Branches whipped and the trees swayed, groaning, as she entered Honey Creek. People scurried here and there, securing awnings and bringing in outdoor furniture. Leave it to Montana to have snow and then turn around a few days later and have a violent springlike thunderstorm in October.

She parked in the hospital parking lot and ran for the building. It wasn't raining, but the wind was lashing her hair against her face so hard it stung. She ducked into the front lobby. The relative calm was a relief after the violence of the coming storm. She headed for the ICU, where she was bound to find Craig…and Finn.

Finn was at Craig's bedside when she arrived, and she spotted him through the glass wall immediately. Glaring daggers at him, she parked herself next to the nurse's station to wait for him. One of the nurse's cell phones rang behind her.

Then the nurse announced, "My husband says they just issued a tornado warning for Honey Creek. Somebody turn on the local news."

The low drone of the television mounted high in the corner of the waiting area was turned up and tuned in to a Bozeman television station. The meteorologist was speaking with contained urgency: "…take cover immediately. Doppler radar indicates rotation in this cloud five miles west of Honey Creek. A weather watcher reports seeing a funnel cloud forming moments ago. Even if a tornado does not fully form, residents of Honey Creek should expect damaging wind gusts of up to seventy miles per hour and tennis ball-sized hail. The storm is moving east at fifty miles per hour and should reach Honey Creek in the next five to seven minutes. Residents are urged to take cover inside a sturdy building and stay away from windows and doors."

Rachel glanced outside in alarm. The daylight had taken on a strange, green-yellow cast she'd never seen before. A phone rang behind her, and a few seconds later a nurse announced, "All nonessential personnel are to take shelter in the basement."

A nurse beside Rachel grunted. "We're all essential personnel."

Finn's voice spoke up from behind her. "Rachel. What are you doing here? You need to get out of here. Head home and take cover."

"I don't think there's time for that, Dr. Colton," the nurse beside her replied. "Look."

Rachel looked where the woman pointed outside and gasped in dismay. A thick column of spinning cloud snaked down toward the ground no more than a mile away. That window faced west. The storm was moving east. Crap. That tornado was coming straight at them.

Finn ordered sharply, "Get Mr. Warner ready to move. Get all the ambulatory patients down to the basement. Get the nonmobile patients away from the windows and into an interior hall. Cover them with blankets so they don't get hit by flying glass. Move!"

Rachel ran after the nearest nurse. "What can I do to help?"

"Take these blankets. Wrap the patients in rooms two and four in them and pull their beds out into the hall. Hurry!"

Rachel took the pile of blankets the woman thrust at her and scrambled to do as ordered. One of the patients was either sedated or unconscious and wasn't difficult to wrap up and roll out into the hall. But the other patient, an elderly woman, didn't seem to understand what was happening and kept pulling the blanket off herself. Rachel dragged the heavy hospital bed out into the hall.

The lights flickered and went out and the hall plunged into darkness. Only the faintest light came from the window in the waiting area down the hall. An emergency floodlight came on somewhere in the other direction, sending enough light toward them to see, but not much more.

"Rachel, get the hell out of here!" Finn snapped as he helped her drag the bed across the hall.

"Too late. The storm's almost here, and you guys need the extra hands."

She darted off to help a swearing nurse who was having trouble getting a bed through a door. They wrestled the bed into the hallway and tucked blankets over the frightened man's head.

Rachel noticed Jolene Walsh farther down the hallway tucking more blankets around Craig Warner with all the tender concern of a mother for a child—or a woman for her lover. No doubt about it. Those two were in love. *Good for them.*

She took a step toward Jolene to help her, but then she heard it. A roaring, tearing sound. Huh. The twister really did sound like a freight train. Coming down a set of tracks straight at her at high speed. She glanced out a window as she ran past an open door and gasped. The entire window was filled with a whirling mass of debris, barely on the other side of the hospital parking lot. Shocked into frozen awe, she stared at the monster coming for her.

And then something big and hard and heavy slammed into her.

"Get moving," Finn barked. "Come with me." He dragged her along by the arm until she started to run under her own power. They raced behind the nurse's station and he shoved her down under the tall desk that formed the front of the station.

He wrapped his arms around her as she spread the last blanket she had around them. He grabbed one end of it and tucked it beneath his hip. The other end he wrapped tightly around them both and over their heads. It was hot and stuffy under the blanket. This was surreal. She was not about to face death, not with Finn Colton's arms tight around her and his cheek pressed against her hair.

"Are we going to die?" she asked blankly.

"Not if I can help it!" he shouted over the roaring wind. "Hang on to me with all your strength!"

That was not a hard command to follow. Her terror was beyond anything she'd ever experienced. But then, as glass shattered nearby, a strange thing happened to her. A calm came over her at all odds with the violence erupting around them. If this were it, so be it. Living or dying was out of her control now. It was up to Fate or God or whatever force controlled such things in the universe. And in the meantime, she couldn't think of another person in the whole world she'd rather spend her last few moments on Earth with.

She might be furious with Finn for believing the worst of her and never giving her a chance to defend herself, but as debris struck her back through the blanket and Finn wrapped his entire body around her protectively, a single stark fact came into crystal-clear focus. She loved Finn Colton. No matter what he'd done in the past. Against all reason, against her better judgment—heck, against her burning desire not to do so—she loved him.

The roaring got louder and the building shook around her. More glass shattered and the wind shrieked its fury, yanking at her with a violence that was stunning. Her eardrums felt like someone was trying to suck them out of her head. She pressed her right ear against Finn's chest and hung on for dear life as the tornado did its damnedest to tear them apart. And wasn't that just the story of their lives? Everyone and everything around them trying to keep them from each other.

Finn squeezed her suffocatingly tight against his chest. All hell broke loose then. Crashes and ripping sounds joined the banshee wail of the tornado as the hospital was literally torn apart around them. The screams of the wind were so fierce she thought the sound alone might kill them. The blanket tore away from them. She clung to Finn with all her strength in the madness, as desks and chairs and computer monitors flew past.

Something hit Finn's shoulder and he grunted in pain. She'd have spoken to ask him if he were okay, but all the air had been sucked out of her lungs. She tried as hard as she could to pull in a breath, but she couldn't manage it. She couldn't breathe! Panic hit her. She started to struggle, but Finn's crushing embrace held her still. Something about him conveyed an assurance that he would take care of her. That she would be all right. That he was in control of this madness and would see her through it safely. Her heart opened even more as the love she'd held at bay all these years flooded through her.

All in all, it wasn't a bad way to die. In the arms of the one man she'd ever loved wholly and without reservation.

The moment passed and she dragged in a lungful of air. The noise was still horrific, but mostly paper, leaves and light debris were flying around now. And then even that settled. The roaring faded as the tornado passed, and a strange stillness settled around them. And then, as quickly as the silence had come, it shattered with nurses yelling for help and doctors yelling back instructions and patients moaning and crying. Someone screamed, but the noise cut off abruptly.

Finn looked down at her like he was as surprised as she was that they were still alive. "You okay?"

"Shockingly, yes. You? Something hit you."

"It was nothing. I've taken worse hits in a football game." He looked around them and then back to her. "Gotta go do the doctor thing now."

"We need to talk—" she started.

Finn jumped to his feet and held a hand down for her. For an instant his gaze met hers, naked and unguarded, and maybe a touch shell-shocked. The tornado had been a profound moment for him, too, apparently. "Later," he bit out. "I think I'm going to be busy for a while."

She took one look down the hallway at the mess and knew that for the understatement of the century that it was. She prayed that the residents of Honey Creek had heeded the tornado warnings and taken cover and that no one had been seriously hurt or killed. But if the destruction here was any indication, the town probably wouldn't be so lucky.

She pulled out her cell phone, but it had no signal. The tornado must've wiped out the cell phone towers. Scouring the corners beneath a blizzard of paper, she spotted a desk phone and plugged its cord into an outlet she found low on a wall where a desk used to stand. Miraculously, the thing still worked. Quickly, she dialed the nursing home. It was on the other side of town. She hoped it had been completely out of the path of the twister.

"Hello?" someone answered in a completely distracted voice.

"Hi, this is Rachel Grant. I'm just calling to check on my mother. Are you folks okay?"

"Yes, we're fine. We hear the hospital got hit, though."

"It did. I'm there now. The building's standing, but there's a lot of damage and debris inside."

"Well, we've got our hands full over here calming down the residents and assessing the damage."

Rachel wished the woman luck and hung up, so relieved she was faintly ill. She stumbled into the hallway and asked the first nurse she saw what she could do to help. For the next hour she moved robotlike through the motions of helping to clean up the worst of the debris and helping see to the most immediate nonmedical needs of the patients. Carrying her telephone from room to room, she made a number of phone calls for patients so they could reassure their families.

All the while, she felt like she was wading through syrup. Maybe was in a little shock. But then, she'd just lived through a tornado, both the physical and emotional kinds.

Eventually, a horde of medics and firemen, volunteers from several nearby towns, descended upon the hospital and her services were no longer needed. Someone suggested she go home and get some rest and make sure her place was okay. And that was when memory of leaving Brownie out on the back porch broke over her in a wash of horror.

She raced outside into the parking lot and stared in dismay at the flattened remains of her car. It was upside down on its roof and stood no more than two feet tall. No time to stand around mourning the remains of her little clunker, though. She had to get home. Make sure Brownie was okay. She took off jogging toward her place, but even that was a slow proposition as she dodged fallen trees and a variety of mangled debris ranging from entire trees to furniture to giant slabs of roof.

The swath of destruction was neither long nor wide, but within it, the mess was breathtaking. She supposed people would say Honey Creek had been lucky, but it was hard to believe as she wended her way home through the main path of the storm.

She turned onto her street and breathed a massive sigh of relief to see that her house was still standing. A tree in the next door neighbor's yard had fallen over and lay mostly in her backyard, and trash littered her front lawn. It looked like she'd lost some roof shingles, and the bathroom window next to where the tree had fallen had taken a stray branch and was broken. But that looked to be the worst of it.

She made her way around the tree, discovering as she did so that it had wiped out the three-foot-tall hurricane fence along one side of her backyard. Annoying, but not particularly expensive or difficult to repair.

She picked her way through the broken branches to the back porch and looked around. Where was Brownie? The porch didn't look bad. Her lawn furniture and grill were still there. Even Brownie's blanket was still in its original spot. But the dog was definitely missing.

"Brownie!" she called. "Here, boy!"

But he was not forthcoming. She knelt down to see if he was hiding under the porch perchance. No luck. A frisson of panic started to vibrate low in her gut. She stepped out into the backyard and shouted again. Nothing. Where was he?

Had he made a run for it after the fence came down? He couldn't have gone far on his bum leg. He'd been limping around on his cast a little better last night and hadn't been whimpering every time he put weight on the leg, but still. He couldn't exactly have headed for the hills on it.

He was still taking antibiotics and painkillers, and he needed both. She had to find him. She set off down the street, yelling for him as she went. But before long she got sidetracked into helping her neighbors as they called out to her. Harry Redfeather's herb shed had been blown over and he was picking through it, trying to recover what supplies he could. He was too old and frail to be climbing all over the unsteady pile of broken wood, and she shooed him away from the remains of the shed and took over the job. But all the while, she kept an eye out for a flash of brown fur.

To their credit, most of the citizens of Honey Creek who hadn't been hit by the tornado turned out to help those who had been unlucky enough to fall in its path. Chain saws roared and portable generators rumbled all through the several-block-long and -wide area. By nightfall, huge piles of tree branches and debris stood along the affected streets. Blue plastic tarps were tied down across damaged roofs, and lights began to flicker on in areas that had lost power during the storm.

But Rachel couldn't bring herself to go home. She wandered up and down the streets of her neighborhood long after dark, calling for Brownie. It was all to no avail. There was no sign of her injured dog. Finally, exhaustion began to overwhelm her panic. She hadn't eaten since noon and was getting shaky and light-headed.

Desolate, she turned her dragging footsteps toward home. The prospect of facing her empty little house alone was almost too much to bear. In desperate hope that Brownie might have come home in her absence to the dishes of food and water she'd left out for him, she picked her way around the stacked woodpile in her yard that had been her neighbor's tree and headed wearily for her back porch. She rounded the corner of her house and her heart leaped in anticipation as she spotted movement at her back door.

But in an instant, she realized she was not looking at a canine form. The shadow crouched over her kitchen doorknob was too big, too vertical for a dog. That was a human. And he looked to be breaking into her house.

"Hey!" she shouted.

The form straightened abruptly. A shadowed face turned her way and then the guy bolted, vaulting the rail at the far end of the porch and taking off around the far end of her house. She might have given chase in her initial outrage that someone was trying to break into her place, but her legs were just too damned wobbly and she was too exhausted to run a single step.

She sagged against the woodpile and dug out her cell phone. Thankfully, it was operational now. She dialed the police station.

"Sheriff Colton," a male voice answered at the other end of the line.

"Hi, Wes. It's Rachel Grant. I just startled someone trying to break into my house. I don't think he got in, but I'm not sure."

"Anything of value in your place missing?"

"I didn't go in. But given that I've still got those contracts I showed you in my briefcase inside, I thought you might want to know."

"Where are you?"

"Standing in my driveway."

"Are you alone?"

"Yes."

"Go to a neighbor's house. Now. Get inside and with other people. You hear me? Don't stop and think about it. Just get moving. Stay on the phone with me until you're with someone. Okay?"

Sheesh. Whoever said men didn't overreact in a crisis was dead wrong. It wasn't as if she were about to die. The would-be intruder was already long gone and probably more scared than she was. Nonetheless, she walked around the woodpile and dutifully knocked on the Johnsons' front door. Thankfully, a few lights were on in their house, powered by a generator she heard rumbling out back like a car with no muffler.

Bill Johnson looked mighty surprised to find her standing there. She spoke into her phone. "Okay. I'm with Bill Johnson. Now what?"

"Stay with the Johnsons until I send someone over to check out your house. I don't want you going into your place alone. Understood?"

Definitely overreacting. "Yes, sir."

"I'll have a deputy out there shortly."

Her neighbors were understanding, and Mary Johnson fed her a ham sandwich at the kitchen table while they waited for Wes's man to arrive. About halfway through the sandwich the delayed reaction hit her and her knees began to shake. That had been really stupid to charge, shouting, at the intruder like that. The guy could've been armed and shot her dead for all she knew. Why on earth would anyone want to break into her house? She didn't have anything of any great value to steal. Her first impulse had to be the correct one: the guy had been after those damning papers from Walsh Oil Drilling. Had Lester Atkins sent someone to get the contracts from her before she had a chance to read and study them? She chided herself for her suspicions. Just because she didn't like the guy didn't mean she had to assume he was a criminal.

And then the rest of her horrendous day hit. The shocking discovery of why Finn had dumped her all those years ago. The terror of nearly dying. The stunning realization that her feelings for Finn were still there. The worry for her mother. The loss of her dog.

She didn't know whether to cry or scream or just go completely numb. She was saved from having to choose, however, by the Johnsons' front doorbell ringing. She flinched, her nerves completely frazzled. Bill waved her to stay where she was and went to answer the door. She heard a murmur of male voices and then Bill stuck his head into the kitchen.

"Deputy's here."

Rachel murmured her thanks to the Johnsons and stepped out into the front hall. And froze. "You? Since when are you a sheriff's deputy?"

Finn shrugged. "Since a tornado came through town and Wes had to draft every able-bodied man he trusts to help keep order. C'mon. I'll take you home."

Chapter 11

Finn's knees were shockingly wobbly. Thank God Rachel was safe. When Wes had called and told him to get over to the Grant place, he'd felt like someone had knocked his feet out from under him with a two-by-four. He hadn't had a moment to slow down since the tornado and to process what it had been like to nearly die with Rachel in his arms. But he needed to at some point. And in the meantime, the idea that something else might have happened to her, when he wasn't around to protect her—it was nearly as bad as that frantic phone call she'd made that had led him to believe she'd been shot.

"You gotta quit making me think you're dying, Rachel," he muttered as he ushered her out of the Johnson house.

She frowned up at him. "Wes knew I was fine. He made me stay on the phone with him until I was with the Johnsons."

"Yeah, well, he didn't share that with me when he told

me to get over here as fast as I could because someone had been seen breaking into your house."

Rachel blinked up at him, looking surprised. "Sounds like your brother was pulling your chain."

Now why would Wes do something like that? Finn scowled. Either Wes was trying to give his little brother heart failure or make the point that Finn's old feelings for Rachel were still alive and well. Wes had laughed his head off when he heard the story of Rachel's phone call about Brownie that'd had Finn tearing down the mountain thinking she'd been shot. *Bastard.*

Without any real heat, Finn murmured, "Remind me to kill Wes next time I see him." He took Rachel's elbow to steady her as they picked their way around the pile of smaller tree limbs left over from a tree that had been blown over by the tornado. The big branches and the trunk had already been cut up into neatly stacked cord wood. Nobody in Honey Creek was going to run out of firewood this winter.

"I checked out your house," he told her. "It's all clear."

"How did you get in?" she blurted.

"The back door was unlocked."

That made her frown. "I wonder if the intruder was breaking in or letting himself out, then."

"Your place isn't messed up like someone tossed it, looking for valuables. At a glance, it didn't look like anything obvious was missing, like your computer or your television. Did you have cash or jewelry in the house? Something small that someone might have known about and gone in specifically to steal?"

Rachel rolled her eyes at him. "Are you kidding? I'm broke. My mom's medical bills are taking everything I've got and then some."

A stab of desire to make it all better pierced him. He

could afford her mom's bills, no problem. If they were married, she wouldn't have to worry about—whoa. Married? Not a chance. He could never trust her not to betray him, and he wouldn't survive losing her a second time. He could never go down that road with her.

"You're sure it's safe to go inside?" Rachel asked in a small voice as they stepped up onto her porch.

"Want me to go first?" he offered.

"If you don't mind." Damned if that grateful look she threw him didn't make him feel like some kind of hero. No wonder Wes liked being sheriff so much. He got to rescue people and get looks like this every day.

Finn stepped into the kitchen and flipped the light switch. Nothing happened. "Looks like you don't have electricity back, yet. Electric company's working on the downed power lines now. Wes expects everyone to get power back by morning."

He felt Rachel's shiver behind him. Since the evening was still unseasonably warm and muggy, he gathered the shiver was less about temperature and more about not being thrilled to spend a night involuntarily in the dark. "Come with me. I'll show you there's no one here."

She tagged along behind him reluctantly as he pointed his flashlight into every room again, looked behind every door and under her bed again and checked in all the closets. She made a little sound of relief when he shined his light on her briefcase standing unopened beside her nightstand. Finally, as they stood back in her living room at the end of his second search, she let out a long, slow breath.

"You gonna be okay now?" he asked.

"Not hardly. But I'll survive."

His eyes were pretty well adjusted to the dark and Rachel looked just about done in. He frowned. Whether it was his usual physician's compassion kicking in or specific concern for Rachel, he didn't know and couldn't care less. Either way, that haunted look in her eyes goaded him to action. He asked, "How can I make it better?"

A frown gathered on her brow. "Now's probably not the time…"

"For what?" he prompted.

"You're a deputy. You probably have other people to go save from the boogey man."

"Actually, I was on my way back to the ranch when Wes called me. Things have pretty much settled down around town for the night." Which was to say, he didn't have anywhere he needed to be right now, and frankly, he'd be glad for some excuse to spend a few more minutes with her. He didn't know what in the hell had happened to him during that tornado, but he did know his compulsion to be with her was stronger than ever.

She shook her head. "We're both wiped out, and I'll say something I'll regret."

Alarm lurched through him. Regret? Was she going to break things off between them for good? Had nearly dying put her life into some new perspective that didn't include him at all? The thought made him faintly nauseous. Why did he care if she didn't want him in her life? After all, he knew better than to make her part of his life. *Although,* a tiny voice whispered in the back of his head, *a little fling wouldn't be such a bad thing, would it?* Maybe he ought to scratch the itch she'd been to him for most of his adult life. Maybe it would get her out of his system once and for all.

But then his better self kicked in. He didn't go to bed with women just to get them out of his system. Regardless of what she'd done to him, it was beneath him to sleep with any woman for purely selfish reasons. Better for her to end it now between them once and for all. He sighed. "Go ahead and say it, Rachel."

Except she didn't say anything at all. She took a deep breath. And another. And then her shoulders started to shake. And then…oh, for crying out loud…those were tears on her face. With deep alarm, he spotted their glistening tracks streaking her cheeks in the dim night.

He didn't stop to think. He merely stepped forward and swept her into his arms. "Hey, Blondie," he murmured. "What's wrong?"

"Everything's wrong," she mumbled, sniffing.

"You lived through the tornado. Your house wasn't blown over. It doesn't look like anybody got into your place, after all. There's nothing to be scared of."

But in spite of his comforting words, she cried all the harder. He tightened his arms around her. He shouldn't be enjoying the woman's distress, but darned if she didn't feel like a slice of heaven in his arms. "Hey, honey. It'll be all right."

Another burst of tears. Maybe he shouldn't try to say anything soothing to her. Flummoxed, he tucked her more closely against him, pressing her head gently down to his shoulder. Their bodies fit together as perfectly now as they had fifteen years ago. More so. Her teenaged skinniness had filled out to slender curves any man would drool over.

He'd buried his nose in her hair and was already kissing it lightly before he realized what he was doing. It might be madness, but what else could he do? It wouldn't be gentlemanly to turn away a damsel in distress.

Her arms crept around his waist as she cried out what was undoubtedly the stress and terror of an awful day. And something moved within him. Deep and fundamental. Profound. Who was he kidding? This was his Rachel. He'd always looked after her. Taken care of her. Comforted her when she needed it. He could no more walk away from her when she needed him than he could order himself to quit breathing. Like it or not, she was a part of him. Weird how his head could be so opposed to being with her, but his heart could be so completely uninterested in what his head thought.

"I'm sorry," she murmured. "I'm getting your shirt all wet."

"No worries. It's better than some of the stuff that gets on my shirts at the hospital."

That got a little chuckle out of her.

"What's on your mind, Rachel?" Crap. The question provoked another flood of tears. Must not have cried out all the stress yet. He guided her over to the sofa and pulled her down into his lap. He maybe should've thought better of that idea before he did it, but it was what he'd always done with her and it had just come naturally to do it. Just like when they were kids, she curled into his lap like a kitten finding its perfect nest, her cheek resting in the hollow of his shoulder. And it felt like…home.

How long she cried into his collar, he couldn't say. But he did know that every minute of it was sheer bliss. And sheer torture. He wanted this woman so badly he could hardly breathe. And yet with every breath he took, he knew it to be a colossal mistake to even consider making her his.

"I'm so sorry, Finn—" she started.

"I think we already covered the 'no apologies needed' bit," he replied gently. "I'm still waiting for the part where you tell me what's wrong so I can fix it."

He felt her lips curve against his neck into a tiny smile. The feel of it instantly had him thinking thoughts that had nothing whatsoever to do with comfort and everything to do with hot, sweaty sex.

Finally, she mumbled, "Brownie's missing."

"I thought you'd taken him to a neighbor's or something."

"I left him out on the back porch this morning. He—" her voice hitched, but she pressed on "—he loves to lie in the sun. The Johnsons' tree knocked over my back fence, and when I got home he was gone. Oh, Finn, he must be scared. And he needs his antibiotics. And he doesn't have his painkillers. He must be hurting so bad after walking around on his leg this long…"

Finn's gut twisted, too, at the idea of her having lost the mutt. Brownie kind of grew on a person. More important, Rachel loved him, and if he was being honest with himself, he'd grown a little attached to the critter, too. "He's a smart old dog. He'll have found somewhere safe and dry to hunker down for the night. He'll show up tomorrow morning bright and early wanting to know where his breakfast is."

"I left his supper out for him, but he didn't come home to eat it."

Finn shrugged. "He might still have been too scared after the storm. Give him overnight to come to his senses. Trust me. When he gets hungry enough, he'll come back to you."

"If he can. Oh, I hope he wasn't hurt or killed in the storm. Something could've fallen on him. Or he could've reinjured his leg and not be able to walk. Or coyotes—"

Finn kissed her. He didn't know what else to do. But he knew Rachel would work herself up into a state of hysteria if he let her. She was exhausted and distraught and in no mood to listen to reason. Not that he blamed her. She'd had a hell of a day. They all had.

At first, his goal was simply to silence her and distract

her. And those were accomplished in the first moment of their kiss. Why he kept on kissing her after his initial missions were accomplished…well, he'd rather not examine that too closely. He really ought to stop this insanity—

And then, oh Lord, she kissed him back. So much for logic and reason. His hand went to the back of her head lest she consider escaping this kiss any time in the next century, and then he let go of everything else. All of it. The restraint and control and sensible arguments against having anything to do with her. The long years of wanting and wondering what it would have been like between them. His ethics and values and codes of personal conduct. His obligations to his family, of his sense of responsibility, of always being the Colton to do the right thing.

He was Finn. She was Rachel. He wanted her. And apparently, she wanted him. It was a miracle. And he wasn't about to walk away from it. To hell with his head and every cursed reason why he shouldn't do this. He'd missed her like a desert missed the rain, like a new shoot missed the sun. She was his life. And for now, that was enough.

He slanted his head to kiss her more deeply, and she met him halfway, her mouth opening and her tongue swirling against and around his as if she were starving as badly for him as he was for her. She moaned deep in her throat and the sound resonated through him more forcefully than the tornado.

"Rachel." He sighed. "My Rachel. Always mine." He kissed her eyelids, her brows, her jaw, every part of her lovely face. Her hands splayed through his hair as he shifted, lowering his mouth to her neck. He lapped at the hollow of her collarbone, then kissed his way up to her earlobe, which he sucked into his mouth and scraped with his teeth lightly, but with enough emphasis for her to know he was marking her as his. She threw her head back, and her thick, honey hair spilled over his hand, cool and silky. He reached for the first button of her shirt and popped it open, baring more of her shoulder to him. His lips encountered the satin of a bra strap, and the sudden need to have it off of her, to have no more obstacles between him and all of her, surged through him. He worked his way down the row of remaining buttons quickly, all but tearing the cotton off her body.

White lace. As demure and sexy as she was. He smiled and lowered his mouth to the valley between her breasts. "My God, you're perfect," he muttered.

She replied breathlessly, "Lucky for me the power's out and there's no way you can see how wrong you are."

"You've always been perfect, Rachel. At least to me."

Her answering laugh was breathless and maybe a little sad.

"I'm not kidding," he insisted. "I've never met another woman like you. You're absolutely perfect."

"And that's why I snap at you and lose my temper and—"

"That's my fault. I can be an insufferable jerk some-times."

"Can I quote you on that?" she replied humorously.

"Sure, if you'll keep on kissing me."

Her hands closed on either side of his head and raised his mouth to hers. "Oh, Finn." She sighed. "This is crazy."

"I know."

Thankfully, she kissed him then and said no more. Her mouth was sweetness itself against his. The shy little girl had grown up into a confident woman, but her essential femininity was still the same, still intoxicating, still entirely irresistible. Her tongue explored his mouth, and she sipped at him like he was nectar from the gods, but he knew the truth. She was the true gift from heaven.

She threw a leg over his hip and straddled his lap in her impatience to kiss him more deeply, and he shifted beneath her until her core was nestled against his groin so tight and hot that white lights exploded in his brain and stringing words together into thought became nearly impossible.

"Clothes. Off…" he gasped out.

She laughed, a throaty purr that all but had him coming undone. "I thought you'd never ask." Her hands worked at the buttons of his polo shirt, and then her fingers were hooking under the garment's hem. She tugged at it and he raised his arms for her. Her hands ran up his ribs, across the ticklishness that was his underarms, then up the length of his arms, which were corded with muscle from the strain of not grabbing her, pulling her beneath him and ravishing her on the spot.

"You've gotten bigger since high school," she murmured.

He groaned. She had no idea what all had gotten bigger, but it was straining with eagerness to feel her flesh.

"Do you still work out?" she asked.

He struggled to focus. Work. Out. "Uhh, yeah. Weights. Run. Swim some."

"Mmm," she murmured as if he were a tasty treat. He about leaped out of his skin as she leaned forward and—merciful heaven—licked his chest. And then her hands were fumbling at his belt and he was pretty darned sure he was going to explode.

"Let me get that," he rasped.

But she pushed his hands away and insisted on doing it herself. His belt slithered slowly from around his waist. He'd swear she was teasing him, drawing it out until he couldn't take a proper breath. And then his zipper started down, one tantalizing tooth at a time. Oh, yeah. She was messing with him.

"Payback is a bitch," he managed to grit out from between his clenched teeth.

Damned if the little tease didn't grin back at him. "I'm counting on it," she murmured.

He lifted his hips so she could push his pants down, and she hooked his boxers on the way. He kicked the tangle of fabric off his ankles. "What's wrong with this picture?" he asked up at her, his fingers hooked in the top of her jeans.

She sighed. "You always were a little slow on the uptake. You have to keep up here, Finn."

He laughed darkly and hooked a finger under the front of her bra, popping the sassy little catch there. And all of a sudden, her breasts were spilling forth in all their glory, pale and shapely. He inhaled sharply. They fit perfectly in his hands, smooth and firm, and one hundred percent Rachel. He closed his eyes. Opened them again. Nope. Not a dream.

He leaned forward slowly, giving her time to reconsider. But she didn't stop him, and his mouth closed upon her breast. She arched sharply into him, and he took more of her into his mouth. His tongue laved her nipple and she cried out. The sound made him freeze in pure wonder. He licked again, and again she gifted him with a cry of pleasure so intense that it sounded like it almost bordered on pain.

He turned his attention to her other breast and was rewarded with gasps that quickly turned into pants of desire. He surged to his feet, pulling her with him, and stripped her jeans off of her in a single powerful yank. She got tangled up in the legs of the jeans and stumbled into him laughing. He bent down and lifted first one slender foot, then the other, and pulled the slim pants off of her. He kissed her hip and then worked his way over to her soft, flat belly. How he got to his knees in front of her, he wasn't quite sure. But he kissed his way down her abdomen while his hands slid up the back of her thighs. His fingers tested the warm crevice of her buttocks, holding her still while his kisses became more intimate.

He felt the moment when her legs went weak and caught her easily. He shifted back to the couch and pulled her down on top of him, savoring the silky glide of her naked body against his.

"Do you know how many times I imagined getting you naked on this couch?" he murmured.

She lifted enough to gaze down at him. "How many?"

He grinned up at her. "At least twenty times a day. And getting you naked in the my truck. And in the hayloft. And under the stars. And in the boys' locker room—"

"The boys' locker room?" she exclaimed.

"Well, not when anyone else was there. But yeah. In the showers. I had some pretty creative ideas about what I could do in the weight room with you, too. Oh, and the biology lab…"

She laughed, and he could swear she was blushing. "Okay, I confess. I had some rather…steamy…thoughts that involved those big lab tables, myself."

"Ha!" He rose up beneath her to capture her mouth with his. To capture all that joy and laughter and draw it into his soul. "Maybe I'll get the key to the high school from Wes and you can show me your ideas."

"Don't you dare, Finn Colton!"

He pulled her down to him an inch at a time, abruptly serious. "I'd dare just about anything with you, it seems."

"Oh, Finn—"

Alarmed at what she might say next, he closed the remaining distance between them. "Kiss me," he commanded.

Her arms looped around his neck and he held her tightly around the waist as he rolled off the couch in a controlled move, lowering her to the floor beneath him. He propped an elbow on either side of her head. Her eyes opened and she gazed up at him, her eyes wide and serious. He gazed into their depths, letting everything he felt for her show in his eyes. For once, he held nothing back from her.

And then he nudged her thighs apart with his knees, positioning himself so she was wide open beneath him. It was all he could do not to plunge into her and take her like a mindless animal.

"You're sure about this?" he asked tightly.

Her answer was no more than a sigh. But it fell on his ears like a blessing. A benediction. And then he did plunge into her in a single strong, steady stroke that left her no room whatsoever to change her mind.

His eyelids wanted to drift closed, to lose himself in the pure wonder of the moment, in the excess of sensation flooding through him. Rachel. Tight. And hot. And wet. And clenching him so tightly he was about to go over the edge this very second. But he forced his eyes to stay open. To continue gazing into her eyes. To see the matching wonder exploding in her gaze. The limpid delight, the spreading, languishing pleasure rolling over her.

The building wonder in her eyes was astonishing to watch. In a matter of seconds her breathing had shifted, becoming shallow and rapid, little gasps of pleasure that ravaged his soul. Her internal muscles pulsed spasmodically, and before his very eyes, she climaxed. Her gaze went unfocused and stunned but never left his.

It was the most incredible, vulnerable, intimate thing he'd ever experienced. And she'd shared it with him. *Him*. He was profoundly humbled by it. Something moved deep in his heart that he couldn't name. But he knew without a shadow of a doubt that he would never forget that moment for as long as he lived. Hell, he suspected that when he died, it would be the last thing he ever thought of.

The joy in his chest expanded and built until he couldn't contain it any longer. He began to move within her, slowly at first, his strokes lengthening and growing in power like a force of nature, wild and uncontrollable. Rachel found the rhythm with him, her breath quickening once more. She arched up suddenly, crying out and then shuddering beneath him in abandon. He drank in her cries but never stopped driving into her. Something within him wanted to make her go completely out of her mind with pleasure.

Her eyes went dark and wide and a smile curved her lips. And still, their gazes remained locked together. They stared deep into each other's souls as their bodies became one and galloped away with both of them.

He felt his own climax start to build within him, his entire body beginning a slow and exquisite implosion that grew and grew and grew. Amazement widened his eyes, and triumph glittered in hers. And then his entire being clenched. For an instant, everything stopped and even time was suspended. He might have been afraid of the power of it, but Rachel was there with him, her arms and legs clinging desperately to him, her soul completely naked before him.

And then the entire universe exploded. He shouted his release and surrendered every last bit of himself to her as he emptied body and soul into her in an orgasm of such power it drained his being. Disbelief shone in Rachel's eyes, and he mirrored the feeling in his own stunned mind. Never, ever, had he given himself to a woman in even remotely that way. But, Rachel…Rachel took it all. And in return, she'd given everything to him of herself down to the very last dregs.

There were no words. He panted as he tried to catch his breath and pushed the damp hair off her forehead. And still they stared at one another. A world of silent communication passed between them. So much that he didn't know how to catalog it all.

He was quite simply…amazed. He'd always known it would be good between them, but he'd never dreamed it could be like this with anyone, let alone her. What was it about her that drew so much out of him? Was this the difference between sex and making love? Or was it a simple matter of them being soul mates, like it or not? Why on earth had they waited this long to find this?

Rachel was the one to finally break the silence. "Wow," she said on a breath.

He laughed, still a little out of breath. "Yeah. Wow."

"Thanks."

"You're welcome. And thank *you*."

She smiled up at him. Silence fell between them again.

"Are you uncomfortable? The floor must be hard."

"I hadn't noticed," she murmured.

Laughter bubbled up in his chest again. Or maybe it was just that he couldn't ever remember being this happy. "How about we adjourn this to your bed so you're not too bruised in the morning?"

"The damage is already done," she replied, smiling.

"Yes, but the next time I may not be so gentle."

Her eyes widened at that, and her body went languid beneath his. Yup, the lady liked that idea. He pushed up and away from her and reached down to scoop her in his arms.

"Who knows?" she murmured, looping her arms around his neck. "Maybe I'm the one who won't be gentle with you."

Chapter 12

When Rachel opened her eyes in the morning to bright sunshine, she was pretty sure she was hallucinating. Finn Colton was actually asleep in her bed beside her. It hadn't been a spectacular dream after all. Sleepy and content, she lay there, remembering the magic of it. At some level, she'd always known it would be like that between them. They were the two halves of a whole and knew each other better than anyone else in the world. No surprise, then, that they were such a perfect match in bed. They could anticipate the other's desires and pleasures at some instinctive level that transcended conscious thought.

At least, that was what it felt like Finn had done with her. At one point, she'd asked him if they taught students how to be fantastic lovers in medical school, and he laughed heartily at that. Finally, he'd murmured that what they had between them had nothing to do with medical school and everything to do with fate.

Whoever said making love with a man couldn't be absolutely, magically, fairy-tale perfect was dead wrong. Obviously, they'd just never found their true soul mate. Or, let fifteen years pass to build the anticipation to epic proportions. The thought made her smile.

A hand passed lightly over her tangled hair. "Good morning, Blondie."

She turned her smile lazily to Finn. "Good morning. Sleep well?"

His smile widened. "I didn't sleep much, but it was the best rest I've had in years. Maybe ever."

"Feeling rested, are you? Maybe I'll have to do something to change that," she teased.

He rolled onto his side and gathered her close. "Don't change a thing, Rachel. You're perfect just the way you are."

She inhaled the spicy smell of him and couldn't resist dropping a kiss on his chest.

He shifted and his mouth was there all of a sudden, capturing hers and drawing her up higher against him. Their bodies fit together like two pieces of a puzzle, and she sighed as their legs tangled together familiarly.

"Sore?" he murmured.

She was a little, but she wasn't about to admit it. She wouldn't trade this morning's soreness from last night's magic for anything in the world. She merely smiled invitingly. "Why? You all tuckered out?"

He grinned. "Not hardly. I've waited fifteen years for you."

A shadow passed over her heart and she frowned. But then Finn was there kissing her so she couldn't talk and then until she couldn't think at all. Their lovemaking this morning was slow and lazy and exquisitely intimate. Finn looked deep into her eyes again as they made love, and it went beyond personal, forced her to completely open her soul to him, and he to open his to her. If she thought she'd known him well before, it was nothing compared to now that they'd given each other these intensely private pieces of themselves.

She reveled in the slow, powerful glide of his body upon and within hers. He knew just how to draw her out, to steal her breath away, to take her to heights of pleasure she'd never dreamed existed. She clung to his muscular shoulders and shuddered her release to the sight of a smile unfolding on his handsome face.

"You're magnificent," he murmured. And then he shuddered with pleasure into her arms.

When they'd both caught their breath, they lay side by side, gazing at one another. And that was how she saw the moment when the first frown crossed his brow.

"What?" she asked, trying to mask the frisson of alarm streaking down her spine.

He swore under his breath. "We didn't use any protection. I didn't even think about it. I don't do this sort of thing often, and I didn't expect to end up in bed with you last night…" He swore again. "I'm a doctor, for God's sake. I'm supposed to think about these things. I'm sorry, Rach—"

She pressed her fingers to his lips. "I didn't think about it, either. And we're both adults, here. I'm as much to blame as you are. But for what it's worth, I haven't slept with anyone in a few years, so I highly doubt I have any contagious diseases."

His frown deepened. "I was more worried about pregnancy—" He broke off abruptly.

Oh. *Pregnancy.* The word thudded between them heavily. It was like someone had punched her in the stomach. Hard. Everything from yesterday came crashing back in on her. For a brief, shining moment, she'd managed to hold all the rest of it at bay. But no more. A new day had dawned. The magic of the previous night was over.

She closed her eyes and released a long, slow breath.

"Please look at me," Finn murmured.

She opened her eyes, but the link between them was broken. They were strangers once more with all their ugly history hanging between them. Amazing that a single word had the power to do that. Pregnancy.

"About that," she started. She took another deep breath for courage and then plunged ahead. "You and I need to talk."

"So talk," he muttered grimly.

"Not like this."

"Why not like this?" he retorted. "It's not like either one of us can deny that last night happened."

But it was just so darned…vulnerable…lying here naked beside him. She had nowhere to hide. Maybe he was right, though. Maybe it was time to quit hiding from him. From their past. "All right, then," she answered. "Here goes. Would you mind telling me why you walked out on me night before last at the homecoming dance? Again?"

He blinked and looked startled, but she waited resolutely.

"Seriously?" he muttered.

"Yes. Seriously. I've spent the last fifteen years wondering what in the hell happened on prom night, and I'm not about to spend another fifteen wondering what the hell happened Saturday night."

His brow knitted into an ominous expression that hinted at surfacing anger. But he answered evenly enough. "I left the homecoming dance because I couldn't stand to be with you any longer."

Stunned, she exclaimed, "And yet you spent most of last night making love to me?"

"My family was at the homecoming dance."

She frowned. "What the heck do they have to do with anything?"

Finn struggled for words, but then he blurted, "They haven't exactly been your biggest fans over the years. And they were all standing there glaring daggers at me for being dumb enough to have anything to do with you. They reminded me of why I can't ever be with you. Of how you betrayed me and broke my heart. I don't think I could survive it if you did that to me again. You all but killed me the last time."

Rachel stared at him. After everything they'd shared last night, after all the intimacy and honesty and heartfelt sharing, he could still say that? Tearing pain bubbled up from somewhere deep inside her. But along with it came a generous measure of anger.

"Speaking of this supposed betrayal, I had a rather enlightening conversation with your brother yesterday before the tornado."

"With Damien?" Finn asked.

She nodded, her fury gathering a head of steam. "I went out to the ranch to confront you. But you weren't there. I cornered your brother in the barn and forced him to tell me why you dumped me the night of prom."

Finn's eyes went dark. Closed. Angry. "Surely you knew I'd react like that when I found out. You knew how much I cared about you. Hell, I was planning to ask you to marry me."

Something sick rolled through her. Oh, God. He *had* been planning to propose. They could've had it all. All those years of blissful happiness and sharing life's joys and sorrows…

"Here's a news flash for you, big guy. *Maisie was wrong.*"

He stared at her blankly. Finally he said in a strangled voice, "I beg your pardon?"

She couldn't stay in bed with him any longer. She had to get away from him. To get dressed. Cover herself and her pain from him. It was too raw like this. She rolled away from him and, horribly self-conscious all of a sudden, reached into her closet for a robe. She flung it about herself and knotted the belt jerkily. When she turned around, Finn was sitting on the side of the bed, a quilt thankfully pulled across his lap.

"Would you care to explain exactly how Maisie was wrong?" he repeated tightly.

Rachel jammed her hands into the robe's pockets, her hands tightly fisted. "I was at a pregnancy counseling center in Bozeman the morning of prom. But not to have an abortion. My mom had just been diagnosed with early-onset Alzheimer's, and I was there to have genetic testing done to see if I had inherited the gene or not."

Finn was staring at her as if he didn't comprehend a word she'd said.

She continued doggedly. "I was not pregnant. Heck, I'd never had sex." She turned and paced the length of her bedroom and back. "You know what's really ironic? I had decided that I was ready to make love with you. That I wanted you to be my first and only."

Finn sat completely still. He might as well have been a marble statue for all the reaction he was showing to her revelations.

She flung a hand at the bed. "I knew it would be like that between us. And I wasn't wrong, was I? We were made for each other. But you had to go and believe a lie. Why didn't you at least give me a chance to defend myself? If you had bothered to ask me about it, I would've told you. The only reason I was in Bozeman having that stupid test done was because I wanted to marry you and spend the rest of my life with you, but I was afraid that I might get Alzheimer's at age forty like my mom did." She paced another lap of the room before adding, "And I loved you too much to saddle you with a burden like that."

Still, Finn said nothing. She paused to glance at him on the next lap, and he looked pale, maybe a little ill, even.

He mumbled, "She'd bought a digital camera that day. She used it to take a picture of you in the clinic. She showed it to me," he finally said. He sounded almost…confused.

"Maisie? I'm sure she did. She's quite the interfering bitch, you know. And I was, indeed, at that clinic. For blood testing. Finn, I was a virgin. I never slept with any other guy, and I bloody well wasn't pregnant. Besides, I would never have had an abortion—and certainly not without talking to you about it, your child or not. I love kids. How could you have thought any of that of me? I *loved* you."

He opened his mouth to speak twice but closed it both times.

She couldn't take it anymore. She was going to shatter into a million pieces, and she darned well wasn't going to do that in front of him. Not after what they'd shared last night. Not after finally knowing the true measure of just what they could've had. Sleeping with Finn Colton had been the dumbest thing she'd ever done in her entire life. Now she would have to live out her remaining years *knowing* what he'd cost them. It had been so much better merely wondering what it could've been like between them. At least then she'd had the comfort of the possibility that they wouldn't have suited one another at all.

She turned on the shower and was thrilled to feel hot water coming out of the tap. The power had come back on sometime in the night, apparently. She stepped under the pounding stream of water. And as she scrubbed the feel and taste and smell of Finn off her skin, she cried her heart out.

The water was starting to go tepid when she finally turned off the shower and stepped out onto the cold tile floor. Shivering, she dried quickly and jumped into the clothes she'd had the foresight to grab before she'd retreated in there.

She opened the bathroom door. Her bedroom was empty. Finn was gone. Her bedroom, her house, her life was the back the way it had been before last night's crazy magic. Some of the light went out of the bright morning, and the colors of her grandmother's quilt seemed a little duller.

The sense of loss within her was every bit as heavy and suffocating as the day her father had died. Something inside her shut down. Grief. She knew how to do that. One foot in front of the next. Make lists. Force herself to do each thing on the list. Sleep. Eat now and then. And eventually, after a very long time, the pain would begin to ease. A little. But maybe not in this case.

First, she had to take a step. Kitchen. She'd go in there. Make herself something tasteless to choke down. Feed Brown—

A new wave of grief and loss slammed into her. Her dog was gone, too. Her desire to do something nice for Brownie had backfired, and his pleasant afternoon on a sunny porch had turned into a disaster. She seemed to have a knack for doing that with the men in her life, apparently.

She turned the corner into the kitchen and stopped, startled. Finn was there. Cooking something on her stove.

"Scrambled eggs okay?" he asked.

"What are you doing here?" she asked blankly.

"We're not done talking."

She frowned. "Yes. We are."

"I haven't apologized yet. I'm not sure how I'm going to be able to apologize adequately for being such a colossal idiot, but I'd like to give it a try."

She sat down at the kitchen table. "It's not as simple as an apology, Finn."

"Okay, so I'll have to find a way to make it up to you."

Pain rippled through her almost too intense to stand. As it was, she had trouble breathing around it. He took the eggs off the stove and shoveled them onto plates beside slices of toast. He set them down and slid into the chair across from her.

"I've just found you, Rachel. I don't plan to lose you again."

She closed her eyes in agony. She couldn't believe she was going to say what she was about to. But for the first time in her life, she knew what she had to do about Finn Colton. "Finn, you never had me to lose. Last night was an anomaly. You and I both know it. It doesn't change anything."

Something dark flickered through his gaze, but he answered steadily, "I disagree. I was wrong to break up with you at prom. You never betrayed me. If I got into a relationship with you now, I could trust you. Don't you see? That changes everything."

It was a struggle to keep her voice even, but she did her best. "Maybe that changes things for you. But not for me. The fact remains that you were all too willing to believe the worst of me. You never gave me a chance to explain myself. You judged me without ever hearing me out. And I have a problem with that. You didn't trust me or our love. And I have a bigger problem with that."

Finn stared at her incredulously. "So what was last night, then? Revenge sex? You knew you were going to rip my heart out and shred it this morning, so you jumped into the sack with me to make sure the destruction was complete?"

"There you go again," she said miserably. "Making assumptions about me. If you really think I'm capable of such cruelty, then clearly we have no business being together."

He closed his eyes and pinched the bridge of his nose with his fingers. Then he said more calmly, "You're right. I apologize. But please understand, this has been an incredibly stressful morning for me. I tend to lash out when I'm this confused and upset and angry at myself. It's one of my worst flaws."

She almost wished he would shout and rant and lose his temper. This tightly controlled, polite version of Finn was painful to see. It was all so civilized, and yet her world was crumbling all around her.

She took a wobbly breath. "I'm sorry, too, Finn. But I just don't see how it could work between us. I've spent most of the last fifteen years hating myself for driving you away from me, even though I didn't have the faintest idea what I'd done wrong. And then I found out yesterday that I hadn't done anything wrong at all. And I realized that I had been far too willing to believe the worst of myself. How can I expect anyone else to love me, or for me to love anyone else in a healthy way, if I can't love myself?"

"So that's it?" he murmured. "It's over?"

She couldn't bring herself to say the words. She looked down at her hands, clenched tightly in her lap, and nodded. His chair scraped. She felt him stand up, towering over her, but she couldn't look up at him. Her eyes were filling up fast with tears, and they'd spill over if she moved a millimeter.

"I'm sorry, Rachel. For last night. For everything. Goodbye."

And then he was gone.

Chapter 13

Rachel stepped out onto her back porch to see if Brownie had come back for his breakfast like Finn had predicted. But the food in the bowl was untouched and his bed of blankets wasn't disturbed. And that was when the last spark of light in her world went out.

She visited her mother after breakfast because it was on the list of things to force herself to do today. Her mom was agitated and upset after the tornado, and for a little while, Rachel was glad of the wet blanket of grief smothering her emotions. Otherwise, the visit would have been deeply upsetting.

She got to Walsh Enterprises a little before lunch to find the place in an uproar. Although the tornado hadn't hit the Walsh building, the hail and flying debris had knocked out a row of windows on the third floor. The accompanying rain had caused a fair bit of water damage on the second floor where she worked. As she picked her way past the mess and the cleanup effort, she was vaguely relieved that her cubicle was on the other side of the floor.

Until she reached her desk. Or rather the remains of her desk. A massive steel pipe lay diagonally across a pile of kindling and plastic that had once been her desk and chair.

"What happened here?" Rachel gasped at the man examining the wreckage. "Who are you?"

"Roger Thornton. Building inspector in Bozeman. Got sent here by the county to help check out structures in town. Make sure they're safe."

"Well, that doesn't look very safe to me," she said in dismay as she edged into her office and peered up into the dark cavern of the ceiling space overhead.

"I've never seen a plumbing main come down like this. Should've been bolted to the ceiling with steel bands. But it looks like they were never installed or were removed for some reason."

"You mean the tornado didn't do this?" she asked, aghast.

He shrugged. "Seems like it's gotta be the twister. But I just don't see how. Good thing you weren't sitting at your desk when it came down. Thing would've killed ya if it landed on yer head."

She stared at the pipe, horrified. "When did it fall?"

"Folks say it came down about an hour ago. I got here a few minutes ago."

An hour ago? Had she not swung by to visit her mother first, she'd have been sitting at her desk when that pipe fell. She stared in renewed horror at her mangled chair. "Have you called the police?" she demanded.

"Why? It's a structural failure caused by the tornado. It's Walsh's insurance company somebody oughta call."

Rachel nodded warily. She might have argued with him

that he shouldn't rule out foul play so quickly, but Lester Atkins spoke from behind her, startling her. "Rachel. Why don't you take the rest of the day off? It's going to take the cleanup crew a while to clear this out. You do have most of your work stored in a backup file or hard drive of some kind, don't you?"

"Uhh, yes. I've got it all in my briefcase."

He glanced at the case she clutched in her hand. "Perfect. Go home. We'll see you tomorrow when we've got you a new desk and computer set up."

She wasn't about to argue with the uncharacteristic kindness from the man. But the idea of going to her lonely home and its painful memories was too much for her. She went over to the senior citizens' center and spent the afternoon helping with the cleanup there. After eating a tasteless dinner, she went out and wandered the streets of her neighborhood, looking fruitlessly for a brindled brown dog with a limp.

Over the next few days, life went nominally back to normal. She got her new desk and computer and started working on the payroll audits Lester had assigned her to. She had to finish the Walsh Oil Drilling audit in her evenings at home. But that was just as well. It gave her something to do besides stare at her walls and slowly go crazy. The final tally for all the embezzled funds over fifteen years ran to in excess of ten million dollars. Mark Walsh must have lived nicely off of all that money.

She printed off a final copy of her report and put it in her briefcase. At lunchtime, she left the building and headed for the sheriff's office. She parked down the street and took a careful look in the parking lot beside the building to make sure Finn's truck wasn't there before she got out of the rental car her insurance company had provided her until she could buy a new car. When she was going to find the time or energy to head up to Bozeman and take care of that, she had no idea. She'd put it on her list of things to make herself do soon.

She stepped into the sheriff's office to the tinkle of the bell over the door.

"Hi, Rachel. How are you doing?" Wes asked warmly as he came out of his office.

She shrugged, dodging his question. It was easier than trying to lie about being just fine, thank you. "I've got the complete, revised Walsh Oil Drilling financial report. I thought you might want a copy." She held the thick file out to him.

He took it and laid it on the counter. "Thanks." He studied her closely enough that she had to restrain an urge to squirm.

"Any word on who might belong to that signature?" she asked in a blatant effort to distract him.

"The State of California claims it can't find the Hidden Pines incorporation documents. I'm going to hire a private investigator to look into it. He might contact you, and I'd appreciate it if you could give him any help you can."

"Of course," she replied. She probably ought to say something chatty along the lines of how strange the weather had been, but she just didn't have the energy for it.

She started to turn to leave, but Wes reached out and touched her arm. "Rachel. How are you really doing?"

She frowned.

Wes continued, "I wouldn't have sent Finn over to your place if I'd known how much it would upset you."

Oh, Lord. What had Finn told his brother about their torrid night together or their disastrous argument the next morning?

"For what it's worth, he's a wreck," Wes commented.

Vague sorrow registered in her heart that Finn was

hurting. She couldn't find it in herself to wish this sort of misery on anyone.

"Is there anything I can tell him for you?" Wes pressed.

She blinked, momentarily startled out of the fog that enveloped her life. "Uhh, no. No message."

"Don't be a stranger, Rachel. If you ever need anything, or you need to talk…"

She glanced up at him, surprised.

He shrugged, looking a little embarrassed. "Just take care of yourself, okay?"

"I will." She left the office, bemused. What was that all about? Was Wes feeling that guilty about throwing her and Finn together, or was there more to it than that? What was going on with Finn?

She knew from the grapevine at Walsh Enterprises that Finn was still in town caring for Craig Warner, who was improving slowly. Apparently, no one but Jolene Walsh was allowed in to see Craig yet, though. Rachel certainly wanted the best care for her boss, but she couldn't help counting the days until Craig left the hospital and Finn left Honey Creek.

She'd done the right thing, darn it. She had to learn to like herself. To come to terms with the fact that she hadn't done anything wrong all those years ago. It was a lot to absorb. She was going to be mature, darn it.

A few days more after her disastrous night with Finn, the fog enveloping her was interrupted once more by Lester Atkins calling her into his office, which was actually Craig's office, which Lester had appropriated while his boss was out sick.

"Rachel, you didn't get Jolene's signature on those documents, like I asked. You've interfered with a very important business deal."

Fear blossomed in her gut and the usual litany started in the back of her head. She couldn't lose this job. She couldn't lose this job....

"I'm sorry, Mr. Atkins. Jolene was too busy signing medical release forms for treatments for Mr. Warner to look at the papers. She said she'd take a look at them later, when Mr. Warner was out of danger."

She thought Atkins might have sworn under his breath, but she didn't quite hear what he mumbled to himself. Then he said abruptly, "I want those documents back. I'll get her to sign them myself."

"Of course, sir. They're at my desk. I'll go get them now."

When she brought the thick file back to Lester, he snatched it out of her hands and immediately thumbed through the stack of documents. She thought he might have slowed down in the middle of the pile, right about where the Hidden Pines drilling contracts were, but she couldn't be sure.

"Did you look at these?" he demanded abruptly.

Startled, she stammered, "Uhh, no, sir."

He glared at her suspiciously. She was such a lousy liar. She felt the heat creeping up her neck against her will. Cursing her fair skin and telltale blush, she mumbled, "I'd better be getting back to work. I have a lot to do."

Still giving her a damning look, he waved her out of his office. She wasted no time leaving and went back to her desk and resumed plowing through the tall pile of tedious payroll records for Walsh Enterprises. Interesting how Atkins had pulled her off the Walsh Oil Drilling records practically the moment Craig Warner had gone into the hospital.

It was dark when Rachel left the Walsh building that evening. She'd stayed late to catch up on the mounds of work Atkins had heaped upon her in what she suspected was an attempt to keep her so busy she wouldn't go anywhere near the Walsh Oil Drilling records again anytime soon. She probably ought to mention it to Wes. But in her dazed state, she was having trouble working up the energy to get around to it.

The warm spell that had spawned the tornado had passed, leaving the night air bone-chillingly cold. It always took her a few weeks to acclimate to the winter's cold each fall, and she wasn't there yet.

As had become her habit, she didn't drive directly home. Rather, she drove slowly down streets along the edge of town, peering into the night for a glimpse of a brindled brown dog with a limp. She figured by now he'd chewed the cast off his leg.

She approached a dark corner behind a row of warehouses, and maybe because her attention was focused on the tall weeds of an empty lot to her right, she didn't see the other car coming from her left. She started out into the intersection, and before she knew it, something had crashed into her car, sending it careening into a spin that threw her forward into the exploding airbag, which slammed her back in her seat, pinning her in place and blinding her to the other car.

Shockingly, the vehicle sped away into the night. By the time the airbag deflated enough for her to see around it, she caught only a glimpse of red taillights disappearing in the distance. Fast.

Stunned, she sat in the car, replaying the last few moments. And something odd occurred to her. The other car hadn't had its headlights on when it barged out into the intersection. Given that it was pitch black out here, that was really strange.

Her brain finally kicked in and she fished her purse off

the floor where it had fallen in the collision. She pulled out her cell phone and called the sheriff's office.

"Sheriff Colton."

"Hi, Wes. It's Rachel Grant. I'm sorry to bother you, but I was just in a car accident."

"Are you hurt?" he asked in quick alarm.

"No. Just shook up. The airbag deployed."

"Where are you?"

She gave him a rough description and he said he'd be there in five minutes. She was to lock her door and not move a muscle in the meantime. Sighing, she leaned her head back against the headrest to wait. Wasn't it odd for him to tell her to lock her door? Shouldn't she unlock it in case she passed out or something? That way he or a paramedic could get into the car easily to treat her. Did he think she was in some kind of danger? The guy who'd hit her had taken off. She wasn't in any danger if he'd fled the scene, was she?

Wes was the sheriff. Probably just erring on the side of caution. It was his job to be paranoid and protect everyone, after all.

Someone knocked on her window and her eyes flew open in fright. Wes. She unlocked the door and started to open it, but he stopped her.

"Stay right there. I want a doc to look at you before you move. He's right behind me. While he's checking you, I'm going to take a few pictures of your car."

On cue, another vehicle pulled up to the scene, a heavy-duty pickup truck. A silhouetted figure climbed out and strode over to join Wes, who was just finishing up. Her heart sank. Finn.

Darn that Wes. Why couldn't he leave well enough alone? Whoever said men weren't nosy matchmakers would be dead wrong. They were as bad as any interfering auntie or momma impatient to be a grandma. Men were just clumsier about it than their female counterparts. The two men strode over to the car.

It was as if someone had thrown a bucket of ice water over her, shocking her system fully awake for the first time in days. She shivered, stunned at the intensity of the emotions coming back to life within her. Who was she kidding? She was as in love with Finn Colton as she'd ever been. *But loving someone doesn't necessarily mean he's good for me.*

Finn had believed the worst of her, and she'd let him. That last part wasn't his fault. It was hers. And until she knew she would never lose her sense of self-worth again, she dared not engage in any romantic relationships.

Her door opened and Finn's achingly familiar voice said, "Don't move. Let me have a look at your neck first."

Oh, for crying out loud. She glared at Wes as Finn reached into the car to slide a big, warm hand carefully behind her neck. "My neck is fine. I'm fine," she groused.

"Why don't you let me be the one who decides that," Finn murmured back, his concentration clearly on examining her vertebrae. "Does this hurt?" He pressed two fingers gently on either side of her spine.

"A little."

"Describe the pain."

"Like a sore muscle getting poked."

"Any nausea? Headache? Blurred vision? Tingling in your hands or feet? Numbness anywhere?"

"No to all of the above."

"Slowly tilt your chin down and tell me if it hurts."

She did as he directed. "It hurts a little. Like I've strained my neck and it doesn't want me to move it."

"I'd say that's a pretty fair description of your injury. You can get out now." Finn held a hand out to her. She would have to shove past it to get out of the car without accepting the offered help anyway, so reluctantly she took his hand and let him half lift her out of the vehicle.

She turned around to survey the damage. The rental car's entire left side was caved in and had a huge, black scrape down its white side. "I guess the car that hit me was black, then?" she said drily.

Wes nodded. "Yup. Nailed you pretty good."

Finn commented grimly, "If he'd hit her much harder, he'd have rammed her car right over that embankment."

Rachel glanced behind her car and gulped. Only a few feet beyond its rear tires was a steep drop-off, at least twenty feet. At the bottom lay a double set of train tracks. If she'd gone over the edge of that, she could've been seriously hurt, or worse.

"What can you tell me about the car that hit you?" Wes asked grimly.

"Not much. I was looking off to my right. Although I did notice its headlights weren't on." An awful thought occurred to her. "*Ohmigosh.* Did I run a stop sign?" She looked back over her shoulder in alarm.

"No. In fact, the other guy was the one with the stop sign."

Rachel frowned. "He must have run it then, because he came at me way too fast to have been stopped a moment before."

Wes nodded. "Given how far your car was pushed beyond the point of impact, I'd estimate he was going fifty miles per hour or so. So there's nothing you remember about the car, Rachel?"

"Nothing. I never really saw it. I was driving along here slowly, looking into the weeds, and then all of a sudden he was coming at me and there was nothing I could do. Then the airbag inflated and I couldn't see a thing."

"Thank goodness for the airbag," Finn muttered fervently enough to make her turn her head and look at him. Come to think of it, he didn't look all that great. "Are you feeling okay?" she asked.

He scowled at her. "I swear you're going to give me heart failure if you keep having these near-death experiences."

She rolled her eyes. "I was in a little car accident. It was hardly a near-death experience. Now, that pipe falling on my desk at work—that could have been a near-death experience."

Wes asked sharply, "What pipe?"

"The one that fell out of the ceiling at Walsh Enterprises and smashed my desk to smithereens. The building inspector said it was a good thing I wasn't sitting at my desk or I'd have been crushed."

The two men traded glances. Wes looked grim and Finn looked furious. "All right, all right," Wes muttered. "So someone is trying to hurt her."

Rachel spun to face him. "I beg your pardon?"

Finn answered for his brother. "Wes let you get mixed up in the Walsh murder investigation by having you give him all those financial records. I *told* him he was going to draw the killer's attention to you." Finn made a sound of disgust.

Wes asked, "Have there been any more accidents or incidents in the past few days like the pipe or this hit-and-run?"

"You don't think the driver hit me intentionally, do you?" she asked, aghast.

Wes frowned. "I can't be certain until I analyze the crash scene fully, but yes. Basically, I do think someone crashed into you and hoped to shove your car over the embankment."

Rachel stared. He had to be kidding. This was Honey

Creek. The world capital of "nothing ever happens around here." Oh, wait. Until Mark Walsh was murdered.

Finn shook his head. "First Walsh. Then Warner. And now this. Someone's trying to hide something over at Walsh Enterprises. And it's too damned dangerous for Rachel to be involved anymore. I'm calling an end right now to her snooping around there for you."

Wes sighed. "You may be right. I may have to go ahead and talk to Peter Walsh. See if he might be willing to poke around the company. He is a private investigator, and he's also a Walsh. He ought to be able to have a look around without arousing too much suspicion."

Rachel interrupted. "Wouldn't it be some sort of conflict of interest to let him help investigate his own father's murder?"

Wes exhaled hard. "Yeah, that's a big problem. It's why I haven't hired him already. And the district attorney would probably have my badge if I did. But I don't know how else I'm going to get inside that place and figure out exactly who's hiding what."

Finn stepped closer to Rachel. And if she wasn't mistaken, he'd gone all protective and he-man on her. It was kind of cute, actually. Well, actually, it was totally hot. "And in the meantime, she's not staying alone. Until you catch the bastard who's pulling this stuff on her, I'm not leaving her side."

Rachel gaped. *Not leaving*— "Oh, no you're not!" she exclaimed. An unreasonable terror of being alone with Finn swept over her. It was hard enough to resist the pull of him when she didn't have to see him at all. But if she was with him 24/7, no way would she be able to control her urges. And she positively *knew* that that would be a disaster.

Finn gave her a stubborn look she knew all too well and

announced, "I'm not arguing with you about this. End of discussion."

Her gaze narrowed. "I'll remind you one more time, Finn. I am not fifteen and willing to be bullied by you. I'm an adult, and no way will I stand for you hovering over me day and night."

"Then act like an adult and make a sensible decision," he snapped.

Wes murmured, "Let me handle this, Finn."

Rachel turned to Wes for support. "They were accidents. Who in their right mind would remove the supports holding up a giant pipe exactly over my desk? And as for the guy tonight, he probably just didn't expect there to be any cars out in this part of town at this time of night."

"What were you doing in this area, anyway?" Wes asked.

"Looking for Brownie," she answered miserably.

"Who?" Wes echoed.

"Her mutt," Finn replied. "No luck finding him?" he asked her sympathetically.

"No."

"I'm sorry."

Tears threatened to fill up her eyes. Since when had she turned into such a baby? She sniffed angrily. She was *not* going to cry in front of Finn. But at least it looked like she'd distracted him from his harebrained scheme to become her personal bodyguard.

But then Wes had to go and say, "I have to agree with you, Finn. I'd feel better if Rachel wasn't alone until we figure out who's behind these accidents of hers."

"Wes Colton, you can stop trying to play matchmaker right this—"

He held up a hand. "I'm speaking as the sheriff. And Finn's right. This is not open to discussion. I'm worried about your safety. Either you let Finn stay with you or I'm taking you out to my family's ranch to stay until I catch your assailant."

"The Colton ranch?" she squeaked.

"Yes," Wes answered, crossing his arms over his chest resolutely.

She glanced over at Finn, who was gaping at his brother. Crap. He thought Wes was serious, too. She glared at both of them. "Wild horses couldn't drag me out to that ranch. And no power on Earth is making me stay there."

Wes's eyebrows went up and he looked prepared to demand to know why. But Finn intervened hastily. "And that's why I'm going to stay with you until this guy's caught."

Rachel glared. "I don't like it."

"Do you have a better idea?" Finn demanded.

"Sure. Hire Peter Walsh to keep an eye on me. He's a trained private investigator. They do that sort of thing, right?"

Thunder gathered on Finn's brow. "Rachel, we need to talk."

She scowled back at him. "No, we don't. We said everything we had to say to each other the last time we talked."

"No, you said everything you had to say. I didn't say everything I wanted to by a long shot."

Alarm skittered through her. The man did not sound happy.

"Uhh, okay then," Wes said uncomfortably. "It sounds like you two have some stuff to work out. Finn, you take Rachel back to her place and don't let her out of your sight until we talk again."

Finn nodded briskly and took Rachel by the arm.

"I am *not* a sack of potatoes to be hauled around wherever you want," she barked.

"Fine. Then walk over to my truck and get into it of your own volition like the adult you claim to be. Otherwise, I'm going to throw you over my shoulder exactly like a sack of potatoes and haul you over there."

Oooh, that man could be so infuriating! And it didn't help one bit that a creeping sense of relief was pouring over her like warm water.

Chapter 14

Finn's big pickup wouldn't fit in Rachel's driveway with the giant pile of fire wood taking up most of it. Nor could he park in front of her house, given the pile of stacked debris awaiting removal. Honey Creek was mostly cleaned up from the tornado, but pockets of town, like this street, weren't quite back to normal. The guys at the landfill had been working around the clock all week to get caught up.

He ended up parking a few houses down on the street and walking Rachel back to her place. For her part, she'd been silent and sullen on the ride back to her house. And frankly, he didn't give a damn. No way was he leaving her alone to face whoever was out to hurt her. An itch to get his hands around the guy's neck and snap it came over him. He took her elbow as she climbed the steps onto her front porch.

"I can go up a few steps by myself, thank you," Rachel muttered.

"Get used to it. I'm not leaving your side." Not *ever,* if he had his way. But one step at a time. First he had to make her safe. Then he'd move on to the subject of their future.

"Really, Finn. Did you *have* to go all caveman on me? I'll be fine. I've been…distracted…since the tornado, and it's made me accident-prone."

Since the tornado, or since their mind-blowing night together? He didn't voice the question aloud, however. No sense provoking open warfare with her if they had to be together for a while. He followed her into her living room and sighed with pleasure as its homeyness wrapped around him like a blanket. He'd always preferred her family's cozy home to his family's cold mansion. They'd been happy together, the Grants.

"I always envied you for having the parents you did," he commented.

"Really?" she asked, surprised, as she set her briefcase down and shrugged out of her coat.

"You were a real family. We Coltons never were."

"I don't know about that," she disagreed. "You guys seem to stick together pretty close."

"My old man is a big believer in survival of the fittest. He saw it as his mission in life to toughen us all up. To make 'men' out of us."

"While his methods might leave something to be desired, I'd say he didn't do too bad a job all around. I don't know your younger brothers all that well, but Duke and Damien and Wes all turned out pretty good."

He shrugged. Maybe. But he was inclined to believe it was in spite of his father and not because of him. "Stay here. Let me have a look around the place and check for bad guys under your bed and in your closet, okay?"

He hated the fear that flickered across her face. Thank God he was here to look out for her. The house checked out fine and he returned to her in the living room. She'd turned on a lamp, and in its warm light he got a good look at how pale and drawn she looked. Her skin had gone almost transparent, and violet smudges rested under her eyes.

His doctor side kicked in. "When's the last time you ate?"

She frowned, thinking, and that was answer enough for him. He headed for the kitchen. "And when was the last time you got a decent night's sleep?" he called over his shoulder.

Her sharply indrawn breath was answer enough to that question, too. It was the last decent night's sleep he'd gotten, too. He considered the odds of them spending tonight in each other's arms again and decided regretfully that it would be too much too soon. He had a lifetime with her to consider. He could behave himself for a few more nights.

Her kitchen was shamefully bare of food, but he found eggs, some cheese and the remnants of a few vegetables in the refrigerator and whipped up omelettes for them. Over the meal, she kept sneaking looks his way that looked like a mixture of disbelief and relief. He'd take that as a good sign.

After supper, he ordered her into the bathroom for a long soak in the hottest bath she could stand. In particular, he wanted her to soak her neck and try to keep the muscles from stiffening up too badly after her car accident. As it was, he suspected she'd be pretty sore for a few days.

She emerged a while later, rosy pink, wisps of her hair curling around her face, wearing a pair of fuzzy pink pajamas that made her look about eight years old. He was ready and waiting with the next salvo.

"Here." He held out two pills in his hand with a glass of water.

"What are those?" she asked.

"Muscle relaxants. Consider them a preemptive strike against the discomfort to come from your wrenched neck."

She took the pills without argument. Must already be starting to feel a little creaky. He held out the mug of hot chocolate he'd made for her next.

That, she was suspicious of. "What's going on here, Finn?"

"I'm trying to make you as comfortable and relaxed as possible before we talk."

"Oh." Caution blossomed in her eyes as she studied him over the rim of her mug.

"Sit down," he ordered gently. He noted wryly that she chose her father's old armchair across the room from the sofa, which was left for him to occupy.

"Finn—"

He raised a hand. "Please, Rachel. Hear me out. I think you owe me that much. I heard you out the other day."

She subsided.

He took a deep breath. He'd been rehearsing this speech for the past several days. But now that the moment was here to deliver it, fear twisted in his gut. So damned much rode on him getting it right.

"Rachel, I love you."

She lurched at that and he thought she made a tiny sound of distress, but he pressed on. "I always have loved you. And I expect I always will love you. You've been part of the fabric of my life forever. You're a part of me."

She shifted restlessly and he waited for her to settle once more before continuing. "I fought that fact for a long time. But it was no use. I love you and nothing's going to change that."

"But, Finn, I already explained that love isn't always enough."

His jaw clenched, but he forced it to relax. "Yes, you did. You also said you had to learn to love yourself before you could love anyone else or let anyone else love you. And I can see where you might feel that way. I happen to agree with you, in fact."

That sent her eyebrows up behind her hot chocolate.

"And I'm willing to wait for you to work through that."

"But I have no idea how long it might take."

He shrugged. "Take as long as you need."

"But you can't know that you won't meet someone else in the meantime. Or maybe you'll lose patience or just… get over me."

He laughed, but there was no humor behind it. "I can assure you, I've tried everything to get over you already. That's not happening."

"So even you agree that we're not good for each other, then?" she challenged.

"When I thought you'd betrayed us, I might have agreed with that. But now that I know what really happened, I'm convinced we're perfect for each other. Admit it. You know I'm right."

She stared into her cup for a long time. Then she raised sad eyes and said, "Love isn't the only requirement for a relationship to work. The timing has to be right. The right place, the right time in life. And then, of course, the love itself has to be healthy and good for both people involved."

"How can love not be good for a person?" he exclaimed.

"Trust me. Loving you over the past fifteen years all but destroyed me."

Pain sliced through him. "Rachel, there was a terrible misunderstanding. That's resolved now. Our love doesn't have to hurt anymore."

She sighed. "Along with love's power to make people feel good comes great power to harm another person. Can you honestly say you've felt great this past week? Wes said you were a wreck. Love did that to you."

"I'll admit, love is a risk. Maybe the biggest risk any person ever takes. But that doesn't mean we should run away from it."

He barely heard her whisper, "But I'm not that brave."

That pulled him up off the couch and across the room to kneel in front of her. "You're one of the bravest people I know. You've faced the loss of your dad, taking care of your mom, being alone, financial burdens, taking care of this place by yourself—heck, you've faced the whole damned town of Honey Creek and not flinched."

"Oh, I flinched, all right. I just didn't let anyone see it."

He smiled gently at her. "Let me help you. Let me shoulder some of the burden for you. No, *with* you. I want to be there for you, Blondie."

"But you don't even live in Honey Creek. You're a busy doctor. Your patients need you. Let's be real, Finn. You can't commute between me and your real life in Bozeman. Besides, you hate this town. You and I both were desperate to get out of Honey Creek. I couldn't ask you to come back. And I can't leave. Not until my mom—" Her voice broke.

"We'll work it out. Just tell me you're willing to give it a try."

"I—" She fell silent. Eventually, she murmured, "I can't make you any promises."

It was better than the outright rejection he'd expected.

He took the mug out of her grasp and set it aside. He took both her hands in his and captured her gaze, gently forcing her not to look away.

"Know this, Rachel Grant. I'm not going anywhere. I'm here to stay in your life. I'll wait for you as long as it takes for you to be ready to love me. I love you, and we *are* going to be together."

"Are you planning on stalking me?" she asked with patently false flippancy.

"Nope. I'm not getting far enough away from you to follow you. I'm going to be right here."

She frowned skeptically.

That, he'd expected from her. He'd laid down the gauntlet. Now it was up to him to follow through on his big words and show her just how much he loved her.

"You probably ought to crawl into bed, sweetheart. You look like you could use the rest. I'll be on the couch tonight, and I'm a light sleeper. No one's getting past me to bother you. Okay?"

She nodded thoughtfully and retreated to her bedroom.

Rachel slept deeply that night, although she figured it had as much to do with the pills Finn had given her as it did feeling safe for once. When she woke up in the morning, delicious smells were coming from her kitchen. That man was going to fatten her up but good at this rate. She realized she was smiling for the first time in a long time.

So. Finn was planning to wait for her, was he?

One part of her was deeply skeptical. That would be the part that remembered him abandoning her without so much as giving her a chance to explain herself. But another part of her, a tiny kernel deep inside her heart, was…hopeful.

If only he were telling the truth. She'd give anything for that to be the case.

When she strolled into the kitchen a few minutes later, Finn was dishing up biscuits and sausage gravy and a fresh fruit compote that looked scrumptious. "Where did all this food come from?" she exclaimed.

"I made a quick run to the grocery store before you woke up. I had Wes come over and sit in front of your house while I was gone."

Horrified that he'd put the sheriff out like that so she could have a nice breakfast, she opened her mouth to protest, but he waved her to silence. Frustrated, she sat down and dug into the delicious fare. She insisted on doing the dishes after breakfast and shooed him out of the kitchen to go take a shower. She opened her refrigerator to put away the leftovers and was stunned to see the thing jammed with food. Suspicious, she opened the pantry. It was fully—fully—stocked. Finn must have bought her three months' worth of food.

Bemused, she let him drive her over to the nursing home to visit her mother, as was her daily habit before work. He let her go in alone to see her mother, which was probably best. Strangers seemed to bother her mother, who worried that she was supposed to recognize them and didn't.

When Rachel came out to the front desk to rejoin Finn, the nurses were all smiling broadly. Clearly, he'd been working his considerable charms on them.

The floor supervisor handed her a sealed envelope, and Rachel winced. This month's bill for her mother's care. At least she would get her second paycheck from Walsh Enterprises today, and it should cover this bill plus a little.

She tucked the envelope in her purse and let Finn escort her out to his truck and drive her to work. He'd tried to talk her out of going to Walsh Enterprises, but she wasn't hearing of it. She needed the paycheck too much.

"Don't be alone and don't leave the building unless I'm with you, okay?" he asked.

"Really. You don't have to—"

He waved a hand. "No arguments. Not until the bastard's caught."

She sighed. Okay, so it felt nice knowing that someone big and strong was looking out for her.

"Are you busy for lunch? I have an errand I need to run and I thought you could come along if you like," he suggested casually.

"Uhh, okay."

"I'll be here at noon," he said. Something thawed a little in her heart. He did, indeed, seem committed to being around for her as long as it took to prove that she could count on him not to leave again.

When she got to her cubicle and bent down to put her purse under her desk, the nursing home bill fell out. She picked up the envelope and opened it idly. And stared. There must be a mistake. The outstanding balance on the account was zero. *Zero.* It should be close to fifty thousand dollars. She picked up her desk phone.

"Hi, Jason. It's Rachel Grant. I think there's been a mistake on my mother's bill."

The floor supervisor at the nursing home laughed heartily. "I was wondering when you were going to open that envelope. It's no mistake."

"I don't understand."

"While you were in visiting your mom this morning, Finn Colton paid off your mom's account."

Rachel gasped. "But it was *thousands* of dollars!"

"He stood right here and wrote a check for the whole amount. Must be nice to have that kind of money, huh?"

Rachel mumbled something and hung up the phone, stunned. It was too much. She dialed Finn's cell phone.

"Hi, Blondie," he answered cheerfully.

"You shouldn't have, Finn. I'll pay you back. I insist."

"Ahh. The nursing home bill. Marry me and we'll call it good."

"Finn!" she said on a gasp. "You can't buy me like that!"

"I know I can't. But I told you I was going to help shoulder your burdens. Get used to it."

"We're going to talk about this when we get home tonight." she said darkly.

"I like the sound of that. When *we* get *home*. Let's do that every night."

"Finn Colton, you are the most exasperating man on the planet."

"Yup, and you love every bit of me."

"I—" She opened her mouth to deny it, but the words wouldn't come out.

"You're welcome," he said gently. "It was my pleasure to pay your mom's bill. She was more of a mother to me over the years than my own mother. It was the least I could do to repay her for her kindness."

Rachel stared at the wall of her cubicle. What was she supposed to say to that?

"Have a nice morning, and I'll see you at noon. Lunch. Don't forget. I love you," Finn said.

She hung up, stunned. Her mountain of debt. Gone. Just like that. The load off her shoulders was unbelievable. She'd had no idea how much it was weighing her down until Finn had lifted it away from her. She was going to find a way to pay him back, though. She hated the idea of being beholden to anyone like that, even if it was Finn, and even if he did have a great explanation for his act of generosity.

Craig Warner's secretary delivered a mountain of payroll records to her from Lester Atkins with instructions to report to him by the end of the day with an audit report. She spent the morning digging through the dust-dry records, sure that the assignment was petty revenge from him for her not getting his precious contracts signed.

The clock registered five minutes till twelve and her stomach started to flutter. She left her desk a few minutes early and headed downstairs to the front door. Sure enough, Finn's pickup truck was there and he was leaning against its side, tall and rugged. Lord, he was handsome. Smiling, she stepped out into the brisk sunshine.

He leaned down to kiss her cheek and her pulse leaped as he held the passenger door open for her. He pointed his truck toward the highway and she frowned. "Where are we going?"

"Bozeman."

"What for?" she asked.

"I have to check in briefly at my hospital. It won't take more than five minutes. But I have to let them know I'm extending my leave of absence for a while. And then I have another errand."

The drive to Bozeman was pleasant. The easy camaraderie they'd shared all those years ago when they'd been young and in love came back to them, and they fell into their usual pattern of fun banter and wide-ranging discussions. She enjoyed his quick mind and his knowledge of seemingly everything under the sun.

The staff of the Bozeman emergency room eyed her speculatively enough that she grew uncomfortable, and Finn didn't help matters when he looped an arm around her shoulders and dropped an absent kiss on top of her head while they waited for his boss to leave a patient to speak with Finn.

As advertised, the stop didn't take long. Finn's boss commented that he was glad Finn was finally taking some of his accumulated vacation time and to go with his blessing.

They got back into Finn's truck, and Rachel frowned at his palpable excitement. "Where are we going?"

"To pick up something I ordered this morning," he answered mysteriously.

"What have you done now?"

He merely grinned…and turned into a car dealership.

"Finn…"

"Shared burdens, kid. Deal with it."

And before she knew it, the keys to a brand-new loaded-to-the-hilt, four-wheel-drive SUV were handed to her. And, no surprise, the title was handed to her as well. The vehicle was paid in full, of course.

"I'm going to kill you, Finn," she muttered direly.

"I look forward to you trying," he grinned back unrepentantly. "I'll follow you back to Honey Creek. And I'm still meeting you when you get out of work to follow you home."

"After this long lunch and given the amount of work on my desk, I'll be late tonight."

"What time should I be there?" he asked.

"Say, six-thirty?"

"Done."

Shell-shocked, she got into her brand-spanking-new SUV and headed back to Honey Creek. The vehicle drove like a dream. It was smooth and powerful and wrapped around her as comfortably as the man who'd bought it for her. She was *not* letting him buy her affections, darn it. She'd find a way to pay him back for this, too, she vowed grimly.

True to his word, Finn watched her walk into the Walsh

building and blew her a kiss when she turned around to wave goodbye. As campaigns went to blow her away, his was proceeding very nicely. And that alarmed her. Things were moving too fast for her to process. He was intentionally sweeping her off her feet, not giving her any time to think. The man was a bulldozer. A really, really sexy, thoughtful bulldozer. But still.

She dived into her work with a vengeance but it was still nearly six o'clock before she finished the report Lester had requested. She printed it off on her computer and grabbed the papers. If she were lucky, he'd already left for the day. She'd just put the thing in his in-basket and pack up to meet Finn. Darned if her tummy didn't go all aflutter at the thought of seeing him again. After she kicked his butt for all the things he'd done for her today, she was imagining all kinds of ways to demonstrate her gratitude.

A smile on her face, she passed the empty desk of Craig Warner's secretary. Drat. A light was on in Warner's office. She sighed and knocked on the door.

"Who is it?" Atkins's voiced called out.

"Rachel Grant, sir. I've got your payroll report."

"Come in."

She stepped into the office. Lester wasn't sitting at the desk like she'd expected. He was standing over by the wet bar. One hand was awkwardly behind his back and he had a strange look on his face.

"Lay it on my desk," he directed.

She crossed the room while he watched and did as he'd ordered.

"Turn around," he barked, startling her.

She whirled to face him. What was wrong with him? And then she saw it. The gun pointed at her. Terror erupted in her gut and her knees all but collapsed out from under her. Belatedly, Finn's warning never to be alone came to mind. Of course, she wasn't alone now. Apparently, she was in the company of a certified lunatic.

Atkins ranted, "You think you're so smart, don't you? Finding those discrepancies in the Walsh Oil Drilling documents. And then you had to go and tell the damned sheriff about them. Ruining all my plans, are you? Well, I won't have it. I won't stand for that. I've worked too hard for too long to let some filthy little slut like you wreck it for me now."

She stared. What on earth was he talking about? Was he the insider behind the embezzlement after all?

"What's going on with the Hidden Pines deal?" she blurted. "Are you involved with that in some way?"

He jolted and the gun wavered dangerously. Yikes. Maybe bringing up Hidden Pines hadn't been such a great idea. But if she could get him talking…keep him talking… she glanced at the clock on the wall—6:02. Lord. Almost a half hour before Finn was supposed to pick her up. Could she keep Lester occupied for that long?

"Tell me about Hidden Pines," she demanded.

"I have a better idea. Come over here, bitch," Lester snarled.

She walked as slowly as she could toward him. He sidled away from the bar toward the window, staying well out of her reach. Although it wasn't like she was about to jump an armed and clearly crazy man.

"Drink that," he ordered.

She looked down at the bar and noticed a glass with a few ounces of clear liquid in the bottom of it. "What's that?" she asked.

"Drink it, or I'll kill you here and now. Everyone's left the building. I've made sure of it. It's just you and me."

She recalled the rows of empty and half-dark cubicles

she'd walked past on her way to his office. He was right. Panic skittered down her spine.

"Drink it!" he repeated more forcefully. The barrel of the gun wavered and then steadied upon her, deadly and threatening.

She reached out to pick up the glass and noticed her hand was shaking. She sniffed at the glass. It didn't smell like anything.

"Drink!" he shouted.

She tipped the glass and took a sip. Oh, God. It was bitter.

"Drink it all or I'll shoot!" he screamed.

Terrified, she tossed down the entire contents of the glass. At least she didn't immediately start choking or convulsing or anything. She turned to face Lester. "Okay, I've drunk whatever that was. Now you can tell me. What was in that? Did you just poison me?" Visions of her future with Finn danced through her mind's eye. They'd been so close to having it all. Had this madman just taken it all away from them? Panic and grief and rage swirled within her at the thought.

"Craig's the only one I poisoned," Lester answered slyly. "Slipped it into his drinks a little at a time. Idiot never had a clue. Just got sicker and sicker. And then that damned doctor had to come along and figure it out."

Finn. He was talking about Finn. Her head was beginning to swim a little. The lights overhead were swaying slightly. Or maybe that was her doing the swaying. "What did you give me?" she asked thickly.

His gaze narrowed. "You'll feel it soon enough. Stupid bitch. Had to go and try to ruin everything my associate and I have worked so long and hard for."

She tried hard to concentrate. He'd said something important. An associate. He wasn't working alone. "Who's your associate?" The word came out closer to "ashoshiate," but it made him scowl either way.

"Do I look dumb? Do I look like I'd tell you something like that?"

"Uhh, I guesh no'…" She'd passed through woozy to stoned in about two seconds flat. She was having trouble following anything the guy said.

Only snatches of his next words registered with her: "…get you out of here…can't kill you here…too messy… find somewhere to stash you first…then kill you…"

The lights spun crazily overhead, and then everything went dark.

Chapter 15

Finn looked at his watch—six forty-five. It wasn't like Rachel to be late. But she had said she had a lot of work to do, and he'd kept her out of the office for nearly two hours at lunch. The look on her face when the salesman had handed her the car keys had been priceless. He'd never forget the wonder and delight in her eyes. He wanted to put that expression there every day for the rest of their lives.

He shouldn't bug her. But worry niggled at the back of his mind. He pulled out his cell phone and dialed hers. It went straight to voice mail. That was strange. He dialed it again and got the same result. Somebody had just turned off her phone.

He leaped out of his truck and hit the ground running. Something was wrong. Very wrong. He reached the Walsh building and yanked on the front doors. Locked. He swore violently. He punched another number into his cell.

"Wes, it's Finn. Get over to the Walsh Enterprises building right away."

"I'm on my way, bro. Talk to me."

Finn heard a siren go on in the background and an engine gun. "I was supposed to pick Rachel up at six-thirty. When she didn't come out I called her cell phone and somebody turned it off. The Walsh building's locked up tight. Do you have a key or can I break in now?"

"Bust the door. I'll be there in five minutes," Wes replied sharply.

Finn had already checked her cubicle and found her purse under the desk by the time Wes came storming inside. They searched the building by floor and found nothing until they reached Craig Warner's office. Over by the wet bar, Finn found several printed papers scattered on the floor and—oh, crap—one of them had Rachel's signature on it. The document was dated today.

"She's been in here," Finn bit out.

Wes glanced at the document and then at the bar. "That glass still has a little fluid at the bottom of it. Someone's been here recently."

"Then where is she?" Finn demanded.

"Hang on. We'll find her. We've been watching this place." Wes had his phone out and was dialing a number. Finn listened as the panic mounted in his gut.

"This is Sheriff Colton. I need you to run back the surveillance tapes of Walsh Enterprises for the past hour. And pull up the entry and exit logs for the security system. Who's gone in and out of the building since, say, six o'clock?"

Finn waited in an agony of impatience for Wes to get off the phone. "Well?" he demanded when his brother ended the call.

"Lester Atkins is the only person to leave the building

since six o'clock. And the security cameras at the rear of the building show him carrying a large cloth-wrapped object outside."

"The bastard's got her," Finn rasped.

Wes was already on the phone again, ordering police units to Lester's home.

Finn paced. Nothing could happen to her. He'd promised her he'd keep her safe! They were going to live happily ever after with each other. Have a home together. Kids. Grandkids. This couldn't be happening.

"He won't be at his house," Finn announced, certain deep in his gut that he was right. "Atkins is too smart to go there. He knows that's the first place we'll look for him."

Wes nodded, thankfully not arguing. "Lester must have figured out that she stumbled onto the embezzlement and the Hidden Pines deal. He needs to get her out of the picture. Silence her."

"My God. He's going to kill her!" Finn gasped.

Wes frowned, working through the logic. "Looks like your suspicions that he was the one to poison Warner were right." Finn looked over at the empty glass standing on the bar. Atkins had access to Warner's office. It would have been an easy matter to slip a little arsenic into all of the man's drinks.

Wes continued, "Good news is he didn't try to kill Warner outright. He used indirect means. Assuming he's behind the attacks on Rachel, he didn't use direct means on her, either. He sabotaged the pipe over her desk and then hit her with a car."

"And that's important why?" Finn asked impatiently.

"He's not a naturally violent criminal. He's probably going to have to work himself up to the idea of killing Rachel outright. I think we've got a window of time before he actually kills her. He's careful. A planner. He'll want to know where he's going to stash her body. How and where he's going to kill her. I think maybe he grabbed her today on impulse."

"Rachel told me he'd given her a pile of work to do today and wanted a report on it by close of business."

Wes frowned. "Then snatching her today might have been a premeditated act after all. C'mon. Let's head out to his place and see what the boys find."

But even as Finn rode out to Lester's home on the outskirts of Honey Creek, he knew the visit would be fruitless. He racked his brain for where he'd take someone if he wanted to kill a person neatly and quietly. But his panic for Rachel was too much. He couldn't think past it.

A half hour later, Wes stood beside Finn in Lester's living room, swearing under his breath. "Nothing."

"What now?" Finn asked, barely containing himself from tearing the room apart.

"Helicopters are searching the surrounding area and the state troopers have set up road blocks for sixty miles around town. We'll find her."

Yeah, but would they find her in time? Or would they find a corpse? Unfortunately, because of his medical training, he knew all too well what a corpse looked like. And the idea of his Rachel blue and still and lifeless made him want to throw up.

"Let's head back to Walsh Enterprises," Wes said. "It's where the trail starts. There has to be a way to track her, damn it."

"Has anyone local got a tracking dog?" Finn asked hopefully.

"A pair of police bloodhounds are on their way down from Butte, but it'll be midnight before they get here," Wes replied.

Finn's gut told him they didn't have that much time.

"Go home, Finn. You can't do any good here. Let us do our job. I'll call you if there are any developments."

Because he couldn't stand here any longer without exploding, he did as he brother suggested. He blinked when his truck stopped in front of Rachel's house, though. Her place was already "home" to him, and in his distraction and terror, he'd driven here. He got out of the truck and went inside.

His knees all but buckled when he stepped into the living room and smelled the vanilla scent that always pervaded the place and reminded him so much of her. He couldn't fall apart. He had to hold it together for her. He tried to sit. To turn on the television and watch the news segments the Bozeman channels were breaking in with to cover the search for a missing woman in the Honey Creek area.

But his agitation was too great for stillness. He straightened up the already neat living room and moved into the kitchen with the intent to eat or maybe clean the sink. Something, anything, to keep his hands busy so he wouldn't tear his hair out.

Where are you, baby? Talk to me!

Rachel regained consciousness slowly, registering small things first. She was cold. And she was lying on dirt. The air was perfectly still around her. And it stank. Something rustled nearby. She wasn't alone, then. She kept her eyes closed as her mind slowly started to work again. Her wrists were tied behind her back. And her ankles were tied together. Her left arm was asleep. She would roll off of it except the movement might alert her captor that she was awake. Gritting her teeth against the pain, she slitted her eyes open. A dark figure moved in the near total darkness, maybe a dozen feet away from her.

It looked like she was in some sort of cave. Slowly,

she turned her head a little to look out of the opening. A mountain loomed in front of her at close range. It was oddly colored, a speckled white in the darkness. And strangely symmetrical. Its sides were smooth and its slope consistent. No trees or gullies marred its side. Odd. Too bad the night was cloudy and no moon shone to illuminate it more clearly.

And why would a cave opening be facing a mountainside like that? Wouldn't a cave open up out of the side of a mountain so she was looking down into a valley. In this area, caves didn't form at the bottom of valleys. She was too groggy to make sense of it, though. Dang, her arm was killing her.

Killing. Was that what Lester had in mind for her? She vaguely remembered hearing him say something to that effect before she passed out. Terror, sharp and bright and sudden, pierced her, doing more to wake her up than a bucket of cold water in the face.

She was not going to go down without a fight, damn it. She and Finn were just finding each other again, and she wasn't about to lose him now.

Lester, silhouetted in the cave opening, tipped a bottle up to his mouth and took a long drink. He shuddered as if the liquid burned. Oh, God. He was getting drunk to work up the courage to kill her.

Finn, where are you? Find me, please. And hurry.

Urgency rolled through Finn. Rachel didn't have until midnight for the tracking dogs to arrive. He knew it as surely as he was standing there breathing and sweating bullets. There had to be something he could do. But what? He finished emptying the dishwasher and turned to stare out the back window into the blackness of the night. The woman he loved was out there somewhere. *But where?*

He took a step forward and kicked something metallic with a clang that startled him. Brownie's food dish. Too bad the mutt wasn't here. Maybe he could track down Rachel. Lord knew, the dog adored her.

It was a thought. If he could find Brownie, maybe the dog *could* track her. But Rachel had been looking for Brownie for a week to no avail. And Finn had only a matter of hours at most to find the dog *and* find her.

Think. Brownie had left during or immediately after the tornado. No one had seen hide nor hair of the mutt since, which meant he'd either died or gone somewhere with few or no people. And given the animal's general terror and state of abuse when he'd come to Rachel's porch, it was a good bet the beast had headed away from humanity.

He refused to believe Brownie had died from exposure or coyotes or the like. The animal'd had enough common sense and survival instinct to drag himself to Rachel's porch for help. He was still alive, damn it.

Okay. People-hating dog. Bum leg. No way could he have gone far on that broken femur. He would need food and shelter. Finn racked his brains on where the dog could find both within a few miles of Rachel's house.

And he hit on an idea. The landfill. It was about a mile from here. Outside of town. Good pickings for a scavenger like a dog. It was a long shot, but chasing it down was better than sitting around here staring at the walls and losing his mind.

He drove to the landfill and got out to examine the chained gates. He was startled to see the chain was merely looped around the gates and wasn't locked. He opened the gates and drove through. The stench was thick enough to stand up on its own and slug him in the gut. He climbed toward the symmetrical mountain of trash and trudged up the rough road carved into its side by the garbage trucks coming up here to dump their loads. A pair of bulldozers were parked on top of the acres-wide mound, quiet and dark in the cloudless night.

"Brownie," Finn called. "Here, boy." He strode across the landfill, calling as he went. He had no way of knowing if the dog would come to him or run for cover from the human who'd caused him pain. He would like to think the dog knew he'd been helping to heal his broken leg.

A cloud of seagulls flushed up in front of Finn, startling him badly. Their cries grated on his already raw nerves.

"Brownie!" he called again. "Come here, boy. Rachel needs you."

He'd reached the far edge of the mountain and had turned around to hike back when he thought he heard something. A whimper. He turned sharply. "Brownie?"

A shape, low and broad, moved in the darkness.

"Is that you, boy?" he asked gently.

Another whimper. The dog always had been talkative with Rachel.

Urgency rode Finn hard. He squatted down patiently, though, and held out one of the dog treats he'd grabbed from the kitchen before he left the house. "Are you hungry? I brought your favorite snack."

A furry shape sidled forward. The fur resolved itself into speckled brown, and the familiar gray muzzle took shape. "Hey, buddy. How are you? Miss Rachel and I have been plenty worried about you."

The dog inched forward, sniffing at the snack. Finn didn't rush the dog but let him come in his own time. Brownie finally took the bone and Finn reached out slowly to scratch the special spot on the back of the his neck. Brownie still had his collar on. Finn held it lightly while he pulled a leash out of his pocket and snapped it onto the collar.

He gave the leash a gentle tug and the dog went stiff. Finn swore under his breath. Lester Atkins could kill Rachel any second. Improvising, Finn pulled out Rachel's nightshirt that he'd stuffed inside his jacket and held it out to the reluctant dog. Lord knew if Brownie could smell anything but trash out here, but it was worth a try.

"We're going to find her, buddy. You're going to help me. Let's go get in my truck and head over to Walsh Enterprises. And if the gods are smiling on me and Rachel, you'll pick up her scent and lead us to her in time to save her."

His voice broke. No way was this harebrained scheme going to work. But he had nothing else. And he couldn't just give up hope. He loved her too damned much for that.

Brownie sniffed the nightshirt deeply and wagged his tail.

"That's right, buddy. We're going to find her, you and me."

Brownie whimpered and danced a little with his front feet as if he were excited at the prospect.

"C'mon. Let's go."

But the big dog balked. Finn swore aloud this time. He didn't have time for this. Rachel didn't have time for this. He pulled harder on the leash. "I'm sorry, but you've got to go with me. Rachel's life depends on this. I swear, I'll make it up to you later. Just help me now, dog."

But Brownie set his feet and yanked back. Finn watched in horror as the collar slipped over the animal's broad head. Crap! The dog turned and took off running, a limping half skip that was faster than Finn would have thought possible. He took off after the dog, frantic to get him back. Everything depended on catching him!

The dog scampered across the landfill, moving rapidly back toward the rear of the massive hill. Finn stumbled in the uneven landscape of garbage bags and dirt, cursing grimly. He couldn't lose Brownie!

The dog started down the steep slope at the back of the fill, which was blessedly covered with dirt and weeds. White plastic bags and bits of trash speckled the hillside, but it was smoother going for Finn. The incline gave the injured dog some trouble, though, and Finn closed the gap quite a bit. Brownie reached the bottom of the hill and paused to sniff the air. The act struck Finn as strange. But at the same time he was grateful for the extra yards the dog's pause had given him.

"Brownie!" he called with frantic, fake cheer. "Do you want another snack?"

The dog looked over his shoulder once, almost as if to check that Finn was still following him, and then took off running again.

Damn, damn, damn.

Brownie ran along the gully at the back of the landfill for a few moments and then veered away from the trash heap and up an uneven dirt slope. It was dark, and boulders littered this side of the narrow valley. Finn lost sight of the dog and darted forward urgently. He had to get that dog back!

There. He caught sight of a dog shape disappearing into an inky black shadow. What the hell? Was that a cave? Maybe Brownie's hideout since he'd run away? Huffing, Finn followed. If he was lucky, the dog had just cornered himself.

Rachel started as a dark shape hurtled forward into the cave low past Lester's legs. *What the heck?*

Lester swore and dropped his whiskey bottle, grabbing for the pistol jammed in the back of his waistband.

And then the shape was headed for her. Rachel recoiled

in terror. Had they invaded the cave of a coyote or a pack of wolves who'd come back to reclaim their home? Was she about to be torn apart? She'd almost prefer being shot to that.

"Hold still, you damned wolf!" Lester shouted.

Her wish to get shot looked like it might just come true as the beast closed in on her rapidly and Lester pointed his gun at both her and the beast. And then she heard a familiar whimper.

Oh my God. Brownie. How he'd found her or what he was doing here, she had no idea. But Lester was about to shoot the dog!

"Hey!" she shouted sharply at Lester. "Stop that!"

The gun wavered as she startled him. He was just drunk enough to be a little confused by an outburst from the supposedly unconscious prisoner.

"Put that gun down!" she ordered.

But unfortunately Lester wasn't that drunk. He snarled. "You wish, bitch. That your dog?"

It was kind of hard to deny belonging to Brownie when the dog had closed in on her and commenced licking her face.

"I love you, too, buddy," she whispered, "but you have to get of here. Go away, boy." When he merely wagged his tail enthusiastically, she said more sternly, "Go on. Shoo!"

Lester laughed. "I was going to kill just you, but now I'm going to shoot your dog and let you watch him bleed first. And then, after you've suffered for a while, *then* I'll kill you."

She didn't waste her time trying to argue with him. He was obviously crazy as a loon. She'd never done a darned thing to hurt him. There was no reason for the man to want to make her suffer. But every minute she could delay him killing her was another minute for Finn to find her. She had faith that their love had to count for something. It had to be of some help in locating her.

"Go on, Brownie," she murmured. "Run, boy!"

Lester was no more than five feet away now, squinting down at her and the dog.

"Lester, who are you trying to kid? You're not going to get away with this. You're not a killer," she said with desperate calm. Anything to distract him. To give her an extra few seconds to convince the dog to leave. The idea of watching poor old Brownie suffer again broke her heart almost worse than the idea of dying.

He laughed wildly, and his words were vaguely slurred when he retorted, "I got away with poisoning that bastard, Warner. Almost killed him, too. One more good dose of arsenic would've had him. And I got away with setting up fake contracts at Walsh that will net me millions. No one's ever going to find your body way out here. In another year or so, this hillside will be covered up with trash and you'll rot beneath it for all eternity."

"Just put the gun down, Lester," she said patiently.

"Not only no, but *hell no!*" he exclaimed.

And then a new voice came out of the darkness by the cave opening. "I'd do what the lady says, Lester."

Rachel's heart leaped first in jubilation at the sound of Finn's voice, and then in terror as Lester spun, gun and all, to face the man she loved.

"He's got a gun!" she shouted.

Finn's silhouette charged forward and went airborne, flying toward Lester. From beside her, Brownie growled and charged as well, going low.

Bang!

The sound of the gunshot inside the stone walls of the cave was deafening. She screamed, but her ears were too full of the report of the gun to hear herself.

All three shadowed shapes fell to the ground. They rolled around for a few moments, and then became still.

"Finn! Oh, God. Finn!" she cried.

"I'm fine, Blondie," he grunted. "You okay? Are you hurt?"

"I'm fine," she answered breathlessly. *Please, God. Let it be true. Let Finn be unharmed.* She loved him more than life itself.

"Just lemme tie up Lester here, and make a quick phone call to Wes," Finn said. "Then I'll come over and untie you."

"Is Brownie okay?"

Finn laughed. "Yeah. I owe the mutt one. He bit Lester's leg and made the guy jerk just as he pulled the trigger. At this close range, I expect the mutt saved my life."

"Good boy, Brownie," Rachel called out. The dog whimpered happily and came over to her to lick her face. Laughing, she tried to dodge the persistent tongue but failed.

It took a few minutes, but then Finn was there, his hands deft and gentle on the knots holding her wrists. Her bonds fell away. She started to move her shoulders and then cried out in pain.

"Easy. Don't try to move all at once," Finn directed. He probed her shoulder joints gently, no doubt checking for injuries, and then apparently finding nothing, rubbed her shoulders lightly. Pins and needles exploded from her neck to her fingertips as her circulation gradually returned to normal.

She wasn't thrilled when Finn passed her the gun and left to guide Wes to the isolated cave. Thankfully, Lester chose to sulk in silence.

But as Wes slapped handcuffs on Atkins and hauled the man to his feet, Lester screamed, "I'll kill you!"

Finn wrapped her in a protective embrace. "Don't worry. He's hog-tied and not going anywhere anytime soon. And I'll take his gun back."

Rachel sagged in relief, and Finn murmured, "It's over, baby. You're safe. Brownie led me right to you."

"I guess we both owe him our lives, then," she mumbled against Finn's chest.

"Yup. That dog's earned being spoiled rotten for the rest of his life. He can even sleep on our couch if he wants. But you and I get the bed all to ourselves."

Wes dragged Lester out of the cave and it wasn't until Atkins's complaints and threats died away that the significance of Finn's words sank in. "Our couch?" she echoed.

"Well, unless you just want chairs in our living room, I suppose," Finn replied. "I'll leave the decorating of our home up to you if you don't mind. I'm no good at that design stuff."

"Our home?" she repeated.

Whoever said men weren't dense at times would be dead wrong. But then, sometimes women were dense, too. And she was feeling decidedly dense at the moment. "Did I miss something here?" she asked.

Finn held her far enough away from him to grin down at her. "We are getting married, right? I almost lost you tonight, and I'm not taking any more chances with losing you again. I'll still wait for you to work out whatever issues you want to work out. But sooner rather than later, I plan to make you my wife and spend the rest of my life adoring you."

Rachel blinked, shocked into a stillness that went all the way to her soul. "Well, then. I guess you've got it all planned out, don't you?"

He laughed and gathered her close. "Not hardly. Life

with you is going to be one surprise after another, if I don't miss my guess. But I can't wait to see what happens. How about it? Will you make me the happiest man in the world and marry me?"

"Oh, Finn." She couldn't help it. She burst into tears and promptly soaked his shirt through.

He stiffened, alarmed. "What does this mean? Are you crying because you're saying yes and you're overcome with joy, or are you saying no and crying because I've made you so unhappy?"

"Of course I'll marry you," she answered through her tears.

Brownie whimpered and pushed between them, and they both bent down to pet him. The dog wasted no time licking the salty tracks off her cheeks. Finn and Rachel laughed. "Guess I'll have to get used to sharing you with the mutt," Finn commented.

"Do you mind?" she asked.

Finn laughed. "Hell, no. Brownie brought us together in the first place and then saved us both tonight. He can be the best dog at our wedding if he wants."

"That sounds perfect." Rachel sighed.

"It will be," Finn replied softly. "No matter what happens in our lives from now on, we'll have each other. And I can't think of anything in the world more perfect than that."

Whoever said men weren't capable of being as tender and romantic as women would be dead wrong. Obviously that person had never met Finn Colton. But for her part, Rachel counted herself the luckiest woman alive to not only have met Finn Colton but also to have won his heart.

She opened one arm and Brownie stepped eagerly into her embrace, warm and fuzzy and wiggly. Finn laughed and kissed Rachel over the dog's head. "Find your own girl to kiss, mutt," he muttered.

Rachel smiled against Finn's mouth. Yup, life was just about perfect.

* * * * *

MILLS & BOON®

are proud to present our...

Book of the Month

Sins of the Flesh
by Eve Silver

from Mills & Boon® Nocturne™

Calliope and soul reaper Mal are enemies, but as
they unravel a tangle of clues, their attraction grows.
Now they must choose between loyalty to those
they love, or loyalty to each other—to the one
they each call enemy.

Available 4th March

Something to say about our Book of the Month?
Tell us what you think!

millsandboon.co.uk/community
facebook.com/romancehq
twitter.com/millsandboonuk